I0706097

The Silence of the Dead

a Charlie-316 Novel

Frank Zafiro | Colin Conway

The Silence of the Dead: a Charlie-316 Novel

ISBN: 978-1-961030-23-7

Cover design by Zach McCain

Original Ink Press, an imprint of High Speed Creative, LLC
1521 N. Argonne Road, #C-205
Spokane Valley, WA 99212

To those who stick. You know who you are.

*"The privilege of absurdity;
to which no living creature is subject, but man only."*

-Thomas Hobbes, philosopher

"No man is above the law and no man is below it."

- Theodore Roosevelt,
New York City Police Commissioner, 1895-97

Prologue

2023

Chapter 1

Detective Wardell Clint paused as he settled into a deck chair at former police Chief Robert Baumgartner's lake house.

"I'm surprised to see you," Baumgartner said.

Clint narrowed his eyes. "What's that supposed to mean?"

Baumgartner spread his hands. "Easy. No hidden messages."

Clint's stare didn't relent. He knew better. There were *always* hidden messages, especially with people like Baumgartner, who, as chief, had spent far more time as a politician than as a cop.

The silence went on longer than it might in any casual encounter. Despite his contempt for the contrived fragility of social conventions, Clint knew how they worked. Silence made people uncomfortable. That made it a useful tool, whether to throw a person off balance or tacitly urge them to fill the quiet by speaking. Often, what was said in those moments could be damning.

Baumgartner, however, matched Clint's silence, beat for beat.

Darla, the chief's longtime girlfriend, finally broke the tension when she arrived with a carafe and a pair of coffee cups. If their lack of conversation surprised her, she didn't show it. She set the container down and slid a cup toward each of them.

"Straight from The Office," she said lightly. "Our number one blend."

Clint took a moment to get the reference. Since retiring, Baumgartner had opened a coffee shop called The Chief's Office. They also served wine and beer in the evening hours. From what Clint had gathered in discussions with others, Baumgartner often spent his days at the business, regaling patrons with stories from his time on the job. Clint figured that was his way of staying in the spotlight. He also believed the chief would much rather be there than sitting with him.

Good. That was one more opportunity to keep the man uncomfortable.

Baumgartner thanked Darla, who bustled away.

When she was out of earshot, Clint said, "I'd have thought you'd marry that one."

Baumgartner cast a glance after her, then reached up and scratched his face. Clint noticed that he'd lost weight since leaving the job, though he remained heavyset. "I would, but she won't marry a cop."

Clint smirked. "You're no longer on the job."

"Once it's in the blood, it doesn't vanish."

If that were true, Clint thought, maybe his visit would actually bear fruit.

"What are you doing here, Ward?"

Clint fought the desire to correct Baumgartner's shortened use of his first name. Baumgartner certainly knew he hated it. At any other time, Clint would have shut down the man immediately. However, he wanted the former chief to think he was getting something over on him. Clint reached into his pocket and removed a digital recorder. He placed it on the table between them and pressed Record. "I am Detective Wardell Clint, Spokane Police Department. I work in the Major Crimes Unit. With me is retired Police Chief Robert Baumgartner. The date is—"

Baumgartner reached out and hit the Stop button. "Quit fucking around and answer my question."

"I was in the process of doing exactly that."

"No, you were grandstanding."

"I don't grandstand," Clint scoffed.

"Tell me why you're here."

"I'm investigating a homicide."

"Who's the victim?"

"Melanie Paz."

Baumgartner squinted in thought. Finally, he shook his head. "Sounds vaguely familiar."

"It should. She was murdered in 2016. You were the chief when it happened."

"I know when I served as chief, Ward."

"Funny how a murdered girl doesn't register, though, isn't it? You must have been busy down at city hall."

Baumgartner's brow knitted in a glare. Clint didn't wither. He had respected Baumgartner's power as the chief. Truth be told, he'd regarded the man more highly than most of the brass he'd known throughout his career. But despite his large personality, Baumgartner never intimidated him. He wasn't going to let it start happening now.

"Melanie Paz," Clint repeated. "Found behind a dumpster on East Sprague, May 18, 2016. Sexually assaulted. Some mutilation. No suspects. Detective Leeanne Hollander assigned. She got nowhere on it. Now I'm working it."

Baumgartner took in his words with a calculating gaze, then said, "Working cold cases, huh? What'd you do to get booted out of the rotation, Ward?"

Clint seethed at the question and chose to answer indirectly. "Don't think you know how things work now. You've been gone a while."

"Not that long," the chief said. He lifted the carafe and poured some coffee into his cup. He glanced up. "Want some?"

Clint ignored the question. "I dug into Paz's case. There were some elements connecting it to previous unsolved homicides in the cold case files."

"What a surprise." Baumgartner set down the carafe. "You're down a rabbit hole."

Clint frowned. He knew his reputation around the police department. Some saw him as a crazy, conspiracy-weaving paranoid detective with no social skills. Others saw him as something worse. None of them could deny his clearance rate, which was the highest one in Major Crimes, an objective fact he took a measure of pride in.

At times, his reputation helped him accomplish his goals. Other times, it proved an obstacle. He still wasn't sure which it would be with Baumgartner.

Clint reached out and pressed the Record button again. "The twenty-sixteen case has some similarities to a homicide investigation you worked in two thousand-five. James Lockett?"

Baumgartner didn't react.

"When I looked into your oh-five case and did some more cross-referencing, I found similarities between it and two much older homicides deeper down in the vault. One from seventy-four and another from all the way back to 1951. Like Lockett, both were *marked* as solved."

"Sounds like you should be interviewing someone from the Law Enforcement Museum and Archives instead of me."

"Fuck LEMA," Clint growled. "I'm not looking for whitewashed propaganda. I want the truth."

"About what?"

"These cases are connected."

"You said they were all solved."

"I said they were marked as solved. It's not the same."

"Sounds like you're chasing ghosts again."

"Forgive me if I trust my insights as a seasoned investigator more than someone who spent the last years of his career playing footsie with politicians."

Clint was surprised to see Baumgartner's muted reaction. Back in the day, the chief's anger was legendary. Now, all Clint got from a direct insult was the slightest tightening around Baumgartner's eyes and mouth.

"If you don't value my opinion," Baumgartner said evenly, "why are you here?"

"I don't need your *opinion*," Clint said. "I need facts. Facts only you know."

Baumgartner stared at him for a long while. Clint sat and waited, unperturbed. Finally, the chief said, "What cases are we talking about?"

Clint told him. As he spoke, he watched carefully for micro expressions to betray Baumgartner's true depth of knowledge. What he saw only confirmed what he had long suspected. Baumgartner clearly recalled the investigation he worked with Detective Dusty Maragas, his partner in 2005. Clint also believed the former chief knew about the 1974 case, too. One of the men assigned to that murder had been the much-revered Augustus Salter, as close to Spokane Police royalty as one could get. The man spawned three generations of Salters on SPD.

Salter was Baumgartner's lieutenant in 2005.

That was a connection.

The 1951 case he dredged up had a more tenuous correlation, Clint had to admit. The two detectives assigned were George Amherst and Walter Pierce. After working that investigation together, Pierce remained on the job for a long career. In 1974, he worked another high-profile homicide—along with Salter—that Clint was certain related to the one in 1951 and the one in 2005.

That made for a direct link in all three cases—Baumgartner back to Salter to Pierce—2005 to 1974 to 1951.

Maybe it was all a coincidence.

Only, Clint didn't believe in coincidences.

He kept these thoughts to himself when he told Baumgartner about the cases, relating only the dates, victims, and status of each. He let Baumgartner fill in the rest, which he knew the man would do. Baumgartner was smart. More than that, he was cunning. He'd see Clint had discovered the tethers connecting these investigations.

When Clint finished, Baumgartner seemed to consider his words for a brief time. Then he motioned toward the recorder. "I'll talk to you—unofficially."

"This is an official investigation."

"If you want to know what I know, it'll be off the record."

"What are you afraid of?" Clint asked. "The truth?"

Baumgartner pointed at the recorder. "Off the record," he repeated.

"I can get a subpoena," Clint warned. "Force you to testify."

"You can," Baumgartner agreed, "but memory's a tricky thing, isn't it?"

Clint scowled. He reached out and snapped off the recorder. "Tell me," he demanded.

Baumgartner appraised Clint. "Some secrets deserve to be kept, especially since most of these are held by the dead. They'll remain silent."

"I turned off the recorder," said Clint. "What more do you want?"

"Same thing anyone wants after a long, tumultuous career. Peace."

"What about justice?"

Baumgartner smiled wanly. "There's a slippery word." He shook his head. "You should walk away from this."

"Why would I do that?"

"Because it's the smart move. If I tell you what happened— if I tell you everything—you won't be able to leave it alone. I know you, Ward. I know who you are." He peered more closely at Clint. "Do you know who you are?"

Clint once more struggled to control the resentment about the shortened use of his first name. "I know myself fine."

"I wonder."

"I wonder how they make Twinkies. What's your point?"

"The point is," Baumgartner said, "there's nothing to solve. It's all done. It's at rest. You poking around?" He shook his head again. "No good will come from it."

"I told you, I'm not looking for good. I'm looking for justice."

"Is that all?"

Clint flexed his jaw and stared back at the former chief.

"Leave it be," Baumgartner said. "Save your career."

"My career is my business." Clint cocked his head. "You seem awfully worried about a little sunshine being cast on these cases. Makes me think I'm right about them."

Baumgartner watched him in silence for a few moments. "You won't give up, will you?" he said, though the chief's tone seemed to Clint more like he was talking to himself. "It's not in your nature."

Clint didn't bother to answer.

"All right." Baumgartner picked up the carafe again. "You sure you don't want some of this? It's a long story."

"Fine," Clint said.

As Baumgartner poured, the two were silent for a few seconds. When the cup was full, Clint reached for it.

"Turn it off, Ward."

Clint froze. He looked up into Baumgartner's direct, piercing gaze. His eyes cut to the digital recorder between them. "I already did."

Baumgartner shook his head. "You'd never give up that easy. You've got a backup recorder."

"Now who's paranoid?"

"No paranoia. Just a belief that past behavior is the best predictor of future performance." Baumgartner's stare did not waver. "Certain habits a man has are unlikely to become more moderate over time."

"You read that in a leadership book?" Clint snapped.

"Do I have to pat you down?" the chief asked, undeterred. "Make you empty your pockets? We're not talking until you turn it off."

Clint stared at him, torn. He didn't like the thought Baumgartner might outmaneuver him at *anything*. He wanted—no, he *needed* to know what the man knew. If getting the information meant compromise, Clint decided it was worth it—in this instance.

As Baumgartner watched, Clint withdrew a second recorder from his pocket. He'd started it rolling before he exited his police car. Now, he set it on the table, next to the first. Very deliberately, he pressed the Stop button. Then he picked up the cup of coffee and took a sip, his eyes never leaving the former chief's. Only when he'd plunked the mug back onto the table did he ask, "Okay if I take notes, at least?"

Baumgartner shook his head. "Use that vaunted Wardell Clint memory."

Clint frowned, but he'd already agreed to Baumgartner's terms. There was no going back now. "Fine," he said. "Let's begin."

The former chief glanced at the morning sun glinting off the lake. "Where do you want to start?" he asked.

"Fifty-one," Clint said immediately. "Amherst and Pierce."

Baumgartner nodded slowly. He closed his eyes, as if collecting himself. Then he said, "Okay. Here's what I know."

Part I

1951

"Man is the cruelest animal."

- Friedrich Nietzsche, philosopher

Chapter 2

George Amherst limped into the Detectives' Office. His new shoes dug into the backs of his heels and the tough leather tore at the corns on both feet. It was barely noon, and he was thinking about stopping by his house to get an old pair of loafers to finish the day.

He'd just returned from eating his lunch outside in the sun. It was a practice he'd developed years ago to take a break from his work—to get away from the constant aura of death and the administration. Some days, Amherst couldn't decide which was worse.

Voices boomed through the bullpen as other detectives carried out their duties. Some conducted interviews by phone. Typewriters clacked as others pecked their way through writing reports. Amherst thought it was a waste of time for detectives to type their own reports. If the city wasn't so damn cheap, they'd hire a few girls to do it and put the detectives on the street where they belonged.

He stopped at the desk next to his. Walter Pierce hunched over an open file, carefully writing on an official report form. Sitting next to Pierce's arm was half of a sandwich. It had been cut at an angle and laid on a piece of wax paper. A shiny apple sat with it.

"You gonna eat that?" Amherst pointed at the sandwich.

Pierce stopped writing and looked up. "What happened to your lunch?"

"I ate it." Amherst rubbed his belly. "Is that a no?"

Pierce returned his attention to the report. "You can have the apple."

"What do I look like?"

"Like a man whose wife has him on a diet."

Amherst's lip curled. "Watch yourself, kid. This job'll make you fat, too." He limped over to his desk and dropped into his wooden chair. It creaked under his weight. "What're you working on?"

Pierce lifted his pen from the paper but didn't bother facing his partner. "Closing the file on the Riverside murder."

"I thought you already did that."

"I would if I ever got time to write."

Amherst noticed Pierce's annoyance and smiled. "Listen to you. It's not like you're writing your grandma. Means and opportunity—" He held up two fingers. "What more do you need?"

"Oh, I don't know." Pierce looked up at a whirring ceiling fan. "How about a suspect, a victim, and a location for starters."

Amherst flicked his hand. "Goes without saying."

"Still needs to be in the report." Pierce lowered his head and started writing again.

"What kind of sandwich is that, by the way?" Amherst craned his neck. "Looks like salami. Did Connie pick that up from Sonnenberg's?"

Pierce dropped a fist on the wax paper. "If I give you the sandwich, will you shut your trap?"

Amherst lifted his right hand like he was swearing in before a judge. "I'll even eat it outside."

"Then here." Pierce pushed the sandwich away.

Sergeant DiCarlo shouted across the room, "Laurel and Hardy, you're up."

Amherst snatched the sandwich from Pierce's desk. "No take backs." He plopped the sandwich onto his own desk and stood. "Let's go."

Pierce pushed his chair back. "I hate being called Laurel."

"Being compared to Oliver Hardy ain't no picnic either." Amherst straightened his tie and fixed his collar as he limped toward the sergeant's office.

"Nice shoes," Pierce whispered.

"I can get you a pair."

"I'll pass."

Amherst glanced at Pierce. The younger detective's pious nature leaked out from behind his mask of indifference. "Have it your way, but it'd save you a few bucks."

Sergeant Geno DiCarlo had thick, dark hair and a caterpillar mustache. He wore the department's uniform instead of a suit as was an option for a man in his position. DiCarlo often claimed it was because he preferred to honor the department, but Amherst knew how cheap DiCarlo was. They'd worked as partners on patrol years before. Plus, Amherst had met some other Italians back in the Great War and those men were notoriously cheap.

DiCarlo tossed a thin file on his organized desk. "We got a missing person. One Josephine Banfield."

Even though he was closer, Amherst didn't reach for the file. "Let the uniforms handle it," he said.

"They have. She's been missing close to twenty-four hours now."

Pierce grabbed the file and flipped it open.

Amherst scrunched his nose. "Why the hot potato?"

"Stop your bellyaching, George. It's an active case."

"She's nineteen," Pierce said. He looked up from the file and eyed his partner.

"Probably playing hide the pickle with her boyfriend." Amherst waved a hand. "We're gonna run out of here with our hair on fire—"

Pierce tapped something in the file. "No boyfriend."

Amherst glanced at the file. "How'd she rate? That's not even a report. It's just some notes. This case goes from the patrol boys to us." He snapped his fingers. "Like that."

"Stop arguing," DiCarlo said. "You go when I say you go."

"Yeah?" Amherst said. "That's how it is?"

"That's how it is. Just like the Army. You remember those days, George? Or is it too far back?"

Amherst straightened and saluted DiCarlo. "Private Amherst, reporting for duty, sir. Let me know how many Germans I gotta kill."

"Hey now!" DiCarlo blurted. "That's not what I meant."

Amherst spun and limped out of the sergeant's office.

"George! George!"

He didn't stop walking. Amherst snatched his fedora and the half-eaten sandwich from his desk and continued outside.

***

George Amherst inhaled on his cigarette as he watched his partner cross the parking lot in long, lanky strides. Walter Pierce's brown suit fit nicely, and his new fedora sat at a jaunty angle. He carried the thin folder in his left hand.

Amherst sort of disliked his partner. It wasn't for anything more than the advantages of youth. Pierce hadn't gotten fat or lost any hair yet. He didn't get winded walking up long flights of stairs. Young, beautiful women still smiled at him.

It was the last which bothered Amherst the most. He hadn't had sex with someone other than his wife in more than two years. Amherst blamed the job. When he started with Spokane Police, he was like Pierce—young, healthy, and virile. Now, he was old, fat, and miserable.

He crushed out his cigarette.

Pierce opened the passenger door and dropped into the car. "DiCarlo's pissed."

"He'll get over it." Amherst stomped the accelerator and they sped from the parking lot. "Where we going?"

"The South Hill." Pierce recited an address on Syringa Boulevard.

Amherst knew the area. It was a ritzy neighborhood with big homes, lush yards, and towering trees. He hated the privileged folks who lived on the hill.

They headed south on Monroe Street. A silence fell over the car as they drove. Pierce took off his fedora and set it on his knee. He pulled out a pack of cigarettes, shook one free, and lit it.

"You can stop doing that," Amherst said.

Pierce eyed him.

"Cupping your cigarette." Amherst lifted his hand from the steering wheel. "Jerry's not gonna get you back here."

"I was in the Pacific."

"Fine. The nips aren't gonna get you either."

Pierce smirked. "Why don't you mind the road?"

"I mind the road fine. I'm just saying you can stop acting out the war."

"Maybe I like smoking this way." Pierce stuck his cigarette between his lips and cupped it.

Amherst sniffed dismissively. "I'm not even sure why you mortar boys worried about being seen."

"This again?"

"What? You guys were lobbing footballs like Sid Luckman or something."

"Maybe you can ease up. I shared my sandwich with you." The cigarette bounced between Pierce's lips as he spoke.

"Eh." Amherst lifted his hand from the steering wheel. "The bread was dry, and there wasn't enough mayo. Connie must be mad at you."

"Jesus, you're ungrateful."

Amherst pushed his hat back on his head. "I'm just saying you mortar pukes fought from the back of the war, while we grunts fought from the front. Those are unassailable facts."

Pierce shook his head.

"Well?"

"Mortar is part of infantry," Pierce said evenly. "We weren't artillery, or in the rear. We were with infantry, at the front."

"*Behind* us riflemen," Amherst corrected.

"How many times do you want me to say you win this argument?"

"It never gets old."

Pierce inhaled on his cigarette. "Riflemen fought harder than mortar. You had it more dangerous. You happy?"

"I'm getting there."

"What more do you want?"

"How much time did you spend in the trenches?" Amherst asked.

"Not this again. Look, it was a different kind of war, okay?"

"It was, and our war was rougher than yours."

"Everyone thinks theirs was the roughest. Are you going to lay this same line on the boys who come back from Korea?"

"That's a conflict, not a war."

"Bullets fly the same, either way."

"If they come back talking like they had it rougher than us, I'll set them straight, too."

Pierce waved his hand. "Shove that up your fat, miserable ass."

Amherst feigned offensive. "Watch your language. Does Connie want you coming home with that mouth?"

The drive up the hill continued in that fashion. Amherst never got tired of finding fault with Pierce. It broke up the tedium of the job.

***

"Joey's a good girl," Bernice Banfield said. She dabbed her eyes with a silk handkerchief. "This isn't like her."

Martin Banfield sat next to his wife on the couch, his back ramrod straight. His face remained expressionless. "Not like her at all," he echoed.

Martin wore a blue suit with a white shirt and red tie. His wingtips were recently polished. Bernice's blue and white print dress appeared expensive as if it might have been from the Bon Marche's spring line.

Pierce relaxed in a wingback chair with one leg crossed over the other, trying to create an air of calm. He balanced his notebook on his knee.

Amherst sat on a piano bench in the corner of the room and observed the interview. He initially planned to stand, but his new shoes made that intolerable. Every time he shifted his stance, pain lanced through his feet. He imagined his heels were bloody by now and the corns were inflamed.

"Josephine still lives with you?" Pierce asked.

"That's correct," Martin said. "Joey goes to school out at Eastern College."

Eastern Washington College of Education was in Cheney, a town about twenty-five minutes southwest of Spokane.

Pierce scratched his cheek with the end of his pen. "Have you checked with her friends?"

The father nodded. "Yes, of course. We're not prone to worry. We told the policemen this earlier."

"We understand." Pierce flashed a practiced smile. "We're just following up. Do you have any other children?"

"Only Joey."

Amherst's gaze flitted about the room. The Banfields lived in an expensive house in a high-end neighborhood. Photographs of the family's world travels, along with trinkets, adorned the walls. He absently reached into his pocket and pulled out a pack of cigarettes. He shook one free and stuck it in his mouth.

Bernice loudly cleared her throat.

"Excuse me, Detective," Martin said. "We don't allow smoking in our house."

Amherst slowly and exaggeratedly pulled the cigarette from his mouth. "What do you do, Mr. Banfield?"

"Pardon me?"

"For work," Amherst clarified. He waved at the photographs on the wall. "To afford all these trips, you must be rich."

Martin's jaw tightened and he smoothed his tie. "I'm an investment banker. I'm not sure how that matters in this situation."

"I'm not sure either." Amherst shrugged a single shoulder. "Maybe it does."

Pierce rolled his eyes and turned back to the couple. "When did you last see Joey?"

"Last night," Martin said. "She told us she was going to the library to study."

"Which library? The one at the college or the one downtown?"

The parents looked at each other. It was clear neither had the answer to that question.

"It's all right," Pierce said. "We'll check them both. You told the officers earlier that Joey didn't have a boyfriend."

"That's correct," Martin said.

Bernice nodded.

"Did she ever have one?" Pierce asked.

"No," Martin said.

"Well." Bernice eyed her husband. "There was that one in junior high school."

"She had a crush on him," Martin said. "I'd hardly call him a boyfriend."

Pierce asked, "What was his name? Just in case."

The parents exchanged glances.

"Bobby," Martin said.

"Billy," Bernice corrected.

"That's right," the husband said. "Billy Wirth."

Bernice's brow furrowed. "I thought it was Weaver. Isn't Billy Wirth the boy from church?"

Martin smoothed his tie again. "The boy from church? The one with the funny teeth?"

"That's the one."

"Huh." Martin eyed Pierce. "It's one of those—Wirth or Weaver. We're relatively certain of Billy, though."

"What about her friends? Can you tell us who she spends time with?"

Amherst studied the photographs lining the top of the piano. Three faces were consistent throughout. Martin,

Bernice, and a young blond girl. Amherst found the most recent picture of the girl, the one in which she seemed the oldest, and grabbed it. The girl stood knee deep in the ocean, the hem of her dress pulled up to her knees.

He turned back to the parents. They were providing a list of friends to Pierce.

Amherst held up the framed photo. "Is this what Josephine looks like now?"

"That was taken last year," Bernice said. "When we were in Hawaii."

"May we take it?" Amherst stood. Daggers sliced across his heels and he winced.

"Yes," Martin said. "If it'll help you bring her home, please have it."

Amherst removed the photograph from the frame and tucked it into his jacket pocket. "I'm going outside for a smoke." He headed for the door, limping as he went. "I'll meet you in the car."

Pierce looked at him. "You want to check her room?"

Amherst paused only briefly. "Let me know if you find anything."

Chapter 3

Amherst had just lit up a second cigarette when Pierce finally returned to the car. The younger detective paused near the hood as he considered where Amherst was now sitting. Pierce shrugged and continued to the driver's side.

Pierce climbed into the car and situated himself behind the steering wheel. He pushed his fedora back on his head. Amherst blew a stream of smoke in the younger detective's direction.

"Why'm I driving now?" Pierce asked.

Amherst's feet hurt but he wasn't going to give Pierce the satisfaction of knowing. He curled his lip. "What took you so long?"

"I was being thorough."

"Barking up a dead tree, more like."

Pierce started the engine and put the vehicle into gear. As he pulled out of the Banfield driveway, he glanced sideways at Amherst. "I don't have all your years of experience when it comes to investigating cases—"

"You don't have to qualify," Amherst interrupted. He took another deep drag on his Lucky Strike. "You don't have as much experience at anything."

Pierce frowned. Amherst took a small measure of satisfaction whenever he saw that reaction. Pierce needed cutting down to size. Like a number of returning soldiers who found a home in the police department, the young man exhibited a sense of entitlement that irked Amherst. It was compounded when these same young men started being promoted to detective after a mere five years on the job.

Not like the old days, Amherst groused inwardly. A man could go years and not get a sniff at being a detective. Amherst was promoted after twelve years, not earning any help from his time in service.

Prior to joining the police department, he'd enlisted in the Army at age fifteen, courtesy of an inattentive processing sergeant and the government's push to increase troop readiness. No one was around to stop Amherst from running off to war. His father was dead by that time and his mother had run off with a traveling preacher, telling the boy he was old enough to care for himself. When she returned home after the romance failed, she discovered her son was off fighting for his country.

By then, he'd fought in the Battle of Belleau Wood on the Western Front, one of the bloodiest campaigns of the war. His mother complained about her son's whereabouts in a local newspaper report. A state senator saw the article and intervened. Amherst was pulled off the frontlines by the War Department and dismissed from the service. The men he'd fought with earned the Distinguished Service Cross awards for their time. He never saw any such recognition.

The older Amherst got, the more it angered him. He glanced at his partner and wondered if Pierce was ever awarded anything for his time in the Pacific. Amherst would never ask because he didn't want to know.

"Have it your way," Pierce said. His frown faded and his tone was once more amiable. "All I'm saying is I might not have your experience, so I make up for it by being thorough."

"Wasting time, you mean."

Pierce kept his eyes on the road while he spoke. "You never know which detail is going to be the one to break open a case," he said solemnly.

Amherst snorted smoke through his nostrils. "Which book did you get that from, rookie?" He shook his head dismissively. "Don't try to make this job more complicated than it is. It's a simple job. You know why?"

"I have a feeling you're going to tell me."

"It's because people are simple. They want simple things. Money, for one. Power. Sex. When they don't get those things, the result is crime. Somebody does something to someone else over one of those three desires. The only part that is marginally difficult—and only once in a while, at that—is when you don't know all the players."

They drove in silence for several blocks. Amherst smoked and looked out the window at the passing homes. Damn, he hated the rich.

"What about this case, then?" Pierce asked. "Money, power, or sex?"

"All three, probably."

"How's that?"

Amherst took a final drag on his cigarette and flicked it out the open window. "Mommy and Daddy got money, so there's that. This little dolly, Josephine, is pushing back against their power over her. That's why she ran away."

"What about the sex?"

"If she's not having it, she wants them to think she is. Goes back to the power struggle."

"You're jumping to conclusions," Pierce said. "You spent all of ten minutes in their living room. You didn't even check out the girl's bedroom."

"You find anything in there worth a tinker's damn?"

"Well… no."

"Exactly." Amherst felt a piece of tobacco on his tooth and scraped it off with his tongue. He reached up and picked it off with a finger, flicking it out the window. "You watch, kid. This case is simple. If the uniforms weren't too busy rousting bums downtown, one of them could've solved it."

"If it's so simple, why are we working it?"

"You ought to know the answer to that," Amherst said. "Back in the Army, I guess the answer would be that she's the colonel's daughter."

Pierce nodded in understanding. "Some things never change, I suppose."

"That's because they're simple."

***

At the downtown library, they quickly determined Josephine Banfield hadn't checked out a book in weeks. The aged librarian at the circulation desk couldn't say if Josephine had been there the previous evening since she couldn't recall Joey's face. When she lifted her glasses to examine the photograph Amherst showed her, the most the librarian could offer was a shrug.

"I'm sorry, officer," she said dryly. "I pay attention to books more than people."

The campus librarian was slightly more helpful. For one, she was younger and stacked. A far sight better looking than the old bird downtown. Amherst snuck an appreciative glance at her cleavage when she leaned forward to study the photograph of Josephine.

"Yes," she said, after a moment. "That's Jo, I believe."

"You mean Joey?" Amherst asked.

The librarian shrugged. "Her friends call her Jo, from what I've heard. They're a boisterous group when they come in to study. I usually get after them to quiet down."

Amherst motioned for Pierce to show her the list he'd acquired from the Banfields. "Any of these names in that group?"

The librarian waited patiently while Pierce flipped through a few pages of his notebook, then held it out to her. She scanned the list, nodding while she read. "I recognize these names, but this isn't the group Jo studies with."

"No?" Amherst asked. "Who, then?"

The librarian thought for a moment, then recited, "Peggy Little, Sharon Cudmore, Steve Corson, Basil Pershing…" She shrugged. "Those are the only ones I know. The others on this list might be her friends, but I couldn't tell you who they are beyond a name on a checkout card."

"Thank you," Amherst said.

The librarian handed the notebook back to Pierce, who asked her to repeat the names she'd mentioned. She complied and Pierce jotted them down. "Officers," she asked, "is Jo in trouble?"

"Why do you ask?"

"The police don't come around unless someone did something wrong."

"Or needs our help," Amherst said. He smiled at her, flexing his charm out of habit.

The librarian's mouth tightened. "Of course. That, too."

"We just need to talk to Josephine," Amherst said. He glanced down at her left hand and saw a small solitaire diamond on the ring finger. So, this one was on the hook but not landed yet. Sometimes those were the best. They wanted one last trip to the fair before summer ended. "Any idea where the group might gather, aside from at home?"

"Just the usual spots, I suppose."

"Which are?"

"The cafeteria." The librarian shrugged. "Maybe one of the malt shops downtown. I don't know what they do away from here."

Amherst reached into his pocket and handed her one of the few business cards he carried. The corners were bent, and the card had a rumpled look to it. "If she comes in again, give me a call, would you, Miss…?"

The librarian took the card as her gaze traveled his length. Her lips briefly pursed before she responded. "Certainly… but you're sure she's not in trouble?"

"Positive." Amherst flashed her a half-hearted grin, realizing his effort to impress the young woman was like throwing grass seed on a sidewalk. "I hope you call."

The librarian nodded unenthusiastically. "If I see her."

His grin faded. He turned and walked away. Just outside the library, the pain in Amherst's feet flared up and he scowled. "Let's find this little brat," he grumbled.

Next to him, Pierce said nothing.

***

The clerk at the Eastern Washington College of Education registrar's office was efficient. A military service background was apparent the moment Amherst laid eyes on him. The man stood straight and tall. He had a fresh buzz cut. His collar was starched, and his shirt perfectly ironed.

Amherst showed his badge.

"How can I assist you, sir?" the man asked, and the practiced nature of his tone sealed it for Amherst. Either Army or Marines, he was sure of it.

"I need the class schedule for these eight students," Amherst said while Pierce handed over his notepad.

The clerk glanced down. "I only see seven here."

"The eighth is Josephine Banfield."

The man nodded without any recognition. He disappeared for a few minutes. Amherst lit a cigarette and shifted uncomfortably in his tight shoes. Pierce stood stoically, seeming to be deep in thought.

The clerk returned with five sheets of paper and slid them across the counter. As Amherst picked them up, he asked, "Where'd you serve?"

The man didn't hesitate. "Big Red One," he replied. The pride in his voice was the first inflection Amherst had noticed in their entire interaction. "Why do you ask?"

"I'm taking a poll," Amherst answered, and turned to go.

Outside, Pierce asked, "What was that about?"

"Just confirming a hunch."

"How's it related to the case?"

"It doesn't," Amherst said.

"Then why ask about it?"

Amherst lit a cigarette. "The librarian gave us guff. The clerk didn't."

"You think it's got something to do with his military service?"

"You don't?"

Pierce shrugged. "I'd imagine."

"The world seemed simpler before the wars."

***

Amherst's mood declined over the next hour as he and Pierce tromped around the college campus. He should have stopped at his house for a pair of comfortable loafers. The pain in his feet was only a part of his problem.

Dealing with snotty professors who didn't like their classes interrupted for official police business was some of the reason. That the first three students they pulled aside were less than helpful only made it worse.

"Joey and I went to high school together," Madelaine Kearns told them. "Sometimes our families have dinner together. But the truth is, we were never really close."

Amherst motioned for Pierce to show her the list of names in his notebook. "Is she friends with any of these kids, do you know?"

Madelaine scanned the names. "Trudy and Perry are in our same social circle."

"Explain what you mean."

"We all went to high school together. Beyond that, our families sometimes socialize and we see each other at church. But we've all drifted apart since starting college."

"Josephine's parents said these were her friends."

Madelaine's expression was pained. "We are, I suppose. Just not..." She trailed off and shrugged.

"Not really close," Amherst finished her thought. He pointed at the names in Pierce's notebook that the librarian had provided. "How about these four?"

"I don't know them," Madelaine said.

After that, they decided to skip talking to the other two names Josephine's parents provided and moved on to those supplied by the librarian. Unfortunately, most of those students were not in their scheduled classes, which further eroded Amherst's patience and raised his suspicion.

He considered going back to the registrar's office but decided to finish the list first. At their final stop, they encountered a French professor seated alone at his desk in an empty classroom. He was in his early thirties and had the soft academic look to him that Amherst equated with cowards, weaklings, and poofs.

The professor's name was Ethan Fromme. He confirmed Sharon Cudmore was enrolled in his class.

"Where *are* your students?" Amherst asked, looking around at the empty seats.

"I released them early," Fromme told him. He motioned toward the stack of papers in front of him. "Today was a test. They're not going to learn anything new after that, so I set them free."

"Was Sharon in class today?"

Fromme closed his eyes and thought for a moment. "Yes, I believe she was."

Amherst pointed at the tests. "Maybe you could confirm it for us?"

"Ah. Of course. Good thinking." Fromme shuffled through the stack and stopped at one sheet. "Yes, here's her test."

"How'd she do?"

"I haven't graded it yet."

"How's she generally do?"

Fromme held out his hand and wiggled it. "*Comme ci, comme ça.*"

Amherst checked the schedules. "You have Josephine Banfield, too."

"I do."

"What kind of student is she?"

"About the same. Though I think she could do much better. She's a bright girl."

"Not a hard worker, then?"

Fromme pursed his lips. "I don't think Miss Banfield is averse to working hard. My guess is she's more than willing to put in the effort when it suits her."

"French doesn't suit her?"

"It certainly doesn't excite her."

"What does, do you think?"

"Adventure," Fromme said. "Unless I miss my mark."

"Adventure, huh?" Amherst looked at Fromme more closely. "The kind of adventure that involves professors?"

Fromme smiled broadly. "Quite possibly, but not me, alas. No, I get the impression her choices might lie more in the extreme."

"Extreme? Like how?"

"Ruffians, perhaps. Scoundrels. Or someone much older." Fromme tilted his head. "Whatever might cause the most distress to her parents."

Amherst eyed the professor with suspicion. "How do you know this? Or are you just blowing gas?"

"I don't *know* it, per se," said Fromme. "Miss Banfield is merely no different than dozens of other students I see every year who are cut from the same cloth."

"The adventure cloth, huh?"

Fromme shrugged. "Perhaps I'm wrong." He hesitated, then asked, "Is she all right, Officer?"

"Why do you ask?"

"You're here, and you didn't ask if Jo was present in class today, which leads me to believe you already know she was not." He spread his hands. "I may be a French professor, but even I can add two plus two."

"You're a real Sherlock," Amherst mumbled. He didn't bother handing Fromme a card. "Next time you see either of these girls, tell them to call the precinct."

"Certainly."

Amherst limped out of the classroom.

Pierce trailed behind. When they were outside again, he said quietly, "You didn't ask him about the war."

"That Sally didn't serve."

"I think he might've."

Amherst shot him a dark look. "Not a chance."

"With the French background, he could've been MIS."

Amherst scoffed in reply. In his experience, those in Intelligence were worse than the officers above him. He couldn't count how many times his unit stumbled into a village that was supposed to be empty only to have it full of krauts, armed to the teeth.

He changed the subject. "In my day, not showing up for class would get you booted out of school," Amherst groused as the two walked back to the car.

"Where'd you go to college?" Pierce asked, surprised.

"I never said I went. You think I'd be wearing out shoe leather if I went to college?"

"I suppose not."

"College isn't for people like you and me, Pierce."

"What kind of people is that?"

"Ones who work for a living."

When they reached the car, Amherst's stomach was grumbling. He directed Pierce to drive to Knight's Diner at Division and Jackson.

"You'll spoil your dinner," Pierce objected.

"Don't worry about my dinner."

The younger detective didn't argue further. When they reached the rail car that had been transformed into a restaurant, Amherst lumbered inside and climbed onto a stool at the counter. Pierce took the one to his right.

Deliberately, Amherst turned over the coffee cup and set his badge on the counter in front of him. When the waitress bustled over with a coffee pot, she glanced at the tin while she filled his cup.

"What'll it be, Officer?" she asked.

Amherst ordered a pastrami on rye. Next to him, Pierce took only coffee. The sandwich arrived quickly, and Amherst tore into it.

"So…" Pierce said. "Their homes next?"

Amherst groaned around a mouthful of pastrami.

"Corson's house is closest," Pierce said. "We could start there."

Amherst flexed his aching feet as he swallowed. "Will you shut up and let me eat?"

Pierce fell silent.

Amherst finished his sandwich and pushed the plate away. He took a long drink of coffee to wash it down. Not the greatest rye pastrami he'd ever eaten, but better than he'd expected from a greasy spoon.

He climbed off the stool, brushing crumbs from his shirt and tie. As he turned to go, he noticed Pierce leaving several coins next to his cup. He almost stopped to rebuke the younger detective, but his pinching shoes made him wince, so he just headed for the door.

Chapter 4

As they walked toward the car, Pierce asked, "Am I still driving?"

"Until I say otherwise," Amherst said, his tone sharp.

The shoes dug deeper into his heels and his limp became even more pronounced, as if he were walking on broken glass. The pair were from a downtown cobbler, a supposed 'thank you' for all the hard work the department did in keeping the city safe. Now, Amherst thought otherwise. The store owner must have another agenda—a secret up-yours he wanted to send SPD. When Amherst had some free time, he'd return the up-yours with relish.

When they dropped into the car, Pierce shifted himself behind the steering wheel. Amherst looked at him suspiciously. "You got some kind of problem with tradition?" he asked.

Pierce glanced sideways at him. "No."

"You suddenly confused about how things work in this town? Meals are on the arm—we don't pay. *That's* a tradition."

Pierce stared straight ahead, not speaking.

"How long have you pulled this act?" Amherst demanded.

"No act."

"You trying to buck the system?"

Pierce sighed. "I left a tip, that's all. The waitress has to make a living, doesn't she?"

"A cup of joe is two bits. You tip two hundred percent?"

"Why do you care?" Pierce asked, turning onto Mission Avenue and driving toward Monroe.

"It sets an expectation. You start paying, pretty soon they think the rest of us should, too. The entire system crumbles."

"Maybe it should."

Amherst snapped his thick fingers and jabbed one in Pierce's direction. "Goddamn rabble-rouser. You *are* trying to buck the system. I knew it."

"No," Pierce said. "I'm one man. I'm not going to change a damn thing, but that doesn't mean I can't pay for my coffee."

"You're going to tell a restaurant owner he can't help out his local copper? He knows how little we get paid to do this job."

Pierce glanced at him again. "This isn't the Army. None of us were drafted."

"Voluntary or not, the pay is crap and you know it. A good meal goes a long way."

"It does, huh? What about the liquor and cigarettes, then?" Amherst frowned.

"And the shoes?"

"Just drive. There's no talking to you."

Pierce crossed the Monroe Street Bridge and turned west, headed into the neighborhood of Browne's Addition. A few minutes later, they pulled to a stop in front of Steve Corson's address. Amherst took in the regal lines of the thirty-year-old home. Not quite as fancy as the Banfield residence, and older. Regardless, it still smelled of money.

Before leaving the car, Amherst untied his shoes. Perhaps loosening them would ease the cutting on his heels and the pinching around his toes. Pierce waited until Amherst grabbed the door handle.

The two detectives walked wordlessly up the sidewalk. Amherst's shoelaces flopped wildly, giving a deridingly unprofessional look. He stopped and reluctantly re-tied his shoes. Pierce stood silently by. When he finished, Amherst stood and hobbled toward the house.

Amherst lit a cigarette while Pierce rapped on the door. Music drifted through the walls. To Amherst's ear, it was blues or jazz. He never understood the difference, only that both genres were distinctly Negro. Such music was like the flu, infecting the younger generation, especially on the east coast and California. He didn't like hearing it in his hometown.

After a long pause, an old man slowly opened the door. He was dressed in elegant clothing but appeared slightly disheveled. Several days' growth of gray stubble covered his cheeks and chin. His deep burgundy ascot was held in place with a gold pin.

"Yes?" he asked Pierce, his tone quavering with age.

Pierce held up his badge and opened his mouth to speak.

"This the Corson residence?" Amherst interjected.

The man's gaze drifted toward him. "I'm Reginald Corson. This is my home."

"Sir, is your son here?"

"He is entertaining guests at the moment."

Amherst smirked. "We heard the music."

Reginald shrugged helplessly. "I've found that no generation understands the music of the one which follows."

"We need to come in and talk to Steve," Amherst said, stepping forward.

At first, Reginald didn't move. Amherst wondered if he might be contemplating resistance or if the old man was just slow to react. The point became moot when Reginald shuffled aside and held the door wider.

"They are in the parlor," Reginald stated, pointing a skinny arm.

Amherst murmured his thanks and lumbered in the direction the man had pointed. The Negro music was already giving him a headache to rival the pain in his feet. He didn't bother to knock at the parlor door. Instead, he pushed it open and stepped inside.

Five heads turned his way. Everyone in the room froze, staring at the new arrivals.

Behind Amherst, Pierce closed the door.

An athletic young man with sandy hair stood in the middle of the room, entwined with a brunette girl. They'd clearly been dancing before the detectives entered. In a nearby oversized chair, a young blond woman sat on the lap of a huskier man with jet black hair. A younger man with a slight build sat on a window seat, his knees drawn up to his chest and a book in his hands. Bottles of beer and glasses of amber liquid dotted several surfaces.

Jackpot, Amherst thought.

He pointed to the record player console. "Turn that garbage *off*," he ordered.

No one moved for a moment. Then the brunette disentangled herself from the man in the center of the room and went to the record player. The music skidded to a silence.

"I'm Detective Amherst, Spokane Police," he said, projecting as much authority as possible with every word. Amherst jerked a thumb over his shoulder. "This is Detective Pierce."

No one answered. They just continued staring. Amherst noticed the athletic, sandy-haired kid swallow nervously. He decided to start with him.

"Your name," he demanded, pointing. "Now."

The sandy-haired one swallowed again before answering. "I'm Steve Corson. This is my house."

"It's your father's house, pretty boy," Amherst corrected. He pointed to the brunette girl, who winced slightly, as if struck.

"Peggy Little," she nearly squealed.

Amherst swung his finger to the chair. The black-haired young man identified himself as Kenneth Marchment. The blonde on his lap was Sharon Cudmore, though her tone held a little too much insolence for his liking.

"Get off lover boy," Amherst instructed her. He motioned toward the nearby sofa. "Sit there."

Sharon stood and did her best to stomp to the sofa. She plopped down and crossed her arms.

Amherst turned to the last remaining person, who still sat on the window seat. "And you?"

"That's Baz," Peggy blurted.

Amherst flashed her a dark look. "Let him speak for himself." He turned back to the handsome young man. "Is that your name, bookworm? Baz?"

"Basil Pershing," he answered.

Amherst nodded, glancing over at Pierce. After spinning their tires in the mud all afternoon, they'd finally caught a break. He turned his attention back to the group. "Here's what's going to happen," he said. "My partner and I are going to talk to each of you out there in the living room, one at a time. While that's happening, the rest of you are going to sit in here and wait. No music, no talking. Am I clear?"

"What's the problem, Officer?" Steve asked. The shock of seeing two detectives in his home seemed to fade and Amherst could tell he was going to be a problem.

"What's your sport, pretty boy?" he asked.

Steve looked at him, momentarily confused. "My sport?"

"What do you play? At the college?"

Steve glanced around at the group before answering almost sheepishly. "Baseball," he admitted.

"Good," said Amherst, unimpressed. "You're the lead-off hitter." He jerked a thumb toward the door, which Pierce dutifully swung open. "Let's go."

Steve hesitated. "What's this about?" he asked, trying to sound demanding.

"It's about five seconds from being an arrest," barked Amherst. He pointed at the beer bottles and glasses of liquor. "Any of you twenty-one? Because if you're not, that's a charge."

"I'm twenty-one," Steve said, a touch of smugness creeping into his voice.

"Good," said Amherst. "Then that's a charge for supplying liquor to a minor. We can talk down at the station instead of your living room. You decide."

Steve looked uncertain. Then he drew himself up and walked quickly out of the room.

Amherst took a moment to look around at the remaining four. "Not a word," he cautioned, before he turned and lumbered into the hallway.

***

In the living room, Amherst could see that Steve Corson still couldn't decide whether to be cooperative or belligerent. The struggle was apparent within the man, though Amherst wasn't entirely sure what drove the dynamic. He zeroed in on what he wanted to know right away, in case Corson decided to get smart with him.

"You're friends with Josephine Banfield," he stated.

Steve looked confused. "Sure, but—"

"When did you see her last?"

"A couple of nights ago." Steve squinted. "Why? Is she okay?"

"A couple of nights ago?" Amherst asked. "Does that mean exactly two, or are you being cute?"

"Look, Officer, I don't mean any disrespect, but—"

"Then answer my question."

Amherst saw the young man's eyes hardening with a mixture of resentment and entitlement. *Here comes the spoiled brat from old money.*

"Answer the detective's question," Pierce interjected, his voice low and flat.

Steve crossed his arms defiantly. "I don't think I care for you coming into my house like this, demanding—"

"It's your parents' house," Pierce corrected, echoing Amherst's earlier response. "Though I don't know for how much longer."

Steve's eyes flared.

"Also," Pierce said, "I don't think the college's scholarship committee would look too kindly on one of their students refusing to do his civic duty when it comes to assisting the police in an investigation. It might even be something they'd revoke a scholarship over, don't you think?"

Steve stared at Pierce, his expression turning nervous. Then he shifted his attention back to Amherst. "Jo's one of my friends. I saw her three nights ago."

"Where?"

"Here at the house."

"Who else was present?"

Steve thought for a moment. "Same group as today."

"Tell me about this group," Amherst said. "You and Peggy an item?"

"Trying to be," Steve said. "She runs hot and cold." The smug look returned.

Amherst wanted to smack the smirk off the spoiled prick's face. He leaned forward and studied Steve. "What about you and Josephine?"

Steve shook his head. "No. I mean, I tried last year, but she wasn't too interested."

"Why not?"

"I'm not her type, I guess."

"What's her type—lover boy in there, or the bookworm?"

"No. Her tastes run more… exotic."

Amherst narrowed his eyes. "Colored?"

"I don't know about that, but she likes her men older. I think."

"Older? Why's that?"

Steve shrugged. "I don't know for sure. I only ever heard about it when she was drunk."

"Who did you hear?"

"No names. She called them her paramours." Steve smiled slyly. "Peggy said paramours were married men, but Jo told her she didn't know what she was talking about. Jo was all mysterious about it. You ask me, I don't even know if they existed."

"Was Josephine a liar?" Amherst asked.

"Not usually. She was a straight line in most ways, but when it came to her love life, she was secretive."

Amherst continued the interview with Steve, trying to find new lines of questioning, but discovered nothing but blind alleys. While he spoke, Pierce jotted in his notebook, not interrupting the process.

When Amherst finished, he cautioned Steve not to talk to anyone about their conversation. "Call the station when you see Josephine again," he added.

"I will," Steve assured him. He hesitated, then asked, "Please, Officer, tell me—is she okay?"

"She ran away from home," Amherst said gruffly. "Now, go wait in your room until we're finished."

Steve looked dismayed, but he turned around and reluctantly trudged up the stairs.

"I'll get the next one," Pierce said, once Steve was gone. "You might consider going a little easier. You get more flies with honey than vinegar."

"These brats aren't brought up to respond to nice. They only respect money and power. Since I don't have any money..."

Pierce shrugged. "Their friend is missing. I think they'd try to be as helpful as possible if we just told them that."

"Or cover up for her," Amherst argued. "Especially if she ran off with some trumpet player or the like."

"I don't think that's it."

He peered more closely at Pierce. "How'd you know about that kid's scholarship?"

"Educated guess."

"Based on what?"

Pierce glanced around. "This place is old money but look a little closer. There's a layer of dust over the mantle. Some of the furniture is worn. Like a household that used to have servants but doesn't anymore. It looks like decaying wealth."

Amherst thought about the appearance of Reginald Corson when he'd answered the door. His clothes had been expensive but frayed, giving off the air of rotting regalness. He nodded, seeing Pierce's point.

"So, when you got him to admit he was a ballplayer," Pierce said, "it only made sense he'd be on a scholarship. If the family could afford tuition, this place would be in better shape."

"That's quite a leap," Amherst said.

Pierce shrugged. "An educated guess, like I said. If it turned out I was wrong, there was still plenty of leverage with his general enrollment."

Amherst glanced around at the living room, seeing it differently after Pierce's comment. "Why not sell the place?" he wondered aloud.

"People adhere to their illusions," Pierce said. He went into the parlor and returned with Kenneth Marchment.

It was immediately apparent to Amherst that Kenneth was not the sharpest knife in the drawer. He was definitely less help than Steve, though Amherst didn't believe it was purposeful on Kenneth's part. The kid seemed to only pay attention to what was at the end of his nose.

"Jo was cool," he said. "A real classy chassis, if you know what I mean."

Amherst blinked, taking a moment to translate the slang. "You mean she was stacked?"

Kenneth nodded. "A little snooty, too."

"What do you mean? You're all rich kids, aren't you?"

"I guess," said Kenneth. "With Jo, it was like all of us were her second-string friends, you know? Like, junior varsity?"

"Do you know where she is now?"

"No."

"Don't lie to me, lover boy."

Kenneth raised his hands in surrender. "Word from the bird, Daddy-O."

"Speak goddamn English," growled Amherst.

"Honest to God," said Kenneth. "I have no idea."

Amherst decided *I have no idea* was likely to be Kenneth's life motto. Lucky for him, his parents had enough money that it probably wouldn't matter. He got to go to college and chase co-eds instead of being drafted and killing communists in Korea.

Kenneth confirmed most of what Steve had said. After Amherst sent Kenneth packing, Pierce brought out Peggy Little.

The young brunette was as skittish as a cat. Amherst took her through the same questions he'd asked Steve and Kenneth. She didn't have any additional information other than confirming what the boys had said. However, her eyes nervously flicked back and forth between the two detectives the entire time.

"What are you hiding?" Amherst asked.

"Nothing," she said, unconvincingly.

"Don't lie," Amherst said. "It's an insult and a waste of time. Do you know where Josephine is?"

"No!"

"Then what is it?"

Peggy swallowed and pressed her lips together. "What they told you about her liking older men, it's true."

"Which older men?"

"I don't know. She met them at parties."

"What kind of parties?"

Peggy shrugged. "Not the kind I go to, that's all I know. Jo said she met a few different men that way."

"Did she mention names?"

"No."

"Did she describe any of them?"

Peggy shook her head. "I don't even know if she was… you know."

"Having sex with them?"

The young woman turned red. "Yes. That."

"Were any of these men professors at the college?" Amherst thought of the French Professor, Ethan Fromme, secretly hoping he was one of Josephine's paramours.

"I don't... I mean, it could be," Peggy said. "There was someone she'd been seeing on campus recently."

"How do you know that?"

"It was obvious whenever she mentioned him."

"But you don't know who?"

"No. Maybe Sharon will. Those two are much closer than me and Jo."

Once Amherst had exhausted his questions with Peggy Little, he sent her home. She asked to say goodbye to Steve, but Amherst merely pointed at the front door. Disappointed, Peggy left.

Sharon Cudmore still had some attitude. She sat on the couch with her arms crossed, scowling. Amherst decided, since his earlier approach hadn't worked, he'd reluctantly give Pierce's suggestion to go a little easier a try.

"Josephine is missing," he said simply.

Sharon cocked her head, suspicious. "Missing? Like kidnapped or something?"

"We don't know," Amherst admitted, though it galled him to give more weight than it deserved to this rich brat running away from home. He justified it by thinking the sooner they found her, the sooner they could move on to other cases.

"Neither do I," Sharon stated firmly.

Amherst spread his hands. "She's not in any trouble. Her parents are just worried about her."

"She's an adult."

"She still lives at home."

"So? It's her home."

Amherst resisted the urge to rub his eyes. These kids thought their parents' wealth and power flowed to them, and it frustrated him. He said, "Look, her parents love her. They only want to know she's safe."

Sharon snorted. "They don't give a hoot about her."

Amherst thought of the photos he'd seen at the Banfield residence. "They've taken her all over the world," he said.

"What does *that* have to do with love?"

He decided he couldn't communicate with this girl in her own language, so he shifted to one he knew better. "If you know where she is and you don't tell me right now, you'll be guilty of a crime. If she—"

"What crime?" demanded Sharon.

Amherst ignored the interruption and powered forward. "If she's been hurt or taken against her will, you withholding information could be what gets her killed."

Sharon's head twitched and she blinked rapidly in surprise. "You think she's... hurt?"

Amherst didn't, but he knew an angle to play with a witness when he saw one. "I think it's possible," he said, softening his tone.

Sharon swallowed nervously. "I thought she was just... off with someone, you know?"

"Who would she be off with?"

"I don't know for sure. She never mentions them by name."

"Them?"

Sharon shifted uncomfortably. "I'm not saying Jo is a tramp or anything, but there have been a few men she's talked about."

"Who?"

"All of them are older. She met them at parties, except for one on campus. She wouldn't say who, but I think it might be Dr. Etherton. He works at the campus clinic."

Amherst felt a small thrill of discovery. Next to him, Pierce wrote down the name. "She told you she was involved with this doctor?"

Sharon shook her head. "That's the thing with Jo. She doesn't really tell us anything. She *implies*. It's all about mystery with her."

"Wonderful," muttered Amherst.

He pressed Sharon for more but got no further information than was already written in Pierce's notebook. Finally, he told her to go home.

Sharon didn't move right away, though. "Do you really think something's happened to Jo?"

"No," Amherst answered impatiently. "But we have to be sure."

That didn't seem to comfort Sharon. She got her purse and left without another word.

Instead of waiting for Pierce to escort Basil Pershing out into the living room, Amherst rose and followed Pierce into the parlor.

His feet felt swollen now. Amherst imagined how his heels looked underneath his socks—bloody hamburger. The shoe salesman would regret handing Amherst this pair.

Basil Pershing still sat on the window seat, though he'd extended his legs out and leaned back against the wall. He was reading when the detectives walked in. Sunlight bathed him like a photo from *Life* magazine. His thick, sandy brown hair was neatly trimmed. He wore gray tweed pants, a white shirt, and a charcoal-colored sweater vest. Of all the students, he was the one most dressed for success.

"What's that?" Amherst asked, motioning toward the book.

Wordlessly, Basil held up the book so Amherst could see the plain cover.

Amherst leaned forward to see it better. "*The City and the Pillar,*" he read, "by Gore Vidal." He shrugged. "Never heard of it."

"I'm not surprised."

"Is it new?"

"A few years old," Basil said. His tone was easy, and he sounded unruffled by the detectives' presence. Amherst decided he'd had ample time to get used to the idea. "I don't think you'd enjoy it."

"I'll tell you what I'd enjoy," said Amherst. "Someone to tell me where Josephine Banfield is."

Basil cocked his head. "All her dear friends less than helpful?"

"Or ignorant," Amherst said. "Why, do you know better?"

"I'm afraid not."

Amherst watched Basil carefully. He appeared younger than the others. His mannerisms seemed practiced and deliberate with an air about him that was starting to smell a little fruity.

"What year are you in college?" he asked.

"Sophomore."

"Really? You look younger than the others."

"I am. I'm seventeen."

That surprised Amherst given the kid's attitude and attire. "Seventeen and a college sophomore? How's that work?"

"I skipped a grade in elementary school," Basil explained. "As a result, I graduated early and got a head start on college."

"What are you, some kind of genius?"

"It doesn't take a genius to excel at public school," said Basil. He put down his book and swung his legs so that his feet were on the ground. "What does my education have to do with Jo?"

Amherst pursed his lips in thought. "Looks like Steve and Peggy are working on being a couple. Seems Ken and Sharon already are. That leaves you and Jo. You two an item?"

Basil scoffed lightly. "I'm hardly Jo's type, nor she mine."

"What's her type?"

"Older, for one."

"How about yours?"

Basil shrugged. "The same, actually."

"You and Jo have the same type?" Amherst asked. "Older men?"

"Did I say that?" Basil smiled coyly. "What's your interest, Detective?"

Amherst suppressed a shudder. He glanced over at Pierce, who didn't react. He wondered if his partner had the same attitude toward degenerates as his own.

"Tell us about the doctor," Amherst said, changing the subject.

"Doctor?"

"On campus."

Basil's eyes narrowed in confusion. "I'm not sure who you're talking about."

"Dr. Etherton," Amherst said.

"Ah." Basil nodded several times as if considering something. "I've seen him around campus. He seems all right, I suppose, as doctors go. I've never gone to him myself. We have a family doctor."

"Is Josephine seeing him?"

Basil burst out laughing. "Seeing? As in dating?"

"He's older, isn't he? That's her type, you said."

Basil's laughter tapered off. "I suppose that's true. But no, I don't think he's actually her type at all. Far too straitlaced. If she's had anything to do with him, it was for medical reasons."

Amherst leaned forward. "What kind of medical reasons?"

"The private kind."

"Don't be funny." Amherst jabbed a finger in Basil's chest. "Why would she go to Dr. Etherton instead of her family doctor?"

"Why do you think?"

Amherst frowned. That was what he'd been afraid of. Basil was either talking about contraception or, worse yet, abortion. "This doctor does those things?"

Basil turned up his hands. "Seeing as how I'm not a girl, how would I know? I'll tell you this, though—she wasn't playing any backseat bingo with the good doctor. You're barking up the wrong tree there."

"I'll be the judge of that."

"Judge, jury, and executioner, I'm sure."

Amherst didn't like Basil's tone or his effeminate manner. "Where would you look for her, smart guy?"

"Parties," Basil answered immediately.

Amherst's interest was piqued. Several of the others had mentioned parties as well. "What kind of parties?"

"The kind where they smoke marijuana. It's all the rage this year. You'd be surprised who is trying out the giggle-smokes, Detective."

Amherst had heard whispers about marijuana parties among the younger generation but had yet to come across one. The bulk of his experience with the drug was occasionally taking it off people he arrested.

"You smoke the stuff?" Amherst asked.

Basil shook his head. "I think marijuana—and most other drugs, for that matter—is for the weak-minded. To each their own, I guess."

Amherst shifted on his feet, wincing in discomfort. These damn shoes. He pulled a chair closer to the window seat where Basil sat and dropped heavily into it. He eyed the young man for a few seconds, his expression hardening. Basil stared back, seemingly unconcerned.

"Tell me more about these marijuana parties," Amherst said.

Chapter 5

They drove southbound along Altamont Boulevard.

"Where we going?" Pierce asked, from behind the steering wheel.

Amherst bent over and untied his shoes. It was a painful, awkward position. "Keep going south until you get to Third, then turn left."

"Aren't we going to follow up on the reefer lead?"

"In a minute." Amherst pulled at his right shoe. He felt lightheaded in this position.

"What about the doctor?" Pierce asked.

The shoe popped off and relief flooded Amherst's extremity. He flopped back into his seat and sighed. "We'll get to him after." Third Avenue was up ahead. Amherst pointed at it. "Second house on the right."

Pierce turned the car and pulled to the curb. He clicked off the engine. "Who're we seeing?"

"You aren't seeing anyone." Amherst opened the passenger door. "Stay here. Listen to the radio."

He climbed out and limped toward his house. He still wore his uncomfortable left shoe, but his right foot was now protected only by its sock. Amherst waddled up the path, like an unbalanced penguin. He climbed the four concrete stairs and entered the house. An aroma of cooking meat wafted to him.

"Gloria?" he called.

"Back here."

Amherst didn't bother checking on his wife. Instead, he limped directly into their bedroom. He tossed the right shoe into the corner, then dropped heavily onto the edge of the bed. It squeaked under his weight. He crossed his leg and untied his other shoe.

"What're you doing home at this hour?"

Gloria appeared in the doorway. A white apron protected a light-green patterned dress. She dried her hands on a dish towel. Her brown hair was pulled back with a red ribbon.

"Why?" Amherst asked. "You hiding something?"

"Only my boyfriend."

"You better not." Amherst peeled the second shoe off and threw it at its mate. It bounced off the floor then clunked against the wall.

"I take it you don't like your new shoes."

"They're goddamn torture devices."

Gloria crossed her arms. "Don't use that language in our house."

"Don't start."

"I won't have you blaspheming the Lord."

Amherst groaned when he stood. "The Lord doesn't care how I talk."

"Yes, he does," Gloria said, "and you know it. If you don't like the shoes, take them back."

"I will. Believe me." Amherst shuffled to his closet and grabbed his most comfortable pair of loafers. The brown shoes had been reheeled once already and were in desperate need of another. The leather was soft and broken in like a well-used first baseman's glove. Amherst slipped them on. They clashed with his black suit.

Gloria raised an eyebrow. "You can do better."

"Not today," Amherst said. "Style be damned."

His torn heels and pinched corns still hurt in the loafers, but the pain was tolerable now. Amherst kissed his wife on the cheek as he passed. "What's for dinner?"

"Beef stew."

He scoffed. "My favorite."

Gloria headed toward the kitchen. She called over her shoulder. "Keep complaining and you can cook for yourself."

"That's not the order of things." He watched her go. "You do the cooking, and I do the earning."

"Keep flapping those gums," Gloria hollered. "That boyfriend of mine is looking better every minute."

Amherst shook his fist in her direction, even though Gloria couldn't see.

"Hurry home," she said from the kitchen. "No drinking with the boys tonight."

"Yeah, yeah." Amherst dropped his hand and gently pulled the door closed behind him.

***

The only confirmed address Basil Pershing provided was in an apartment building on Trent Avenue across from Union Station, the city's train depot. A large clock tower stood in the middle of the building. Powerful-looking engines remained silent on multiple tracks with seemingly endless lines of cars stacked behind them. Downtown Spokane abutted the depot.

"I'll never get this," Amherst said.

Pierce glanced at him as he slowed the car. "Get what?"

"Rich kids from decent homes come down here looking for trouble."

Pierce pulled the car to the curb and parked. "This is a couple blocks from police headquarters."

"Right under our noses," Amherst said.

"Wasn't there a speakeasy in this building?"

Amherst popped open his door but didn't get out. "What're you saying?"

"Seems like a lot happens without us knowing it."

"This ain't that." Amherst flicked his hand.

"Then what are you angry about?" Pierce asked. "Citizens coming downtown for their kicks? They've been doing it for years." He pulled the key from the ignition. "They're not going to do anything illegal where they live. Not where their neighbors can see."

Amherst grumbled. "Still," not feeling the need to add more. He stepped onto the sidewalk and slammed the door. He adjusted his fedora.

The five-story Coeur d'Alene Building loomed above them. The fleabag hotel stood at the corner of Trent and Howard. A restaurant and small grocery store filled the lower floors.

Amherst limped toward the hotel. "How's anyone smoking that stuff around here without the world knowing it?"

"Without us knowing about it is what I'd like to know." Pierce spun and backpedaled. He waved a hand toward the train depot. "Maybe the engines mask the smell."

"It was a rhetorical question."

"Then why ask it?" Pierce faced forward and walked a half-pace behind him. "Grumpy bastard," he muttered.

Amherst yanked open the door and entered the small lobby. The black and white linoleum floor shined as if recently mopped. A hint of PineSol struggled to mask a generation of body odor and cigarette smoke.

A gray-haired man in a wrinkled white shirt and purple vest hunched over the front desk. His pencil ticked feverishly on a small paper. A black telephone and shiny chrome bell sat on either side of him. Hooks littered the wall with a variety of keys dangling from them. An expensive-looking camera sat on the back counter.

Amherst stepped forward. "Who you got?"

The clerk looked up, surprised to see someone standing there. "Sir?"

Pierce also moved toward the front desk. He pushed his hat back and tilted his head to study the newspaper.

"Got a hot tip?" Amherst tapped the clerk's racing form. "Those are the ponies running at Playfair, right?"

The clerk swallowed and his eyes darted between the detectives. "Sir?"

"I'm Detective Amherst." He thumbed toward his partner. "That's Detective Pierce."

"Sir?"

"This one's a broken record," Amherst said. "Maybe I should smack him upside the head and see if he skips."

The clerk swallowed and slid the racing form off the counter. He clutched it to his chest.

Pierce leaned an elbow on the counter. "What's your name?"

"Vern."

"Well, Vern," Pierce said, "we hear you allow marijuana smoking in this building."

Vern's face slackened. "Sir?"

Amherst lifted his hand. "Time to see if he skips."

The clerk hopped away and bumped into the back counter. The fancy camera shifted to the edge. "The basement," Vern blurted. "They're in the basement."

"Look at that," Amherst said. "The record's playing again."

***

Vern led the way down a set of rickety stairs. "There used to be a speakeasy down here, you know."

"What'd I tell you?" Pierce asked from behind.

"Keep it to yourself," Amherst said.

Light bulbs drooped from a line attached to the wall. It descended with the staircase. Water dripped nearby. Muted music drifted upward along with a skunky smell.

To Vern, Amherst asked, "How'd these junkies find this hideaway?"

"Sir?"

Amherst grabbed the clerk when they reached solid ground and spun him around. He stuck his finger in Vern's face. "Every time you 'sir' me, I know you're lying."

The clerk tried to move back, but Amherst's fingers dug into his arm.

"How'd the hopheads find out about this Cracker Jack box?"

Vern winced and covered Amherst's hand with his own. "I told them. They were smoking in a room and I— You're hurting me."

Amherst eased his grip but didn't let go of Vern.

"Some of the other guests were complaining," the clerk said. "So I told them about the basement."

"What do you get out of the arrangement?" Amherst's lip curled. "They pay you extra?"

Vern swallowed.

"Well?"

"I don't get money. I promise." Vern tried to tuck his arms into his chest like a turtle pulling into his shell, but Amherst held on to him.

"What do you get?" Pierce asked.

"Sir?"

Amherst's fingers dug into Vern's arm and jerked him closer. "Don't start with that crap again."

The clerk grimaced, then licked his lips and looked away.

"The girls?" Pierce asked. He looked at Amherst. "What're they trading?"

Amherst slapped Vern with his free hand. "Spill." His fingers dug harder into the clerk's bicep.

"Pictures. They let me take pictures." Vern closed his eyes and shook his head. "Nothing more."

Amherst let go of Vern. He pulled Josephine Banfield's photograph from his jacket pocket and shoved it into the clerk's face. "Seen this one?"

Vern rubbed his bicep as he pulled back, as if trying to study the picture. His eyes narrowed and he cocked his head. "No. Never."

Pierce pushed the clerk's head closer to the photograph. "Take another look."

"I never seen her. I never forget a pretty girl." Vern lifted his chin. "And that one's a cutie."

"You better not be lying." Amherst said.

"Why are you looking for her?" Vern asked. "Is she missing or something?"

***

No one scattered when Vern pulled the sliding door to the side. Ten teenagers and college-aged men and women lounged on ratty couches and old recliners. A couple of the girls sat on the laps of their boyfriends with their arms draped around the others' shoulders. Two boys slouched as if they'd just gotten home from a hard day's work. A haze hung in the low light of the basement reefer den. The pungent odor reminded Amherst vaguely of burning rope.

An old bar counter sat behind the group. Soda bottles and trash from the local hamburger dives accumulated on its top. An annoying sound emanated from the battery-operated radio.

"Turn the garbage off," Amherst ordered as he waved away the marijuana haze.

One of the women laughed. "Come off it."

"Yeah, man," a teenager said. He held a homemade cigarette in his hand. "That's Les Paul and Mary Ford. Don't you know the hits?"

Amherst smiled. "Yeah, I know the hits." He motioned the kid to stand up. "Come here, you."

"Take it easy," Pierce said.

"Mind your business," Amherst muttered. To the teenager, he said, "Get up."

The kid looked eighteen, maybe even twenty, and had that privileged appearance the Catholic ones got after attending years of private school at Gonzaga. He languidly left his recliner, put the marijuana cigarette on the edge of the coffee table, and moved toward Amherst. "What?"

Amherst slugged him in the gut. The teenager dropped to the ground and clutched his belly.

"How's that for a hit?" Amherst asked. "Wanna hear another?"

The others in the room sat up straighter. The girls who were sitting on their boyfriends' laps slid off and straightened their skirts. One of the men reached up and clicked off the radio. Silence hung over the room.

"Now that we've got your attention," Amherst said, "it's time to remember your manners."

Vern tried to slink away, but Pierce grabbed him and pushed him into the corner of the room. He angrily pointed at the clerk.

"I'm Detective Amherst. He's Detective Pierce. First thing we're going to do is get each and every one of your names. Including you, mouthpiece." Amherst patted the head of the teenager still gasping for air. "Let's go."

Pierce pulled out his notebook. For the next five minutes, they identified everyone sitting in the former speakeasy.

When they finished, Amherst pulled Josephine's photo from his jacket. "Now, who wants to stay out of trouble?"

The girls all raised their hands. Soon, the boys had their hands in the air, too.

"Great," Amherst said. "First one who tells me where to find this girl stays out of jail." He turned Josephine's picture and held it out.

They all scrambled closer to see it, but the looks on their faces told the story. None of them knew Josephine.

"We were told," Pierce said, "she hangs out with people like you."

"Not us," someone blurted. Amherst didn't catch who said it.

"Give us another place," Pierce said, "where you types smoke this crap."

Calvin, the teenager who smart-mouthed Amherst, raised his hand. He had settled back onto the couch and continued to rub his belly. "The only others I know are in the colored neighborhoods. You think she might go there?"

"I don't know, Calvin." Amherst said. "You tell me." He flashed Josephine's picture again. "She look like the type of girl to hang out with the coloreds?"

Calvin swallowed. "No, sir."

Amherst shoved the picture back into his pocket. His gaze cut to Pierce. "What do you want to do?"

"Let's get a wagon started," Pierce said. "Book 'em all."

One of the girls grabbed her boyfriend's arm and said, "No!" Amherst couldn't remember her name.

"It's a lot of paperwork," Amherst said, "and we still gotta interview the doctor."

Pierce motioned toward the group. "We can't ignore them."

Amherst frowned. He would have hoped the younger detective could have seen the bigger picture. "You got one minute," Amherst said to the dopers. "Eat the evidence."

"What?" Pierce said.

Calvin grabbed the marijuana cigarette from the edge of the coffee table. He shoved it in his mouth and swallowed. "That's it," he said. "There was nothing else but that roach."

The others nodded. Someone muttered, "Nothing."

"We know about this hangout now," Amherst said. "Vice will be back to talk with you about your pusher. Understand? You better not hold out on them."

Pierce shoved his hands in his pockets and looked at his shoes.

Amherst crossed his arms. "Now, all of you, scram."

Everyone jumped to their feet. They raced by the two detectives, through the basement, and up the stairs. It sounded like a bunch of horses. Amherst imagined the speakeasy had heard that sound once or twice in its heyday.

Amherst glared at Vern. "As for you, shutterbug. You let these hoodlums come back, we're gonna charge you with running a drug house. Got it?"

Vern's eyes widened. "I wasn't."

"Maybe pornography, too," Amherst said.

"But," the clerk stammered. "But." He didn't add anything beyond his simple protests, including, Amherst was glad to see, no lying, obsequious *sirs*.

"But nothing. You know the rules now." Amherst eyed Pierce, who stood sullenly with his shoulders slumped. "Let's go."

Chapter 6

"What's your problem?" Amherst asked.

Pierce gripped the steering wheel. "I don't have a problem."

Amherst laughed. "You look like my wife does when I tell her to ease up on the spending."

They were on the highway, headed back toward Eastern Washington College of Education.

Pierce lifted a hand to say something but refrained. He dropped it back on the steering wheel.

"Go ahead," Amherst said. "Spit it out."

"You going to shovel some nonsense about what's said in this car being sacred?" Pierce's gaze cut to Amherst. "Because I'm not buying it."

"I was going to tell you to stop being a crybaby."

"A crybaby?" Pierce's face tightened. "I'll have you know—"

Amherst pointed ahead. "Watch the road."

The car had drifted onto the shoulder and was about to run into the scrub brush.

Pierce's attention returned forward, and he pulled the car back within their lane. He inhaled deeply. "You shouldn't have let those dopers go."

Amherst tugged a pack of cigarettes from his jacket. He didn't offer one to Pierce before lighting up.

He ignored the younger detective's outburst. Instead, his thoughts drifted to his feet. They felt better now since switching to his loafers. The heels still hurt and the corns pulsed, but it no longer felt like his feet were in a vise. Amherst had helped a salesman out of a jam and the bastard repaid the favor with a less-than-quality pair of shoes. The detective wasn't going to forgive that transgression.

"Well?" Pierce asked.

Amherst blinked. "Well, what?"

"What have you got to say?"

"About?"

"The dopers."

Amherst studied the burning end of his cigarette. "It wasn't the best use of our time."

"You asked me what I wanted to do, and I said—"

"Listen," he interrupted.

"No," Pierce said. "You listen. I get you're the senior detective, but I'm not new to this job."

The other detective droned on. However, Amherst ignored him. He caught occasional bits like "society's menace" and "devil's weed" while thinking about Gloria's beef stew. It wasn't his favorite meal, but Amherst found if he concentrated on his wife's cooking, he could blot out the rant of administrators, the bleating of church preachers, and his mother-in-law's blathering whenever she visited.

Amherst hoped there were more potatoes in the stew than carrots. He disliked it when Gloria got a deal from the grocer and went heavier on the other vegetables. Amherst figured himself a meat and potato man, not a meat and carrot man. Eating too many vegetables put him precariously close to being a vegetarian and every one of those weirdos he knew was a closeted fag.

"And that's all I've got to say about that," Pierce finally said.

Amherst rolled down his window. He inhaled a final time on his cigarette and flicked it out the window. "Feel better?" he asked.

Pierce's face reddened. "No."

"Well, if you're gonna start barking again, can you do it softer this time? I need to catch up on some Zs."

Pierce grabbed the steering wheel with both hands and glowered. He remained pleasantly silent the rest of the way to Cheney.

***

They drove about the campus for ten minutes, zigzagging their way as they checked directional signage for anything that remotely looked associated with a medical purpose. The buildings sported names like Showalter, Hargreaves, and Martin but none of them revealed which purpose they supported.

"I remember when this was called Cheney Normal School," Amherst said.

Pierce said under his breath, "You remember when Lewis and Clark discovered this area."

Amherst motioned with his hand. "Pull over."

Two women walked along the sidewalk—a brunette and a redhead. They wore knee-length skirts and clutched textbooks to their chests. They laughed as they chatted.

The car glided to the curb in front of the women, and Amherst hopped out. He winced as soon as his feet touched the ground.

The women stopped walking and fell silent.

"Afternoon, ladies." Amherst flashed his best smile which neither returned. They eyed him with cool suspicion. "I'm Detective Amherst. Spokane Police. Where can we find the campus doctor?"

The young ladies exchanged confused glances. The brunette raised an eyebrow. "You mean the nurse?"

Amherst shook his head. "I mean Dr. Etherton."

"Oh." The brunette glanced at her friend, but the redhead looked down.

"What?" Amherst asked.

"Nothing." The brunette said. "Dr. Etherton isn't on campus." She pointed over Amherst's shoulder. "He's downtown."

"We were told he's the campus doctor."

The brunette smiled politely. "No, sir. He's affiliated—"

"Recommended," the redhead corrected. She still didn't look up and her cheeks were now flushed.

"Right." The brunette nodded. "He's *recommended* by the school nurse. Anyone can go wherever they want."

Amherst thumbed over his shoulder. "So, Etherton's downtown?"

The two women nodded, but only the brunette made eye contact.

"Thank you for your time," Amherst said.

The young ladies turned and hurried down the sidewalk.

Amherst dropped back into the car. His gaze remained locked on the departing women. "Maybe I should have gone to college."

"What'd they tell you?" Pierce asked.

"The doctor's downtown."

Pierce cocked his head. "Cheney has a downtown?"

***

Doctor Karl Etherton's office was in a painted brick building on First Street. Underneath the office's sign was the painted invitation—*Additional Parking in Rear.*

The single-story structure stood shoulder-to-shoulder with brick buildings on either side. An accountant filled the space to the east while a real estate office took the office to the west.

Pierce found a spot on the street near the real estate office. A heavyset man in blue slacks and a white shirt lounged on a wooden bench in front. The two detectives climbed out of the car and headed toward Etherton's practice.

The fat man coughed. "That spot is for my customers."

"City parking," Pierce said.

Amherst contemptuously flicked his hand. "Mind your business, fatso."

"Looks who's talking, fatso."

Pierce bumped into Amherst when he suddenly spun around. "Leave it alone," Pierce said.

"You calling me fat?" Amherst asked over his partner's shoulder.

The real estate man stood. "I should stand next to you, so people think me thin."

"You'd need to stand next to a blimp," Amherst countered.

"Why do you think I want to stand next to you?"

Pierce pushed Amherst back. "Ignore him."

"That's it!" Amherst yelled. "I'm coming back for you!"

"Yeah?" the real estate man said with a laugh. "Bring a sandwich."

Amherst had no idea what the insult meant but he wanted to thump the man. Pierce wrapped his arms around Amherst and moved him forward. "You're too old to be acting this way."

***

Amherst sulked in the corner with his arms crossed while Pierce spoke with the receptionist. She was a youngish woman with cat-eye glasses and a tight blue blouse. Amherst was so upset he couldn't enjoy the opportunity of chatting up the woman.

"Dr. Etherton is finishing with a patient," the receptionist said. "I'll let him know you're here."

Pierce nodded, then turned to Amherst.

"Look at you," Pierce whispered.

Amherst frowned. "What?"

"You look like a tea kettle about to squeal."

"That guy." Amherst lifted his chin toward the window. "I should've busted him in the mouth."

"What would that accomplish?"

"He would have learned not to insult a cop."

Pierce rolled his eyes. "He didn't know we were cops."

"He should have."

"Well, he didn't. Besides, so what if you're fat?"

Amherst's jaw dropped. He glanced at the receptionist before whispering, "I'm not fat."

Pierce shrugged. "If you say so."

"I'm big boned."

"Courtesy of a terrible diet."

"I should bust you in the mouth, too."

Pierce cocked his head. "You're not as young as you think you are."

"I'm only forty-nine, which is young enough to whip your—"

A door in the rear opened and closed, and the two detectives stopped talking.

Footsteps walked up the hallway and the receptionist reappeared. "You can go in now. Dr. Etherton just finished with a patient. It's the office all the way in the back."

Amherst led the way to the doctor's office. Two leather chairs with chrome arms stood in front of an elaborate mahogany desk that reminded Amherst of the ones all the brass had in their offices at the station. Awards and other certifications hung on the white walls.

Karl Etherton stood combing his hair in front of a small, hanging mirror. He saw Amherst and Pierce enter the room by their reflection in the mirror. "Gentlemen," he said. "Have a seat."

Amherst raised an eyebrow as he flashed a look at Pierce. The younger detective shrugged in response.

Etherton slipped his comb into a back pocket, then patted his dark brown hair. He moved his head left and right as he checked his reflection. "Vivian said you wanted a word."

"Cary Grant's got nothing on you," Amherst said.

The doctor turned. "That's nice of you to say."

Amherst frowned. The doctor had missed his sarcasm.

"Please, gentlemen, sit." Etherton dropped into his chair. "I don't need you both towering over me."

Pierce settled into a chair. Amherst considered standing for the interview but, after a moment, thought better of it. Better to take the weight off his sore feet. He sat in the chair nearest the door.

Etherton steepled his fingers. "What can I help you with?"

"Josephine Banfield," Amherst said.

The doctor cocked his head, looking as if he were trying to recall her. Or maybe he did recall her and was considering whether to share that fact. Amherst hoped the vain doctor wasn't going to be a problem. "She's been a patient of mine," Etherton finally said. "What about her?"

"What'd she come to you for?"

"That's privileged medical information." The doctor's brow furrowed. "Why are you here?"

"She's missing," Amherst said. "We thought it might have had something to do with her visit."

"An adventurous young woman gets a physical, then goes missing, so you interview her doctor?" Etherton's smile was salesman perfect. "Someone's been listening to too many episodes of *Dragnet*."

"That's what she had done?" Pierce asked. "A physical?"

Amherst leaned forward in his chair. "We heard it was something else."

"Like what?" The doctor's smile never faltered. "Rumors and innuendos abound in a college town, Detectives. Trust me, I've heard it all. So try me."

"We heard Josephine came for an abortion," Amherst said. "Maybe some contraception."

The doctor's smile faltered. Pierce cocked his head and looked at Amherst.

It was then Amherst realized the absurdity of his accusation. "What I meant to say—"

Etherton held up a hand to interrupt him, then flicked his fingers to brush away Amherst's concerns. "You're fishing, Detective, and you're doing it without a worm on your hook."

Amherst shifted uncomfortably in his seat. He thought he caught Pierce smiling but it quickly vanished.

The doctor continued. "I'm not going to tell you anything about Josephine except she came here, and I examined her. She was fine when she left. She walked past Vivian on her way out."

Pierce asked, "Why do some go through the back door?"

Amherst snapped his fingers as he thought about the earlier patient who left via that route. "Yeah, Doc. Why do they need to sneak out the back?"

"You got me, Detective." Etherton chuckled and held his wrists out. "Take me away now."

Amherst cast a sideways glance at Pierce. The younger detective stared ahead, studying the doctor.

"Some of our patients park there," Etherton said. His hands flopped to the desk. "It's easier for them to leave out the back. If it's going to look suspect, I'll put a stop to the practice going forward."

Amherst recalled the invitation to park in the rear plastered on the practice's window. He grabbed the chair's chrome arms. Holding onto something made him feel oddly safe. For whatever reason, he'd already stepped on himself multiple times in this interview. He wanted it to end.

"If there's nothing else," Etherton said. His gaze bounced between the two detectives.

Amherst bounced to his feet and grimaced as the loafers rubbed against his sore spots. He didn't like being dismissed by anyone, much less an arrogant doctor with flicky fingers.

Pierce lingered in his chair a moment longer. He slowly rose to his feet. "Thank you for your time."

Amherst didn't bother saying thanks. He entered the hallway and headed back toward the receptionist. He glanced over his shoulder. Only Pierce followed.

Vivian was bent over her desk, thumbing through the latest issue of Look.

Amherst leaned an elbow on the counter. "Hey, doll," Amherst whispered.

She looked up with bored eyes. "Not interested." Her attention immediately returned to the magazine.

Pierce moved toward the front door and waited.

Amherst waved off the receptionist's dismissal. "You remember a girl named Josephine Banfield?"

Vivian flipped a page. "What about her?"

"What'd the doctor see her for?"

"That's none of your business."

Amherst snapped his fingers in front of her face. "I'm a cop, girlie. Everything's my business."

Vivian looked up and studied his eyes. Then she glanced down the hall. Not seeing Dr. Etherton, Vivian whispered, "She thought she might have a venereal disease."

Amherst straightened. "Did she?"

Vivian rolled her eyes. "Bladder infection." She returned to flipping magazine pages.

"You saw her walk out of here?"

The receptionist clucked. "Well, she didn't fly."

Chapter 7

"Pretty full of himself, wasn't he?" Pierce commented as they pulled away from the curb.

"Typical doctor," said Amherst. "Smooth talker."

"Like apple butter," Pierce agreed.

"You believe him?"

Pierce considered before answering. "Hard not to believe his arrogance. How much of that comes from being a doctor, do you think?"

"As opposed to what?"

"Family money. I'd be surprised if he didn't come well-heeled."

It was Amherst's turn to consider. "Could be. He sure acts like it. Whether it's the MD after his name or his social standing, he reminds me of every officer I knew in the war."

"There's more than one kind of officer," Pierce said evenly.

"Maybe in your war. In mine, there was just one—the dumb bastards telling the sergeants to blow their whistles and send us over the edge of the trenches to charge the goddamn machine guns."

Pierce shrugged. "Different war, I suppose," he said. "I had some good leaders in the Pacific."

"If you think so, it's because they were as good at bullshitting as this doctor."

Pierce didn't reply.

Amherst glared at him, wondering if Pierce was the kind of cop who would kiss up to the sergeant or, worse yet, the lieutenant. He hadn't seen it yet, but one thing was for sure—no one liked a bootlicker. "You didn't answer my question," he growled. "Did you believe him?"

"I don't know," said Pierce, keeping his eyes on the road. "No real reason not to, but he didn't entirely sit right, either."

Amherst muttered, "That's what I thought." Etherton may not know where Josephine Banfield was. He might just be an arrogant, rich, son of a bitch, but Amherst guessed the doctor had some dirt on him, all the same.

Call it a hunch.

"What if it's more about type?" Pierce asked.

"What the hell does that mean?"

"Etherton. He's Josephine's type. Say she's not into him specifically, but someone like him."

Amherst scoffed. "So we should go knock on the door of every doctor we think might be sleazy enough to play backseat bingo with a college girl?"

Pierce grinned. "Backseat bingo? Now you sound like that kid."

Amherst scowled at him. "What kid?"

"The one from Corson's place. Pershing. He said the same thing."

"Pull over," Amherst told him.

Pierce glanced sideways. "You want to drive now?"

"No, I'm going to knock your block off."

"Aw, come on. I'm just yanking your chain."

"You called me a faggot."

"No, I didn't. I said you sounded like that kid, Pershing."

"Who's a fruit," Amherst insisted. "Now, pull over."

Pierce kept driving. Finally, he said, "Why does everything have to be a fight with you, George?"

Amherst opened his mouth to reply, but nothing came out. Neither he nor Pierce spoke each other's names very often. When they did, it was last names that were used. Calling him by his Christian name struck Amherst as purposeful on Pierce's part.

He gave some thought to the question. The more he contemplated it, the more it seemed like a riddle, not a question.

"I don't start it," he finally said. "It's other people who do."

Pierce drove in silence, not looking at him.

"It is," he insisted.

"Okay," Pierce replied in a subdued tone.

Amherst frowned and waved a hand dismissively. He glanced down at his watch. "Head back to the station," he said. "I'm done for today."

Pierce tilted his wrist to look at his own watch. "We still have half an hour. That's time enough for one more lead."

"Station," Amherst repeated.

***

Once Amherst was at his desk, he collected his car keys and refolded his lunch bag. Without another word to Pierce, he stood to head for the door. Before he could take his first step, however, Sergeant DiCarlo appeared.

"Laurel and Hardy," the sergeant bellowed at them. He seemed to have recovered from any regret over using the moniker during their previous conversation. Or maybe he just forgot.

Amherst hadn't. He snapped to attention, staring straight ahead. "Yes, Sergeant!" he bellowed back.

DiCarlo frowned. "Ease up on the grudge," he told Amherst. "It's not healthy. It'll eat your insides."

"Yes, Sergeant!"

DiCarlo sighed and shook his head. He glanced at Pierce, as if considering getting a briefing from the junior detective. Several other detectives watched the scene surreptitiously while they worked. Amherst remained at attention, enjoying the sergeant's discomfort. He knew tradition mandated the supervisor confer with the senior detective on the case, especially when there was such a lopsided difference in their experience. Pierce had barely a year as an investigator. Amherst was a veteran detective. Even DiCarlo couldn't buck that tradition without repercussions. The men watching would make note of it and the sergeant would lose their respect for not giving seniority its due.

Of course, Amherst knew he was pushing his limits, too. If DiCarlo let him get away with mouthing off, he'd also lose a measure of respect from the other detectives for that. It was a fine line to walk, but Amherst had no pity for the sergeant. He chose his path. It wasn't Amherst's fault DiCarlo couldn't resolve it by sending him to the stockades for his impertinence.

DiCarlo's response surprised him.

"At ease, Detective," he snapped, and Amherst heard the steel of an NCO in DiCarlo's tone. He knew the man had ended the war as a staff sergeant but the way the Army threw around rank and medals in late '45 kept Amherst from being impressed with either.

Out of habit, though, Amherst shifted positions to stand at ease.

"Now, fall out and take a seat," DiCarlo added.

Amherst hesitated. The sergeant, he realized, had essentially beaten him at his own game. He'd pushed his insubordination as far as he could without crossing the line, so if he didn't go along with DiCarlo's orders now, he'd be looking at some form of punishment. Maybe a formal reprimand, maybe a suspension without pay.

Despite this, Amherst remained in the stiff at ease position for several seconds before complying with the sergeant's direction. Scowling, he lowered himself into his desk chair, his cheeks warm with embarrassment.

"You find this Banfield girl yet?" DiCarlo asked. His voice was congenial once more, seeming to have already forgotten their battle of wills.

"No," Amherst said.

"Leads?"

"A few."

DiCarlo waited for him to continue. When Amherst didn't, the sergeant twirled his first finger. "And?"

"What do you want me to say?" Amherst lifted his hands and shrugged. "The little princess is a bit loose, it seems."

DiCarlo's thick brow knitted. "She's some kind of floozy?"

"Sounds like it. Got a thing for older men, too."

The look of concern on DiCarlo's face deepened. "Which older men, precisely?"

"We're still working on that."

"Right now, you think she's a runaway? Not any kind of kidnapping?"

Amherst snorted. "You ask me, she's a spoiled rich girl searching for something strange in order to shock her parents. We'll find her."

"That's your job," the sergeant reminded him.

Amherst leaned forward, lowering his voice. "Why the big push?" he asked. "I get that she's from a rich family, but—"

"They're not just rich," DiCarlo interrupted. "They're connected."

Amherst chewed on that. A city like Spokane was more of a large town when it came to social circles. There were maybe a dozen different families influencing most of what was important. Whether that was the mayor, the chief of police, the newspaper, or various business interests didn't matter because, in Amherst's experience, all were interwoven to a degree that made them monolithic. He thought of them simply as "the machine." It wasn't the only one he had encountered in his life. The Army was a machine, too. Its methods and operations had chewed up thousands of men and left the European battlefield littered with corpses. By the grace of God, or simple luck, Amherst had avoided being one of those casualties before his mother's intervention got him yanked from the trenches. His return to Spokane and subsequent hiring by the department five years later was little relief. He simply exchanged one machine for another. Like the Army before it, he knew better than to run afoul of this machine.

"We'll find her," he told DiCarlo.

The sergeant looked uncertain. He cast another glance at Pierce but didn't ask the junior detective anything. Finally, DiCarlo said, "Do it tomorrow, then. Report in as soon as you do."

"Yes, Sergeant," Amherst said, keeping his voice low enough to avoid another conflict, but making his point all the same.

DiCarlo flashed him a dark look before he walked away.

Once the sergeant was out of earshot, Pierce said, "That's what I was talking about earlier. Why pick a fight with the sergeant?"

Amherst turned his gaze toward Pierce. Slowly he rose from his chair, glaring at him. Once he was standing, he growled, "Fuck you," and lumbered painfully from the bullpen.

***

That night, Amherst simmered on the day's events while he ate Gloria's beef stew. He knew a cop's life wasn't meant to be one of luxury, but most days he ended up in a foul mood by the time he made it home.

He thought about that and realized it wasn't the truth. Not anymore. For the past couple of years, he'd been miserable before lunch. There was always something. If it wasn't some cobbler trying to be wise with ill-fitting shoes, it was putting up with DiCarlo acting like an Army officer or being partnered with a kid like Pierce. Running into fat civilians giving him lip. Or good-looking dames *not* giving him any lip.

So, playing babysitter for the rich and connected when their little brat ran away didn't sit well with him.

Well, not babysitter exactly, but Amherst couldn't think of a better term for rounding up a wayward tramp like Josephine Banfield. It was a job for the uniforms if it was a job for the police at all. He shouldn't be wasting his talents on it.

That was how the machine worked. Grinding everyone to a nub.

"You all right, dear?" Gloria asked.

Amherst nodded.

"You like the stew?"

He wanted to reply that there were too many goddamned carrots and not enough potatoes, just like he'd feared. But Amherst knew complaining about supper was a good way to get the cold shoulder later. With his aching feet and the simmering anger in his gut, the last thing he wanted was to get denied in the bedroom when the lights went out.

"Delicious," he said blandly, and slurped the stew from his spoon.

Gloria smiled woodenly at him.

Chapter 8

When Amherst arrived at work the next morning, Pierce was already there. As he dropped the bag containing the bad shoes onto his desk, his partner said, "I worked up a few different leads."

"Aren't you just a busy bee?" Amherst couldn't help his mockery, but he was in a better mood today. His old shoes might lack the stylish luster of the ones in the bag, however, they felt better on his feet.

Pierce ignored the sarcasm. "I figured we have two different avenues to pursue," he said. "Degenerate doctors or reefer parties."

"Why not both?"

Pierce nodded excitedly. "That was my thinking, too."

"I wasn't serious," Amherst said scornfully.

"If they overlap, we might be onto something."

Amherst crossed his arms. "How are doctors and reefer parties going to overlap? We're talking two completely different elements of society—professionals and lowlifes."

Pierce shifted in his seat, then adjusted his tie. "Well, if Joey—"

"Stick with calling her Josephine," Amherst told him.

"Why?"

"It's part of being professional. Plus, if you stick to the formal when you talk to people, and they slip into some kind of nickname, that tells you something. If you give them the nickname and they use it, it tells you nothing."

Pierce nodded in understanding. "Got it. Good advice."

Amherst liked that Pierce was still willing to learn from him. It didn't outweigh all the other reasons he wished he had a veteran detective for a partner, but it made it more bearable.

"Now, tell me why we should be talking to either one of these."

"That kid, Pershing. He said Josephine hung out at marijuana parties. I think it's important where he told us, though."

"In the parlor?"

"No, in a rich person's house." Pierce tightened his tie knot and leaned forward. "Maybe this girl is running around on the bad side of the tracks and we'll come across her in a place like that old speakeasy. But I think it's more likely she's getting her kicks at homes like the Corsons'."

Amherst stared at him, thinking it through. The idea wasn't rock solid, but it wasn't quicksand, either. "Wait," he said. "Why'd you say doctors?"

Pierce shrugged. "I was thinking of smooth, rich guys like Etherton. I checked into him some more, by the way. Did you know he was divorced?"

"How would I know that?"

"I called Vivian, the receptionist. She told me the doc divorced his wife two years ago. She moved away after. Get this—when he dumped her, she'd just had their kid."

"Some people are assholes, I guess."

"Anyway, that's why I had doctors on the brain. I should have said wealthy degenerates." He cocked his head. "Though I suppose some of them could be doctors."

Amherst gave the theory more consideration. In the end, the best leads they had were that Josephine Banfield was promiscuous, liked marijuana, older men, and parties. Pierce's suggested avenue of investigation could conceivably lead to her. It wasn't like they had much else to go on.

"All right," he said gruffly. "We'll test your theory. For today, anyway."

"Where do you want to start?" Pierce asked. "Socialites or marijuana smokers?"

Amherst held up the bag on his desk. "The cobbler."

***

The shoemaker was apologetic and fell over himself to make it right. Of course, this occurred after Amherst slammed the uncomfortable shoes onto the counter and accused the shopkeeper of being an anti-police Nazi sympathizer.

"I've never even been to Germany!" Bernard Schmidt cried.

"Your parents were." Amherst leaned over the counter. "Or your grandparents."

The cobbler clutched the shoes to his chest and moved out of Amherst's reach. "But not me. I love America." His eyes widened with fear. "The police, too."

"Then what's with the shitty shoes, Fritz?"

Schmidt swallowed. "They didn't fit right?"

"Hell no, they didn't fit right. They tore up my feet. My heels look like hamburger and my corns feel like they've been hammered. I got treated better by your countrymen and they were shooting at me."

"I'm an American," Schmidt said. "Ever since birth." He lifted the shoes. "Let me remeasure your feet. I must have made a mistake."

"You're damn right you made a mistake." Amherst slapped the counter. "I should run you in for assaulting my feet."

"Please," Schmidt said. "I'll make it right, Detective."

Several measurements later and after a brief examination of Amherst's swollen feet, the cobbler promised to make the necessary alterations.

"It might take a few days," Schmidt said apologetically. "I may need to make new ones."

Amherst shrugged. As long as the man got it right, he could wait a few days. He really needed a new pair of shoes.

By the time he left the cobbler's shop, Amherst was hungry again. Gloria hadn't felt well that morning, so he'd been forced to make his own breakfast. Toast and jam didn't exactly stick to his ribs.

He directed Pierce to The Family Table on Monroe. His partner frowned but didn't argue. Inside, Amherst ordered eggs, bacon, and hashbrowns. Pierce had coffee.

While he ate, Amherst eyed Donna, the waitress who served them. He'd taken her for a tumble a few years back, but now he noticed a ring on her finger. Between her new jewelry and the thirty or so pounds Amherst had packed on since their moment of glory, he wondered if there was any chance for a repeat performance.

"You still haven't answered my question," Pierce said, his tone far too petulant for Amherst's liking.

"What question is that?"

"Socialites or smokers?"

"Smokers. There's gotta be fewer dens in this town than rich people burning the funny stuff."

Pierce opened his notebook. "I talked to Singleton in Vice. He gave me a few addresses for hopheads."

"He just *gave* them to you?" That didn't sound like Singleton.

"If we arrest anyone, we book them under his name. He gets the credit."

Amherst smirked. *That* sounded more like Singleton.

Pierce continued. "I did some checking around, too. There are some big shots we might want to visit."

"Why?"

"Singleton mentioned a few. I did a little digging on the others."

"What'd you find?"

"Some who were affiliated with the college. Also, a few complaint calls that didn't become arrests," said Pierce. "Oh, and I talked to the school secretary at Lewis and Clark High. She and I grew up on the same block."

"A secretary? What'd you talk to her about?"

"Secretaries always know the best gossip. You'd be surprised how much you can learn about a family from what their high school son or daughter says and does in the hallowed halls of educational institutions."

Amherst peered closely at Pierce. "You did all that before I came in this morning?"

"Some. The rest was last night, after you left."

Amherst nodded his approval but then wagged a warning finger at him. "Don't make a habit out of those late nights," he said. "Not unless you want those bone-dry sandwiches Connie makes to get even dryer, if you know what I mean."

"Is that your way of saying nice job?"

"It's my way of saying if you work late too often, some of it better be with a Sally on the side, because the missus isn't going to like it. You know how an unhappy wife can be."

"I don't, actually." Pierce drained the last of his coffee and left some coins next to the cup. "I'll be in the car," he said.

Amherst shrugged and turned back to his plate. He made short work of the hashbrowns. When he'd finished mopping up the last of the egg yolk with his toast, he pushed the plate away and wiped his mouth with the napkin. Then he smiled and winked at Donna as he stood. He dug in his pocket and pulled out a couple dollars. Amherst normally didn't pay for a meal here, but since Donna served them, he thought he'd better. He wasn't delusional enough to think he'd get a roll in the hay by paying for his meal. Amherst simply didn't want Donna running her mouth and his business getting back to Gloria.

Wives were like mushrooms, Amherst thought. They thrived best when they were kept in the dark.

***

The first location was a bust. A construction crew was inside a building on Market Street, gutting the place for renovation. One of the workmen said a Mexican restaurant was moving in.

"Mexican?" Amherst's face pinched. "Who wants to eat that shit?"

Pierce shrugged. "I've eaten it."

"Of course you have."

At the second stop, an unnamed bar on the edge of downtown, the pungent stench of loco weed hung in the air. A slightly confused doorman blocked their entrance. He was heavyset and in his thirties. "Hey now, we paid for protection."

"Who'd you pay?" Pierce asked.

The doorman cleared his throat. "You know."

"No, I don't. That's why I asked."

Amherst moved in closer and put his hand on Pierce's shoulder. "Relax, Mac. Your secret's safe with us."

"This is bull." The doorman waved his hands. "They said they'd protect us from this kind of harassment."

"*Who?*" Pierce asked.

Amherst smiled. "We're looking for a missing girl." He flashed Josephine Banfield's picture to the doorman. "Her parents are worried. We're not looking to cause you or your patrons any trouble. You paid for protection, and you got it."

The doorman eyed the photo. "She ain't never been here."

"All we want to do is ask your patrons if they've seen her," Amherst said. "We'll be in and out in ten minutes. You can go about your business."

The doorman nodded. "All right, fine. But only you." He nodded toward Pierce. "He's got too much of a hard-on for us. Who knows what he'll do?"

Anger flashed in Pierce's eyes.

"He's got you there," Amherst said to his partner. "Gimme ten minutes. If I'm not out in in that time, come in guns blazing."

The doorman's eyes widened. "Ten minutes?"

"You better encourage your patrons to talk fast."

***

Amherst was out in eight minutes. "What a waste of time."

Pierce raised an eyebrow.

"One guy smoking mooter. The rest were drinking beer. All of them older than me." Amherst shook his head. "None of them saw Josephine."

Pierce followed Amherst to the car. "You should have let me come in with you."

"And waste eight minutes of your life? You should be thanking me."

"I wasted it outside," Pierce said.

"Jesus, you're a stick in the mud."

Pierce was quiet for a moment, standing at the car door but not opening it. Then he asked, "Who did that guy mean? When he said he paid someone."

"Vice, probably."

"Not Singleton, though, right?" Pierce said, his tone unsure. "He gave me these spots."

"Yeah, he did, and one of them is turning into a taco joint." Amherst leaned his elbows on the top of the car. "Look, Vice is its own world. Most likely, they got a racket going with a few of these places around town. Not just smoking dens but dirty bookstores, peep shows, brothels, you name it. They get a little pay to look the other way. Everyone understands the arrangement comes with the occasional loud arrest to make things look above board to the public, see?"

"We were supposed to be that arrest," Pierce muttered, getting it now. "Saving them the trouble."

"Why do the work if someone else will do it for you and thank you for the privilege?" Amherst asked.

Pierce shook his head in disgust. "We're never going to beat this if that's how we operate."

Amherst let out a chuckle that dissolved into a coughing fit. When he finished, he wiped his mouth and sighed. "I've got a news flash for you—we are never going to beat crime. All we can do is manage it. Keeping certain activities confined to certain areas is a pretty good way to do that."

"That's a defeatist philosophy," said Pierce.

"No, it's a realistic one."

"So, Singleton is in on the racket?"

"Let me tell you something you should have figured out on patrol," Amherst said, opening the car door. He gave Pierce a hard stare before he got in. "Don't ask stupid questions."

***

Their third stop was a large farmhouse in the unincorporated portion of the county. A dusty and dented 1946 Buick Special was parked in front.

Amherst and Pierce climbed the stairs to the rickety porch. Amherst entered without knocking.

Three people were present in the front room, a man and two women.

Both women were brunette. One of them was topless, her blouse and brassiere draped carefully over the back of the padded bench where they sat. She made no effort to retrieve her clothing or cover herself. This made Amherst think she was either a prostitute or extremely high. Neither possibility stopped him from admiring her bosom.

Pierce looked away from the woman's bare breasts.

The man stood. "Afternoon, gentlemen." He wore a dingy white shirt and black slacks. His shoes were scuffed. "What can we do you for today?"

Amherst swept his jacket to the side, exposing his badge and gun. He introduced himself and Pierce.

"A little out of your jurisdiction," the proprietor said.

"We're commissioned in the state of Washington." Amherst closed his jacket and pulled his sleeves back in place. "That means we can effect an arrest anywhere within her borders."

"You're running a house of prostitution," Pierce said, "and I smell marijuana, too."

Amherst frowned. *Always the boy scout.* He pulled Josephine Banfield's picture from his pocket. "You seen this girl?"

"No," the proprietor said.

"What about you two?" Amherst flashed the photograph to the two brunettes.

They both shook their heads.

"Didn't think so." Amherst tucked the picture back into his jacket. "Will the word *arrest* change that for any of you?"

The two women shook their heads again, their expressions panicky.

The proprietor pulled his wallet from his back pocket and removed several bills. He set them on the table in front of the two brunettes. "Have either of you lost these, I wonder?" he asked with faux innocence.

Amherst didn't bother with any charade. He simply swept the money off the table and pocketed it.

Pierce clenched his jaw and looked away.

***

"Why's it bother you so much?" Amherst asked.

They were pulling up to an address in the Manito neighborhood, headed to see one of the socialites on Pierce's list.

Pierce turned off the engine. "What are you talking about?"

"It bothers you," said Amherst. "The little tastes that come with the job."

Pierce took the key from the ignition and slid it into his jacket pocket. Then he reached for his notebook. "You don't have to worry about me," he assured Amherst.

"I'm not worried. I'm curious."

"You know what? I liked you better with tight shoes. You weren't so curious then." Pierce opened the car door and got out.

Amherst shrugged and followed.

A colored servant answered the door and, after a brief wait, escorted them to the library. The doctor who waited there was named Covington. He was a slightly rotund man with a Teddy Roosevelt mustache and a haughty expression Amherst immediately wanted to slap off his entitled, pudgy face.

"I'm not quite certain what you're asking me," Covington said, once Pierce had made a few cautious forays into questioning him. Amherst recognized the need to be circumspect, but Pierce's oblique queries left the doctor understandably confused.

"Let's try this," Amherst interjected. "What's your affiliation with Eastern College?"

"I'm an alumnus," the doctor replied stiffly. "Not that it's any of your business, I support the school with a pre-medical scholarship, as well."

"Go to any events?"

"Certainly."

"Parties?"

"Yes, of course." Covington shook his head. "This is highly irregular, Officer. What is this about?"

Amherst ignored him. "I don't mean champagne and tuxedo affairs. I'm talking about more informal gatherings."

"That distinction does nothing to mitigate the question I just asked—what is this about?"

Amherst worked his jaw momentarily and exhaled. "It's about girls, Doctor. You like girls?"

"What are you implying?"

"It's not an implication. It's a question."

"Of course, I like women. I'm married, after all."

"How about younger ones?" Amherst asked. "Say, college girls?"

The doctor drew himself up, though it was less impressive than it would have been if he'd been younger, taller, and had less of a belly. He glared hotly at Amherst. "I don't care for your insults. What makes you think you have the right to come in here and—"

"This." Amherst held up his badge, cutting off the doctor's angry rant. "And the fact that a nineteen-year-old girl is missing."

The heat didn't leave Covington's eyes, but his expression softened slightly. "How does that concern me?"

"We don't think she's missing so much as she might be having herself a weeklong party."

"I still don't—"

"You're exactly the kind of guy she enjoys spending time with. Since you're affiliated with the college, we're talking to you."

The doctor's eyes widened, then narrowed. "That's… well, that's preposterous."

"How do you know it's preposterous?" Amherst asked, pulling Josephine Banfield's photograph from his jacket pocket. "We haven't shown you her picture yet."

"I don't run around with young women," Covington snapped. "That's how I know—"

Amherst thrust the photo towards the doctor's face. Surprised, the man stared at it. Amherst watched his expression carefully. He saw no sign of recognition from Covington.

"Sweet little number, isn't she?" Amherst asked, still watching his expression.

Doctor Covington scowled. "You are a vile man," he said. "I'd like you to leave."

***

None of the other socialites were any more helpful than Covington. Some responded to Amherst with horror while others became defensive. All of them eventually demanded the detectives leave their residences or places of business.

Amherst crossed Zepp the jeweler, Leighton the railroad man, and Vanbiesbrouck, who was just wealthy, off his mental list of potential suspects. The surprise and disgust in their reactions was not feigned. Besides that, their connections to the college, the Banfields, and the other names on Pierce's handwritten list were tangential.

There were several people whose prickly responses and defensive attitudes made him suspicious. Even their names made him apprehensive—Chabot the banker, Bailey the restaurant mogul, Doctor Mayhew, and a lawyer named Schmautz. Especially Schmautz, the fucking kraut. Much like Etherton, Amherst was certain these men were undoubtedly up to no good. Whether that involved Josephine Banfield was another matter.

Pierce remained largely silent throughout the latter part of the day, seemingly resigned to how Amherst chose to approach these interviews. His only protest came early, right after they left Covington's house.

"Might not be the best idea to talk to these people quite like that," the younger detective suggested.

Amherst snorted. "It's the *only* way to talk to them. If you try the mother-may-I routine with these types, they'll eat you alive."

"I don't think they're used to it."

"That's the point," Amherst snapped.

After that, Pierce kept his opinions to himself.

By the end of the day, despite all the interviews, they still had nothing. Amherst felt frustration creeping in. More than being assigned a "go find your sister and tell her dinner's ready" sort of case. This new strain of frustration was two-fold. One part came from their lack of progress and dealing with arrogant doctors all day long. The other part came from a nagging voice in the back of his head.

It was a voice that told him maybe Josephine Banfield wasn't bed-hopping or looking to scandalize her parents. Maybe she was actually in trouble.

He had no more proof of this now than the moment Sergeant DiCarlo dumped this case on them. Yet he couldn't shake the sensation. He'd learned to trust his gut, both in the trenches and on the street.

"You want to run down anything else?" Pierce asked, glancing at his watch.

Amherst did the same. Fifteen minutes to quitting time.

"Let's stop at the smoking den in the Coeur d'Alene building again," he said. When Pierce gave him a questioning look, Amherst scowled. "What? It's on the way to the station."

Chapter 9

They got nothing from the converted speakeasy other than a surly attitude from Vern, the shutterbug clerk. Still, Amherst felt good about checking. Maybe reefer dens weren't Josephine Banfield's terrain. He was starting to think this was so. That was the thing about working a case—it was as much about eliminating probabilities as it was discovering them.

Amherst didn't realize how much he stunk like marijuana until they reached the detectives' bullpen and Singleton, who was camped out near their desks, let out a whistle.

"Amherst, you reek."

"That's just you," Amherst retorted. "You forgot to wipe your ass again."

"At least I can reach mine, tub o' lard." Singleton waved his hand in the air. "You smell like skunk."

Then Amherst realized what Singleton was talking about. "We've been out doing your job, fighting the rise of reefer madness."

"You make any arrests?"

"No."

Singleton frowned. "What good are you?"

"None," said Amherst, dropping into his chair. "Guess we should work Vice, huh?"

Singleton shook his head and stalked away.

Amherst watched him go, shaking his own head as well. He turned to Pierce. "How long do you figure he was waiting here, just to find out if we brought him any spoon-fed collars?"

Pierce shifted uncomfortably. "I did promise him some arrests, but that was before—"

"You want to haul some hopheads in tomorrow?" Amherst interrupted. "Would that make you happy?"

"Finding this girl would make me happy," Pierce said quietly, sitting at his desk.

Amherst's demeanor softened. "Yeah, me, too."

Pierce gave him another odd look like the one he'd given when Amherst suggested they stop at the marijuana den in the Coeur d'Alene Building.

Amherst scowled back. "If we don't make some headway soon, not only will DiCarlo be in our business, but he'll slap us with the next case coming down the pike, too. I don't like to fall behind. Once you do, you never catch up."

"It's not like we'll ever run out of cases," said Pierce.

"You're the expert now?"

"No." Pierce shifted in his chair, reaching for his hat. "What's the plan for tomorrow?"

"I'm not sure. I need to sleep on it."

"Good enough." Pierce stood and said good night. A moment later, he was gone.

Amherst wanted to follow, but he hesitated. Then he rose and went down the hall to the records room. Laboriously, he spent over an hour looking for any information on the four socialites whose responses he hadn't liked. He realized while he worked that Zepp was probably a German name, too. Not that it mattered anymore. More and more, people seemed concerned about communists, not Nazis. He understood why, but the idea of letting the Germans off the hook didn't sit well with him. They may not have technically been Nazis when he fought them, but based on what eventually happened, he suspected all Germans had the potential for evil.

Hell, he thought to himself. Maybe everyone did.

However, neither Zepp nor Schmautz had any criminal record he could find. Same with Bailey. Doctor Mayhew, however, had two arrests. One was for family assault. Not surprisingly, his wife had declined to cooperate with the investigation, so all that existed in the record was the incredibly succinct patrol report and an even more terse follow-up from a detective.

That surprised Amherst. How bad must the fight have been for the uniforms not to defer to the doctor? Just chalk it up to family concerns and move on. It happened every day if the dust up was insignificant. Everyone understood that families fought. Brothers fought each other. So did sisters, though less often. So did husbands and wives. If it wasn't beyond a bruise or a split lip, most cops didn't want to intrude on a family matter.

Mayhew spent a night in jail, though. Or part of one, at least. Sure, the charge was never filed, but for a doctor to be booked, it meant the incident was more than the typical spat.

Amherst scanned the report, finding the injury description. "Injured forearm" was all it said. Since there'd been no further investigation after the initial response, the extent of the injury remained unknown.

Still, Amherst thought, *smacking your wife isn't the crime of the century.*

Mayhew's other arrest was more interesting, at least in terms of the case he was currently investigating.

Possession of Marijuana.

Once again, the details in the report were sparse. Amherst read them carefully.

```
    On 5/11/50 at approximately 11:43 PM,
this officer did respond to the listed
address on the complaint of an assault.
Upon arrival, officers determined that
the combatants had already fled the scene.
This officer did detect the distinct odor
of Marijuana on the premises. A search of
the parties present was subsequently
conducted. Suspect #1, DR. EDGAR MAYHEW,
was found to be in possession of three
hand-rolled Marijuana cigarettes, for
which he was placed under arrest. Suspect
denied ownership of the narcotics and
stated that someone must have put them
```

into his pocket during a recent party.
Suspect did not provide further details
of the party, its location, or who was in
attendance. He was booked into jail in
accordance with policy. The narcotics
were logged into evidence.

The officer who wrote the report, Anthony Cirrelli, was a veteran patrol cop who Amherst knew. Cirrelli was devoutly Catholic and his views on law enforcement were in lockstep with the tenets of his faith. Poor Mayhew had no chance of talking—or bribing—his way out of the arrest.

Yet, no charges were filed.

Amherst flipped to the detective's report.

This detective did review the details
of the arresting officer's report. Due to
irregularities in the arrest procedure
and the comparatively minor nature of the
offense, it was determined that further
investigation did not serve the public
interest.

The scant paragraph told Amherst volumes, but not as much as the signature of the investigating detective.

Singleton.

Amherst exhaled heavily. Singleton giving Doctor Mayhew a walk didn't matter. Perhaps the man spilled his guts about the parties in exchange for leniency on the assault charge. However, had that occurred, Singleton would've likely written it in his report. Amherst decided it didn't matter how or why Mayhew walked. He still had this arrest to use as a lever. He thought back to Pierce's question when the younger man left for the day.

The plan for tomorrow, Amherst thought, *is to roust Dr. Smokehound.*

∗∗∗

That evening, Gloria was full-on sick. Her coughing and congestion told Amherst he was fending for himself when it came to dinner. He made sure she didn't have the plague or anything, left her a glass of water on the bedside, and went out to dinner at The Shack.

As he ate his steak, he wondered if Dr. Mayhew was just another dead end. So far, every lead in the Josephine Banfield case seemed to be. He was used to some leads being nothing and others not panning out entirely, but most of the cases he worked eventually had a trail to follow. The tracks may be faint and intermittent, the direction not entirely clear, but there was *something* there.

What did they have? A missing girl who might not be missing, despite what his gut told him. Rich men, some of whom were keen to sample young tail. Or smoke some goof-butts. Perhaps both, if Pierce's theory held any water. Amherst had yet to see any crossover between the social degenerates and the weed smokers, and didn't know if it was the key to unlocking this case as Pierce thought.

The steak was juicy and tender. Amherst chewed slowly, savoring each bite while he thought.

Maybe they should take another run at her college friends. Corson and that crew, including the pansy, Basil Pershing. One of them might have been holding out information, though Amherst doubted it. Their rich attitudes had been on display, but he'd been rough enough with each of them to get past their defenses.

So, was Mayhew the best lead?

Amherst decided, the answer was yes.

When he finished the steak, he left behind enough to cover both the meal and a tip. He might not see the world the same way Pierce did, but he wasn't on duty either. There were unwritten rules about the job, and Amherst believed in respecting them.

Back home, Gloria had fallen into a snore-rattling sleep. Amherst grabbed a blanket and pillow from the closet and made up the couch. Then he poured himself a whiskey. He sat and sipped long into the night.

Chapter 10

Amherst lumbered into the bullpen in a foul mood. His head hurt from the whiskey, and he'd slept poorly. Gloria was still in bed when he woke up, so he was on his own for breakfast again. He didn't bother with toast or even coffee. Once he grabbed Pierce at the station, they'd go straight to a diner.

He'd barely reached his desk when Sergeant DiCarlo threw a monkey wrench into that plan by barking, "Amherst! Pierce! My office, now!"

Amherst winced at the noise. He also noticed DiCarlo hadn't called them Laurel and Hardy, which didn't bode well. He glanced at Pierce to see if the man knew anything about this but the blank stare he got in return answered that question. The two of them followed DiCarlo into the broom closet of an office the sergeant kept.

"Close the door," DiCarlo ordered.

Amherst didn't move. Pierce reached past him and swung the door shut.

"What in the Sam Hill are you two dumbasses up to?"

"Easy, Sarge," Amherst said, pumping his palms toward DiCarlo. "Pierce here is a Mormon and I've got a headache."

"I'm not Mormon," Pierce muttered.

"Well, I've got a headache, and you act like one."

"To hell with your headache," DiCarlo growled. "I've got an ass ache. Or I would, if there was anything left of my ass after the lieutenant got through chewing it off this morning."

"What'd you do?" Amherst asked.

"Don't be funny. What do you think you're doing, running around town and haranguing prominent citizens?"

"Haranguing?"

DiCarlo pointed a finger at him. "You know what I mean."

"We're looking for a missing girl," said Amherst. "The case you gave us a couple of days ago."

"Now, you're being cute," DiCarlo seethed. "A regular Jack Benny. What do you need to talk to these people about?"

"The missing girl."

DiCarlo's finger shook. "I'm warning you. One more smart comment and you're off this case. I'll have you investigating stolen hub caps for the next year. Maybe send you to the juvenile squad."

Amherst grimaced and raised his hands. "Look, we were being thorough. Everyone we talked to is either associated with the college somehow, or with each other, or with the Banfields."

The sergeant's expression didn't change. "You didn't just talk to them. You were rude and unprofessional."

"That's a matter of opinion."

"It's a matter of fact."

"Why, did one of them complain?"

"*All* of them complained!" snapped DiCarlo. "Some to the chief, some to the goddamn mayor."

"Language," Amherst said, jerking his head toward Pierce. "Mormon, remember?"

"I'm not Mormon," Pierce repeated.

"See?" DiCarlo said. "He's not Mormon but I'm starting to think you're a moron. What good did you think would come from upsetting the apple cart like that?"

"I thought I might shake something loose and find the girl," said Amherst.

"Oh, you shook something loose, all right."

"See?"

"Did you find the girl?"

Amherst frowned and glanced downward. "Not yet."

"Uh-huh." DiCarlo took a deep breath and let it out. "I realize your style is that of a bull in a China shop, but you've got to tone it down on this one. Understand?"

Amherst regarded him coolly for a few seconds. Then he said, "Here's what I understand, Sarge. On the one hand, we've got a rich family whose daughter—*adult* daughter, by the way—has run away or is missing. I assume they're putting pressure on the department to find their girl, right?"

Reluctantly, DiCarlo nodded.

"Well, that trail of breadcrumbs has led us to people who happen to run in the same social circles as the Banfields, or at least exist at the same rarified heights. So, in order to find Josephine, we've had to upset a few of those people, who are now putting pressure on the department to stop." He turned over his hands. "Who wins? Either we upset the apple cart to find Josephine or we don't and the Banfields drop the hammer on us for not doing enough. Which is it?"

DiCarlo stared at Amherst for a long time. Finally, he pointed toward the door. "Get out of my office, Detective. Go find Josephine Banfield, and leave the doctors alone."

"Sergeant…"

"Out," DiCarlo repeated.

***

"That was pleasant," Pierce said, once they were in the car and away from the station.

Amherst waved off the comment. He didn't feel like giving any more air to the DiCarlo situation.

"Where to?" Pierce asked.

Amherst rubbed his tired eyes, then glanced outside the window. "Let's go to the Skyway."

"The café out at Felts Field? What's out there?"

"Breakfast. I'm hungry."

His partner frowned but didn't argue.

An hour later, after a plate of eggs and hashbrowns were washed down with two cups of coffee, Amherst felt ready to face the day. Back in the car, he gave Pierce an address.

Pierce put the car in gear, then stopped. "We were there yesterday. That's Doctor Mayhew's address."

"Keep playing detective. You're good at it."

Pierce kept his hand on the shifter but didn't release the clutch. Amherst waited for him to spout some nonsense about what the sergeant said earlier but it never came. After a few seconds, Pierce turned his attention to the road. The car lurched forward, and they were on their way.

Doctor Mayhew answered his own door, unlike the first time they'd come when it was the housekeeper. He stood in the doorway and glared at Amherst.

"You didn't get the message?" he sneered.

Amherst grinned. "I'm what they call a little slow, doc."

Then he drove his fist into the doctor's gut.

Next to him, Pierce muttered a curse. Amherst kept his gaze on Mayhew. The pained, utterly shocked expression on the doctor's face brought him more satisfaction than slapping cuffs on any misdemeanor perpetrator. Hell, maybe more than a few low-range felons.

Amherst moved forward, his large frame bumping the slender Mayhew backward into the foyer. Pierce stepped in behind him and closed the door.

"You..." Mayhew gasped, his breath not entirely returned.

Amherst grabbed him by the shoulder and walked him to a nearby chair. With a shove, he deposited the much smaller man into it. "Tell me about the marijuana party," Amherst said.

Mayhew stared at him, still in shock from getting slugged in the gut. This new information seemed to compound the expression. "Wha—at?"

Amherst balled his fist. "That last one was about one quarter strength, doc. I can throttle it up if you need me to. Increase the dosage, so to speak."

"You..." Mayhew croaked.

"Maybe do your arm like you did your wife's," Amherst growled, leaning forward and glaring.

"No," Mayhew quickly answered. He held up a hand as if to ward off another blow.

"The marijuana party," Amherst repeated.

Mayhew swallowed hard. He took a few moments to catch his breath. Finally, he said, "What do you want to know?"

***

They spent the rest of the day running down the information provided by Doctor Mayhew.

Unfortunately, it seemed that marijuana smokers were similar to drinkers in that they did most of their imbibing at night. At one of the houses Mayhew identified as hosting parties, they got no answer at the door. Amherst made a note to return during the evening hours. Maybe tonight, in fact. With Gloria sick at home like she was, this would be a good night to put in some overtime.

After a grilled ham and cheese at the counter of Silverdale's, they continued their tour of the locations Doctor Mayhew provided. Their luck didn't improve; if anyone happened to be home at the residences they checked, they definitely weren't hosting any parties at the time.

"Why do you even care?" a snooty wife named Marlene Fitch asked him. Her husband Daniel, who ran a real estate firm that focused on commercial properties in the downtown area, was off at work. "What people do in their own homes—"

"—is still subject to the law," Amherst interrupted her. "Otherwise, it'd be all right to murder someone, as long as you did it on your own property, wouldn't it?"

Marlene fixed him with a nasty look. "That's not what I meant, and you know it."

"Do I?" Amherst said. He affected a posh tone with an edge. "You know, right now doesn't seem like a good time. I'll come back later. Maybe a lot of later, in fact."

Her expression didn't relent but Amherst saw that she took his point. "I'd like to avoid those visits," she said tersely.

Amherst held up Josephine's photograph. "When did you last see this girl?"

Marlene took a long look at the photo. Finally, she shook her head. "Sorry. I wish I had seen her, if it meant keeping you off my back."

He slipped the photo back into his pocket. "Who comes to your parties?"

"Cut me a break, mister. No one likes a gossip."

That made Amherst smile. He bet Marlene Fitch was the kind of woman who absolutely lived for gossip. "You either tell me now," he said, "or I come back and see for myself."

Marlene crossed her arms. "We don't hurt anyone. It's no different than having a highball."

"Names," Amherst demanded.

So Marlene gave him names. The ones she reluctantly rattled off didn't surprise him or Pierce. Amherst made note of some of the names that didn't crop up, including Covington. Or Etherton, for that matter.

Most of them, he recognized as people he and Pierce had already talked to. He was starting to see how the social circles overlapped. On the surface, everyone in the upper class belonged to the same group. In fact, thanks to Pierce thinking to ask, he'd learned most went to the same two churches on the South Hill.

Once Amherst pushed past the common denominator of money, cliques started to form. Old money versus new was the first he noticed. Then came finer distinctions, such as bankers versus restauranteurs. However, the one that interested him the most was the straightlaced versus the party crowd.

Oh, they all went to parties. The champagne and tuxedo kind of events he'd asked Covington about. Not all of them went to the kinds of parties Daniel and Marlene Fitch threw. Fewer than half if his math was even close to right.

Amherst thanked Marlene, whose deep frown told him she didn't appreciate his gratitude one bit. He didn't care. His frustration was seeping back in again. All the running around they'd done today was the equivalent of spinning their wheels in the snow. A lot of energy expended without much forward motion.

"What do we know?" Amherst asked aloud as they drove toward the station at the end of the day.

Pierce took a drag and blew out the smoke. Amherst noticed he'd stopped cupping his cigarette, at least some of the time. "Rich people can get away with pretty much anything."

"That's a revelation for you?"

Pierce shook his head. "Seeing it up close is like having your nose rubbed in it, that's all."

Amherst slouched in his seat. "Hardly anyone knew Josephine, except through family events," he said. "Church, square parties, that's it. What's that tell us?"

"She either doesn't like smoking pot or she does it with people her age."

"Even the kids her age haven't seen her in days."

"So they say."

"You didn't believe them?"

Pierce seemed to consider the question as he turned the car onto First Avenue. "I think they told us as much of the truth as they're likely to."

"What the hell does *that* mean?"

"They have their secrets, but they don't know where she is."

"So, marijuana parties are a dead end. That leaves us with her type. Older men, probably your Cary Grant type. Most likely wealthy since that's her crowd."

"Maybe another doctor," said Pierce. "Someone like Mayhew?"

Amherst pursed his lips, thinking of Professor Fromme at the college. "It could just as easily be a professor or a bartender." He wriggled his feet. They were still sore from the bad shoes, but he only noticed it now when he stood for a long time or walked too far.

That's what we did. Walked too far down a bad road.

"We've got to reload," Amherst said. "Go at this from a different angle."

"You still think she's shacking up somewhere? Trying to make mommy and daddy mad?"

"I don't know," Amherst said quietly. He remembered Sharon Cudmore saying how the Banfields didn't really love their daughter. That almost certainly wasn't true, but it could be true that Josephine *thought* they didn't. In that case, running off with someone who would scandalize the family was a response that made sense to him.

Yet it didn't *feel* like that was the case. Not at all. At least, not completely.

Pierce tapped his thumb on the steering wheel. "I keep thinking about what you said."

"What's that? I say a lot."

"About why people do the things they do."

"Oh." Amherst nodded. "Money, sex, power."

"I think you're right," Pierce said.

"Of course, I am."

"There's money all around this. Sex, too. And power."

"How does that help us find Josephine Banfield?"

Pierce drove in silence for a few moments. Then he said, "The rumor she's got an older man for a lover? That part is true, I think."

"I think so, too."

"She's been away from home two nights now."

"I know."

"Seems like a long time for a tantrum."

"Maybe she's good at throwing them. Spoiled, rich kid, and all."

Pierce didn't answer right away. Then he said, "I hope so."

***

As they walked into the station house, Amherst decided he'd get DiCarlo to approve the overtime, then start by checking in with the Banfields. Maybe Josephine was already home, and they were so full of themselves they didn't think to report their daughter had returned. If that weren't the case, him checking in would reinforce the image that the Spokane Police took her disappearance seriously. He could use the Banfields on his side when the roster of socialites whined to the chief and mayor again.

Amherst waved for Pierce to follow him to the sergeant's office. The door stood open, so he poked in his head. "Sarge?"

DiCarlo looked up, his expression etched with concern. "Where've you been? You haven't checked in for hours."

"We're here now."

Amherst braced for another onslaught regarding his interview tactics and the tender sensibilities of Spokane's elite. Then he caught a strange element to DiCarlo's expression. He wondered for a second if something had happened to Gloria. Maybe she was sicker than he realized and had to go to the hospital. His stomach lurched at the thought.

"What is it?" he demanded.

"Did you find the Banfield girl?"

Amherst shook his head. "Not yet. Why?"

DiCarlo reached up and smoothed his thick mustache. "We've got another one missing."

Chapter 11

Floyd and Marith Jensen sat together on a threadbare couch and stared up at Amherst and Pierce. Floyd held Marith's left hand while her right clutched a tissue to her chest. His face held stoic resolve while panic washed over hers in crashing waves.

Two cigarette butts smoldered with long ashes in a blue ceramic ashtray on the wooden coffee table. An unframed photograph of a dark-haired woman lay next to the ashtray.

The Jensens lived in a modest home on Addison Street in the shadow of Gonzaga University. A cross hung near the front door and several pictures of Jesus adorned the living room walls. The house smelled of recently cooked bacon.

Pierce pointed at the photograph. "Is that Shirley?"

"Yes," Marith said. She pushed it forward. "That's for you. We thought you might need it."

Amherst grabbed it, gave it a once over, and turned it to show Pierce. After the younger detective looked at it, he nodded. Amherst tucked the picture inside his jacket pocket.

"When's the last time you saw your daughter?" Pierce asked.

Floyd looked at his wife and Marith said, "Yesterday, right before dinner."

Marith wore a well-worn, blue housedress underneath a tattered, foam green sweater. Her salt and pepper hair was disheveled as if she'd recently run her fingers through it.

Pierce jotted in his notepad. "Does Shirley normally eat with you?"

"Yes," Floyd said. "With Marith, I mean."

"She skipped last night," the wife added. "Shirley was meeting some friends."

Amherst thumbed in the direction of the Jesuit university. "Does your daughter go to Gonzaga?"

Floyd shook his head. He sported the uniform of a city bus driver. His hat rested on his knee. "She's taking a year off to work."

"You're okay with that?" Amherst's brow furrowed.

"We couldn't afford to pay for school," Floyd said, "Things are a little tight around here."

The small house was tidy but most everything inside looked as if the Jensens had been given hand-me-downs. Based upon the number of religious artifacts on the walls, Amherst imagined the Jensens tithed mightily to their church. Probably a Catholic branch of Our Lady of Infinite Suffering where heavenly glory was achieved through financial sacrifice. The Jensens were probably going to be in the front row at the pearly gates.

Amherst smirked and Pierce eyed him questioningly.

"She's a smart girl," Marith said.

"No doubt," Amherst said. He dug his cigarettes from his jacket pocket. "You didn't worry when she didn't come home last night?"

"Well, no," Marith said. "I went to bed early. I thought Shirley came home after I was asleep."

Amherst slipped a cigarette between his lips. He lifted his chin in Floyd's direction. "What about you? Did you see your daughter last night?"

"I drive the late shift," Floyd said. "Three to midnight."

"So you miss dinners most nights?" Pierce asked.

Floyd nodded. "I get a couple with the girls every week."

"Not driving tonight?" Amherst asked.

"I'm supposed to." Floyd nervously pulled at his hat. "Some of the guys are covering my route until I get back."

Pierce asked, "Does Shirley go out at night a lot?"

The husband and wife exchanged glances, then they both nodded.

"She always comes home before midnight," Marith said.

Coming home before midnight had little to do with protecting a woman's honor. Amherst had done plenty of bad things with a lot of good girls and almost all of them took place before midnight.

"She's a good girl," the wife added.

"As good as she is smart?" Amherst asked. He lit his cigarette and inhaled.

"What's that supposed to mean?" Floyd asked.

Pierce rolled his eyes at his partner. "What about breakfast, Mrs. Jensen? Did you see Shirley this morning?"

Marith shook her head. "I thought she must've gotten up early." She wiped her nose with the tissue. "I checked her room, and her bed was made."

"She does that every morning?" Amherst asked. "Get up early and make her bed?"

The woman nodded. "She works the lunch counter at Newberry's. Somedays she'll walk downtown."

"Heck of a walk," Amherst waved a hand.

Floyd shrugged. "Not so bad. Just a couple miles."

Marith smiled. "Shirley likes the exercise. On bad weather days, she rides the bus."

"Does she have any friends?" Pierce asked.

"Lots of them." Marith nodded. "She's real popular."

"Can you tell us their names?"

Marith glanced at Floyd. "Well, there's Sally and Norma."

Floyd looked at the ceiling. "And Evelyn."

Amherst exhaled a plume of smoke. "Last names, too. If you got their addresses or phones numbers, that'd be a big help."

The couple looked at each other. Worry passed through their eyes.

"Phyllis?" Floyd said eventually.

Marith's eyes widened. "Yeah, Phyllis." She turned to Amherst. "Phyllis Helppie. I know where she lives."

***

"What's this about?" Phyllis Helppie asked.

She was an attractive nineteen-year-old who supposedly lived with two other women her same age. They shared an apartment on the lower South Hill that overlooked downtown. Her roommates were out with their boyfriends.

Phyllis clasped her hands in front of her waist. She wore a pink sweater and a gray tweed skirt. Her feet were bare. Amherst couldn't stop staring at them.

"When's the last time you talked with Shirley Jensen?" Pierce asked.

"Shirley? Why?" Phyllis glanced at Amherst. "Has something happened?"

Pierce shrugged. "She hasn't come home."

"That's not like her." Phyllis's face pinched with concern. She walked over to the couch and sat.

The detectives followed her. Amherst stayed focused on the woman's feet. The damn things may have been the most perfect feet he'd ever seen. They didn't have any corns, and her heels weren't torn up by any lousy shoes. What he wouldn't give just to massage them. Maybe play 'this little piggy' with the girl.

"So the last time?" Pierce prompted.

"Golly," Phyllis said. "I talked to her yesterday."

"What did you talk about?"

"Work mostly." Phyllis caught Amherst staring at her feet. She harrumphed and brought her legs up underneath her. She faced Pierce as she repositioned her skirt.

Amherst straightened and cleared his throat.

"Where do you work?" Pierce asked.

"Newberry's. I work in women's clothing. Shirley works at the lunch counter, but she wants to get out of it. Too many leering businessmen." Phyllis glared at Amherst. "Men in general is more accurate."

He smiled.

Pierce tapped his notepad. "Did Shirley mention a boyfriend?"

"She's had a few, but she quit talking about them."

"Why's that?" Pierce asked.

"Because people are terrible gossips."

"What do they have to gossip about?"

Phyllis crossed her arms under her breasts. "I really shouldn't say. I don't want to be as bad as them."

"Shirley's missing," Amherst said. "We don't know what will help us find her. Maybe you know something. Maybe you don't. We won't know until you tell us."

Phyllis twisted her lips.

"Please," Pierce said.

Amherst pulled Josephine Banfield's photo from his pocket. "What about this girl? Do you know her?"

Phyllis leaned in. "Never seen her. Who's she?"

"She's missing, too," Amherst said. "For several days now."

"Both of them?"

"That's right," Pierce said. "Two women missing in a matter of a few days."

Phyllis shifted in her seat and her skirt moved. Her feet were now exposed, but Amherst no longer cared.

"Shirley met a guy about six months ago," she said. "A real smooth talker. She gushed about him all the time until they broke up. Now, Shirley doesn't tell me much because she's quit talking around the people at work. We mostly gab about nonsense. Who's on the radio or what's playing at the matinee. That kind of thing."

"Back to this boyfriend," Pierce said. "Do you know a name?"

"Yeah," Phyllis said. "Steve Corson."

Amherst straightened.

"Steve Corson?" Pierce said.

"That's right."

Amherst's heart pounded and he heard blood hammering in his ears. He wanted to scream with excitement. There was a connection between Josephine Banfield and Shirley Jensen.

"How'd Steve and Shirley meet?" Pierce asked.

"The lunch counter." Phyllis shook her head. "The attention Shirley got there never stopped."

"Why'd they break up?"

"Shirley never said. All she told me was she'd never date a guy from Browne's Addition again."

"Sounds like solid advice," Amherst said.

He headed for the door.

***

Reginald Corson opened the door to his house. "Detectives?"

"Where's your son," Amherst asked.

"He's in his room, studying. I can get him—"

Amherst shoved the man aside. "We'll find him."

"You can't come inside," Reginald protested.

"Upstairs?" Amherst glanced back at Pierce.

The younger detective nodded once, clearly bothered by their forced entry.

Amherst didn't let it trouble him, though. He took the steps as fast as his weight, age, and sore feet would allow him to move. When he made the second floor, he wheezed like an Oldsmobile with a busted piston.

Pierce passed him and went down the hall. He stopped outside a room blaring jazz.

"I'm calling the police," Reginald hollered up the stairs.

"Tell them to send a transport car," Amherst called back. "For when we arrest your son."

The music stopped suddenly.

Amherst bounded down the hall. He twisted the knob and threw the door open.

Steve Corson stood in front of the stereo with a record in his hands. Surprise registered in his eyes.

"You dumb bastard," Amherst said. He crossed the room.

"What'd I do?"

Amherst slapped the record from Steve's hand, then he grabbed the younger man by the shirt.

"Shut the door," he ordered Pierce.

Pierce turned and closed the room off from the rest of the house.

"What's going on?" Steve asked. His voice rose several octaves in fear.

"Where is she?" Amherst demanded.

"I told you," Steve said. "I don't know where Jo is."

"No, pretty boy." Amherst pulled the younger man closer. "Where is Shirley Jensen?"

"Shirley?" Steve looked at Pierce in contrived confusion.

Amherst balled his fists into Steve's shirt. "You know her!" He put his nose against Steve's. "Don't lie and tell me you don't. I can smell your lies."

Steve lifted his hands and turned his head. "All right, all right! I know her!"

"Where is she?"

"I haven't seen her in months."

Amherst let go of Steve with his right hand and held the fist in the air. "I'm smelling a lie."

"I swear!"

"Why'd you break up?" Pierce asked. He was leaning against the door.

"What?"

Amherst slugged the young man. He held on to Steve's upper arm and didn't let him bend over. "You heard my partner. Why'd you break up?"

Steve held his stomach. "She was crazy."

"Crazy?" Amherst glanced back at Pierce. "How so?"

"She thought she was pregnant."

"Bullshit," Amherst said. "Her friend would have told us."

"If you don't believe me, ask Baz."

"Basil Pershing, your fruity friend?"

"Hey man," Steve said. "That's not cool."

Amherst shoved Steve away. "How's Basil involved in this?"

Steve hunched as he rubbed his stomach. "Basil was with me when I met Shirley at Newberry's. I went out with her a few times, but they became friends."

"Basil knew she was pregnant?" Amherst asked.

"Shirley wasn't pregnant, man." Steve tapped a finger against his temple. "It was all in her head."

Pierce moved closer. "In her head how?"

"She missed her period, but that was it." Steve straightened. "I'm telling you. Ask Baz. He went with her to the doctor and everything."

Amherst's lip curled. Now he had a second connection between Josephine Banfield and Shirley Jenson.

"What doctor?" Pierce asked.

Steve waved a hand. "How would I know? They went, not me."

"Where's Basil live?" Amherst asked. "I'll bet that's something you know."

Chapter 12

Basil Pershing lived on the smallest lot on Nora Avenue in Northwest Spokane. Amherst recognized right away the house actually sat on a half-lot, a variation allowed in the aftermath of the war to accommodate the booming need for new homes. Pierce's war, though—not *his* war. When Johnny came marching home, he needed a place to live and raise a family, so savvy businessmen chopped up lots to put more houses on fewer square feet. Many who didn't go to war took an opportunity to trade up.

The house itself was well-kept and light blue with white trim. As Amherst pounded on the door, he wondered if Basil's father had been in the most recent war or just ended up in a cracker box house on a half-lot because of bad luck.

A woman with a vaguely confused look answered the door. The smell of baking bread drifted out of the cracked opening. The woman wore a blue housecoat and an apron splashed with flour. Her iron gray hair was drawn into a loose bun with several thick strands hanging loose. She was thin and her face was etched with age.

"I'm afraid I'm not interested in whatever you might be selling, sir," she said, and started to close the door.

Amherst reached out and stopped the door in place. He also jammed his foot in the opening but hoped she didn't close it on him. His sore feet didn't need any additional battle wounds this week.

"We're not salesmen, Mrs. Pershing. We're police detectives." Amherst held up his badge. "I'm Amherst. That's Pierce."

"Oh, my. Has something happened to my boy?"

"He's not here?"

She shook her head. "He's gone to the store for me. Is he all right?"

"Why would you ask that?"

Her eyes flitted quickly between the two men. "You're here, and I didn't call. Please tell me my boy isn't hurt."

"Not that I'm aware of," said Amherst. He removed his hat with his right hand but kept his left resting on the door, just in case. "Can we come in and speak with you, Mrs. Pershing?"

She stood blinking in apparent indecision for a few seconds before nodding. She moved aside and let them enter.

The delicious aroma of fresh-baked bread made Amherst's stomach growl, but he ignored it. He followed Mrs. Pershing into a cozy living room. A pair of chairs flanked a small round table with a large radio. Photographs lined the wall. Amherst noticed many of them featured a young man in uniform. Even if the photos hadn't been so old, he would have recognized the style of uniform.

His war.

So, Basil Pershing's father *had* served.

Mrs. Pershing offered them the two seats, but Amherst demurred. "We're fine, but please, sit. Unless you need to check the oven?"

"No, the loaves are cooling." She perched on the edge of one of the chairs. "What's this about, sir?"

"We're working on a case. Your son may be able to help us with some information."

"He's not in any trouble?"

"I suppose he could be, if he doesn't help us. He's not a suspect, if that's what you mean."

"What kind of case is it?" she asked.

"What's your name?"

"Doris."

"Doris," Amherst mused. "Beautiful name."

Doris didn't react to his compliment.

"Where is Mr. Pershing?" he asked.

A shadow crossed her face. "My Paul is gone," she said, her voice lowering.

"In the war?"

She nodded. "He fought in both of them, you know. In the trenches and then in the Pacific. He signed up to go back in right after Pearl Harbor."

Amherst's brow furrowed. "How'd he manage that?" he asked. "Age-wise, I mean."

Doris smiled sadly. "He lied, both times. Probably the only lies the man told in his entire life. The first time, he joined at sixteen, claiming he was eighteen. After Japan attacked Hawaii, he signed up again, saying he was thirty. Both times, the Army believed him, or at least, they didn't look very hard."

Amherst glanced at Paul's picture, feeling an affinity for a man he never met. They both lied about their ages so they could fight in France. Yet Amherst didn't think once about signing up after the Japanese attacked Pearl Harbor. He was already a police officer and believed his experience was needed at home. "I'm sorry to hear he didn't return," Amherst said solemnly, meaning every word. "May I ask…?"

"Guadalcanal," Doris said, the sadness in her voice tinged with pride. "They say it was a turning point in the war."

"It was," Pierce said quietly from behind Amherst. "I was there."

Doris tilted her head to look past Amherst. "I know it's crazy to ask, but sometimes it can be a small world. Is there any chance you might have known my husband? Paul Pershing?"

"No, I'm afraid not."

She sighed. "I thought so. There were so many men in that battle. So many in the war."

Amherst paused a moment out of respect. He noticed Doris was still an attractive woman for her age and wondered why she hadn't remarried. He couldn't think of a tactful way to ask at the moment, so he held the question. Instead, he brought the conversation back to the topic at hand. "You said your son was at the grocery store?"

"Yes. He should be back soon. I'm certain he'll be more than happy to assist you if he can."

"Does Basil spend a lot of time at home?"

"Heavens, no. I swear, he almost lives at the library and out at the college." Her face beamed while she spoke of her son. "Bassie is what they call a prodigy, though I think genius might be a better word for him. Did you know he skipped two grades? One in primary school and another in high school. He earned several scholarships and he's already a sophomore at the college."

"Bassie, huh? That's what you call him?"

Doris nodded. "Although, Basil is actually his middle name. I chose it, after my grandfather."

"What's his first name, then?"

"Jack. Paul insisted we name him after the general."

Amherst didn't have to ask which general. He nodded appreciatively. He'd admired General "Black Jack" Pershing, too, and, like many Americans, credited him with forcing the Germans to the bargaining table.

"He didn't tell us Basil was his middle name," Amherst said, feeling slightly foolish for not finding that information during their initial interview.

Doris smiled. "When he started school, there were two other Jacks in his class. He came home after the first day and said he was Basil now. He wanted to be the only one."

"Sounds like he's a smart kid," Amherst said flatly, irritated that the kid had got one by him. "Tell me, Doris, do you know much about his social life?"

"Oh, I don't think he has much of one," Doris said. "Too much studying to do. You know, people think everything is easy for geniuses, but the truth is anything but. Even with the gifts God gave him, he works three times as hard as anyone else."

Amherst showed her the photograph of Josephine Banfield. "Do you happen to know this girl?"

Doris shook her head. "Should I?"

"Not necessarily. How about this one?"

Doris peered at the photo of Shirley Jensen. "I think… maybe. Does she go to Our Lady of Lourdes?"

"Good question."

The front door rattled and swung open. Basil Pershing stepped inside, clutching a paper sack in the crook of one arm. His keen eyes took in the scene but showed no surprise at seeing the detectives.

"To what do we owe the pleasure?" he asked, swinging the door shut.

Doris Pershing rose from her chair and hurried to her son. "They need your help, Bassie, that's all."

Basil nodded impassively. He handed the bag of groceries to her. "The bread smells delicious, Mother."

Doris smiled at him like he'd just cured polio. Amherst suppressed a smirk.

"Why don't we speak out back, gentlemen?" Basil suggested. Without waiting for their reply, he brushed past Amherst and headed toward the rear of the house.

Amherst didn't like witnesses dictating terms, but Basil was nearly to the back door before he could react. He lumbered after him, wondering if the effeminate young man would try to flee. But Basil merely opened the door and held it for both detectives, following them outside into the small backyard.

"What can I do for you?" he asked amiably.

"Shirley Jensen," Amherst said, watching for his reaction.

"What about her?"

"Where is she?"

Basil glanced at his watch. "Well, if she's finished work, I assume she's at home by now."

Amherst grabbed him roughly by the arm and shook him. Basil let out a small yelp. "Don't play games with us,"

Amherst said. "We know you're best pals with her. We know about her and Steve Corson. Now, talk."

Basil's face fell. He glanced away, then shrugged his arm out of Amherst's grasp. "What do you want to know?"

"Start with her and Steve."

"There isn't much there. Steve is like every other entitled rich boy in this town." He stared pointedly at Amherst. "People—and especially women—are things to possess and control for their own needs."

"I thought he was your friend."

"Please. Do you see Steve Corson, or any of his ilk, being friends with someone who lives in a house like mine?"

"We talked to you at *his* house," Amherst said. "Everyone there talked about you like you were one of them."

"I have the girls to thank for that," Basil said. "They like me. They trust me because I'm different than the other boys."

Amherst clenched his jaw but said nothing.

Basil sighed and shrugged. "The boys simply go along because it's the path of least resistance."

"Did Shirley Jensen trust you?"

"Did?" Basil narrowed his eyes. "Why are you using the past tense? Is she all right?"

"She's missing."

The young man's eyes widened, and his hand flew to his mouth. Amherst read the action as genuine, almost involuntary.

"When did you see her last?" Amherst pressed.

Basil stared at him, still shocked. After a few moments, he recovered enough to sputter, "The night before last. We got malts and she talked about the classes she was going to take next year, after she'd saved enough for tuition." His eyes glistened with tears. "She's going to be okay, isn't she?"

Amherst was taken aback at the display. Since meeting the young man, he'd projected a sophisticated, aloof affect, like someone who didn't care about much. Seeing Basil vulnerable like this softened Amherst's opinion of him.

"We need to find her," Amherst said, easing his tone. "If you can think of anywhere she might go or who she might be with, that'd be helpful."

"Yes, of course. Anything you need."

"There's something else," Amherst added. "Steve Corson said there might have been some medical irregularities concerning her."

Basil brushed at his eyes, nodding. "She thought she was pregnant."

"She wasn't?"

"No. Just a late period, is all. Almost a week off schedule, I guess."

"Steve said you took her to see a doctor."

Basil smiled. "I told Steve that to calm him down. He made a big show of calling Shirley crazy but make no mistake, he was worried she was in a family way."

"She didn't see a doctor, then?"

"She went for a checkup, yes. I took her myself. I told Steve how I held her hand all the way through so he'd stop prattling on about it. The boy was worried he might have to marry her."

Amherst glanced at Pierce but couldn't read his partner's stoic expression. He turned back to Basil. "What doctor did she see?"

"I believe it was Dr. Etherton," Basil said.

Another thrill shot through Amherst, an even stronger one than when he'd made the connection between Basil Pershing and Steve Corson. Etherton treated both missing girls? This was the kind of link that they could build a case upon.

"Why would she see him?" he asked. "Did you send her to him?"

Basil shook his head. "Shirley couldn't go to her family doctor, so I told her how Dr. Etherton helped Jo."

"A man known for his discretion."

Basil hesitated, then nodded. "I suppose so. Nothing untoward, mind you, just discreet. Shirley is an adult, after all. Her medical business is her own."

"You ever hear of Dr. Etherton messing around with his patients?"

Basil scrunched his brow. "You asked me that before, about Jo."

Amherst stared at him, waiting.

"My answer is the same," said Basil. He glanced at Pierce, then turned his attention back to Amherst. "Dr. Etherton is very handsome and I'm sure he enjoys the benefits of his good looks and financial status. I'd imagine seeing patients is strictly forbidden."

Amherst grunted. "Anything else you can share about Shirly, Jo, or Dr. Etherton?"

"I… I hope you find her," Basil said, his voice hitching while he spoke.

Amherst set his jaw. "We're going to do our best, son."

***

Amherst dropped into the passenger seat and pushed his hat back on his head. "Find me a call box."

Pierce dropped the car into gear and left the Pershing's neighborhood. He drove up to Indiana Avenue, stopping a few blocks later.

Amherst slid out of the car, not bothering to close the door behind him. He opened the call box, hoping to find a bottle of something an enterprising patrolman might have left behind. Unfortunately, there was only the phone.

He lifted the receiver and said, "Detective Amherst. I need an address search."

A second passed before an operator replied. "Go ahead for address."

"I need a home address for Dr. Karl Etherton." Amherst spelled the last name phonetically. "That's Karl with a K."

"Copy, Dr. Karl Etherton," the dispatcher said. "Will you call back or are you waiting?"

"Waiting."

Pierce climbed out from behind the wheel and walked over. "What're we doing?"

"Getting an address." Amherst cradled the receiver between his ear and shoulder. He removed a pack of cigarettes from his jacket and shook one free.

Pierce pulled a Zippo from his pocket and ignited it, holding it out so Amherst could light his cigarette. "You took it easy on the kid."

"Who? Pershing?"

"Who else?"

"Bullshit." Amherst's face warmed.

"We're going to do our best, son." Pierce tried his best to imitate Amherst's voice, but he sounded like Buffalo Bob from *The Howdy Doody Show*. "What the hell was that?"

"Stick it in your ear. I can go easy when the job requires."

"Could have fooled me."

Pierce chuckled. "Maybe you're going soft."

Amherst sneered. "You calling me queer?"

"No, I was just saying—"

"Sounds like you're calling me queer." Amherst slapped the call box with his palm. "It ain't the first time you suggested that, either."

"Take it easy," Pierce said. "Jesus. I'm only busting your chops."

Amherst inhaled on his cigarette. "I'll bust your chops you keep playing that song."

Pierce pulled out his own pack of cigarettes and lit one. He turned when he exhaled.

"I was feeling for the guy," Amherst said, "if you gotta know. His dad fought in my war and died in yours. Left behind a widow and a kid. I know what it's like to be that kid, that's all."

"It's no skin off my nose."

"Besides, he's young and soft-hearted. His friend is missing."

"I get it," Pierce said. "I'm all for you being nice once in a while."

Amherst opened his mouth to retort, but the operator returned to the line. "Detective?"

"Here."

"Dr. Karl Etherton lives on Sumner Avenue." She rattled off the house numbers.

Amherst repeated it back to her.

"That's correct."

Pierce stuck his cigarette between his lips, then hurriedly dug out his notebook. He jotted down the address.

"Got it?" Amherst asked.

"Good to go."

Amherst said thanks to the operator before ending the call.

"We're not going out to the clinic to see Etherton?" Pierce asked.

"Look at the time. He's a doctor. No way he's working this late." Amherst tossed his cigarette into the street. "That's his home address. Let's go, Jeeves."

****

Even in the fading remnants of dusk, Dr. Karl Etherton's home was impeccable. The two-story affair was painted white with black accents. The front door was bright red. A two-car garage extended off the side of the house.

The yard looked freshly mowed as if the landscapers arrived that day and carefully manicured the grass. Amherst hadn't seen a lawn so meticulously sculpted since his time on a military base. He appreciated the attention paid to it.

The first and second story windows were large, and many rooms were lit up. No lights came from the basement windows, though.

Amherst and Pierce parked in front of the house and got out. They started up the walkway.

"Guy must be a Rockefeller," Amherst said.

Pierce nodded. "It's a nice place. I'll give you that."

"He leaves on every light like he's got stock in Washington Water Power."

"Maybe he does."

They each took a different side of the door and Amherst banged on it with the flat of his fist.

"What do you bet he's got a butler?" Amherst asked.

"Gonna call him Jeeves, too?"

"No."

"Why not?"

"Because maybe his butler's involved." Amherst raised an eyebrow. "Wouldn't that be something?"

"Can I help you fellas?" Dr. Etherton called from the side of the house.

Amherst and Pierce turned to look.

Etherton stood there with a gardening spade and a small, ceramic pot. In the middle was a leafy green plant. He wore a short-sleeve plaid button-up and a pair of tan Chinos. Leather gloves covered his hands.

"A little late for playing in the dirt," Amherst said. "Ain't it, Doc?"

"You don't approve of my hobby, Detective?"

Amherst descended the front steps and crossed the lawn. "I heard you doctor types were into golf."

"Whoever said 'golf is a good walk spoiled' hit the nail on the head."

"Wanna take this inside?" Amherst asked. "Away from the neighbors?"

"Out here is fine. I've nothing to hide."

Pierce stepped further around the corner. "You working in the backyard?"

"I heard a racket and thought I better come investigate. I take it you have some more questions about Josephine Banfield?"

"Actually," Amherst said. "We want to ask about Shirley Jensen."

Etherton tapped his spade against the side of the potted plant. "Shirley Jensen?"

Amherst pulled Shirley's picture from his jacket pocket. "Remember now?"

The doctor's brow furrowed. "Why are you asking me about her?"

"She's missing." Amherst held the photo up higher. "Well?"

Etherton set down the potted plant and the spade. He put his hands on his hips, seemingly unworried about dirt smearing his tan pants. "Is this going to happen every time a young woman goes missing—you come and talk to me?"

"There better not be another one," Amherst said. He flapped Shirley's picture. "You gonna tell us if you know this girl or not?"

"She came into the clinic."

"For what?"

The doctor crossed his arms. "She has rights to her privacy."

Amherst jammed a finger in his chest. "She's missing, Doc. Fuck her privacy. Why'd she see you?"

Etherton's lips pursed. "She thought she was pregnant."

"But she wasn't?" Pierce asked.

"No."

"How'd you find that out?" Amherst asked.

"The usual way. Tests, questions. All above board. You can ask Vivian. She was working that day."

"Fine," Amherst said. "What's Vivian's last name?"

"Why?"

"Because we're going to talk with her."

"No," Etherton said. "You can come by the clinic tomorrow, at a civilized hour, and interview her there."

"Why?" Amherst asked. "So you can intimidate her? We're going to interview her now."

"She's a respectable young woman, Detectives. She doesn't need—"

"Don't tell us what she needs." Amherst kicked the ceramic pot and it exploded. The green plant whirled into the yard.

Etherton looked calmly down. "That was uncalled for."

Amherst grabbed the doctor by the shirt and pulled him close. "Either tell us your receptionist's full name or we're gonna run you in for interfering with a police investigation."

"By all means," Etherton said. "Feel free to arrest me. When Vivian's father finds out what you did, I'm sure he'll have something to say about it. He's an attorney. A very busy one. He'll appreciate my efforts to protect their family time."

Amherst glared at Etherton, not moving. The doctor wasn't intimidated and that pissed Amherst off.

Etherton cocked his head. "No witty retort? Then perhaps you should leave." He lifted his fingers and flicked them in a *shoo* gesture.

Amherst's lip curled, and he reached for his handcuffs. "You mealy mouthed—"

"George," Pierce said. He shook his head.

"What?"

"Remember our talk with DiCarlo."

Amherst balled his fist around the handcuffs. Something was fishy about Etherton, but he couldn't put his finger on it. If he arrested the doctor on a chippy charge, a lawyer would stick the paperwork up Amherst's ass. The sergeant's, too. If Amherst was going to arrest someone rich and connected after the tongue lashing he took earlier, he better be right.

He shoved Etherton away. "You're lucky."

Etherton steadied himself and adjusted his shirt with a tug. "My plant wasn't so fortunate, now, was it?"

Amherst turned and walked toward the car. His feet hurt but he wasn't going to give Etherton the satisfaction of seeing him limp.

"Thank you for your time," Pierce said and hurried after his partner.

***

"What do you want to do now?" Pierce asked.

"I want to bust that smooth-talking prick in the mouth." Amherst took his hat off and swatted the glovebox with it.

"That won't help."

"Why'd you have to thank him?"

Pierce cast a sideway glance. "I was trying to keep you out of hot water. You want me to leave him steaming under the collar, fine. I can do that."

Amherst swatted the glovebox again. "Hell."

"Where to next?"

"The station."

"We calling it a night?"

"I don't see no use in chasing our tails any further. As far as we know, Shirley Jensen might be out with a boy she doesn't want her friends and family bothering her about."

Pierce set his wrist on the top of the steering wheel and draped his hand over. "You really think that?"

"I don't know what to think," Amherst said. "I'm tired as hell. All I wanna do is eat some dinner and get some shut eye."

Pierce nodded. "Let Gloria take care of you, huh?"

"She knows which side her bread is buttered."

"King of the castle," Pierce said. "Sounds like you got it whipped."

***

When Amherst entered his house, no aromas greeted him. His already sour disposition worsened.

"Gloria?" he called.

She didn't answer.

He checked the kitchen but there was nothing on the stove and the dinner table was clear.

"Huh," Amherst muttered.

He opened the bedroom door and flicked on the light. Gloria was in bed with the covers up to her chin.

"Turn out the light," she groaned.

"You didn't make dinner," Amherst said.

She squinted at him. "I'm sick."

"I worked all day."

"I've had my head in the toilet, throwing up my guts, George. You don't want me touching your food."

Amherst stared at her for several moments. Eventually, he said, "Fine," and snapped off the bedroom light. He closed the door louder than was necessary.

He wasn't in the mood to go out. He did that last night. Besides, he was tired. Amherst didn't bother looking for anything fancy to cook. Instead, he made a peanut butter and jelly sandwich. That way, when Gloria asked what he had for dinner, he could make her feel terrible for leaving him to his own devices.

Amherst ate his pitiful dinner over the sink and thought about Dr. Karl Etherton. He wondered what kind of meals the doctor ate and where he went when he wanted to dine out. The guy seemed the fancy type. It was easy to hate Etherton. Amherst disliked any guy who caught a break because of his looks or family connections.

After his sandwich, Amherst grabbed a pillow and blanket, then headed toward the couch.

He flopped down and stared into the darkness of his house.

King of the castle, my ass.

Chapter 13

Amherst was up, dressed, and in the kitchen before Gloria arose. She shuffled in and stared at him.

He stood near the sink, sipping coffee from a white mug. An empty plate, a knife, and the butter tray sat out on the counter.

"Everything all right?" Gloria's voice sounded like sandpaper. She sniffled and pulled her fleece robe tighter around her.

"Why wouldn't it be all right?"

She lifted her chin toward the plate. "You're making your breakfast."

"Had to make my dinner last night, too. Getting to be a regular bachelor."

Gloria cocked her head. "I'm sorry, George. I wasn't feeling well."

"I wonder if Sergeant DiCarlo would let me tell that story for a runny nose."

"I'd bet he'd let you stay home if you had the shits and were barfing your guts out. I've got the flu or something."

Amherst studied her. She looked like hell. He admitted to himself that he wouldn't want to be working if he had the runs. Still, if he went soft on her now, who knew where it would end?

The bread popped in the toaster.

"I'll get that," Gloria said.

Amherst waved her off. "Stay back. I don't need any of whatever crud you're carrying. I got work to do."

He grabbed the two slices of toast and tossed them onto the plate. Amherst lifted the lid off the butter tray. The block inside looked sort of like butter but something was off. "The hell is this?"

"It's Nucoa."

"Margarine?"

"It's supposed to be healthier for you."

Amherst sneered. "Why are you messing with my happiness, Gloria?"

When she didn't respond, he reluctantly cut off a healthy slice. Her face pinched with disapproval.

"You don't need that much," she said.

"Leave it be."

She silently watched him slather the margarine on the first piece. When he went back for more, Gloria said, "I'm feeling better. Thank you for asking."

"You ain't looking it. Where'd you catch that cold, by the way? Your secret boyfriend?" He slurped the last bit of coffee in his cup.

Gloria eyed him. "You know that's all nonsense to get you jealous. The only one of us around here with any secret lovers is you."

"Hey," Amherst said. He pointed the empty mug at her. "Enough with your lip. Go back to bed."

Suspicion clouded her eyes. "You really going to work this early? Is it the case you're working on?"

He nodded. "Had trouble sleeping because of it."

"What is it?"

"Two missing girls."

Gloria craned her neck to see Amherst better. "You thinking they're dead or something?"

He wrapped the toast in a napkin and slipped them into a jacket pocket. Amherst covered his mouth with a hand and slipped by her on the way to the front door.

"George."

When he looked back, Gloria said, "I hope things work out okay."

Amherst kissed his hand and threw a smooch to her. She didn't bother catching it, though.

"I'm sorry for the lip," she said. "I didn't mean nothing by it."

"Go back to bed," he said and slipped out the front door.

***

"You're here early," Walter Pierce said.

Amherst looked up from his desk. "Why's that a shock to everybody? I get to work early sometimes."

"Not since I've started." Pierce dropped into his chair. "What're you working on?"

"The Banfield and Jensen cases. Making some notes, prepping the reports."

"Yeah?" Pierce leaned forward and rested his elbows on his knees. "What's our plan of attack today?"

"We're getting a search warrant for Etherton's clinic and his house." Amherst held up the paperwork. "While we're searching the clinic, we'll talk with Vivian."

"Collaborate the good doctor's story."

"Or poke holes in it." Amherst shoved his chair back as he stood.

Pierce looked up. "Where you going?"

"We are going to see the judge."

"I just got here."

"Suit yourself."

Amherst headed for the exit.

Pierce trotted alongside him. "Hold up."

"What's the problem?"

"You're full of piss and vinegar this morning," Pierce said.

Amherst shoved the door open and exited the building. He descended the stairs. He hardly noticed the pain in his feet. "I'm driving."

"Where's the first stop?" Pierce asked.

"I told you," Amherst said. "The judge's house."

"We're not stopping for breakfast?"

"Not today."

Pierce's face tightened. "I didn't eat."

"Whose fault is that?"

Amherst dropped into the driver's seat of his car and started the engine.

After Pierce settled in, he said, "I don't get you, George."

The car lurched away from the curb.

***

Judge James W. Ziskin was perturbed from the moment the detectives entered his library. Though the magistrate was already dressed in an expensive suit and drinking coffee, he complained about the early hour.

"I will be in chambers at the courthouse by nine," he said, his tone one of irritation. "I keep to business hours, gentlemen. Couldn't this have waited?"

"I apologize, Your Honor," said Amherst, clutching the warrant paperwork to his chest. "But this is a time-sensitive case."

Ziskin frowned and held out his hand. "Give it to me," he said tersely.

Amherst pushed the paperwork into his hands.

The judge settled into an overstuffed chair. He took his time cleaning the lenses of his glasses before he began to read. Amherst shifted on his sore feet, waiting impatiently and glancing at his watch. Even if Ziskin read slowly and asked a number of questions, there was still plenty of time. He wanted to be at the clinic when it opened.

Next to him, he heard Pierce's stomach grumble.

A few moments later, Ziskin looked up sharply. "Is this some kind of terrible joke, Detective?"

"No, Your Honor. I'm deadly serious."

Ziskin scowled. "You had better be," he said in a menacing tone. "Asking to invade the privacy of a man of Karl Etherton's standing. A doctor, no less."

"You know him personally, Your Honor?"

"I know many people, Detective. Spokane is a small city."

Especially when you're talking about the rich and powerful, Amherst thought, but he had the good sense not to say it. "If you don't feel comfortable reviewing the paperwork, sir—"

"Don't be ridiculous. My objectivity isn't a concern." Ziskin shook the paperwork, making it rustle. "Besmirching an upstanding citizen of Spokane, however, is."

"Please, read the affidavit," Amherst said calmly, though his insides were screaming to snatch the papers from the judge's hands. "The probable cause is there."

"For your sake, it had better be." Ziskin returned to his reading. Amherst glanced at Pierce, who remained stoic. Should he have waited for Pierce to provide input on the warrant application? No, he decided. He believed he had enough probable cause to merit a search of the clinic, at least. The doctor's house was admittedly a stretch but if they found any evidence at the clinic that pointed them in that direction, he could re-apply on that count.

Another minute passed in near silence. The ticking of the grandfather clock accentuated each moment. Amherst remained still and was grateful Pierce did the same. The only other sound was the scrape of paper when Ziskin went to the second page of the affidavit.

The judge finally lowered the paperwork with a frown. He reached up and removed his glasses, giving Amherst a stern look. "This is what passes for probable cause in your mind, Detective?" He held up the affidavit in disgust. "There is nothing here."

"All the facts are there," Amherst said firmly, keeping his tone respectful.

"Perhaps so, but facts are just facts. They do not necessarily equate to probable cause." He shook the papers again. "You've done a satisfactory job of succinctly summarizing the facts of your case. But those facts are woefully inadequate when it comes to supporting a search warrant."

"Your Honor—"

"I'm seriously baffled by this," Ziskin interrupted him. "The only spurious connection I see between these missing girls and Dr. Etherton is that both were patients of his."

"That's right, and the clinic is dodgy."

"Dodgy? If you mean the doctor is engaged in unsanctioned procedures, there's no evidence of that. Just your stated suspicion, which is both unfounded and unsupported." Ziskin leaned forward. "Really, Detective, have you thought this through? If both girls had a savings account at the same institution, would you apply for a search warrant for the bank and Chairman of the Board's home? If they both took the same train to Seattle, would I be reading a request for the railroad office and President's home as well?"

"Your Honor…"

Ziskin flicked his wrist, flinging the paperwork toward Amherst. It struck him lightly on the chest and fluttered downward. He grabbed the pages before they fell to the ground. The judge regarded him disdainfully. "If this is the kind of police work you're doing on behalf of the citizens of this city, Detective Amherst, then I weep for the fate of these poor girls who are missing. I believe it might be time for me to have a frank discussion with the Chief of Police." He pointed to the door. "Get out."

***

The drive from downtown Spokane to Cheney was nearly twenty-five minutes. Why the state decided to build a college so far away from the city it was intended to serve would forever boggle Amherst. However, there wasn't anything he could do about it now but accept it.

Neither detective said much during the drive. Both were lost in their thoughts. Amherst stewed over Ziskin's rebuke. He remembered a day when all a judge needed to approve a search was the word of a cop, even if that word came with a knowing wink. Now, apparently, a written warrant wasn't enough. Next to him, Pierce remained silent. Amherst wondered briefly what the younger detective thought of the judge's decision.

When they arrived in Cheney, Amherst pulled curbside in front of Etherton's clinic.

"Should one of us go around back?" Pierce asked.

"We can see the back door through the window." Amherst pointed. "We're fine sitting here."

"The sign on the window says they open at nine." Pierce checked his watch. "We still got thirty minutes. I'm gonna find something to eat." He popped open his door. "Want anything?"

"I'm good."

Pierce left the vehicle and headed east.

Amherst rolled the window down and lit a cigarette. His thoughts returned to Judge Ziskin. He was certain the department's administration would hear about it. The only question was whether the chief would express his displeasure through the chain of command or summon Amherst to his corner office to do it himself.

The cigarette burned down while he sat brooding. Amherst crushed it out and lit another. He decided it didn't matter. There was doing things right and there was doing the right thing. He'd gone through much of his life concerned mostly about the first, but sometimes the second mattered most.

He was on his third cigarette when Pierce strolled back up the sidewalk. Amherst watched him in the rearview mirror. His partner carried two paper cups. Pierce stepped off the curb and walked to the driver's side of the car.

"Here," he said and handed Amherst a cup of coffee.

Amherst accepted it.

Pierce looked at the clinic. "About time for them to open."

"Vivian hasn't showed up yet."

"Maybe she's running late." Pierce sipped his coffee.

"It happens, I guess, but why's it got to be today?"

A car pulled up behind them and a young blonde climbed out. She walked to the clinic door and pulled on the handle. When it didn't open, the woman leaned left and right as if trying to get a better view inside. She knocked on the window.

"Hey," Pierce said, and the woman turned. "They're not open yet."

She frowned. "No flies on you."

"You got an appointment?"

"What business is it of yours?" The woman knocked on the window again.

Pierce walked over to the sidewalk.

Amherst quickly crushed out his cigarette, then got out of the car.

"Hey, smart mouth," Amherst said. "You got a problem with authority?"

The woman's gaze bounced between the two detectives. "Who are you?"

"Spokane Police," Pierce said. He waggled his thumb between himself and Amherst. "We need to ask Vivian a couple questions."

Amherst pulled his jacket to the side to reveal his gun and badge. "You know her?"

"Yeah, I know her," the woman said. "What of it?"

"What's her last name?" Amherst asked.

"Heimbigner. Vivian Heimbigner."

Amherst returned to the car. He set the coffee cup on the hood before walking to a call box at the end of the block. He opened the door, found an empty bottle of rye, and muttered, "Small town bastards." Amherst lifted the receiver and said his name.

An operator came on the line. "Go ahead."

Amherst said, "Connect me to city dispatch."

The Cheney operator didn't reply but Amherst heard some clicking on the line, followed by silence. He eyed the empty bottle, frowning. After a short wait, a familiar voice greeted him and asked what he needed.

"Look up the phone number and address for Vivian Heimbigner. Not sure of the spelling."

"Heimbigner, copy. Hold the line."

While Amherst waited again, he realized Vivian's last name was almost certainly German. He never noticed before that he was surrounded by so many krauts. Before he could formulate any further thoughts on the matter, the operator returned. "Detective, there's a V. Heimbigner listed on Seventh Avenue. I have the name and number when you're ready."

Amherst glanced up and down the street. There wasn't a phone booth anywhere nearby.

"Hey, doll," he said, "would you call the number and see if Vivian's home? Maybe ask when she'll get here? We're at her work now and the place is closed. We're following up on an investigation."

"Sure thing," the operator said. Her monotone response carried more than a hint of irritation.

Pierce abandoned the bratty blonde and approached. "What's going on?"

"Dispatch found Vivian's address. They're calling to see if she's home."

Another woman, a chesty redhead walked up to the clinic and peered into the window. Pierce called out, "They're closed."

The redhead frowned, looked around, and walked over to the bench sitting in front of the real estate office. She sat and crossed her arms and legs.

"Detective?" the operator said.

Amherst pushed the phone tighter to his ear. "Yeah?"

"Vivian is at home. Her boss told her not to come in today."

"Did she say when she got that call?"

"Last night. That's all she said."

Amherst lowered the phone and glanced at his partner. "Etherton called last night and told Vivian not to come in today."

Pierce slapped his hands. "That jackrabbit."

Amherst lifted the receiver again. "Get patrol units to Dr. Karl Etherton's house right now. He lives on Sumner Avenue. Also, send a unit to Vivian Heimbigner's house and another one to Dr. Etherton's clinic on First Street in Cheney."

"Copy," the operator said.

Amherst slammed the phone back onto its hook and shut the call box door with a bang. He stalked back to the car with Pierce on his heels. The two hurriedly climbed into the car. Amherst dropped the transmission into gear and the vehicle lurched from the curb. Amherst's coffee cup fell over and spilled its contents over the hood. He cranked the wheel, cutting across traffic, and turned the car around.

The detectives sped back toward the highway.

***

It took fifteen minutes to arrive at Dr. Etherton's house. Amherst exceeded the speed limit with the car's siren blaring. Pierce put the whirring red light on the dashboard. Vehicles moved to the side of the road as they blasted past.

Three patrol units were parked in front of the Etherton estate. A fourth car, a '49 Oldsmobile Coupe was also there. Several patrol officers huddled together on the lawn.

Many neighborhood women stood on their porches and watched the policemen.

Amherst pulled his car to the curb. He and Pierce hopped out as soon as it stopped rolling.

"Who's driving the Olds?" Amherst hollered.

One of the uniforms motioned at the car. "It's registered to a Doris Pershing. I checked it when I arrived."

Amherst slowed. "Pershing?"

"It's on the registration," the officer called. "I saw it with my own two eyes."

"What's she doing here?" Pierce asked.

"We're about to find out," Amherst said. He waved at the uniforms. "Two of you, go around back. One of you, with us."

The two detectives hurried up the pathway and climbed the stairs.

Pierce rang the bell and Amherst pounded on the door with the flat of his hand.

"Etherton," Amherst yelled. "Open up! We wanna talk with you."

Officer Norman Woodward stared up from the pathway. He was in his mid-twenties and bright eyed. "What's this all about?"

"Missing girls," Pierce said.

Woodward shifted his duty belt and trotted toward the house. An enthusiastic smile creased his face. "All right."

Amherst pounded the door again. "Etherton!"

"You think we try again for a search warrant?" Pierce asked.

"Etherton!"

"You lock down the house," Pierce said, "and I'll run back and write it."

"Back door's ajar!" called one of the officers from the rear of the house.

Amherst glanced at Pierce and cocked his head. "You hear that screaming?"

Pierce's brow furrowed. "What screaming?"

"What about you, Woodward? You hear that screaming, don't you?"

The officer's smile faded, and he shrugged. "I'm not sure."

"There's a right way to do this," Pierce said.

"We tried that. Kick the door, Woodward," Amherst ordered. His feet hurt too much to do it himself.

The young officer's face widened with excitement. "Really?"

"Let's go in the back door," Pierce said.

Amherst waved him off. "No time. I hear screaming." He eyed the young patrolman. "Don't you?"

"Well, yeah." Woodward said. "I think I do." He hurriedly climbed the front stairs.

Pierce held up a hand. "Let's think about this, George."

"We're past that," Amherst said.

Woodward reared back and booted the door. It splintered and crashed inward.

Amherst drew his gun and entered the house. Pierce and Woodward followed.

At first, there was only the ticking of a grandfather clock in the living room. In a surreal moment, Amherst was reminded of a similar clock in the judge's library, ticking away while he waited for the man to read his warrant application. He shook off the thought and pressed forward. As they moved through the living room, a sound became clear—a low moan for help.

Amherst glanced back at Pierce and Woodward. "I told you I heard screaming."

Chapter 14

While Pierce and Woodward climbed the stairs to the second floor, Amherst quickly swept through the opulent first. He saw no one. He listened for another call for help, but none came. The tick of the clock and the tramp of feet above him were all he heard. As Amherst passed near the rear door, he waved for one of the uniform patrol officers to come inside.

"Hold the front door," he ordered. "No one in or out."

The officer nodded briskly and hustled past him.

Amherst started another pass through the ground floor, looking for the door to the basement. Pierce and Woodward came down the stairs just as he reached for what he'd thought was only a closet. The door swung open, revealing a set of stairs that descended into darkness.

"*Help*," came a slow, weak moan.

Amherst pointed his gun down the staircase. He felt along the wall for a light switch. When his fingers fumbled across it, he pressed. There was an audible click but no light.

"Woodward!" he barked. "Flashlight."

Behind him, a patrol flashlight flared. Padding lined the walls of the staircase. A moment later, Woodward appeared at his shoulder to lead the way down, but Amherst stopped him.

"Give it to me," he said.

Woodward didn't argue. He handed over the flashlight. Amherst took it in his left hand and extended it in front of himself. Then he started down.

He heard the groan of leather and the jangle of equipment behind him as Woodward followed. Pierce's lighter steps were barely discernible. Amherst took in the sounds like second nature and focused on what was before him.

Step by creaking step, Amherst descended. Another moan for help punctuated the stuffy silence. Amherst's first instinct

136

was to hurry but he knew better. Etherton might be lying in wait, ready to spring a trap. Amherst saw plenty of ruses in the war, though far fewer while on the job. However, something was off about Etherton. He believed the doctor might conduct an elaborate ploy to kill them before he faced a kidnapping charge.

Amherst reached the foot of the stairs. The entirety of the basement lay to his left. He turned and inched his way forward, the wavering flashlight slicing through the darkness. He saw a couch, a radio, and a workbench.

On the far wall, the light swept across the still face of a young woman.

Amherst stiffened and stopped.

Even from where he stood, he could see it was Josephine Banfield.

Amherst surged forward. Behind him, he heard Woodward follow. A moment later, there was a click, and the basement was flooded with light. Amherst wheeled toward the sound, but saw it was Pierce, who had found another switch at the bottom of the stairs.

The expression on Pierce's face was utter shock.

Next to Amherst, Woodward stood in place. "Mary, Mother of God," he whispered in horror.

As if in answer, another low moan came from behind Amherst.

He wheeled around. Against the far wall, three figures hung from shackles riveted to the wall.

Josephine Banfield.

Shirley Jensen.

Basil Pershing.

Both women hung limply from their shackled wrists, their heads lolled to the side. Blood streaked Shirley Jensen's slack features. Josephine Banfield's face was covered in what looked like black dirt, but Amherst suspected was dried blood.

Both their throats were slit. Thick, bright red wetness glistened down the front of their nude bodies, spilling onto the ground and pooling there. Neither woman moved.

Basil Pershing twitched and let out a low moan.

Amherst surged forward, holstering his gun.

The young man hung from a single shackled wrist, his naked chest awash with the same bright red as both women. He seemed to sense Amherst when he drew near and lifted his head. A bruised knot adorned his cheek. Basil's eyes were laced with terror, and he tried to shrink away from Amherst.

"No," he cried. "No more."

Amherst stopped in front of him. He cast his gaze around frantically for a key to the shackles but saw none.

Pierce pressed his fingers to Josephine Banfield's slashed throat, hoping for vital signs. Amherst knew she was already gone, that both women were. Only the young man was alive.

Amherst reached out and touched Pershing on the shoulder. "It's okay, son. You're safe now."

The young man moaned again.

"Go upstairs," Amherst said to Woodward. "Find a phone and call it in. Stay off the radio."

Woodward stumbled backward before wheeling away, as if grateful to be leaving the bloody dungeon.

"Hey," Amherst said, stopping the patrolman after two steps. Woodward looked back.

Slowly, the detective told the shell-shocked officer what assets he wanted dispatched to the scene.

"Repeat it back," Amherst said.

It took three attempts before Woodward got it right. Amherst was patient with the young officer. He'd seen this kind of response on the battlefield. Only after Woodward's tramping feet retreated up the staircase did Amherst turn to Pierce.

"They're gone," Pierce told him. "Both of them."

Amherst nodded. "We need a pair of bolt cutters."

Pierce's gaze flicked to Basil's shackled wrist. Without a word, he turned and left.

Amherst looked around the room again. Still no key. He spotted a fixed blade knife on the floor a few feet away but kept looking around for a blanket.

Nothing.

He helped Basil to his feet. Then Amherst shrugged himself out of his jacket and eased it around the young man, draping it over his free shoulder. The material hung almost to Basil's knees. He gripped the opposite side, clutching at the hem and pulling it close to cover his naked frame.

"How long ago did he leave?" Amherst asked gently.

"What?" Basil said, staring confusedly back at him.

"Etherton. How long ago was he here?"

A panicked expression came over Basil. His eyes filled with tears that spilled down his cheeks. His chin quivered, and when he spoke, Amherst was certain he'd never heard a man's voice sound so small.

"You didn't catch him?" Basil asked.

***

Pierce returned with bolt cutters he'd borrowed from a neighbor. Together, he and Amherst clipped the manacle holding Basil Pershing to the wall. The young man collapsed forward but Amherst caught him. He wrapped him in his jacket and supported Basil as they climbed the stairs. Rather than take him out front where the neighbors could see, Amherst stopped Basil in the living room. He guided the young man toward the couch, but Basil shook his head violently. Amherst helped him sit on a chair instead. They waited together in silence until the ambulance arrived. Once the medics started their treatment, Amherst assured the young man he'd see him at the hospital.

Through it all, the terror never left Basil's eyes.

Amherst returned to the basement dungeon. Pierce studied the slain women, pain and disgust evident on his face. When he saw Amherst, he held up a key.

"Found it on the workbench," he said.

The two men stood still for a few moments. The right way to handle the crime scene was to touch nothing else. Basil had been alive, and that trumped evidentiary concerns. Once life-saving measures were completed, protocol dictated they lock down the scene and leave it undisturbed.

Amherst eyed Pierce, who stared back. The junior detective still held the key poised in the air like a question.

There's the right way and there's the right thing to do.

Without a word, the pair moved in unison to the shackled young women. Working together, they freed both from their bonds and lowered them gently and respectfully to the floor.

It was during this time that Amherst noticed something else.

Both women were missing the ring finger of their left hands.

***

The crime scene took the entire day to fully process.

Once the victims were removed, Amherst made certain the photographers shot the dungeon in exceeding detail. Every pain-inducing tool on the workbench. The sound padding that covered the entire interior of the basement. The manacles bolted to the walls. The dried brownish blood that seemed too old to have been from the recently deceased. Even the mundane items, like the radio on the table, which Amherst imagined Etherton listened to during his sadistic activities.

The newspaper reporters showed up quickly. Amherst's pet news hounds expected to get their usual inside access, but he rebuffed them. They loitered with the rest of the news crowd and the other onlookers herded halfway up the street by patrol officers.

The brass showed up next. First Sergeant DiCarlo, then the lieutenant. They were followed by the captain and eventually the chief himself. All entered Etherton's house full of bravado but fell completely silent once they saw what was in the basement. There were no recriminations, but Amherst knew those would come later. Two beautiful young women had been murdered. One of them belonged to an important family. The only one he saved was the wrong kind of boy.

Somebody would have to shoulder the blame.

Once he was sure the investigation was on track at the crime scene, Amherst and Pierce left for the hospital. Despite the fact it had been hours since Basil's rescue, when they arrived, the detectives still had to wait for the doctor to finish treating him. The physician, a gruff old man who lit up a cigarette in the hallway while he spoke, reported on Basil's injuries.

"He's got a few contusions." The doctor exhaled a plume of smoke. "Multiple cuts, but most are superficial."

Etherton was playing games, thought Amherst. *Torturing him.*

"The worst injuries are a pair of puncture wounds," said the doctor. "Here and here." He touched his outer left thigh and upper right chest, just below the collar bone. "They're deep but luckily no arteries were severed."

"Can we talk to him?"

The doctor shook his head. "You were both in the war, right?"

Wordlessly, both men nodded.

"Well, call it shell shock or battle fatigue," the doctor said, blowing out a stream of smoke, "but this boy's worst injuries are not of the physical variety. He needs time. Must you talk to him right away?"

Amherst considered. A statewide bulletin had already been issued for Karl Etherton. He doubted there was anything Basil Pershing could tell them that would further cement his captor's guilt or help them locate him.

"It can wait," he said.

***

They went to the clinic next.

Vivian Heimbigner met them with a key and saved them the trouble of kicking in the door. Given the simmering anger brewing in Amherst, he would have welcomed the opportunity, sore feet and all.

While the secretary stood by in silence, the detectives sorted through the doctor's records. The office and its files were clean and orderly, much like Etherton's home. The stark contrast between the businesslike setting and the horror of the man's dungeon kept coming back to Amherst while he thumbed through the records.

"It's really true?" Vivian asked, in a wavering voice.

"I can't tell you anything about—"

"I got a call from a girlfriend who knows the Banfields," Vivian said. "She said Dr. Etherton killed both of those girls. Is it true?"

Amherst considered, then tersely nodded.

"Oh my God," she whispered, sinking into a chair. "Oh my God."

Amherst watched her. He had a crazy thought that maybe she was in on it with him the entire time, his sexy, sadistic apprentice. When her tears fell, he believed they were genuine.

"I worked for him," she said in a shaking voice. "For two years." She looked at Amherst, then at Pierce. "That could have been me instead of them."

"Nothing ever seemed off about him?" Amherst asked, keeping his tone neutral.

"No," she croaked, the tears falling harder now. A sob hitched in her chest, and she put a hand to her mouth.

Amherst grabbed a box of tissues and held it out to her. Vivian plucked several and pressed them to her face.

"Oh my God," she repeated.

Amherst replaced the tissue box. Quietly, he said, "We could tell there was something going on with him."

"Not killing people!" Vivian sobbed.

"No, we didn't think so, either." Amherst didn't add how they were all wrong on that count. Instead, he said, "Something shady, though. At the time, we thought maybe he was fooling around with patients or...?" He trailed off hopefully.

Vivian's sobs continued. In between, she said, "Of course, he was seeing young girls. They loved him and he loved them."

"Young men, too?" Amherst asked.

"Not that I saw," Vivian said, dabbed her eyes with the tissue. "It seems like there was a lot I didn't know about him."

"Were these other young women his patients?"

She nodded. "Most of them, at one time or another."

"He didn't just do checkups, did he?"

"I told you—"

"I don't mean playing hanky-panky. I mean, he was some kind of Dr. Discretion for these girls."

Vivian hesitated, her sobs slackening. She looked up at Amherst with red-rimmed eyes. "If I tell you, will I get in any trouble for what he did?"

"No," Amherst assured her. "You won't."

Vivian wiped her eyes. "Can I get some water? Then I'll tell you everything."

"Sure," said Amherst.

Vivian got herself a glass of water. After she drank the entire amount, she refilled it and took another sip. Then she was true to her word. She pulled several files as examples, showing them the notations and explaining what they meant. A picture of Etherton's true practice quickly emerged. He treated anyone who came in, but specialized in discreetly handling the problems of prominent, wealthy women.

"Not just college students?"

Vivian shook her head. "Wives, too, though that happened less often."

"Using these codes—stomach cramps to mean abortion, headaches for venereal disease—is that legal?"

"I don't know," Vivian said. She fixed him with a meaningful look. "I'm just a secretary. I didn't know what was going on."

"I understand," said Amherst. "You just answered the phone and didn't know a thing."

"That's right."

"I'll put it in my report exactly that way. Now, tell me the rest."

***

That night, Gloria was still sick but looked on the mend. She seemed to sense his mood as soon as he arrived home.

"George, honey, it's late," she said, though without any accusation. She slid on a cloth mitt, removed his dinner plate from the oven, and peeled away the foil.

"My case broke."

"In a good way?"

He looked at Gloria. They'd been together since he returned from the war. Young love. She'd stood by him through a lot, not the least of which was his fooling around. Somehow, she managed to seem like she still cherished him.

"George? Did it break in a good way?"

Amherst didn't answer. Instead, he motioned toward the plate in her hand. "What's for dinner?"

Chapter 15

In the morning, they interviewed Basil Pershing.

Sitting up in the hospital bed, the kid finally looked his age. It was as if all the mature artifice had been stripped away and he was once again a child. Still too young to join the military, unless Basil took a page from his father's book and lied about his age. If Amherst thought he might do such a thing, he'd tell him about his time in the trenches. Anything to keep the kid out of the conflict in Korea.

Basil's slight frame was huddled beneath the blankets. His mother, Doris, sat next to him, hovering watchfully. When Amherst asked her to wait outside, she objected until her son intervened.

"It's all right, Mother," he said, his voice barely audible. "I don't want you to hear these things."

Doris Pershing hesitated, then reluctantly rose and left the room.

Amherst settled into the chair she'd left vacant. "Son, I need you to tell us what happened." He rested a hand on the boy's shoulder.

Slowly, haltingly, Basil Pershing explained. After the detectives told him Shirley Jensen was missing and asked about her seeing Etherton, Basil went to see the doctor by himself. Since he had escorted Shirley Jensen to the clinic when she'd needed Etherton's services, he suspected Josephine Banfield might have gone to see him as well but needed to know for sure. During his visit with Shirley, Basil was struck by how handsome and charming the doctor was. He had even wondered if Etherton might share similar sexual inclinations, but when Basil saw how the doctor interacted with women, he put it down to wishful thinking. Thus, he was surprised by Etherton's overtures toward him when he later came to ask the doctor about Shirley.

"I should've known better," Basil said softly, "but he's very magnetic. Very convincing. When he invited me to his house the next morning, of course, I went."

"Did you two…?"

Basil nodded, seemingly unashamed. "In the living room. He sat on the couch and I…" Tears welled in his eyes again. He looked directly at Amherst. "That's why…after…when you saved me… I didn't want to wait on the couch."

Amherst swallowed thickly and motioned for him to continue.

"He suggested we go somewhere more comfortable," Basil said. "That's when he took me downstairs. That's when I saw Jo and Shirley."

"They were still alive?"

Basil tried to answer but could only let out a moan. He nodded instead. After a while, he continued in a choked tone. "He put those chains on my wrists," he said, his voice hoarse. "He cut on me. If one of the girls screamed, he threatened to kill them. This went on for a couple of hours."

"He only used the knife?" Amherst asked. "There was no more sex?"

Basil shook his head. "Once he started hurting me, I could see that was what did it for him. Pain was the most important thing. Pain, and power." He swallowed again and let out a wavering breath. "He killed Jo to show me his power. Then Shirley. He took his time with them. He didn't stop until we heard sirens."

Amherst sat and listened, dejected, as Basil described the rest. Once he heard the police drawing near, Etherton struck him in the head with the butt end of the knife, stunning him. Then the doctor stabbed a dazed Basil on his way toward the stairs before dropping the blade.

"I watched him disappear up those steps," Basil whispered. "I heard the door slam. A little while later, I heard your voices."

"How long?" Amherst asked. "How long after?"

"Moments," Basil said, his eyes misting again. "Forever."

We were that close, Amherst thought. *That close.*

***

Sergeant DiCarlo escorted the two detectives to the chief's corner office as soon as they arrived at the station. There, Amherst detailed everything he knew. Occasionally, he looked to Pierce to add details or simply confirm them. Through it all, the chief listened with a tight-lipped scowl.

Amherst didn't take that as a good sign.

"Was this doctor a known homosexual?" the chief asked.

"I don't keep track, sir."

"Don't give me any lip," the chief snapped. He glanced at the lieutenant. "What did Vice say?"

The lieutenant answered immediately. "His proclivities were not publicly known, sir."

The chief grunted and turned back to Amherst. "This secretary at the clinic, she's the only one who knows about what's in those files?"

That's when Amherst knew how this would go.

***

"They're going to bury it," Amherst told Pierce.

The partners sat across from each other in a booth at The Park Inn. They had finished eating and were on a second cup of coffee. Each smoked a cigarette.

"They can't bury it," Pierce said. "It's too big. Too many people know."

"You watch," Amherst said. "They'll lock it down and keep all the right names out of it."

"They're not that stupid," said Pierce. "This is too big. Keeping it under wraps will only create another Black Dahlia situation."

Amherst pursed his lips, thinking. Pierce had a point. The Los Angeles Police Department had been too secretive with the 1947 sensational murder case. The secrecy created a mystique that only fueled interest. Amherst knew most agencies took their cues from LAPD, both in training, policy, and lessons learned. "So, maybe they show enough early on to satisfy everyone's surface curiosity," he said. "Then, they quietly slide it back into the file drawer. Either way, it's still getting locked down."

"They can't bury it," Pierce repeated. He took a drag on his cigarette. "They won't."

"I don't care if they do," said Amherst. "I only care about one thing."

"I know."

"How do you know?"

"It's the same thing I care about," said Pierce.

Amherst tapped some ashes onto his empty plate, wondering if it were so. "What's that?" he asked evenly.

Pierce didn't hesitate. "The son of a bitch is still out there."

Amherst nodded. "That's right."

***

Murder warrants were issued for Karl Etherton, in addition to kidnapping and assault charges. Efforts to locate him were unsuccessful. Despite Amherst and Pierce working the case hard, there was no sign of the doctor.

For several weeks, the newspaper and radio stations featured the case. It even got a write up in *True Detective*. Unfortunately, the reporter misspelled Amherst's name "Amhurst." In all publications and televised interviews, the chief carefully crafted the way he wanted the story told. This got the message to the population at large. The chief made it clear Karl Etherton was a monster, a sexually depraved murderer whose twisted, sadistic tastes included both women and men. The details of his homemade dungeon, at least those deemed suitable for public consumption, were described in disgusting detail.

The community paid rapt attention, at first.

Basil Pershing was not named, described only as "an unnamed juvenile male," though his true identity made it into the rumor mill within a matter of days.

Josephine Banfield and Shirley Jensen were painted as naïve young women, seduced by a handsome, charming, and ultimately evil older man. Their unfortunate deaths were a tragedy, but otherwise an aberration.

After a month, the chief stopped talking about the case. People seemed more than willing to forget the terrible event.

Things like this did not happen here.

Spokane was, after all, a family city.

Interlude I

2023

Chapter 16

"How much of that was true?" Detective Wardell Clint asked.

Robert Baumgartner turned over his hands. "You've read the reports. You tell me."

Clint stared at the former chief, trying to suss out his game. How honest was Baumgartner? Usually, a good indicator of the truth was when someone shared something uncomfortable or which made them look bad in the eyes of the listener. Another indication was when the person divulged a secret.

Baumgartner clearly wasn't uncomfortable with the details of the Etherton case. He certainly didn't worry about looking bad about something that happened in 1951, not in Clint's eyes or anyone else's, since he wasn't even alive at the time. There were no indicators of a lack of veracity coming from those corners.

What about secrets?

It seemed Baumgartner had shared a few.

Clint reached out and took a sip of water from his glass. The coffee was gone now. Long before Baumgartner shared how Amherst and Pierce figured out Etherton was their man, Darla had returned to the patio table with a pitcher of water and two glasses. As she took the coffee setting away, she said, "If you're still here come lunch, I put some sandwiches in the fridge. Other than that, you're on your own. I'm taking the boat out."

"Sightseeing?" Clint asked as she walked away. Darla's skin was tanned to a light bronze.

"She fishes," Baumgartner said. He'd waited until she was out of earshot to resume his story.

Now, the former chief watched him. Those eyes missed little, if anything. Clint had seen that keen gaze of appraisal many times during Baumgartner's career. Some of those instances had been directed at Clint himself.

"The reports from back then are sparse," Clint said, "and there are some missing files."

"The basement flood in seventy-two." Baumgartner shifted in his seat. "Something like forty percent of the records were destroyed."

Clint already knew that. "Amherst never got his man, you know," he said. "He died in 1974, haunted by that failure."

"How do you know he was haunted?"

Clint opened his file and pulled out two yellowed newspaper articles. "Amherst was quoted in two local news articles in 1968 following the Richard Speck murders in Chicago. Apparently, the similarity between the cases wasn't lost on the people of Spokane."

"Maybe Speck was Etherton in disguise," Baumgartner said dryly. "That sounds like a conspiracy right up your alley, Ward."

Clint's lips tightened. Baumgartner was tossing around his shortened first name like a fighter throwing jabs. Its incessant use was wearing on him, but Clint couldn't let the former chief know he'd found a soft spot, or the man would work it harder. The interview might go off the rails and all his work would be for naught. Clint smiled humorlessly. "Speck was Speck. We both know he wasn't Etherton."

"No, he wasn't." Baumgartner turned his water glass with his thick fingers. "I'm impressed you found those articles, though."

"I don't single source my investigations. I cast a wide net."

"I've never doubted that. The trouble with you has never been finding information. It's how you interpret what you discover. The less you find, the more you tend to fill in with your theories."

"Fortunately for me, the Etherton file wasn't one of those destroyed in the basement flood," Clint said. "Since it remained an open, linked homicide, the file was kept indefinitely. I pulled it from archives and read every scrap of paper in it."

"If it was sparse, that shouldn't have taken long."

"I said the official reports were sparse. The file contained more than that," said Clint. "There were notes, too, from Amherst. Many of them were from the immediate aftermath of the murders. He checked on Basil Pershing a few times early on, for instance. But mostly, he focused on the killer. Amherst recorded facts, questions, his theories about where Etherton might have gone. It went on for years as he ran down increasingly marginal leads regarding the killer's whereabouts."

"Sounds obsessive," Baumgartner observed dryly.

Clint heard the barely disguised sarcasm in the former chief's voice. With an effort, he ignored it and forged ahead. "There were scraps of paper dating up to his retirement. There were even several written after that, in Pierce's hand, detailing how Amherst kept checking back on his unfinished business, asking if there'd been any sightings of Etherton, and pointing to other cases outside of Spokane that seemed potentially similar. Then, of course, there was the follow-up in seventy-four. Plenty of notes and reports in that file."

Baumgartner didn't look surprised. If anything, he looked disappointed that Clint was aware of this information. "I know," said the chief.

"How is that?"

"I read the file."

Clint narrowed his eyes. "Why?"

"I had my reasons, like you."

"*My* reasons are I've been officially assigned to work cold cases. I've made some interesting connections between these supposedly solved cases and multiple unsolved murders." Clint leaned forward. "What were *your* reasons?"

Baumgartner stared at Clint for several seconds, not speaking. Finally, he said, "Ward, have you ever heard the expression, let the dead lie in peace?"

"No," Clint shot back. "Have you ever heard the creed of the homicide investigator?"

Baumgartner frowned, as if Clint had just made a smart chess move that irked him. Clint knew the chief had heard the creed. He waited for him to say the words. When he didn't, Clint recited them.

"We speak for the dead," he said solemnly.

Baumgartner glanced down, thinking.

Clint wanted to smile. After all the jabs, he'd landed an uppercut. He waited patiently. He had nowhere else to be and nothing else planned for this day.

Baumgartner lifted his glass and took a healthy drink. His Adam's apple bobbed several times. When the former chief set the glass down, it made an audible plunk. Baumgartner studied Clint, then asked, "What else do you want to hear about?"

"Don't be coy. Let's talk about what happened in seventy-four."

Baumgartner drummed his fingers on the tabletop. "You should have walked away from this earlier, Ward. There's still time. I'll give you the opportunity to do it now."

"Not a chance," Clint said, tight-lipped. "Keep talking."

Part II

1974

*"What strange phenomena we find in a great city,
all we need do is stroll about with our eyes open.
Life swarms with innocent monsters."*

- Charles Baudelaire,
French poet

Chapter 17

Detective Walter Pierce leaned against the door of the Chevy police vehicle, smoking and waiting. He kept to Lucky Strike, the same cigarette he'd lighted up since the war. Other brands were introduced over the years and became trendy, but Pierce kept to the old standby. If it was good enough for the C-rations, which sustained him during the war, it was still good enough today.

The waiting, though, was for something new.

Some*one*, actually.

When he spotted the young man striding jauntily toward him, he frowned. Pierce had been a police officer for twenty-eight years, all but five of them as a homicide detective. As such, he didn't often see the fresh faces spilling out of the academy and into the patrol division. Even if he did, they tended to be nearly invisible elements at a crime scene, easy to ignore.

There would be no ignoring this kid, however.

He was to be Pierce's goddamn partner.

The idea galled him. He'd worked hard during his own patrol stint, right after the war, and earned his position as a detective. He endured a year of being treated like a tagalong by his first partner, George Amherst, before finally earning some credibility with the man and within the unit.

However, this kid was assigned to Major Crimes right out of the chute.

Despite his distaste, though, Pierce couldn't get too worked up over it, since it was technically his own doing.

Officer Augustus V. Salter was taller than Pierce by a couple of inches or so. Pierce pegged him at six-one. The kid was lanky and reminded Pierce of a big-pawed, spastic puppy that still had growing to do, though the kid's demeanor was more confident than that. The officer's uniform was brand-new and so was the equipment adorning it. In Pierce's day, veterans got the first pick of new gear. Rookies got hand-me-downs. It seemed Spokane P.D. was as screwed up now as the rest of the world.

"Are you Walter?" Salter asked.

The voice was deeper than Pierce expected, registering somewhere in the mid-range rather than the high-pitched child's tone he'd imagined.

"Detective Pierce," he answered, sending the kid a clear message.

We're not to first names yet.

Salter was undeterred. He held out his hand. "I'm Auggie."

Pierce cringed. Augustus was an unfortunate name without truncating it to that of a cartoon character or what a child might name a stuffed animal. If Salter's parents slapped him with the nickname, they must have hated their kid. That might mean the guy had childhood issues he hoped to work out from behind the safety of a badge. On the other hand, if Salter pinned the moniker upon himself, he just might be an idiot. The only hope was a childhood friend called him Auggie and it stuck.

"You're Officer Salter," Pierce corrected, since the kid was clearly a slow learner.

"That's right." Salter kept his hand extended, showing no discomfort.

Pierce took Salter's hand. He gave the new officer a firm grip and was pleasantly surprised when he got the same in return.

"You missed roll call," Pierce said flatly, dropping his hand.

Salter froze. His eyes turned panicky. "I did?"

Pierce let the kid's flustered emotion ride for a few seconds, saying nothing. He didn't personally enjoy inflicting the discomfort on him. It was Pierce's duty to do so, since the boy had never experienced a drill sergeant like most cops who had military experience prior to being hired. Worse yet, Salter wouldn't get a standard patrol coach until he went back to complete the academy after the ongoing World's Fair ended and he eventually cycled back to the field again.

"No one told me," Salter said.

"You used to being told everything?" Pierce asked. "That what they did in college?"

Confusion seeped into Salter's worried expression. "Well, yeah… that was kind of the whole point."

"Seems to me the biggest point of college for the last decade has been avoiding the draft."

Salter's ears tinged red and his cheeks flushed. "Not for me. I went to learn."

"Did you learn how to tell time?"

"No one told me about roll call," Salter repeated.

Pierce took a long drag of his cigarette, wondering if he'd made a mistake taking on this kid.

The World's Fair required a massive hiring glut of new officers. Once the city went through all the military vets, what remained was some bottom of the barrel shit, in Pierce's opinion. People who never thought of being cops responded to the call for applications. Inflation was high and jobs hard to get, so it was no surprise when some of the applicants turned out to be unworthy.

The problem worsened when the powers-that-be realized they had underestimated the number of officers necessary for the six-month long event. Officially called the International Exposition on the Environment, everyone simply called it Expo. Once the city's administrators realized they'd under-hired for the event, they scraped another layer off the bottom of the barrel, mere weeks before President Nixon arrived for the opening festivities.

"What was your hire date?" Pierce asked.

"April Fourth," Salter responded immediately, as if eager to get something right.

Pierce muttered a curse. That was a scant six weeks ago. "How much of the Academy did you get through?"

"Percentagewise?"

"No," said Pierce, exhaling smoke in barely disguised frustration. He already knew the training lasted sixteen weeks. He wanted to know what Salter had learned. "What classes did you complete before they jerked you out and threw you into service?"

"Oh." Salter thought for a moment, then began to recite. "We went through criminal law, of course, and ethics."

Pierce rolled his eyes. "How about something useful? Physical training?"

"A little."

"Handcuffing?"

"Some."

"Can you fight?"

"Fight?" Salter seemed confused by the question.

"You weren't in the service," said Pierce. "I need to know if you can fight."

"I boxed a little."

"When?"

"At summer camp."

Pierce groaned, then he asked, "How about pistol training?"

"We shot a few times before qualifying."

"You passed?"

Salter nodded.

Pierce drew in some more smoke, appraising the rookie. So, what did he have here? A green college kid who got through the first month of the academy. Probably barely knew which end of the .38 went toward the suspect.

You asked for this.

Pierce exhaled, still staring at Salter. He recalled Salter's uncle, Claude Beetner. Claude and Pierce served in the Pacific together, a pair of Spokane boys who discovered each other after Guadalcanal and spent the rest of the war watching each other's back. Claude's sister, Edith, called Pierce a few weeks ago to report her son Augustus had taken a job with the Spokane Police and request he keep an eye on the kid.

He couldn't deny her. Not after what Claude did for him on Okinawa.

When Pierce heard the latest batch of undercooked recruits were being thrown into the field, he called in a favor of his own to make sure Salter was assigned to him. Most of his reason for doing so was to fulfill his promise to Edith and honor Claude. Better Salter come to him than be teamed up with some old patrol bull who was still collecting free booze and cigarettes downtown.

Pierce had a self-serving reason, too. The personnel shuffle was huge and its ripple effect would result in Pierce being partnered with someone. It was unavoidable. Since his last partner retired three years ago, Pierce had been joyfully working alone. If he got another detective now, that partnership might stick for the rest of Pierce's career. Instead, if this kid rode around with him for six months, essentially a tourist in a uniform, Pierce could fly solo after Expo ended and hopefully spend the rest of his career that way.

Sergeant Fadelin initially hated the idea. There may not have been enough coaches in patrol for all the new recruits but there were still some regular patrol officers who could take them on. When Pierce pointed out Salter had college, though, the man relented.

"You want to babysit, Pierce, that's your business," Fadelin said, and signed off on the assignment.

Looking at Salter now, Pierce could see some of Claude's features in his face. Not a spitting image of his old friend, but an unmistakable family resemblance. Pierce wasn't going to like being reminded of Claude every day for the next six months.

What's done is done, he thought. Only way through is forward.

Pierce flicked his cigarette butt away. Salter watched it fly to the curb, his expression distasteful. Pierce could tell the rookie wanted to say something about littering. That was one of the many causes his generation seemed to champion these days—they had their priorities all screwed up. When the kid held his tongue, Pierce figured that was one point in the boy's favor.

"Get in," he told Salter, and reached for the door handle.

Salter scrambled to the passenger side of the car. Once inside, Pierce started the engine. The big block ran rough. The department repurposed patrol vehicles for detectives after their best miles were used up. Pierce had meant to take the car to the garage to see if the mechanics could smooth out the idle, but the past couple of weeks were busy with the Expo kickoff headlining the reasons why.

"You think I'll be in trouble?" Salter asked.

"For what?"

"Missing roll call." He didn't sound scared, only disappointed, like he'd missed a potentially game-winning field goal.

Pierce put the car into gear and pulled away from the police station. "Only patrol schlubs go to roll call," he told Salter.

It took a moment for Pierce's words to sink in. Then Salter said, "Why'd you say—"

"If you're going to be a good cop, you've got to know the score." He glanced at Salter, then back at the road. "This isn't college. Nobody is going to tell you everything. A lot of people will lie to you. Most, in fact. You've got to set a foundation of knowledge. Know what is what, so you'll know when they're lying."

"Okay," Salter said.

"You've got a lot to learn," Pierce said. "The brass is throwing all of you out here to the wolves just to make the city appear safe for all the tourists. It's not doing you any favors."

"I suppose not."

"I'm trying to teach you something."

"Far out."

Pierce grimaced. "First lesson—don't talk like a hippie."

"Second lesson, you mean." Salter's voice had a slight edge to it. His confidence was back. "First lesson was don't trust your coach."

"Close. First lesson was people lie." He drove in silence for a block, then said, "Do people really call you Auggie?"

"Since I was a kid."

"Why'd your parents pick Augustus?"

Salter nodded. "It's a family name. My grandfather was the first Salter to cross the Mississ—"

"Third lesson," Pierce interrupted. "Drop Auggie. It's stupid. Go by Gus."

The rookie didn't answer right away. After a few blocks, he asked, "Where are we going?"

"Crime scene," Pierce said. "A murder." He turned right on Maxwell. "You might as well learn some things while you're here."

"I didn't hear about a murder."

"You didn't hear about roll call, either."

"Because you lied about it."

"I was teaching you something," Pierce said, rolling down his window to let in the cool spring air. Homicide scenes had a stink of one kind or another to them, and he wanted to enjoy some fresh air before this one. "You didn't hear about this murder because the department didn't want you to."

"The department… what do you mean?"

"They're keeping it quiet."

"Why?"

"The mayor and the chief don't want anything in the press that might besmirch the reputation of the country's newest All-American City," Pierce said. "Or stain the World's Fair. You can plan on most dirty little crimes that happen over the next six months to stay dirty little secrets."

"That sounds like corruption," Salter said earnestly.

His naivete made Pierce laugh.

***

Pierce drove west and descended Boone Avenue toward the mobile home park.

Salter leaned forward. "It's too bad about the amusement park, huh?"

"Things change," Pierce grumbled.

The younger man was talking about Natatorium Park, the city's once pride and joy even though it had been privately owned. Trollies used to shuttle attendees to and from the park. Pierce never rode one; they'd stopped operating before he ever got the chance. The park featured a variety of attractions for nearly seventy years. A change in ownership and dwindling patronage resulted in the park's recent conversion to a mobile home community. It was yet another transformation in Spokane that Pierce hated.

"I never got to go," Salter said. He stared at the shiny metal boxes. "Would you live in a mobile home?"

"What'd I say?"

Salter turned to him. "Excuse me?"

"I don't like to repeat myself."

"You said…" Salter lowered his eyes as if recalling something. "Things change."

"That means stop talking."

The younger man crossed his arms and set his jaw. The pout was hard to miss. Salter's confidence needed a good ding, Pierce thought. Rookies, especially those with no experience and little training, shouldn't walk around with false bravado. Addressing superior officers in a conversational tone wasn't done while still in the training car.

At the bottom of the hill, Pierce didn't turn into the mobile home community. Instead, he turned left. A patrol car blocked access to the small neighborhood. Only a few homes resided along this strip of road known as North Evergreen Street.

Pierce stopped the car and rolled down his window. He stuck his head out and waved his arm in the air. The patrol car crept backward, clearing the lane. Pierce pressed the accelerator and moved his car forward.

Salter craned his neck as he took it all in—the witnesses standing on their lawns, the other cops, a fire engine, and the medical examiner's vehicle. His mouth lowered and he appeared to be having fun. "Check it out."

Pierce didn't fill the silence with a bunch of chatter. It wasn't done to put himself in a better mood before walking up to the crime scene. He'd been in the business of death for too long to worry about something like that. Pierce knew what needed to be done, and he would perform his job to the best of his ability.

He remained silent because he didn't want to engage Salter in further conversation. Pierce hated to suffer fools, and most cops Pierce knew had the same attitude. They dealt with idiots throughout the day, so their tolerance level was usually low. This was different than the policeman in a social setting who loved being the center of attention, regaling guests with stories of daring-do. Every day, rookies balanced precariously on the razor's edge of fool and guest. At least they usually had some academy training to add a little patina to their outlook.

Right now, Pierce believed Salter leaned toward the category of fool.

Although, Salter might have it worse than most rookies. He was college-educated and partially trained at the academy with no military experience. Pierce thought he could see the rookie's trajectory after just a few minutes together—being a career cop was going to be hard for Salter.

Pierce parked the vehicle in front of a single-level home and got out. He stood by the car and lit a cigarette. As he smoked, Pierce considered the neighborhood.

They were in a natural cul-de-sac. Behind the houses to the east was a hill. The river flowed behind the houses to the west as it wound its way south. There were no houses to the south, just a dirt lot lined with bicycle tracks. It appeared to be the neighborhood hangout for kids.

A cluster of older citizens stood in the front yard of a nearby house and watched the police activity with curiosity.

Salter came around the car, his head swiveling about. "Where's the body?"

"On the river's edge." *How could the rookie not piece that together for himself?*

Pierce inhaled on his cigarette as he waved at an approaching sergeant.

"Shouldn't we go check it out?" Salter asked.

"They'll still be dead when we get there."

"Right." Salter glanced around, seemingly embarrassed by his question. "Right."

Sergeant Philip Boyd neared. He was a shorter man with dark features and a bushy mustache. Boyd held out his hand. "Good to see you, Pierce. How's the wife?"

"She's fine," Pierce lied. "Yours?"

"Angry as ever." He smiled now, the grin of a man guarding a handful of good cards.

Pierce cocked an eyebrow.

Boyd chuckled. "Whenever Elaine's in a bad mood, she bakes. There's an apple pie waiting for me tonight. I'm the luckiest man alive, I tell ya. I rile her up in the morning and she rewards me for it when I come home." His chuckle turned into a full laugh now.

Salter looked around as he shuffled nervously.

Pierce took another drag on the cigarette. Smoke drifted up to his eye and he blinked uncontrollably. "Dispatch said we caught a floater."

"Couldn't have been in there too long." Boyd motioned toward the water. "Not even bloated."

"That's new." Pierce tapped his cigarette.

"Hey," Boyd said, "you going to Woodward's retirement party tonight?"

Pierce nodded. "Looking forward to it. Woody's always good for a story or two." He glanced at Salter and grumbled, "Get your hands out of your pockets."

Salter jerked his hands free. "Sorry."

Boyd eyed Salter. "How do you rate?"

"Sir?" Salter asked.

Pierce tossed his cigarette into the middle of the street. "Let's go."

"Aye, aye, Boss." Sergeant Boyd spun on his heel and walked away.

Salter fixated on the cigarette smoldering in the roadway.

"Focus on what's important," Pierce said to him and headed after the sergeant.

Chapter 18

The nude body was male. The pasty white form lay on the recently cut grass of the back lawn. Wickets and colorful balls were scattered about—a morning croquet game paused by death.

A blond woman watched from behind a kitchen window.

Pierce, Salter, and Boyd stood ten feet from the body.

"Who pulled the victim from the water?" Pierce asked.

Sergeant Boyd thumbed toward the roadway. "My guys. It got caught on the rocks, so they grabbed it and pulled it in."

"You didn't call out Fire?"

"Who wants to wait for those guys?"

Pierce couldn't argue the point. "Who found the body?"

Boyd cocked his head toward the house. "The kids who live here. They came out for a game of Smack the Ball before school and discovered it. Hell of a way to start the day. The mother kept them home. They're in their room if you want to talk with them. At least, they'll have a story for tomorrow's recess, huh?"

Pierce looked at Salter who stared at the dead man. The rookie's jaw hung loose. "You all right?" Pierce asked.

Salter didn't respond. Instead, he gaped at the unmoving form.

Boyd patted Pierce on the back. "I'll leave you to it. Holler if you need anything." He turned and moved toward the patrol officers standing at the edge of the house.

"Officer Salter," Pierce said. When that didn't get a reaction, he pushed the rookie on the shoulder. "Hey."

Salter slowly turned to him. Pierce had seen the look before—a world war and a career in the police department provided many opportunities to witness the first time someone saw the dead up close. It's one of the reasons Pierce disagreed with the department hiring anyone without prior military experience.

"You'll get used to it," Pierce said.

Salter nodded but it was apparent his mind was still on the body. He swallowed with great difficulty.

Pierce didn't want to spend any more time coddling the rookie, but he needed to get Salter in the right frame of mind. He asked, "What do we know right now?"

"Sir?"

"We've been on scene for several minutes. Before we examine the body, we've established some other truths. What are they?"

Salter straightened. His brow furrowed as his eyes darted back and forth.

Pierce frowned. "Think about the topography."

Salter cocked his head. "Sir?"

"That's a college word, isn't it?"

"I know what it means, but—"

Pierce interrupted because they couldn't stand around all day. "Did the killer dump the body on those rocks over there?"

Salter turned and looked at where the victim had been discovered. "Probably not. He'd have had to walk through this yard to do it."

"Right," Pierce said.

"Unless he lived at this house."

"Which would be pretty stupid."

Salter's eyes widened. "We'll interview the homeowner, right? Just in case it was them?"

Pierce sighed. "Yes. Just in case."

Salter smiled like a beginning chess player does when they snatch a pawn.

"But it's unlikely," Pierce said. "Highly unlikely. So the killer dumped the body where?"

"In the river?"

"Are you asking me or are you telling me, Officer Salter?"

The rookie nodded once. "In the river."

"Where in the river?"

Fear flashed through Salter's eyes. "How can I know that?"

"Where should we focus our attention, Officer Salter? Upstream or downstream?"

"Downstream. Wait. I mean, upstream. The body came downstream. That's what I meant."

"Okay," Pierce said. "There's a point up on Boone Avenue, in the cul-de-sac where we parked. There are no homes. Could the killer have dropped the body in the river there and the body floated around the bend?"

Excitement passed over the rookie's face. "Maybe."

"No," Pierce said. "It's doubtful."

"Why?"

"There were no car tracks in the dirt."

"Maybe…" Salter's eyes darted about. "Maybe the killer parked where we did and carried the body. That could happen." Another smile and another snatched pawn.

"A dead body is a lot of weight."

"You've carried one?"

"I have," Pierce said. He left out that it occurred during the war and the dead man had been Salter's uncle. "Getting a body in and out of a car would be a pain in the ass. Carrying it to the water would have been a struggle. The killer would likely park as close to the water as possible."

Salter motioned toward the street. "Maybe the killer lives in the neighborhood so he didn't have to drive. He wouldn't have the problem of getting the body in and out of the car."

"If a killer goes to the trouble of dumping a body," Pierce said, "he'll do it away from the neighborhood he lives in. You don't shit where you eat. We're back to the same issue we started with."

"We still have to interview the neighbors just to make sure?" Salter's stupid smile returned. He believed he snatched yet another pawn off the board.

"Yes, Officer Salter." Pierce's shoulders slumped. "We'll interview the neighbors."

He should have never started suffering the fool.

Pierce turned his attention to the victim. The body lay on its back with the arms positioned by its side. The dead man stared up into the morning sun.

Pierce squatted next to the victim. He started to study the dead man's face but heard Salter shuffle forward. Pierce glanced over his shoulder. "Put your hands in your pockets," he said.

Salter stared at his palms. "You told me to take them out."

"Now I'm telling you to put them back in." He turned his attention back to the body.

"Why?" Salter asked.

Pierce inhaled deeply. "So you don't touch anything."

"What's there to touch?"

Pierce looked back, not bothering to hide his frustration.

Salter didn't notice since he was glancing around the yard. His hands were on his hips.

"Put your hands in your pockets," Pierce ordered.

The rookie's attention returned to the detective. They stared at each other for several seconds before Salter jammed his hands into his pockets.

"It's good practice at a crime scene," Pierce said, "especially for dumb ass rookies who want to touch everything like they're grabby, goddamn babies and end up ruining evidence in the process."

Salter's eyes widened.

"Follow directions when I give them to you. This isn't a college field trip." Pierce pointed at the body. "Understand?"

"Yes, sir."

"Now, open your eyes and close your mouth."

Pierce turned back to the body. As Sergeant Boyd pointed out, it wasn't bloated so it likely went in the water recently. The victim appeared to be roughly twenty. There were no visible tattoos or scars. Dark bruises covered the torso and legs. Someone had beaten the man, yet there wasn't any damage to the victim's face that couldn't be explained as a scratch from an errant branch sticking out of the riverbank.

Salter shifted his position to get a better view of the body. His hands remained in his pockets as he leaned. Pierce was happy to see the rookie's earlier revulsion was replaced by curiosity.

Pierce's attention was drawn to the right wrist. A deep ligature mark ran around it.

"Maybe he jumped," Salter said.

"He didn't jump."

"Lots of people jump from the Monroe Street Bridge." The rookie pulled his hand from his pocket and pointed in the direction of the bridge, as if Pierce didn't know where the goddamn thing was.

"He didn't jump," Pierce repeated. To stop the rookie's train of thought, he added, "From anywhere."

"If he did, it makes perfect sense."

Pierce dropped his chin to his chest. "How's it make sense?"

Salter waved his hand at the body. "He's got all those bruises, right? I figure maybe he hit the water, and it busted him up really bad. Then the river pushed him down here and he hit some more rocks on the way."

"Are you saying he jumped in naked, Officer Salter? Or did his clothes get ripped off in the water?"

Salter's lips pinched. "Probably naked. Maybe he had an episode or something. Like those guys coming home from Vietnam."

"Not everyone who comes home from the war has an episode."

Salter shrugged. "Maybe this guy did."

Pierce looked up into the blue sky. He hadn't even made it to lunch, and he regretted his decision to work with Claude Beetner's nephew. "Were you on the debate team, Officer Salter?"

"No."

"Then why do you argue with everything?"

"I don't argue with everything."

Pierce stared at him.

Salter stuck his hand back in his pocket. "I wasn't on the debate team."

"If he jumped from the bridge, you've gotta explain the lack of clothing, his bruising, and the ligature marks."

"Ligature marks?"

"Around the wrists," Pierce said. He motioned toward the right wrist. "Someone bound this man, killed him, and threw his body in the river."

Salter leaned over and studied the left hand. "Geez, you're right."

"I know I am."

"I think someone cut off one of his fingers, too."

Pierce stiffened. "What?"

"There." Salter pointed at the body with his boot. "Yeah. That's what it looks like."

"Let me see." Pierce stepped to the other side of the victim. He bent and grabbed the dead man's arm. With a slight twist, the left hand flopped open.

The ring finger was missing, cut off just below the second knuckle.

***

Pierce stared at the mutilated hand for several moments as names and memories from a case long filed away flooded back to him. Detective George Amherst, Dr. Karl Etherton, Basil Pershing, Josephine Banfield, and Shirley Jensen.

He had seen two other hands with their ring fingers missing—Josephine's and Shirley's. Both had been cut off by Dr. Etherton before he killed them. He ran out of time before he could do the same to Basil.

No one had heard from Etherton for twenty-three years. Could the doctor have returned? Or had he been killing all along and they only now found another victim? Was it possible Etherton had changed his modus operandi? Pierce considered the possibility of a copycat killer but rejected the idea. The department never released the details of the missing ring finger to the public. If anything, it was a horrible coincidence and Pierce was jumping to a conclusion.

"So, yeah," Salter said. "He probably didn't jump."

Pierce blinked and looked at the rookie.

Salter nodded absently as he stared at the body.

The detective no longer had the energy for the kid. He flicked his hand. "Wait at the car."

"Did I do some—?"

"Get the fuck out of here!" Pierce snapped.

Salter backpedaled several steps before turning. He walked away with his shoulders slumped and his hands tucked into his pockets.

Sergeant Boyd noticed the altercation between the detective and the rookie. He ambled over. "Things not going well?"

"They're going fine. I just need some space."

"Uh-huh."

Pierce crossed his arms. "I've seen what I need. Send the photographer down. Let's get some snaps, then the medical examiner can collect the body."

Boyd's eyes narrowed. "You sure everything's all right?"

"I'm fine."

The sergeant lifted his hands in mock surrender. "You don't need to tell me twice. I'll notify the photographer."

"Ask the uniforms to talk to the neighbors. See if they saw anything suspicious in the last day or two."

Boyd nodded. "We're already on it."

Pierce forced a smile. "Thank you."

"Just trying to make your life easier, Pierce." He pointed at the detective. "Don't forget the going away party. Let's have a beer and forget all this nonsense."

Forget? Pierce knew that wasn't going to happen.

Chapter 19

"We're not going to talk to the neighbors?" Salter asked.

"The uniforms will do that," Pierce said. "We've got other work to do."

"Like what?"

They were driving eastbound on Boone Street, headed back to the Public Safety Building. The structure was built in 1970, but it still felt new to Pierce. Now and then, he found himself driving on autopilot to the old police station. He'd almost done that now because his mind was on Detective Amherst. Salter's question jolted Pierce back to today, and he casually eyed the rookie.

"Who's the victim?" Pierce asked.

Salter turned his palms up. "I don't know." He noticed Pierce's repeated glances. "Right. We've got to identify the victim."

"There you go."

"How do we do that?"

"We'll check with the girls in Records about reports of missing white males in their twenties." Pierce lifted his hand from the steering wheel and waved it. "If we find a similar report, we check with the assigned dick to confirm or deny if our deceased is a ringer."

"If we can't find one?"

Pierce's hand landed back on the steering wheel with a thud. "Then our work is cut out for us. The medical examiner will fingerprint the body, and we search through possible matches."

Salter frowned. "How long does that take?"

"Forever. One fingerprint card at a time."

The in-car radio crackled with communications between uniformed officers investigating a collision. The officers assigned to the World's Fair were on a separate channel to keep the amount of their transmissions from clogging the airwaves.

"I don't understand what they're saying," Salter said.

"You will." Pierce turned down the radio's volume. "Someday."

He wasn't a Field Training Officer. Maybe on another day, he'd help the rookie learn the various codes and the clipped lingo officers used to make their jobs easier. That wasn't today, though. His mind was too busy with memories he barely thought of anymore.

"How many dead people have you seen?" Salter asked.

"Stow it, kid."

Pierce turned off Boone and accelerated toward the Public Safety Building. The quicker he could get away from the rookie and focus on finding a killer, the happier he'd be.

***

"Hiya, handsome," Hazel Thompson said. She leaned an elbow on the counter and flashed a smile at Pierce. Her eyes darted to Salter. "Who's the baby?"

She was in her late thirties with long brown hair. Hazel wore a blue mod dress with a white collar. A silver necklace dangled over her large breasts, and a gaudy bracelet circled her wrist. She was one of the records clerks and had been in the role for almost ten years now.

Pierce thumbed at the rookie. "This is Officer Salter."

Hazel's brow furrowed. "He have a first name?"

"No," Pierce said. "He doesn't."

Salter stepped forward with his hand extended. "Hi, I'm—"

Pierce intercepted the greeting and covered Salter's hand with his own. "This kitten has claws, Officer Salter."

Hazel feigned being hurt. "He's a little young for me, Detective." Her smile returned. "You, on the other hand."

"I'm married."

"That's what they all say." Her eyes twinkled with mischief.

Pierce pushed Salter away from the counter. "We need your help."

"More than you know."

"We're looking for Missing Persons reports."

Hazel stuck her tongue out. "Official business. Blech." She grabbed a mimeographed form and pen from a box. "All right. What are we looking for?"

"White male. Eighteen to twenty-two years old. Blue eyes. Brown hair. No distinguishing marks."

As Pierce spoke, Hazel wrote. When he finished, she looked up.

"That's it?" she said. "Not a lot to go on."

Pierce shrugged. "A body was fished out of the water a couple of hours ago. Didn't have any clothes on."

Hazel's lips pursed. "So no identification?" She nodded. "Gimme a minute and I'll check the recently reported missing. That'll at least cover the last forty-eight hours."

She turned and walked away.

Salter watched her appreciatively. "She's a nice-looking woman."

Pierce whispered. "If you stick around, there'll be plenty of opportunities for you to get in trouble. You better decide what kind of cop you want to be because you can't take back any wrong decisions."

The rookie's gaze bounced between Pierce and Hazel. "Listen, man—"

"Detective," Pierce corrected.

Salter raised an apologetic hand. "I'm not hung up on the whole sex thing. People can be with whoever they want. It's totally cool."

Pierce's jaw hardened and his eyes narrowed. "If you compromise your integrity with a woman, you'll compromise it with the job."

The rookie cocked his head. "That makes no sense."

"When you're around long enough it will. Trust me, I've seen it too many times." Pierce's gaze slid to Hazel as she dug through a box of papers. "Plenty of attractive women will turn your head. That uniform will turn theirs. If you don't know what's right, you'll always do wrong."

Hazel returned with two pieces of paper. "These are the only missing persons reports we got that fit what you're looking for." Her bracelet clacked on the counter when she set the papers down for Pierce to review. Salter stepped closer. "If you want me to go back further," Hazel said, "I can."

Pierce shook his head. "These are fine." He scanned the first report. "Good." When he looked at the next, he said, "This one won't work."

Salter leaned in. "Why not?"

Hazel looked closer, too.

"There." Pierce pointed at the Distinguishing Marks section. "This one had his appendix removed. Our victim didn't have a similar scar."

"How could you tell with all that bruising?" Salter asked.

Pierce pushed the unneeded report away and Hazel collected it.

"This is the one," Pierce said. He pulled out his notebook and jotted the relevant information into it.

Hudson Dorsey was twenty years old. He had blue eyes and brown hair. The man lived on the South Hill. The report was taken by a patrol officer and assigned to Detective Kevin Fay.

"How long have you been on the job?" Hazel asked Salter.

"Leave him be," Pierce said. He pushed the report back to the clerk.

"I'm not doing nothing," Hazel said. She mashed her lips together. "I already said he's too young."

"Hazel," Pierce said, "they're never too young for you."

Her face brightened. "You sweet talker. What have you heard?"

Pierce turned to Salter. "Let's go."

***

The Spokesman-Review was spread open on Detective Kevin Fay's desk. Two donuts sat nearby on a small paper plate. Fay held a cup of coffee in his left hand while running his right hand over the paper. His lips moved while he read.

Fay was a large man with soft jowls and pudgy hands. Round glasses perched on his nose. He'd been a detective for more than a decade and spent all that time in the General Detectives pool. The man aspired to no further greatness.

Pierce walked up to his desk. "Kevin."

Fay looked over the rim of his glasses. "Yeah?" His eyes cut to Salter and distrust flooded them.

"Where are you at with that missing person report on Hudson Dorsey?"

Fay slurped coffee before setting the cup on his desk. He leaned back and looked up at Pierce. "Why do you want to know?"

"Uniforms just fished a body out of the river. We're wondering if it might be him."

"You thinking I fucked up or something?" Fay's upper lip quivered. "That maybe I didn't do my job?"

"I'm trying to make a positive ID on the victim," Pierce said. "He was nude, and the ME hasn't pulled fingerprints yet."

Fay lifted his chin toward Salter. "Who's the kid?"

"I got a trainee."

"With some of that Expo money?" Fay's brow furrowed. "That's some bullshit. We could use some trainees over here, too. We're buried in cases."

Pierce eyed the donuts and newspaper but held his comment. Instead, he said, "Hudson Dorsey?"

Fay wiped his mouth with his hand. "Hold your horses." He reached over the newspaper and grabbed a manila folder. "I didn't get anywhere with it."

Pierce accepted the file and opened it. There were only three pieces inside it—an initial call sheet, a small page of Fay's barely legible notes, and a photograph of Hudson Dorsey.

The young man in the picture was handsome and smiling. He bore a resemblance to the dead man pulled from the river.

Pierce showed the photograph to Salter. "What do you think?"

Salter studied it. "Yeah. Maybe."

Fay craned his neck to see the photo. "That's Dorsey's senior picture. He's a couple years older now."

"His parents filed the report?" Pierce asked.

"The mother," Fay said. "Father ain't around."

Pierce tried to read Fay's notes, but he couldn't decipher the man's scrawl. "What'd she say?"

"It's right there." Fay tapped the folder.

"I can't read your writing," Pierce said.

He turned the folder so Salter could see. The rookie shook his head.

Fay clicked his tongue against the back of his teeth. "The kid didn't come home after a couple of days and his mother was worried."

Pierce curled his lip. "A twenty-year-old was living with his mother? What's his problem?"

"She didn't say."

"You haven't done any more follow-up?"

Fay turned his palms up. "I've been busy."

"I can see." Pierce glanced at the address, committing it to memory. Then he tossed the folder onto the newspaper but held on to the photo of Hudson Dorsey. "I'm keeping this."

"Do I have much choice?"

"Enjoy your donuts," Pierce said.

"I'm trying," Kevin Fay called after him, "but I keep getting interrupted by assholes!"

Chapter 20

They drove in silence.

Pierce welcomed it. Over the past three years, his car had been a near-silent cathedral, allowing him to process his thoughts without interruption. Only the light background chatter of the police radio and the passing sounds of traffic were audible. Often, when the rambunctious detectives' office became distracting, he went for a drive so he could think and avoid intrusions from idiots like that fat bastard, Kevin Fay.

He didn't have anything against heavyset people. Amherst had been a side of beef himself, with plenty of marbling. Fat didn't bother him. Lazy and incompetent did. They were fools of a different feather.

Images flashed in his mind as he drove north and then east. The horrific basement dungeon Dr. Karl Etherton had constructed. The slack bodies of Josephine Banfield and Shirley Jensen hanging from shackles on the wall. Their missing ring fingers. Basil Pershing, the terrified young man who survived, thanks to Amherst's willingness to do the right thing, even if it was technically the wrong way to go about it.

Etherton had to be how old now? Pierce tried to recall the man's age when he and Amherst interviewed him in fifty-one. Thirty? Thirty-five? Certainly no younger. Which put him in his mid-to-late fifties now. He might even be in his early sixties.

Pierce was no expert, but he'd read the initial report the FBI disseminated after forming its Behavioral Science Unit a couple of years ago. The report introduced the term serial killer, which Pierce thought sounded pretentious, but he supposed it was accurate. Mostly, the report made it sound like being a serial killer was a young man's game, with most of them in their early-to-mid thirties. Etherton fit that profile in 1951, but not any longer.

"Why am I here?" Salter interrupted.

"Be quiet," Pierce answered, still focused on Etherton.

People don't change, he thought. Not without concerted effort or a traumatic catalyst, at least. Kevin Fay had been a lazy patrol officer, for example. Now he was a lazy detective. On the other hand, Amherst had changed for the better. His old mentor became far more dedicated, perhaps even obsessed, after the Etherton case. Less concerned about haranguing a cobbler over free shoes and cadging free meals and more focused on investigating cases, especially Etherton's. Amherst hung onto that grudge long after retirement.

That was the exception, though, wasn't it? Most people's personalities never changed substantially over the years. So, if Etherton was a sadistic killer at thirty-five, why wouldn't he still be one at almost sixty?

Pierce could think of no reason why he wouldn't. That begged the next question. Where had he been for twenty-three years? Was he back and, if so, why?

"I'm serious," Salter interrupted again. "What am I doing here?"

Pierce scowled. "I told you to be quiet."

Salter looked around. "We're in a car, driving somewhere. I assume Hudson Dorsey's house. There's no crime scene for me to compromise. Seems like the perfect place to talk."

Pierce stared ahead. "Do you know why God gave you two ears and one mouth?"

"So I could listen twice as much as I speak," Salter said. "But there's nothing to hear, only silence."

"And you felt like you had to say something, is that it?"

"I had a question. Should I raise my hand next time?"

Pierce glanced sideways at him. The rookie was starting to sound a little crusty already. Salter didn't have the time in uniform to develop that attitude, but Pierce let it slide—for now. "Was that your question? Why you're here? Sounds like something for a philosophy classroom."

"I meant, why am I with you?"

I'm asking myself the same question, kid.

"All of my classmates were posted with experienced patrol officers, working around Expo," Salter pressed. "But I'm with you."

"Sad to be missing the festivities?" Pierce asked dryly.

Salter shook his head. "I can go down on my off time to see the good stuff, like the IMAX theater. And I'm glad I missed Tricky Dick's big speech on opening day."

"You've got a problem with the President?"

"Only that he's crooked."

"Nixon's a law-and-order man," Pierce said. "Tough on crime, especially drugs."

"A war on drugs?" Salter shook his head. "That'll never work, same as Prohibition failed."

"Heroin and booze are two different things."

"Chemically, maybe. The rest is a social construct."

Pierce turned on Wellesley Avenue and headed east. "Do you have any thoughts of your own or do you only parrot what your professors said?"

"I don't need a college professor to tell me the President is a liar."

Pierce slammed on the brakes and pulled to the side of the road. When he turned to Salter, the young officer's expression was shocked. "Here's a hard and fast rule while you're in my car," Pierce growled. "Don't badmouth this country. You didn't even serve. Instead, you hid behind a college exemption. You haven't earned the right to criticize."

Salter's face hardened. "I didn't dodge the draft. I played within the rules and went to college. It's not like I ran to Canada."

"The ones who ran to Canada are traitors. That's another matter entirely."

Salter drew in a breath, as if trying to calm himself. "I probably wouldn't have been drafted anyway."

"Why's that? You win the lottery with your birthdate?"

"No. I've got a kid."

Pierce's eyes narrowed. "You're married?" Edith hadn't mentioned that to him when she called.

Salter shook his head. "No."

"If you've got a kid, why the hell not?"

"Frida didn't want to. She says marriage is archaic. Just another form of property transfer that keeps the old world in place."

Pierce gaped at him. This Frida woman sounded like a hippie, dialed up to the extreme. He didn't want to entertain whatever crazy philosophy she might be operating under. "You allow that?"

Salter appeared confused. "Allow?"

"Oh, Jesus," muttered Pierce. "Never mind. Where's the kid in all this?"

"He lives with her and her parents on their farm, up in Springdale." He wiped his palms on the front of his uniform pants. "We were both only eighteen when she got pregnant. Since she wouldn't marry me, everyone thought it was best if they lived there and we..." He trailed off.

Pierce took a moment to unclench his jaw. He shook his head in disbelief at the revelation. Edith's omission made sense to him now. She was probably worried his debt to Claude might not be enough to overcome Pierce's disdain for Salter's irresponsible behavior.

"No sense of duty," he said, more to himself than to the rookie. "That's what's wrong with this country."

"I wasn't talking about the country," Salter said evenly. "I'm talking about the President."

"The President *is* the country." Pierce could barely believe he had to explain this. Then again, given what he'd just learned about Salter's attitude toward responsibility, perhaps it made sense.

"No." Salter shook his head. "That's where you're wrong."

Pierce leveled a finger at him. "You're a rookie. You don't know a goddamn thing. Not about life and not about this job."

"I know about—"

"You don't know shit. Your job is to learn, do what I say, and only speak when spoken to. That's three things. Is that too much for you to handle?"

"I can handle it fine," Salter said, "but you still haven't answered my question. Why am I here when all my classmates are in patrol?"

Pierce turned back to the road. He released the clutch and the Chevy lurched forward. "Because I thought maybe you were smarter than the others," he said. "Seems I was wrong."

***

Deborah Dorsey was a thin woman in her mid-forties with a slight hook to her nose. Pierce imagined she could have easily played a witch in a stage production of The Wizard of Oz. Her black hair sported a few strands of light gray, visible even though it was pulled into a tight bun. She wore a loose-fitting dark purple dress adorned with a red and black floral pattern.

Her severe appearance aside, Deborah was initially very warm when they arrived. Her brow furrowed, and her gaze bounced between the uniformed Salter and Pierce, who was in a suit. It was clear she was struggling with the dissonance.

Once Pierce identified himself as a detective, however, Deborah dissolved into tears. "Don't tell me," she wailed. "I don't want to know."

Salter stepped forward and put a consoling hand on her shoulder. Deborah immediately enveloped him in a hug and sobbed even louder. Salter froze when Deborah first wrapped her arms around him, but quickly recovered and returned the embrace, patting her gently on the back.

Pierce stood by and watched. Had she reacted to the uniform or the fact that Salter was younger and closer in age to her son? Pierce waited for her dramatic reaction to taper off.

Once Deborah seemingly cried herself out and pulled away from Salter, she bustled to a tissue box on the counter. She withdrew several and pressed them to the edges of her watery eyes. Then she faced them again.

"What happened to my boy?" she asked.

"We're not certain yet that anything has," Pierce said. "We're following up."

"You're a liar."

The virulence of her accusation surprised him. He'd seen this kind of whiplash behavior before, though not often. It seemed Deborah Dorsey was a bit crazy.

"When did you see Hudson last?" Pierce asked, ignoring her outburst.

Deborah glared at him for a few moments, then her expression softened. "He's been gone three nights now."

"Is that unusual?"

"Of course, it is. Why do you think I reported him missing right away? Hudson is home every night. He even goes to bed at the same time I do."

"What time is that?"

"Nine P.M. Why do you ask?"

"Routine questions, ma'am." Parents often mistakenly thought their teenagers were safely tucked in bed when they'd actually sneaked out and were up to no good, partying and indulging in the nightlife. Pierce had no doubt Hudson Dorsey was among their number. "Does your son have a family doctor?"

Deborah looked at him strangely. "Dr. Carlson. Why?"

"Again, routine questions."

"They don't seem routine."

"Trust me ma'am. They are." He waited a beat, then continued. "Now, did Hudson mention any problems recently? Arguments with friends? Anything like that?"

"No. He and his friends are a gay lot."

Pierce tilted his head at the word 'gay.' For much of his generation, the term was an innocuous synonym for happy or carefree. It'd taken on a different meaning over the past decade, coming to mean homosexual. Deborah was around Pierce's age, so she might still be out of touch enough—

"In both senses of the word, I suppose," Deborah added, resolving his unasked question.

"Meaning your son is…"

"Yes, Detective. He's homosexual, if you must know. He and his friends are a fun, happy group. Though I doubt that matters to you."

"I don't know if either fact matters," Pierce answered calmly. "But thank you for telling me."

"You'd have figured it out quickly enough, once you spoke to his friends."

"Who are his friends?"

"Kerry Chabot is his best friend. There are some others, but they sort of come and go. I never got to know them."

"Kerry is a boy?"

"Yes. Spelled K-E-R-R-Y."

"Do you have an address or a phone number for Kerry?"

Deborah nodded. She stepped through the open doorway to the kitchen and rummaged through a drawer. When she returned, she had a small address book. She recited a phone number and house address. Pierce wrote it down in his notebook.

"Where is Hudson's father?"

"Peter is a soldier. He's still in Vietnam."

Pierce hesitated. The very last American combat troops had left Vietnam a year ago. President Nixon had made a big deal about it, citing it as fulfilling his "peace with honor" pledge. If Peter Hudson remained there…

"He's M.I.A.," Deborah confirmed. Tears misted her eyes. "We're waiting to hear if he's an unlisted P.O.W. We're still hopeful he'll come home."

"I'm sorry," Pierce said automatically. He wouldn't have asked the question if he could have read Kevin Fay's notes. The detective might have told him the complete truth, instead of saying the father wasn't around. Instead, Fay fucked with Pierce, knowing he was about to lose his missing person case. Pierce wouldn't forget the slight.

"He's been missing since sixty-one," Deborah continued. "He was one of the first advisors, sent over by President Kennedy."

Pierce nodded slowly as Deborah dabbed at her eyes. Goddamn Fay. Pierce's interview made a right turn when it should have stayed on course.

"The worst part—" Deborah sniffled, then wiped her nose. "Peter was a good father. I think he might've loved Hudson more than me. Those two were thick as thieves whenever they were together. Then Peter got his orders. We celebrated Hudson's tenth birthday a couple of months early, just so Peter could give him a BB gun. Hudson loved that stupid thing. Played with it every day, pretending to be his father." Deborah looked down at her hands. "Ever since Peter shipped out, it's been me and Hudson. We moved back to Spokane to be closer to my family."

A memory tugged at Pierce. Standing with Amherst in the home of Dorothy Pershing, hearing about another fallen soldier and another fatherless son, Basil Pershing. Then the missing finger on Hudson's left hand flashed in his mind's eye.

Pierce pushed the thoughts away and focused on the moment. He wished he had a photograph of the victim by the river to show Deborah for confirmation, though he wasn't certain he'd have used it. Any mother would struggle with seeing such a sight. He imagined Deborah might melt into a puddle again.

He noticed family photos hanging on the wall, so he stepped closer to examine them. A dashing man in a uniform sporting a Green Beret stood ramrod straight in one of them. A younger version of Deborah and a child stood beside him.

"That's Peter," she said and forced a smile. "Such a handsome man."

Pierce glanced around until he found what looked like a recent photograph of Hudson. It showed a grinning young man seated cross-legged as he looked into the lens. The angle of the shot was such that Pierce was almost certain Hudson Dorsey was the same person as the naked victim they'd found that morning. It was better than the photograph from Kevin Fay's file.

Why hadn't the other detective taken that one?

"Thank you, Mrs. Dorsey," Pierce said. "We'll be in touch."

***

Compared to the modest house the Dorseys lived in, Kerry Chabot's brick home was positively wealthy. As he rapped on the front door, Pierce steeled himself for the attitude he almost always encountered from people who were well off.

The young man who answered had shoulder-length hair, held in place with a thin leather headband. Piece guessed him to be seventeen or eighteen years old. He wore a blue denim shirt and a vest of fringed leather. His blue jeans matched his shirt. A pair of thick sandals completed the look. It was one Pierce knew well.

Hippie.

"What's shaking, squares?" the kid asked, sizing Salter up as he stood in the open doorway.

"Are you Kerry?" Pierce asked.

The kid scoffed. "I'm Terry. Kerry's my brother."

"Is he home?"

"No." Terry crossed his arms. "What's this about?"

"How about your father or mother?" Pierce asked. "One of them home?"

"Why?" Terry demanded.

Pierce brushed aside his jacket to expose his badge. "Police business."

Terry's lip curled.

"Who is it, dear?" called a female voice from deeper in the house.

Terry tilted his head to shout over his shoulder, keeping his eyes on Pierce while he did so. "It's the pigs, Amelia. They want to hassle Kerry."

Pierce's jaw tightened. Of all the derogatory terms he'd endured over the years, that was the only one that worked him up.

An elegant woman in a flowing, cream-colored one-piece pantsuit strode into view. She appeared to be in her thirties. "Oh, come now, Terrence. Don't use such horrible words."

Terry sneered. "You saw what those pigs did to my friends at the Nixon protest a couple weeks ago."

The woman waved his words away. "They were being rude. The World's Fair is no place for politics." She regarded Pierce and Salter, giving Salter more than a casual once over. She seemed bothered by his uniform.

Her long blonde hair was styled in gentle curls, a scarf woven through the golden tresses. Her curves were unmistakable beneath the light material. She bore an open expression, but Pierce could see it was also calculating underneath. She reminded him of Tippi Hedren, from that film with the killer birds, only shrewder.

Holding out her hand, she said, "I'm Amelia Chabot."

Pierce took her hand awkwardly, since Amelia had proffered it almost as if she expected him to kiss it instead of shake it. She didn't seem put off by his reaction, however, and dropped her other hand over the top of their clasped hands. "What can we do for you, Officer?"

"We'd like to speak with Kerry," Pierce said.

"He's not here, but please, gentlemen, come in." She released his hand and stood aside, sweeping an arm.

Pierce stepped through the door, followed by Salter. Nearby, Terry glowered at them.

"Run along, dear," Amelia told him. "The adults need to speak."

"I *am* an adult," Terry said petulantly.

"Of course you are."

"I'm nineteen."

"Yes. Now, run along."

Terry crossed his arms. "Don't talk to me like you're my mother, Amelia. You're not."

Amelia didn't appear flustered by his behavior. "No, I'm only your stepmother. Should I ask your father to intervene?"

Terry glanced at Pierce and Salter before wheeling around and stomping off, muttering to himself.

"Forgive my stepson," said Amelia. "Do either of you have children?"

Pierce shook his head. In his peripheral vision, he saw Salter nod slightly.

Amelia didn't seem to notice, keying mostly on Pierce. "Well, if you ever do, you'll learn they go through more than one stage of life where they simultaneously believe themselves uniquely aware of every perfect truth in the universe and also convinced their parents are certifiable morons." She leaned forward conspiratorially. "That goes double if you're a stepparent."

Pierce gave her a tight smile to acknowledge the observation. He wasn't here for parenting lessons, but he wanted to keep her in a favorable mood toward the police.

"Let's speak on the veranda," said Amelia. "The sunlight is wonderful there this time of the morning."

She turned on her heel and led the way. Pierce followed with Salter in tow.

The veranda was wide, with a table in the center. Flowers and vines rimmed the edges. A man with a thin mustache sat at the table, drinking coffee and reading the financial page of *The Wall Street Journal*. He looked around sixty, but his hair was as jet black as a Sicilian. A second cup sat in front of an unoccupied chair. A half-empty French press was in the middle of the table.

Amelia stopped near the vacant chair, then paused and turned. "Would you gentlemen like some coffee?"

"No, thank you," answered Pierce.

"It's no trouble. I can pop into the kitchen for cups."

"That's all right."

"It's Peruvian," she said temptingly, her voice turning slightly sing-song.

"They said no, Amelia," the seated man said gruffly. "Let it be."

"Of course." She waved a hand toward him. "Officers, my husband, Frederic Chabot."

Chabot rose from his chair. Pierce offered his hand and got a businesslike shake from Chabot. Salter did likewise.

"What's this about Kerry?" Chabot asked as he sat down again, his gaze firmly affixed to Salter. Amelia settled into the other chair.

"We need to talk to him," Pierce said.

"What kind of trouble has he gotten himself into that requires a detective and a patrolman?"

"None," said Pierce. "He might be a witness who can help us."

"A witness to what?"

Pierce shrugged. "Actually, it's more for background information."

"Background, huh?" Chabot peered more closely at Pierce. "Do I know you?"

"I don't think so," Pierce lied.

He remembered Chabot. The banker had been one of the rich men he and Amherst interviewed while running down leads in the disappearance of Josephine Banfield. Back then, Amherst handled most of the interviews while Pierce took notes. Chabot had been compliant yet arrogant, as he recalled, with a much more age-appropriate wife.

Chabot continued to watch Pierce, clearly trying to place him. Finally, he seemed to give up, and said, "Kerry hasn't been living at home for some time. He knows I don't approve of his sinful behavior."

"Sinful? What do you mean by that?"

Chabot smirked. "If that's a real question, you're not much of a detective."

Pierce glanced toward Amelia, who smiled warmly at him, before asking Chabot, "You consider homosexuality to be a sin?"

"*I* don't," Chabot said. "God does."

"Where does Kerry live now?" Pierce asked.

"In a den of iniquity, full of counterculture freaks," Chabot said primly. He eyed Salter. "You understand."

"I meant," Pierce said, "do you have an address?"

"Terry drove me there once, when I tried to talk some sense into his fairy of a brother. Kerry didn't listen and I haven't bothered to go back since."

"Perhaps we could talk to Terry, then?" Pierce doubted the hippie would do much more than chant anti-police slogans at him, but he had to try.

"You're welcome to that one, too," Chabot said. "He's a skip and a jump away from the commune himself."

"I'll take you," Amelia said. She rose from her chair and took Pierce by the arm. Her hands were warm, even through his jacket sleeve. Pierce noticed her nipples protruding against the thin cream cloth of her jumpsuit.

Pierce muttered a thank you to Chabot, who gave a terse nod in reply and returned to reading his newspaper. Then Pierce followed the man's wife. Salter lagged behind.

Amelia led them back into the house and toward the front door. Once they were out of earshot, she said, "I won't subject you to any more of Terry's outbursts. Kerry's living in a group home on Sinto Avenue. It's a couple of blocks from Post Street."

"Which direction?"

Amelia pursed her lips. "Toward the Valley?"

"East, then. You don't know the address?"

"No, but you can't miss it. The entire front of the house has been repainted to resemble a giant flower."

At the door, she gave Pierce's arm a friendly squeeze and held him back as Salter stepped outside. She leaned close to his ear. "If you need any more information from me, Detective, Frederic works very late on Wednesdays."

***

The heat from Amelia's breath in Pierce's ear had mostly faded by the time they reached the house on Sinto. The flower mural covering the entire front of the dwelling was probably supposed to be a sunflower, but the artist's ability was suspect. The peeling paint on the rancher certainly didn't enhance the effect, either.

Pierce didn't have to announce their presence. Three people were sitting on the porch smoking. As he and Salter walked along the sidewalk, one of them noisily whispered, "The cops." The mouthy resident snatched the cigarette they were sharing and hurried inside. A moment later, Pierce caught the pungent odor of marijuana floating on the cool spring air.

"You own a suit?" Pierce said.

Salter eyed him. "Yeah."

"Wear it tomorrow. Your blues are as bad as a foghorn."

The rookie dragged his hand down the front of his new uniform. A look of sadness crossed his face.

Pierce's gaze swept across the front of the house again as he strode up the walkway. Dark curtains blocked the front windows. There was no screen door, though he spotted the hinges where one had been. A few feet to the side of the porch stood a pile of stacked rocks draped with black cloth and an unlit candle in front of it. He wondered briefly what sort of new age hippie ceremonies these people conducted here.

The couple that remained on the porch was a man and a woman, both in their early twenties. She had dirty blond hair that hung nearly to the small of her back, with thin, small braids sprinkled throughout. Her peach-colored tube top covered a mostly flat chest. She wore a pair of tie-dye cloth pants that looked like bell bottom pajamas. The man wore matching pants. Instead of a shirt, he wore only a vest fashioned from a dress shirt. His hair spilled past his shoulders and a red bandana adorned his forehead.

"Well, if it isn't the fuzz," said the woman, her high voice reminding Pierce of the actress, Goldie Hawn.

Pierce slid his jacket aside to show his badge and confirm her suspicion. "I'm Detective Pierce. This is Officer Salter."

"Good for you," muttered the woman.

Pierce focused on her partner. "What's your name?"

"Brandon Treviling, man. What's going on?"

"Is Kerry Chabot around?"

"No, man. He's out."

"Out where?"

"Just…" Brandon lifted his hand and fluttered his fingers. "…out."

"Because it's still a free country," added the woman. "You dig, pig?"

Pierce gave her a hard stare. "What's your name?"

She crossed her arms. "Don't you need to read me my rights if you're going to interrogate me?"

"Miranda doesn't work that way," Pierce said. "Now, what's your name?"

"Sunshine Afterglow."

"Your real name."

"That is my real name." She returned his stare. "I don't answer to anything else."

Pierce turned to Salter. "I smelled the distinct odor of marijuana when we approached. Did you?"

Salter looked momentarily flustered, then nodded and cleared his throat. "Yes. I did."

Pierce turned back to the couple. "I also saw your friend go back inside with what appeared to be a marijuana cigarette. Do you know what that adds up to?"

"A whole lot of bullshit," the woman said.

"Close," said Pierce. "It adds up to probable cause."

"Probable cause, my ass," the woman said. "He's a rookie and you're teaching him how to further corrupt the system."

Pierce raised an eyebrow. "Probable cause means I can go into that house and search for the marijuana cigarette and the person who had it. Anything else I find in the process is fair game. A lot of people can go to jail. We can make an entire day out of it."

Brandon didn't seem fazed by the threat, but he put a hand on the woman's knee. "Leave it alone, Patricia. Be like water."

Patricia frowned and crossed her arms but said nothing.

Pierce returned attention to Brandon. "Now that we understand each other, when do you expect Kerry back?"

"I wasn't snowing you, man. People here come and go as they please. Kerry might be back in five minutes or five hours. He might not ever come back." He shrugged. "We don't live in your rigid world."

"Does Kerry have a job?'

Brandon shook his head. "Not really. What's this about, anyway?"

Pierce considered whether to share his purpose. His gut told him Brandon was some sort of de facto leader in the communal home, so he made his choice based on that. "We're investigating a murder," he said. "Someone Kerry may have known."

"Who?"

"I can't say. Ongoing investigation."

"You're lying," Patricia interjected. "Kerry would never hurt anyone. He's a sweet kid."

Brandon nodded in agreement.

"He's not a suspect," Pierce said, though at this point he couldn't rule it out entirely. A good detective let the facts tell the story. Hudson Dorsey's missing ring finger told him Kerry Chabot was an unlikely suspect. "He might be able to help, though."

Brandon eyed him for a few seconds, then asked, "The person who was killed, was he like Kerry?"

"Meaning…?"

"Meaning did he love men? Was he gay?"

Pierce leaned forward slightly. "Why do you ask?"

Brandon spread his arms. "Because Isaac was, and he's dead, too."

"How'd Isaac die?"

Brandon looked surprised at the question. Next to him, Patricia curled her lip in disgust and shook her head.

He was murdered, Pierce realized.

"What's Isaac's last name?"

"Hermitage," Brandon said quietly. He motioned to the stacked rocks near the porch. "We made a shrine for him."

Pierce glanced over at it, then back to Brandon. "When did this happen?"

"Jesus," Patricia said, exasperated. "You're the heat. You should know."

Pierce ignored her, focusing on Brandon.

"A little over a week ago," he said.

"Do you know what happened?"

"No, but if I had to guess, I'd say it was a bad trick."

Pierce's eyes narrowed. "Isaac was a hustler?"

"He made money the only way he knew how," Brandon said.

"Why do you think it was a john who killed him?"

"Because that's all he did, man. He was either here, grooving with us, or he was out there, hustling. He told me he needed to make good while the opportunity was still there."

"Opportunity?" In Pierce's experience, there was always a market for young men or women.

"Expo, man. It might be about the environment or whatever, but with all those people who come to see the Fair, there's plenty who wanted what Isaac was offering. He was making a lot of bread before he died."

Pierce knew Brandon was telling the truth. Despite the clean-cut, wholesome face of the World's Fair, the event had an underside, not unlike when the carnival came to town. The influx of tens of thousands of people into the city meant tens of thousands of vices came right along with them. People who served those sins were just as likely to see a windfall as the hotels and restaurants downtown.

"Are you going to tell me who else got killed?" Brandon asked.

Pierce shook his head. He withdrew a plain business card and held it out. "Have Kerry call me when he gets home."

Chapter 21

"I'm hungry," Salter announced as Pierce drove toward the station.

Pierce cast a side-eye glance at him. "We're working a murder."

"It's after two. Lunch was at eleven during the academy. I guess I'm just used to it."

"We don't operate on academy time."

"Yeah, I get that." Salter sounded dejected.

Pierce drove in silence for several blocks, then said, "There's a candy bar in the glove box. We'll get something more substantial after we make a stop at the station."

Salter pressed the button and dropped open the glove box. When he pulled out a Marathon bar, he said, "Oh, man, I love these. They're my favorite."

Pierce sulked. They were his favorite, too. He didn't want to imagine he had anything in common with the rookie.

While Salter unwrapped the chocolate bar and chewed, Pierce found a parking spot near the Public Safety Building. The two of them made their way inside. Pierce headed straight to the secretary's desk just outside the detectives' bullpen. Sylvia Cornell was typing but paused long enough to toss a potato chip into her mouth.

Sylvia was roughly Pierce's age and had started in the secretary pool around the time he was promoted to detective. She was a quiet, dark-haired woman, who most of the older detectives considered frigid because she'd rebuffed their advances. Pierce got along with her, probably because he never propositioned her.

She stopped typing when he approached and leaned back. Her gaze flicked over Salter and back to Pierce, giving him an expectant look. "Let me guess—you brought me a nice BLT for lunch."

"Sorry, no. I need to know who has the Isaac Hermitage case."

Sylvia answered immediately. "Barenz and Fletcher. Is that all you need?"

Pierce nodded. "Thanks."

He turned to go. After a few steps, Sylvia called after him, "Bring me that BLT next time."

Pierce lifted a hand in acknowledgement and kept walking.

He found Barenz at his desk, but not Fletcher. Joe Barenz had a slight paunch on his otherwise athletic body. His dark brown hair was meticulously combed, and his thick, drooping mustache extended down the side of his mouth to his jawline. He wore a lime green suit with a white shirt and white shoes. Barenz must have recognized the purpose in Pierce's gait, because he asked, "What do you need, Pierce?"

"You caught a case a week and a half ago. Isaac Hermitage?"

Barenz nodded. "The hippie queer? Yeah, that's ours."

"Get anywhere on it?"

"What, are you the sergeant now?"

Pierce fought the urge to pop Barenz in the nose. Why did everything have to be difficult? A third of the detectives he knew just wanted to be left alone. Another third would leap at the chance to help out. The last third would leap just as far to mess with him. Today was full of ones from that final group.

"I might have a related case," Pierce said.

"Yours is a peter puffer, too?"

"Have you got anywhere on it?" Pierce tried again.

Barenz took a deep breath and let it whoosh out as he shrugged. "The kid was a hustler. How many different ways can that go bad?"

"A lot," Pierce said.

"Exactly."

"Have you narrowed it down more than that?"

Barenz narrowed his eyes. "I don't think I like your tone, Pierce."

"I don't have a tone. I have a question. Stop busting my chops and help me out."

Another voice broke in. "What's going on?"

Pierce turned to see Chuck Fletcher, a tall, thin man with short wavy hair standing nearby. He wore a blue and tan plaid suit over a yellow shirt. The pant bottoms flared toward the toes of his black loafers. Fletcher held a pair of paper coffee cups.

"Pierce here is asking about our fluff case."

"That one's going in the unsolved drawer." Fletcher curled his lip. "Trust me."

"Why?" Pierce demanded.

Fletcher's gaze drifted to Salter, who stood behind Pierce. "Who's your bodyguard?"

"Never mind," Pierce said. "Let's stick to this case of yours."

Fletcher ignored him. "What's your name, kid?"

"Gus," Salter said immediately.

"Gus what?"

"Salter."

"Gus Salter," Fletcher mused. He looked at Barenz. "Never heard of him."

"Me, neither," said Barenz.

"You a rookie, kid?" Fletcher asked Salter. "Or just on a field trip?"

"He's with me," Pierce growled.

"Whoa, take it easy, babysitter," Fletcher said, carrying the cups to Barenz and handing him one. "Why do you care about our case?"

"I caught a floater this morning that might be related." Pierce said, his voice still low with frustration. "I'm checking to see if you've made any progress."

Fletcher shook his head. "A whole lot of dead ends. Little fag lived in some hippie house on Sinto. He hustled the downtown bars. Our theory is he met someone dangerous, and it went bad for him."

"Any suspects?" Pierce asked.

"No."

"So, you're going to chalk this up to him being a casualty of the underground life? Is that it?"

Fletcher held up his hands again. "Hey, what can I say? You dance with bears, you get mauled."

Pierce stood still, seething in silence. Then he extended his hand, "Your case file. Let me see it."

"I thought we already established you weren't the sergeant," Barenz said, but Fletcher waved his hand at him.

"Give it to him," Fletcher said. "It's Pierce. He'll probably ask the sarge to give him the case. Better that it stays unsolved for him than us."

Reluctantly, Barenz opened a desk drawer and flipped through the folders inside. He drew one out and handed it to Pierce. "Here," he said, "but unless you get it transferred to you, I want that back today."

"So you can pretend to work it some more?" Pierce asked. "Or pad out your case drawer?"

"Fuck you, Pierce. You judgmental prick."

Pierce didn't respond. Instead, he turned and left the bullpen. He heard Salter following him, so he headed straight to the interview rooms and, stepped inside one. Impatiently, he waited for Salter to join him before closing the door.

"What are we doing in here?" Salter asked.

"I don't want to be near the Bobbsey Twins right now." More accurately, he didn't trust himself with either of them when his blood was up. "My desk is within earshot of theirs."

Salter reached up and rubbed the back of his neck. "Is that the way things are around here?"

"It's one way."

"I don't get it. Aren't we all on the same team?"

"Supposed to be."

"Those two were so… hateful. I mean, so what if Hudson or Isaac are gay?"

Pierce dropped the Isaac Hermitage file on the interview table. "If you ever spent any time in a foxhole, you might understand it better."

Hell, he thought, knowing both those detectives *did* serve was the only thing that kept Pierce from socking them in the jaw.

Salter shook his head slowly. "I don't think I could ever understand," he said quietly.

Given the rookie's family situation, Pierce didn't doubt it. He flipped open the case file and checked the date of the report. Nine days ago. He ran his finger down the page and stopped halfway. In the box for identifying marks, he found what he was looking for. The letter L was written and circled, signifying the left side, followed by the words third finger—missing.

He closed his eyes, his mind flashed back to Josephine Banfield and Shirley Jensen. Hudson Dorsey from this morning. Now, nine days ago, Isaac Hermitage.

Etherton was back.

Somehow, he was back.

"Are we taking their case?" Salter asked. "Like that other detective said?"

"Yes," Pierce said. "We're taking their case."

***

Hazel Thompson leaned forward on the counter. "Back so soon?" A broad smile spread across her lips. "I knew you couldn't get enough of me."

"I need the Etherton file," Pierce said.

Her eyes cut to Salter, then went back to the detective. Her brow furrowed and she straightened her arms. "I thought you said—"

"I know what I said," he interrupted. His tone was sharp.

Hazel stood fully upright now and grabbed the silver necklace dangling around her neck. "Everything all right, Walter?" Concern filled her eyes.

He waved off her question. "How long will it take?"

"It's in the archives." When Pierce scoffed, Hazel quickly added, "I'll have to send someone to get it."

Salter shifted nervously behind him.

Hazel tugged on her necklace. "I would never have sent it away, but you said."

Pierce shook his head. "Get it," he said with a softer tone. "Please."

"Yeah, sure," Hazel said.

He turned and headed for the west doors.

Salter muttered, "Thanks, Hazel." The rookie clomped after Pierce.

***

"I think Hazel likes you," Salter said.

"Keep it to yourself."

The rookie dropped his hand into the bowl of popcorn as he returned his attention to the menu. They were at Domini's, a sandwich shop in the newly constructed Washington Trust Bank building. The tower went up the previous year. Even at this odd hour, the small restaurant was crowded with out-of-towners. It was an unfortunate result of the World's Fair—every restaurant within walking distance of downtown remained busy throughout the day.

Pierce pushed the bowl of popcorn toward the rookie so he could open the Isaac Hermitage file. Once it was situated properly, Pierce began to read.

Hermitage's body was discovered near the train tracks off the East Sprague Corridor, an area known for prostitution and illegal drug transactions. The body was fully clothed.

An autopsy revealed Hermitage had been beaten in a similar manner as Hudson Dorsey. Hermitage had severe bruising about the upper torso and legs, but not a single mark on his face. Ligature marks around his wrists revealed he'd been bound before his death.

Someone—Pierce presumed Dr. Karl Etherton—tortured Hermitage for a significant amount of time before killing him. According to the autopsy, there was no evidence of strangulation. No bruising around the throat. No petechial hemorrhaging in the eyes. The medical examiner had drawn blood and sent it to the lab for testing, but results were not back yet.

Photos accompanied the file and Pierce began sifting through them.

Salter asked through a mouthful of popcorn, "What kind of sandwich are you getting?"

Pierce looked up from the homicide report, irritated at the interruption.

The rookie swallowed his popcorn. "Never mind."

A waitress approached and Pierce closed the file. She didn't need to be exposed to a stranger's death.

"Ready to order?" she asked.

Pierce didn't wait for the rookie to speak. He said, "Ham and cheddar on French. Cup of coffee."

When the waitress finished writing in her orderbook, she shifted her gaze to Salter.

The rookie's brow furrowed. "How big are the sandwiches?"

"Big." She held her hands several inches apart.

Salter glanced at the wall. Pierce followed his gaze to the clock. It was almost four o'clock now. The detective wondered if the rookie was worried about ruining his appetite for dinner.

"A Ham and Swiss," Salter said. "Does that come with lettuce and tomato?"

"No vegetables," the waitress said. "What kind of bread?"

Salter glanced at Pierce.

"Hurry up," the detective said. "She's busy."

The rookie glanced at the menu. "French, I guess."

She made a notation in her orderbook. "Anything to drink?"

"Coke." Salter shoved some popcorn in his mouth.

"We've got RC."

The rookie nodded. "That's fine," he said while chewing.

Pierce's jaw tightened. "He'll have coffee, or he'll have water."

The waitress raised an eyebrow and her pen hovered over the pad.

Salter flopped back into his seat. He watched Pierce for a moment before announcing, "Water."

The waitress walked away.

Pierce slid the file off the table and put it on the booth next to him. "Children drink soda."

"But I like it."

"I like candy and puppies," Pierce said. He leaned forward and lowered his voice. "If any of these maggots out here get a whiff of you being weak, they'll tear your heart out until you're lying in the dirt."

Salter's eyes widened.

"Act like a man. Everything you do while you're in that uniform, you do it like the whole world is watching. Because they are."

The rookie glanced around the restaurant.

"This isn't a game," Pierce said.

"I know."

"No, you don't. You've never been in a war. You've never had to fight for your life. Right now, everything you know about being a policeman comes from *Adam-12* and comic books."

Salter said, "I've read *The New Centurions*. I know the score."

Pierce shook his head. Joseph Wambaugh's book let everyone believe they had an inside track on what it was like to be a cop. That was like the morons who saw *Patton* and thought they understood what it was like to be overseas fighting Hitler. Nothing replaced having actual boots on the ground.

Several quiet moments passed between the two men. Finally, Pierce sighed. "I said it before, I'll say it again. You've got a lot to learn, Gus."

"Hey, man, I'm not a moron."

The waitress returned with two plastic trays—massive sandwiches were on each. She slid a tray in front of each man.

"Anything else?" she asked.

"I'm gonna need some foil and a bag," Pierce said. "I'm taking half of this home."

The waitress set the bill on the edge of the table. "I'll be back."

Salter's gaze drifted to the bill, then back up to Pierce.

"What?" Pierce asked.

"I heard stories, that's all. About free stuff, you know?"

"Whatever you heard, that shit doesn't fly with me."

"I'm glad," Salter said. "I wasn't sure what I'd do if…" He trailed off as he picked up the first half of the sandwich, his eyes widening. "These are huge."

"Good luck eating it all."

"Oh, I will." He lifted his chin toward the receipt. "I got this, by the way."

"No," Pierce said. "We go Dutch."

Salter bit into the sandwich.

"Nobody takes when you're with me," Pierce said. "Understand?"

The rookie nodded as he ate.

"We always pay our way. That way nobody owns us. Got it?"

Salter swallowed. "Yeah. I got it."

"Never let anybody own you. Whatever you do, make that your priority."

***

Someone hollered, "Show us your titties!" and the men in the bar cheered wildly.

Pierce didn't bother to look back for the voice or the woman, in all likelihood.

"Don't like girls?" the bartender asked.

He had shoulder-length hair and a faded *Bomb Hanoi* T-shirt. The burn scar down the side of his neck gave Pierce the impression he might have seen action in Vietnam.

"I like them fine," Pierce said, "but I already have one."

"Ain't no sin in looking."

Pierce wasn't sure about that.

The bartender slid a glass of whiskey on the counter and announced the total. Pierce laid a bill down and pulled the drink closer to him.

"Holler when you need the next," the bartender said. He moved away to help another patron.

Pierce turned on his stool and surveyed the scene.

The bar was packed for this time of night. It was a few minutes after nine, too early for most joints to be hopping like this, but the party seemed to have kicked off well before Pierce arrived.

The Back Forty was a cop-friendly bar on the west end of downtown. Its owner was supposedly friends with many of the younger officers in the department. It had quickly grown into the department's hangout du jour.

Pierce sipped his drink. He grimaced when the taste bit his tongue.

A rock and roll song Pierce thankfully hadn't heard before played loudly over the jukebox. On the dance floor, several younger men gyrated with women Pierce knew weren't their wives. The women bounced and jiggled as if no one was looking. The wriggling was inappropriate as far as Pierce was concerned but he'd seen it everywhere for years now—from television shows to movies. Even when he went to places like this. Women no longer respected themselves.

Pierce's generation would never go for the annoying rock and roll music, the wild dancing, or the outrageous displays, which is why Pierce thought it weird that Norman Woodward would have his retirement party here.

The man of the hour slow danced with his head pressed against the ample breasts of Hazel Thompson. She wore a billowy white shirt over blue slacks. Hazel held Woodward in the way a mother holds a sleeping son, but her eyes were on Pierce. Hazel winked, and Pierce lifted his drink in acknowledgment.

Sergeant Roland Fadelin sidled up to Pierce, a bottle of Olympia between two fingers. "Look who it is."

"Rollie." Outside the office, Pierce dropped the pretense of rank, especially since Fadelin was many years his junior.

Fadelin turned his attention to Woodward. "Ol' Woody thinks he might finally have a shot with Hazel the Horrible."

Pierce knew Fadelin was making a play on words by calling Hazel a whore—whorrible. It was a term Pierce had heard many in the department used about the records clerk.

"Men in glass houses shouldn't throw stones," Pierce said.

Fadelin abruptly turned. "The fuck is that supposed to mean?"

Pierce shrugged.

"You're a judgmental sort, Walter," Fadelin said. "You know that?"

"So I've heard."

The sergeant sipped his beer and his eyes narrowed. "Joe and Chuck came to me about some fireworks with you."

Pierce smirked. "Whatever they told you, they were happy to give up that file."

"Then why'd they have a case of the ass?" He waved his bottle around. "They said you bullied them into it."

"You know I didn't do that."

"Yeah, well." Fadelin kicked the bottle back for another drink. "You should have come to me about it."

"You know how things are. The cases are connected, and I needed—"

"I don't wanna know." Fadelin tapped Pierce's glass with his bottle. "Not until tomorrow anyway." The sergeant's face pinched. "What the fuck is with this music?" He wandered off, still complaining.

Norman Woodward stepped away from Hazel and noticed Pierce. He waved and stumbled over. "Heya, fella!"

"Woody."

Woodward flopped forward and put his elbows on the bar. "That Hazel. She's really something."

Hazel was now talking with another officer. Pierce had seen him at several crime scenes but couldn't recall the man's name. That was the curse of being on the department for so long.

"What're you drinking?" Woodward asked. His words sloshed together.

"Whiskey."

"Barkeep." Woodward slapped the counter. "Another round for me and my friend."

"I'm good," Pierce said.

"Pshaw." Woodward put his arm around Pierce's shoulder. He lowered his voice conspiratorially. "Tell me something— when are you calling it quits, buddy?"

"I don't know."

"You should grab Connie and move down to California with us."

"Why would I do that?"

"Because that's where we're all going. Gordon and Larry are already in Los Angeles. Hank is in the process of moving. As soon as I sell my house, the wife and I are gone."

Pierce looked into his glass.

"Why would you want to stay here?" Woodward asked. "There's never any sun."

"We've got sun now."

"For three months, then it turns shitty with snow."

Pierce smirked. "You want to hang out with movie stars and Mickey Mouse?"

"Donald Duck, too, if I'm lucky." Woodward laughed and shook Pierce's shoulder. "You and Connie should seriously join us."

"Maybe." Pierce feigned searching for someone. "Where's your wife, Woody?"

"At home. You think I'd bring her to one of these parties? I made it this long without her finding out about my girlfriends." Woodward slapped Pierce's back, then grabbed his whiskey from the bar. "Why ruin a good thing?"

Woodward stumbled into a throng of people and landed in the bosom of a tall brunette. She laughed as she grabbed his head and mashed him deeper into her chest.

Everyone but Pierce cheered.

Hazel made eye contact with him and lifted a hand, telling Pierce she'd be over in a minute.

He set his drink down and left.

***

Pierce tromped up the stairs to his Browne's Addition apartment building. He carried the Hermitage file in his left hand along with the remaining half sandwich from Domini's. His keys jangled as he unlocked the front door. Pierce stepped into the lobby and locked the door.

The nearest apartment opened, and Lois Macy stuck her head out from behind the door. The elderly woman wore thick glasses and a sleeping bonnet. "Mr. Pierce," she said, her tone reprimanding. "It's a little late."

He held up the folder. "My job, Mrs. Macy."

Her mouth puckered. "Have you been drinking?"

"A little."

"I don't allow alcoholics in my building, Mr. Pierce."

"It was just a nip, Mrs. Macy. Part of a retirement celebration."

She huffed. "You policemen should know better. That's why I allowed you to move in."

"Yes, ma'am."

"Don't make me regret my decision." Lois Macy pushed the door closed. The lock turned and a security chain slid into place.

Pierce climbed the stairs to his apartment. It smelled musty, like someone else lived there. He'd only been in the unit for three months. The furniture wasn't his; it belonged to Mrs. Macy. She'd rented the apartment to him furnished. The others in the converted mansion were younger working women. Pierce was the only man. Perhaps others on the department would look at Pierce's living arrangements as a blessing, but he considered them humiliating.

He was too old to be alone now.

Connie didn't feel that way, though. She was living in their house, finding her happiness and discovering her soul. Those were her words. He'd never say such trivial bullshit. Pierce wanted to believe her journey of nonsense started with that goddamned book, *Jonathan Livingston Seagull*. However, he knew it began long ago with all the time he dedicated to the job. He took her for granted. One day at a time—no, one late night at a time—her resentment built up until she couldn't stand him anymore.

Pierce opened the avocado green refrigerator door and grabbed a can of Olympia. He flopped the Hermitage file and his bagged sandwich on the table, then he popped open the can.

He and Connie were in a trial separation—again, her words, not his. Pierce thought a trial separation meant living apart and working to reconcile. But several different men had spent nights at their house over the past couple of months. Pierce wasn't naïve. He knew what Connie was doing with them in his bed. Pierce finally stopped watching the house after he asked Connie for a divorce. She seemed relieved by his request.

Pierce had never cheated on Connie. Never once did he step out on her, even during the trial separation. His integrity demanded he honor their marriage vows. He wouldn't compromise them just because she was treating them like trash.

He flipped open his notebook and considered his observations from the Hudson Dorsey scene earlier in the day. Pierce also reviewed the Isaac Hermitage case file. His gaze drifted back and forth between the notebook and the file.

Pierce was halfway through the beer when he grabbed the telephone from the nearby counter and pulled it to him. The chord snagged on the nearby chair, and he jerked it free. He dialed a number from memory.

It rang several times and a woman answered. "Amherst residence."

"Hi, Gloria. It's Walter. Is he still up?"

"You bet," she said. "Hold on." She hollered away from the phone, "George, phone for you."

A second line picked up. "Hello?" Amherst's voice was weak.

"It's me," Pierce said.

Gloria hung up the other line.

"It's a little late for a social call," Amherst rasped.

"This isn't a social call. Can I come by tomorrow morning?"

"What've you got?"

"He's back," Pierce said.

The line went silent for several seconds. "You sure?"

"Unfortunately."

Amherst sighed. "I'll be here."

"Want me to bring anything?"

"I got everything I need. See you later."

Pierce hung up and leaned back. He sipped his beer and let his thoughts drift to a killer he thought long gone.

Chapter 22

When Pierce arrived at the department the next morning, Officer Salter stood waiting next to Pierce's desk. The rookie wore a charcoal gray suit, white shirt, and black tie. The right pocket hung heavy. His badge was pinned cockeyed to his belt. Salter's hands were in his pants pockets as he casually looked about. He didn't hear Pierce approach.

"Get your hands out of your pockets," Pierce said.

Salter jumped and yanked his hands free. "Good morning."

"Where's your gun?"

The rookie pulled it from his jacket pocket. "I asked the front desk officer for a shoulder holster."

The front desk officer also acted as the supply officer.

"What'd he say?" Pierce asked.

"He said I was out of uniform and that rookies in the academy didn't need a shoulder holster." Salter dropped the gun back into his jacket pocket.

A thick envelope sat on Pierce's desk. Scrawled on it was the note—We put a rush on these.

Pierce grabbed the packet and opened it. Inside were photographs of Hudson Dorsey's crime scene. Pierce shoved the pictures back into the envelope and handed it to Salter. "Hold this."

As he turned to leave, Detectives Joe Barenz and Chuck Fletcher entered the bullpen. Barenz wore a blue suit jacket over white plaid slacks. His wide paisley tie hid most of his white shirt. Fletcher sported a brown polyester suit with white piping around the pockets. His white loafers looked recently shined.

"Look who it is," Barenz said. "Detective Pierce, friend to the homos."

Fletcher chuckled. "Defender of perverts."

"Give it a rest," Pierce said. He jerked his head toward the exit. "Let's go," he said to Salter.

"Check out the rookie," Barenz said. "Pretending he's a detective now."

Salter's expression hardened, but he remained silent.

"Hey, Pierce," Fletcher said. "Vice called. They thought you might like to know there's a bunch of pretty boys working Sprague right now. Maybe you can save them."

Barenz waved. "Maybe your rookie should go undercover since he likes playing dress up so much."

Pierce and Salter left the two detectives to cackle between themselves. They walked over to the Records department. Hazel Thompson noticed Pierce as he approached the counter. She wore a long-sleeved green shirt and a matching skirt.

"What happened to you last night?" she asked.

"Had to get home."

"Likely story." She frowned. "You didn't want to talk with me?"

Pierce motioned toward Salter. "We're here to pick up the Etherton file."

Hazel followed his gesture. "Nice threads," she observed, then waved the rookie away. "Will you give us a minute?"

Salter shuffled back several steps.

"Why are you making this so hard?" Hazel asked.

"I don't know what you're talking about," Pierce said.

"It's 1974, Walter. We women didn't fight for our liberation not to take advantage of it."

"I'm married."

Hazel rolled her eyes. "Divorce filings are public record, Walter. They print them in the newspaper."

He grimaced.

"It's time for you to face the music," Hazel said. "Let me help you through."

His face warmed. Pierce didn't like people knowing his business. "You got that file?"

She reached under the counter and pulled it out. Hazel's eyes darkened. "Good luck, Detective." She tossed the file onto the counter and walked away.

Pierce turned to see Salter watching him. "What?"

"Nothing," the rookie said.

"Good. Keep it that way."

***

"Who lives here?" Salter asked as he seemingly considered the house with the unkept lawn.

Pierce slipped the Chevy into Park. "A friend."

Salter glanced at him. "Aren't we gonna work the murders?"

"What do you think we're doing?" Pierce climbed out of the car and slammed the door.

The rookie hurried up the pathway behind him.

"Is it okay if I go in with you?"

Pierce handed the Etherton file to Salter. "Acquaint yourself with that while I'm talking."

They climbed the steps. The door opened before Pierce could knock.

Gloria Amherst stood there in blue polyester slacks and a floral blouse. She reached out and hugged Pierce. When they broke their embrace, her gaze flicked to the rookie. "Who's this?"

"Gus."

She cocked an eyebrow. "He's a little young for detective, isn't he?"

"He's in the training car."

"What is he? A prodigy or something?"

Pierce smiled kindly. "He's a rookie."

Gloria rolled her eyes. "What's the world coming to when they've got homicide detectives training rookies?" She thumbed over her shoulder. "George is waiting for you. He could hardly contain himself all morning."

Pierce stepped inside. The house smelled different than in years past. It reeked of illness, like death lurked somewhere nearby waiting for an opportunity to sneak in and deal its awful business.

Amherst lived in the guest room now. He'd spent the last two years mostly confined to a hospital bed. He could hobble to the bathroom and back with the help of crutches. If he needed to go anywhere, Gloria pushed him around in a wheelchair.

A television played a morning talk show as Pierce and Salter entered.

Amherst lay covered by a light brown blanket. A tube ran from an oxygen tank up to his nose and draped over the back of his head. The tank hissed. It looked like an uncomfortable position to lie in.

Even though Pierce saw him once a month, he never got used to the weight loss his former partner suffered. Amherst maybe weighed a hundred forty pounds now.

Amherst waggled a hand. "Turn that shit off."

Pierce spun the knob on the television and the volume dropped.

"Who's with you?" Amherst asked. His voice was strained.

"That's Gus," Pierce said.

Salter smiled awkwardly from the corner, the way a prized cow might at the county fair if it could do such a thing.

"Looks like a baby," Amherst said.

"Blame the Expo."

Amherst eyed Salter. "He come from another agency?"

"No. He's still in the academy."

"You're shitting me." Amherst attempted to whistle but it came out as a half-hearted wheeze. "What kind of circus are they running down there?"

"No circus," Pierce said. "I asked for a partner as good as you and they sent me him."

Amherst smirked. "Smart ass."

Pierce allowed himself a smile. "It's good to see you, George."

Amherst struggled to shift himself into a better position.

"Need help?" Pierce asked.

"Mind your business," Amherst grumbled. His face purpled as he strained to push himself upright further.

Amherst had a stroke last year, his second. The former detective had two heart attacks prior to the strokes. Amherst couldn't pronounce his medical affliction, so Pierce never fully learned its nature. All Pierce knew was his former partner's circulatory system was revolting against him. As such, the doctors amputated Amherst's left leg above the knee.

Salter opened the Etherton file and studied it.

"What'd you bring me?" Amherst asked.

"Isaac Hermitage," Pierce said. He opened the Hermitage file and set it on Amherst's lap. He flipped to the crime scene photographs. "Found last week near the train tracks. Missing ring finger, left hand."

Amherst's gaze snapped up to Pierce.

Pierce opened the envelope he'd found on his desk that morning. He fanned out the photographs. "This is Hudson Dorsey," he said. "He was fished out of the river yesterday."

Amherst's attention dropped to the pictures.

"He, too, was missing his left ring finger."

"Son of a bitch," Amherst muttered. His face hardened and Pierce recognized the calculation in his eyes as he examined the photos. "Different M.O.s," he noted critically.

"Maybe Etherton didn't get a chance to dump the bodies back then. Maybe we were on him too fast."

"There's something else." Pierce looked in Amherst's dim eyes. "Both Hermitage and Dorsey are gay."

Amherst pressed his lips together, staring down at the file. "That's different."

Pierce didn't answer, letting his old partner work through his thoughts.

"Then again," Amherst said, after a moment, "there was the Pershing kid in fifty-one. Etherton swung both ways even back then."

"He did."

A silence overwhelmed the room as Amherst slowly flipped through the photographs. Eventually, he looked up. "Do me a favor and light one up."

Pierce reached into his pocket and pulled out his pack of cigarettes.

Amherst leaned slightly. "You smoke, kid?"

Salter looked up from the case file. "No, sir."

"Too bad. I'm not allowed to partake anymore, so I appreciate it when anyone does it for me."

Pierce flicked his lighter and inhaled. He exhaled over Amherst's bed.

Amherst closed his eyes and breathed deeply. "Gloria quit smoking around me." He opened his eyes. "She's worried about me croaking. Can't bear the thought of being alone." He smiled wanly. "Truth be told, that woman is better than I ever deserved."

Pierce wasn't going to argue against that statement.

For several minutes, Pierce smoked, and Amherst reviewed the Hermitage file. He asked a couple questions about the Dorsey crime scene.

"Not sure what you think I can do," Amherst said, when he'd finished. He slid the Dorsey photographs back into the envelope.

"I want your take on it."

"I think you got it right. He's changed his game with the dump jobs, but it's him. He's back." Amherst handed Pierce the envelope. "Hard to believe, isn't it?"

Pierce nodded.

"Brings up a lot of questions," Amherst said.

"It does. Any thoughts as to the answers?"

"Not just yet." He paused, then asked, "You and Connie still Splitsville?"

Pierce glanced at Salter. The rookie didn't look up from the file he now pretended to read.

"I'm gonna take that as a yes," Amherst said.

"I asked for the divorce."

"Too bad. She was a good woman."

Pierce tucked the envelope into his jacket pocket. "Still is."

"As for this mope." Amherst closed the Hermitage file and held it up. "You'll find him. You have to." His gaze was one of intense pleading. "It's not like I can."

Pierce nodded wordlessly.

Amherst grunted in response, but Pierce heard the message in that sound. A promise made and one accepted. Then Amherst leaned and caught the eye of Salter. "Listen to what he says, kid. Pierce here is the kind of cop I wish I would've been."

Pierce accepted the file. "You did all right, George."

"I made some amends." Amherst rested his head against the hospital bed. "Too little, too late."

***

Vivian Kessel neé Heimbigner's hand shook as she lit the thin cigarette. Pierce's lip curled. Not at Vivian's smoking but at her goddamn cigarette. Connie had switched to Virginia Slims about the time she started reading those self-help books. When Pierce first saw a Virginia Slims advertisement, he thought it quaint. Telling women, "You've come a long way, baby," seemed a harmless bit of encouragement. Now, he believed the tagline was an insidious bit of feminism snuck into every pack of cigarettes sold.

She inhaled deeply, then exhaled a plume of smoke toward the ceiling. "How many times do I have to tell you this, Detective? I haven't heard from Dr. Etherton since he took off all those years ago."

Pierce and Salter had gone directly to see Dr. Etherton's former receptionist at her home after leaving Amherst's. She lived on Rockwood Boulevard, a twisting arterial through a tony neighborhood. Vivian was forty-five now but had maintained herself in the manner wealthy socialites were apt to do.

A year or so earlier, *The Spokane Chronicle* did a fluff piece on her husband, a real estate heir. Pierce almost skipped the article but noticed Vivian standing with two teenage boys. Within the first few paragraphs, the reporter prattled on in fawning prose about their landscapers, maids, and private tutors for Vivian's Harvard-bound sons. Pierce never bothered to finish the piece.

They were in her immaculately decorated living room. Expensive artwork hung on the walls. Bronze statues of Greek gods stood in the corners. The sofa and chairs seemed as if they'd never been sat upon.

"We believe he might be back," Pierce said.

Vivian snatched the thin cigarette from her lips. "What gave you that impression?"

"A couple of recent murders bear a striking resemblance to the ones committed in fifty-one."

She touched her sternum. "Am I in danger?" Her eyes darted to Salter. "Is that why you brought the extra detective?"

"He's only observing," Pierce said. "Don't worry about him."

"How can I not worry?" Vivian paced about the room. "You tell me he might be back. Do you think he blames me for anything?"

Pierce shook his head.

"I didn't do anything wrong." She stopped and pointed at Pierce. "You would have made me give you all those files anyway, right?"

"That's right. We would have gotten a search warrant."

She jammed the cigarette between her lips and inhaled. "Goddamn him." Vivian exhaled toward the ceiling. "This can't be happening."

Salter held the Etherton file and continued to read it, much the way he'd done while at Amherst's house.

"I know I've asked these questions before," Pierce said, "but if any detail has come back to you, please let me know."

"Nothing," Vivian said. "There's been nothing. Believe me, if there was, I'd tell you in a heartbeat. I don't want Dr. Etherton back in my life. In fact, I wish I'd never heard of him."

Pierce studied Vivian for a moment as she fiddled with that stupid cigarette. He wanted to tell her she'd come a long way since her receptionist days, but he figured she'd miss his sarcasm.

Besides, the bitterness he felt wasn't meant for her anyway—it was for his soon to be ex-wife.

***

Pierce dropped into the driver's seat and started the car.

Salter climbed into the passenger seat. "Where next?"

The Chevy lurched away from the curb. "We'll work the Hermitage leads," Pierce said.

"What about Dr. Etherton's family?" Salter asked.

"They're all gone," Pierce said. "He divorced his wife a couple of years before the murders in fifty-one. She took their baby son and moved back to Boise. His parents are dead, and anyone else with a shred of relation to the man moved after the killings."

They headed down Monroe Street.

Salter opened the Etherton case file. "What do you think about talking with Jack Pershing?"

Pierce cast a sideways glance. "He goes by Basil, his middle name. Why would we do that?"

"Never mind."

The detective held up his hand. "No. Tell me what you're thinking."

"Well, he's the one who got away, right? Maybe this Etherton guy feels like he missed out and will want another crack at him."

"Sounds like a *Dragnet* episode."

"Yeah." Salter closed the file. "You're probably right. But it would explain why he is focusing solely on gay men."

Pierce thought it over. He knew Pershing had enlisted in the service shortly after the events in fifty-one. Amherst had gone to see him before the young man left for basic training. At that point, the detective was still working the Etherton case whenever he could, a dutiful tradition Pierce had continued after his partner's retirement. Amherst's interview with Pershing didn't net any new information. Afterward, he told Pierce he regretted putting the man through the pain of reliving the most terrible events of his life. As a result, Pierce had left Pershing alone after that, despite pulling out the case file and walking through it regularly.

Still, it had been more than twenty years since Amherst's interview. Those wounds should have scarred over by now, he figured.

Besides, Etherton was back. At the very least, if Pershing was still around, he deserved to be warned.

"It might be worth a conversation," Pierce allowed. "Those Hollywood types have to get their ideas from somewhere."

Salter looked mildly pleased with himself.

"Though I don't know if Pershing is still in Spokane or not. Many of the people from the fifty-one case have passed on or moved away."

"We could check the phone book," Salter suggested.

Pierce pulled over to the curb.

"What are we doing?" Salter asked.

"Call box." Pierce pointed at the small enclosure attached to the telephone pole. "I need to check in."

He pulled his keys from the ignition and got out. Pierce hurried to the box, slid the key into the lock, and opened it. He ignored the half-empty whiskey pint bottle tucked in the corner and dialed the number for the detectives' division. Sylvia Cornell answered. "Spokane Police Detectives. How may I help you?"

"Sylvia, it's Pierce. I need an address if you can find it."

"Fire away."

"Basil Pershing." He spelled both names for clarity.

There was a pause while Sylvia searched. Then she said, "I've got one up on the South Hill."

"Great. Give me the address." Pierce scrawled it in his notebook. "You got any messages for me?"

"Only one. A Kerry Chabot called. He said he's home if you're still looking for him."

"When did it come in?"

"A couple of hours ago."

"If he calls back in, let him know we're on the way."

Pierce hung up. "Change of plans," he said after climbing back into the car. "We're following up on Hudson Dorsey."

Chapter 23

Kerry Chabot was actually wearing makeup.

Pierce had to look closely to be certain. Sure enough, it was there. A little rouge, along with some eyeliner and mascara. No lipstick but a light lip gloss with sparkles in it.

The image itself wasn't shocking. Pierce had seen drag queens before. He knew actors wore makeup, even the tough guys. However, the queens slathered it on, adding a wig and a dress. As for the actors, the makeup was only visible in person, not on TV or film, which was the point of the stuff in the first place.

Kerry Chabot used the stuff in the same way a woman might and Pierce found the effect somewhat disconcerting.

The young man sat on the porch of the flower house next to Brandon Treviling, who had flashed a peace sign at Pierce and Salter as they approached. There was no way Pierce was returning the gesture, but he acknowledged it with a dip of his chin. He half-expected Salter to respond with the peace sign. The rookie surprised him by restraining his college urges.

"Is it Huddie?" Kerry asked before Pierce could start his own line of questioning.

"Why do you think it's him?" Pierce countered automatically. Deep inside, he knew Karl Etherton was responsible for both deaths. Even so, Pierce was driven by decades of doing his job the right way, of confirming facts he already knew to be true because the opportunity to confirm those facts existed. That included eliminating Kerry Chabot as a suspect.

Kerry drew in a wavering breath. The thin young man wore jean shorts and an oversized dress shirt that was unbuttoned halfway, exposing his hairless chest. The sleeves were rolled up to the elbow, and the tails were tied in a knot that dangled at his thighs. He held a cigarette in his trembling fingers.

"I haven't seen him. I called Huddie's house. His mother told me he was missing, and a couple detectives had come around. Now you're here."

Tears formed in Kerry's eyes. When they spilled out, his mascara ran, forming thin black streaks on his face. "You think he's okay?"

Pierce ignored the question and asked, "When did you see him last?"

Kerry considered, dragging shakily on the cigarette. "Two nights ago." Some smoke escaped his mouth before he turned his head and exhaled. He glanced at Salter and added, "I think."

A small thrill went through Pierce. This was likely the night Dorsey was murdered.

"What time?"

"Up until nine-thirty or so. We got high…" he trailed off, looking nervous.

Pierce waved a hand. "We don't care about that."

Kerry hesitated.

"Ask your friend," Pierce said. "They were smoking it yesterday when we showed up."

Kerry glanced at Brandon, who gave him a reassuring nod.

"It's cool," Brandon said quietly. "If they're not reading you your rights, you're safe. Tell 'em the rest."

Kerry turned back to Pierce. His eyes darted between Salter and him. "We got high here at the house, then cleaned up to go out. We went downtown together but split up pretty quickly."

"Why?"

Kerry hesitated again. Now, his eyes shifted to Brandon before returning to Pierce. "We met people," he said evasively.

"You were hustling?"

"Listen." He swallowed with some difficulty. "If I'm going to be—"

"We're not vice," Pierce interrupted. "We're homicide." He felt stupid including Salter in that designation, but it was better than trying to explain the situation.

The rookie proudly put his hands on his hips, and his heavy jacket pocket flopped about.

Pierce continued. "We don't care about marijuana or prostitution. We're trying to find the man who murdered your friend. You get me?"

"Oh, Christ," Kerry said. "He's really dead?" He glanced at Brandon. "Oh my God."

Brandon screwed on a sympathetic expression. "Bummer, man. I'm sorry. Huddie was a decent cat."

Kerry dropped his head and wept.

Pierce and Salter exchanged glances.

The crying went on for a minute before Pierce cleared his throat. "Kerry," he said.

"Yeah," Kerry muttered with a nod. "Yeah." He looked up with wetness shimmering on his cheeks, along with a smudge of mascara. "What was the question?"

"Why'd you and Hudson split up after you got downtown?"

"We were hustling," Kerry softly admitted.

"How long has Hudson been doing that?"

"Only a few weeks."

"How'd he start?"

"I saw how much money Isaac was raking in, so I gave it a go. Huddie saw me making money, so he decided to do the same." Realization seemed to strike Kerry. His face pinched into a pained grimace and new tears streamed down his cheeks. "Oh my God. This is my fault. This happened to him because of me."

Kerry hung his head and sobbed again.

"No," Pierce said firmly. "Someone else did this, and you're going to help me find him."

The sobbing continued.

Pierce set his jaw. He counted to five slowly, giving Kerry a chance to compose himself. When the young man's crying jag showed no signs of abating, he reached out and smacked his shoulder. Kerry yelped in surprise and jerked backward. He looked up at Pierce, shocked. Even Salter seemed astonished at what Pierce had done.

"You hit me," Kerry said.

"I need you to focus."

"You can't hit me."

Pierce leaned forward. "What you're going through is hard, but Hudson is dead. He was murdered. Finding his killer is more important than your grief."

Pierce knew the interview could go either way at this point. Kerry might pull his act together and be a good witness or this interview would go off the rails. He could dissolve into a tear-squeezing lump or become indignant and refuse to help, either of which was bad. If that happened, Pierce would have to return later and try to overcome the negative vestiges of this first contact.

Luckily, Brandon intervened. He dropped a hand onto Kerry's shoulder and spoke earnestly. "Remember, man. You've got to be like water."

The physical contact and the philosophical gibberish worked. Kerry gathered himself. He bobbed his head and took a deep breath, letting it out slowly. "Okay," he whispered. "Yes."

"When was the last moment you saw Hudson that night?" Pierce asked.

"I had just come back from a quick date," Kerry said. "He was leaning against the wall."

"What wall?"

"In the alley behind the bar."

"Which bar?"

"Rags to Riches."

Pierce knew the place. It was on Main, not far from the bar where Norman Woodward had celebrated his retirement. Patrol cops and vice detectives scornfully called it "Fags and Bitches" due to it being a well-known bar catering to gays and lesbians. He'd never had a reason to go into the place, but he knew it was frequented by drag queens and hustlers alike.

"The alley behind is where you meet your tricks?" Pierce asked, though he knew the answer.

Kerry nodded. "It's dark back there, so the shy ones and those who are closeted don't have to worry about being seen."

"Closeted?" Pierce had never heard that term, but from the context, he could guess what it meant. "You mean secret gays?"

Salter eyed him with surprise as if he should have known the term. Pierce scowled and the rookie looked away.

Despite everything, Kerry smiled sadly. "The way you put it makes it all sound so adventurous, doesn't it? Like a secret agent or something. But yes, it means men who are living a lie. They come to that alley for the truth."

Pierce shifted uncomfortably. He masked his discomfort by shaking out a cigarette. As he lit up and inhaled, he considered what Kerry said. A possible scenario in his mind filled out significantly. Etherton was a predator who hunted his victims. In fifty-one, his method was to lure his prey to him. Now, it appeared he went to them.

Evolution, he thought.

"So," Pierce said, motioning for Kerry to continue, "you get back and Hudson's standing against the wall in the alley. And?"

"We chatted for a few minutes, sharing a cigarette. Then a man came along, and Huddie left with him."

"Can you describe the man?"

"It was dark. What I could see was very average."

"How tall was he?"

"About your height. Maybe a little more."

"Thin?"

"No, but he wasn't fat either. Like I said, it was dark. He looked like an average guy. But older."

"How old?"

Kerry shrugged. "I mean, after thirty, it's all old to me, man."

"Was he old enough to be your grandfather?" Pierce asked.

"If everyone involved got busy young, sure."

Pierce wanted to pepper Kerry for more descriptors but decided to circle back to that later. Instead, he said, "I take it Hudson didn't return from that trick."

"No."

"Did that make you worry?"

"Not really. I got one myself shortly thereafter. Huddie was still gone when I got back, but I figured he had landed another trick or was on a long date." He glanced up at Pierce and shrugged. "Sometimes they want you longer than a French."

Pierce kept his expression flat. Salter, on the other hand, seemed surprised that Kerry had openly admitted to oral sex with another man.

"Had you ever seen the man Hudson left with before that night?"

"I *think* so."

Pierce's brow furrowed. "What do you mean, you *think so*?"

"We've only been doing this for a short time," Kerry said, "but we've both already managed to acquire some regulars. Repeat customers, you know?"

"I understand the term. Was this man a regular?"

"I *think* it might have been Dr. Strangelove."

Pierce squinted. "Like the movie?"

A smile creased Salter's face as recognition set in. He had obviously seen the film.

Kerry wiped the tears from his eyes. "Huddie called him that because he liked to play games. Act things out."

"What kinds of things?" Pierce asked.

"Different scenarios. Sometimes it was a sweetheart date. Sometimes he liked to tie Huddie to the bed and pretend to hurt him."

Pierce maintained his composure, but electricity zinged through his body. "That's why the nickname?" he asked. "Because he had strange requests?"

Kerry nodded. "That, and because he's an actual doctor."

***

After the interview, Pierce drove without direction, deep in thought. In the passenger seat, Salter was blessedly silent, leaving Pierce to think things through.

Kerry Chabot's description of Dr. Strangelove was generic, but it fit within the parameters of Etherton's basic body style and potential age. The younger man would likely never be able to identify a photograph or pick Etherton out of a lineup, but at least he'd provided something.

It seemed clear to Pierce that Etherton was back. He'd changed his M.O. since fifty-one, but Pierce saw those changes as more of an evolution than a deviation. The world today was different than the one that existed twenty-three years ago. Etherton had adapted.

Pierce would need to go see The Vice King, that was certain. Get a handle on the hustler scene. That was the best route to finding Etherton. Hunt where the hunter hunts.

Pierce crossed the Spokane River on the Division Street Bridge and turned onto the recently renamed Spokane Falls Boulevard. Prior to the arrival of the World's Fair, the street had been known as Trent Avenue. The powers that be deemed the old name too plain for the Expo tourists.

As they cruised past the State Pavilion, Pierce slowed for traffic. The park was full of people, moving from one attraction to the other. A massive white pavilion that covered several exhibits came into view. Elsewhere, large metal sculptures meant to be butterflies stood sixty feet high. The massive creations were scattered throughout the park, their colorful cloth wings shifting in the breeze. Nearby, the clock tower stood guard over it all.

"Crazy how many people are here," Salter said quietly, looking out the passenger window. "The park sure is beautiful, though."

"Used to be the train station," Pierce said.

"Yeah, I know. They only tore it down like two years ago."

Pierce stopped for the traffic light and looked at the surging crowd crossing the street to enter the park. He glanced to his left at the Coeur d'Alene building. "There used to be a reefer den in the basement of that building," he said nostalgically. "Before that, it was a speakeasy."

"Okay," Salter said. "That I didn't know." He glanced at Expo again. "Lots of changes."

Pierce stared at the entrance that led down to the illicit location. "I liked it better before," he muttered.

"What's that?"

He roused himself and noticed the light had turned green. "Nothing."

"What's next?" Salter asked.

"We go to Vice," Pierce said. "Get some background on any degenerate doctors we can find."

"What about Pershing?"

"Him and any other witnesses from fifty-one can wait," said Pierce.

***

Sergeant Mike Singleton was one of the most senior men on the police department. Pierce knew this because Singleton came on the job a few years ahead of him. Most others knew it because the man never failed to remind people of the fact.

Landing in Vice as a brand-new detective, Singleton had somehow managed to remain in that assignment throughout his entire investigative career. When he was promoted to sergeant, his first assignment was to command the Vice squad. Most new sergeants went to graveyard patrol, but not Singleton.

Pierce was never sure if Singleton had dirt on a few decision-makers or if he remained in Vice for the simple reason that no one else wanted the job. In any event, his decades-long presence there had earned him the moniker of The Vice King.

"Walt!" Singleton brayed in his raspy voice as soon as Pierce entered the Vice office, which was set off from the rest of the detectives. "What're you doing here? You get lost?"

Pierce didn't answer until he reached the sergeant's desk. Several other desks were scattered across the room, but all of them were empty. "Is today a holiday I didn't know about?" Pierce asked, motioning toward the desks.

"All my boys are out working," said Singleton. "Expo has us hopping. Perverts galore." He sounded downright giddy about the development. "Who's your junior?"

Pierce motioned toward the rookie. "Gus Salter."

Salter smiled and Pierce cringed. The guy looked like he was ready to sing for the glee club.

Singleton laughed. "Oh Christ, Walt. Lemme have this one. You know how much damage I could do with a babyface killer like him?"

Salter's eyes widened. "I'm still in the academy."

Singleton waved dismissively. "Screw that. We'll get you an exception, kid. I know people."

Pierce grabbed Salter by the collar of his suit jacket and pulled him back. "I came here for a favor."

"Hey," Singleton said, "did you hear who finally pulled the plug?"

"Woodward." Pierce nodded. "I went to his party."

Singleton shook his head. "No, not him. Cirelli. Guy had almost forty years on the job."

Pierce hadn't heard. He wondered why such a celebrated career didn't get a loud send-off. Then he realized the answer—Officer Anthony Cirelli was a quiet, religious man who probably asked for no hoopla. That's how Pierce would want his career to end.

"You know what that means?" Singleton asked. Before Pierce could answer, the sergeant jerked both thumbs toward his chest. "Badge number one, right here."

Pierce tried to appear interested. The practice of exchanging tins so each officer's badge number represented his seniority had been abandoned in the late sixties, but the lexicon hung on when it came to pronouncing seniority. "They'll have to start calling you the Badge King," Pierce said, "but right now, I have a question for The Vice King."

"What do you need?"

"Tell me about the hustler trade behind Rags to Riches."

Singleton frowned. "What's to tell? It's the same as always." His gazed flicked to Salter. "Is he even old enough to hear this stuff?" Singleton busted up at his own joke.

Pierce heard something rattling deep down in the man's chest while he laughed. It didn't sound good, but it was none of his business. "Just run it for me real quick. Make sure I don't have the wrong idea."

"All right," Singleton said.

He acted as if he were doing Pierce a big favor, but the detective knew Singleton loved to hold court and display his acumen. He took pride in his deep knowledge of the twisted and dark deeds Spokane residents did when they thought no one was looking.

"It's your basic freakshow," Singleton explained. "Fags, lesbians, drag queens, you name it, it's their place. All out in the open, because, hey, that's all okay now."

Pierce's brow furrowed as he listened. A lot had changed since he came on the job. Women's liberation had cost him a wife. The civil rights movement didn't cause much of a dent in Spokane due to the small black population. Homosexuals were becoming more prominent now, but Pierce didn't fault them except for their behavior. He didn't like normal men and women flaunting their sexuality in public either. Pierce missed the days of decorum.

Singleton continued. "The hustlers work the alley behind the place. Queer Alley, they call it."

"They?"

"We." Singleton shrugged. "Don't be such a Nancy." He lifted his chin toward Salter. "You sure I can't use him for a bust or two? I'll send him back without a scratch."

"No," Pierce said, and the rookie looked relieved. "What about activity? Is it around the clock?"

"No, just during the hours of iniquity. Maybe ten until two or three in the morning. Depends on traffic, though."

"Is there a lot?"

"Before Expo? Not a ton. A steady trickle for a couple three hustlers to make some scratch. Over the last few months, though, it's picked up. More demand resulted in more supply, like with the hooker trade. It's been hopping. Can't wait for this fucking fair to be over. My guys were going to do a sweep a couple of weeks ago, but we got caught up in something else, so it got delayed."

"Something else?"

Singleton shook his head. "You don't want to know."

Pierce knew immediately that meant kids. Singleton was right—he didn't want to hear about it. "Any hard cases?" he asked.

"Beatings, you mean?" Singleton shook his head. "No, no one has decided to tune up fags for a while now." He smiled. "It's funny, actually. On the one hand, Expo brought out all this extra vice, right? More hookers, these hustlers, all that. People doing the dirty. On the other hand, it put all the locals on their best behavior."

"Outside of this..." Pierce searched for the right word. "...this Expo surge, there's a lifestyle, isn't there? A subculture or whatever?"

"Sure, but good luck differentiating that from the tourist trade."

"Do you keep tabs on the people who frequent the hustlers?"

"Keep tabs?" Singleton shook his head. "This isn't the fifties, Walt. We don't label folks as known homosexuals anymore. If we catch them in the act, we pop them for public indecency. If we can prove prostitution, they get a patronizing beef. Outside of that, it's a new world. Age of Aquarius and all that. Live and let suck."

"Can we get a look at your arrest records?" Pierce asked.

"Sure," Singleton said. "Why not?"

***

The pair spent the next hour sifting through files. Pierce instructed Salter on what to look for—white males older than fifty associated in any way with male hustlers.

"Not just arrests," he told the rookie. "Mentions of any kind. If you find a doctor, put a star by that name."

The work went slowly. A couple of Singleton's detectives ambled in at one point. The two looked like shifty operators—long hair, beards, and shirts hanging outside of their dirty jeans. Even their leather shoes were scuffed. The Vice detectives gave Pierce and Salter an odd look but didn't ask any questions. After checking in with Singleton, the pair left again.

"How far back are you going to go?" Singleton called out to Pierce and Salter after another forty minutes had passed. "Prohibition?"

Pierce decided that was their cue to leave. They'd worked back to the week before Christmas, so that gave them six months' worth of activity. The list Pierce had compiled had more than a dozen names on it, along with home and work addresses.

"Thanks for the assist, Mike," Pierce said, as he and Salter headed to the door.

"Happy hunting," Singleton rasped after them.

***

George Amherst despised the rich. The man had not been shy about telling Pierce this sentiment or expressing it to the wealthy themselves. His vitriol hadn't transferred entirely to Pierce, but he understood Amherst's frustration. His entire professional life, Pierce encountered men and women who seemed to think they were a cut above everyone else because of their money. Most of those same men and women also believed a different set of rules applied to them.

He supposed, in some ways, they were right.

But Pierce didn't have to like it.

Their first stop was Doctor Scott Lynch, an optometrist. Lynch's immediate reaction was to threaten to throw them out of his office and sue them for slander. Then Pierce reminded Lynch of his arrest in February.

"I was *not* arrested," Lynch snapped. "The officers were quite clear on the matter."

Pierce looked over Salter's shoulder at the list. Lynch's name had a star and a minus sign next to it. The star was for doctor and the minus meant there was no arrest, only a contact and a report. He also noticed the listed physicals Salter had jotted down put Lynch at five-ten, though the man was clearly several inches shorter. Pierce wasn't sure if the rookie made a mistake or had merely copied an error by the contacting officer.

He turned back to the sneering doctor. "You're right. All we have is a police report about what happened the night you *weren't* arrested." He paused, then added, "In great detail."

After that, Lynch was cooperative. Not that it mattered much. His broad face and ruddy features made it clear to Pierce that Lynch wasn't Etherton. Age might change someone's features but not to such a degree as to make them unrecognizable.

Even so, Pierce followed protocol. He asked Lynch the necessary questions. Salter recorded the doctor's answers, as he'd been instructed to do during the drive over. Then they moved on.

Dr. Ralph Townsend was a cold fish. The preternaturally thin man with sunken cheeks had a greasy feel to him. Pierce imagined it was entirely possible he'd have occasion to cross paths with Townsend again. The doctor was dismissive about having been detained in March while picking up a hustler and wasn't moved by Pierce's not-so-subtle references to this becoming public knowledge if he didn't cooperate.

"I like young men," Townsend said snippily. "I don't care if you approve."

"It's not about approval," Pierce said. "We're working on a case involving one of those young men being hurt."

"I am a doctor." Townsend drew himself up and looked down his nose at Pierce. "I do not hurt people. I heal them."

Pierce labored through the rest of his obligatory questions, but knew it was only for form's sake. Townsend's physical appearance didn't fit Etherton or what Kerry Chabot had described any more than Lynch had. Besides, if the young hustler had seen Dorsey leave with Townsend, he would have described getting frostbite in the process.

Dr. Michael Andrews wasn't at his office, so they contacted him at his home on South Post Street, just above Cannon Hill Park. He appeared warmer than the other doctors, but all his contrived charm rang false to Pierce. Where Townsend was cold, Andrews had an underlying current of explosiveness. Pierce had the sense the man could snap and start yelling at any moment, despite his outwardly suave façade.

Andrews didn't invite them inside. He wore expensive slacks and a dress shirt. From deeper in the house, bass-heavy music played, further grating on Pierce's nerves.

"I'm sure there's been a mistake," Andrews said smoothly, after Pierce had explained their purpose.

"Detectives detained you in the alley behind Rags to Riches," Pierce said. "The only mistakes in the report were spelling errors."

Andrews cocked his head. "You're a gruff one, aren't you?"

The doctor's tone struck Pierce as not quite effeminate, at least when compared to someone like Kerry Chabot. Andrews was arrogant but in a velvety, condescending way.

Behind Andrews, a chorus of singers chanted about a love train.

Effete. That was the word. Underneath that, the volatility Pierce had sensed. He decided to push a little and see if some of it came out.

"Doctor, I'm trying to keep these inquiries private—"

Andrews broke into a broad smile that didn't touch his eyes. "Now we move to poorly veiled threats? So quickly from the carrot to the billy club." He shook his head and tutted. "Detective, I don't know anything about what you're investigating. I am a physician of internal medicine with a respected practice. I'm on the board of the children's hospital. I—"

"Do you have a girlfriend?" Pierce interrupted.

Andrews's smile didn't falter. "I have several. One is the daughter of a city councilman. She would be appalled to hear about this line of questioning, as would her father."

"Now who's making threats?" Pierce countered.

Andrews shrugged. "What's good for the goose is good for the gander." He drew in a deep breath and let it out. "Look, Detective, I have no quarrel with the work you're doing. I admire it, in fact. It is essential to the public good. But I can't help you. The only reason we are speaking at all is because a few months ago, I made the ill-fated decision to take a shortcut though an alley on my way to my car from the Davenport. A brutish detective accosted me and created a story out of whole cloth. The only truth to his tale was that I was passing through that particular alley. Much to my relief, I wasn't arrested for this fiction, and I thought that would be the end of it."

He eyed Pierce with a condescending glare.

"Apparently," Andrews finished, "I was incorrect in that assumption."

Pierce knew he wasn't going to get any further with Andrews. He was like most of the doctors and other big shots he'd dealt with throughout his career. Self-righteous with nothing except their own status to be self-righteous about.

He uttered the rote thanks he reserved for these moments and left Andrews standing in his doorway, watching them go with a haughty expression.

"I don't like that guy," Salter said as they returned to the car.

"You're not supposed to like any of them."

"Good, because I don't." Salter paused, then asked. "Shouldn't we be reading them their rights, though? Because of Miranda?"

"No."

"But the Supreme Court said—"

"Where'd you hear about Miranda?" Pierce interrupted. The ruling in US v. Miranda wasn't even a decade old, but the recitation of a suspect's rights had entered the popular zeitgeist like a virus. "At the Academy?"

Salter shifted in his seat. "Not yet, but one of my professors—"

Pierce held up a hand. "Do me a favor, F. Lee Bailey. Don't worry about procedures. Especially the ones you don't understand."

Salter's confused look shifted into a pout. "I thought—"

"You thought wrong. Were any of those men in custody? No, they weren't. Which means Miranda doesn't apply."

"Seems like it should," Salter said carefully.

Pierce kept his eyes on the road, trying to remain patient. Like it or not, he'd become this kid's mentor. He might as well do a thorough job of it. "A suspect has to be in custody and we have to be asking guilt-seeking questions before we're required to read them their constitutional rights," he explained.

"Standing on someone's doorstep asking general questions doesn't meet either criteria."

"Oh." Salter sounded dejected.

"This isn't T.V.," Pierce said, "or a college classroom."

The next three names on their list were solidly middle class. No doctors in that group. Two of the three worked in offices downtown, but Pierce imagined they were more like cogs in a corporate machine than executives.

Butch Kelso, the first, lived alone and was unapologetic. His angular features and blond hair immediately put him in the unlikely column in Pierce's mind.

"Don't you gentlemen have something better to do than hassle me?" Kelso complained. "All I did—"

Pierce interrupted him by simply raising his hand. "Just a few questions, sir, and we'll be on our way."

Brian Armstrong was immediately nervous when they contacted him at his office. He cast several glances over Pierce's shoulder toward his boss's office across the room. Having his nightlife become public at work seemed to be the extent of his worry, though. None of his reactions to Pierce's queries gave the detective any concerns.

Gerald Parr was at home, sick. He answered their questions in a raspy, congested voice while his wife looked on suspiciously.

He was not Etherton, either.

"These last three are all too young," Salter said in the car, "and none of them are doctors."

"Estimating age can be tricky," Pierce told him. "And we don't know for certain that whoever Etherton is pretending to be now is a doctor."

"But Kerry Chabot said—"

"Remember what I said about people lying to you?"

Salter paused. "I don't think Kerry was lying."

"No," Pierce admitted, "but witnesses aren't always reliable. Memory is impressionable. Besides, even if Kerry remembered right and is telling the truth, there's still the probability this Dr. Strangelove lied to Dorsey about being a doctor."

"Etherton was a doctor, though."

"He was."

"Doesn't it make sense he'd pose as—"

"How difficult do you think it is to create a new identity?" Pierce interrupted.

Salter considered the question. "Hard?" he guessed.

Pierce shook his head. "It's easy, though maybe slightly less so now than back in fifty-one. All you need is a birth certificate that matches your gender and approximate age. Use that to get all the other pieces of identification and you're set."

"I thought it would be tougher than that."

"What *would* be harder," Pierce continued, "is getting doctor's credentials in that fake name. Unless Etherton was willing to go through the entire process of becoming a doctor again, he'd have to risk passing off fake documents. Diplomas, medical certificates, the whole lot. All it'd take is one phone call to verify the medical certificates and everything would fall through."

The pair drove in silence for a block, then Salter asked, "Would anyone actually make that call?"

"Wouldn't you?"

"I don't know," Salter said, his tone quizzical. "I mean, people automatically trust doctors. It wouldn't be like he was pretending to be a doctor—he is one. Only his identity is false. He can demonstrate his knowledge and skills, right?" Salter shrugged. "People are trusting. They might never check."

Pierce didn't answer right away. The rookie had a good point. Maybe Etherton's paperwork wouldn't hold up to the kind of scrutiny Pierce might give it, but Salter's scenario was possible. Hell, it might even be *probable*.

"He'd set up a private practice," Pierce said, thinking out loud. That's what Etherton had done in 1951.

"Or work at one of those outreach clinics," Salter added. "They're always desperate for doctors. How close are they going to look?"

Pierce nodded slowly. Then another thought occurred to him. Working at an outreach clinic that served the poor and unfortunate might also serve up potential victims for Etherton. A variation on his old tactic of letting the prey come to him.

"Not bad, Gus," Pierce said grudgingly.

Next to him, Salter grinned.

"Problem is, we've got no more doctors on the list."

Salter's face fell. He looked over the list to be sure, then swore lightly. "I thought I was onto something."

"You might be," Pierce said. "There's one other doctor we can go see."

"There is?"

***

Dr. Aaron Carlson had a quiet family practice near the Shadle Park Mall. Pierce parked the car on the side of the building.

Salter looked up from his notepad. "He's not on the list."

"He's Hudson Dorsey's family doctor."

"Oh, right. His mom told us that."

The waiting room was empty. A woman in her early fifties in a conservative dress was closing the receptionist station. She glanced up at them as they entered.

"I'm sorry," she said immediately. "Dr. Carlson isn't seeing any more patients today."

Pierce flashed his badge. "We just need a minute."

"Oh, my," said the receptionist. "Is there a problem?"

"No. Can you get the doctor, though?"

"Certainly, I'll—"

"What is it, Officers?" The deep resonant voice came from the first open door in the short hallway nearby.

Pierce glanced up at the doctor. He was a handsome man, much like Etherton had been. However, his good looks had a rugged feel to them, more James Coburn than Etherton's Cary Grant.

Another dead end, Pierce thought. He forged ahead anyway.

"Do you mind if we ask you a few questions, Doctor?"

***

After they left Carlson's office, Pierce glanced at his watch. Then he said, "It's almost five. I'll drop you at the station."

"You get to take the car home?" Salter sounded impressed.

Pierce shook his head. "I have some more work to do."

"On this case?"

"No," Pierce said dryly. "I'm doing some sideline work on the D.B. Cooper hijacking." When Salter gaped at him, he added, "Don't be an idiot. Of course, it's this case."

"Well, if you're working, I'm working."

"There's no overtime approved." Pierce knew he could probably get Sergeant Fadelin to okay the expense, but there was no guarantee.

"That's the job sometimes, isn't it?" Salter asked.

Pierce glanced over at him. "Yeah," he said. "That's the job sometimes."

***

They drove past Queer Alley, but it was empty.

"We'll come back later," Pierce said.

In the meantime, they stopped off for dinner at Reed's Diner. Pierce ordered a steak with fries and coffee. Salter asked for a patty melt.

"And coffee," the rookie added, glancing sidelong at Pierce.

Pierce noticed but pretended he hadn't. Instead, he looked around the refurbished restaurant. "This used to be The Family Table," he said.

"Really?" Salter feigned interest in the history of the place.

"Amherst loved the place."

"I read in the file how you two worked the fifty-one case together," Salter said, all of the artifice falling away from his voice now. "There are some pieces missing in that file that I was wondering about."

"Like what?"

"When did you know it was him?" He glanced around and lowered his voice. "Etherton, I mean. That he was the killer."

Pierce leaned back, considering the question. "I think we both knew something was off about him on our first visit. As far as knowing he'd been the one to take those girls and Pershing prisoner?" He shrugged. "I wasn't sure until we were parked outside of his clinic in downtown Cheney, waiting to execute a search warrant. We learned through dispatch that his receptionist—"

"Vivian Kessel, right? We met her."

Pierce nodded. "Heimbigner back then, but yes. Etherton told her the night before not to come in to work. That was when I knew."

"How?"

"It just clicked. We'd been pressuring him. Why else would he instruct her to stay home that morning?"

"Could be lots of reasons," Salter said.

The waitress arrived with the food and slid the plates in front of them. Pierce thanked her and reached for a knife and fork. He could hear the steak still sizzling and the meaty aroma brought his hunger raging up. He cut off a chunk and put it in his mouth, chewing.

Salter lifted his patty melt and took a bite, mirroring him.

"You're right," Pierce said, swallowing and cutting another piece. "There could be any number of reasons, but you asked me when I knew. Not when I had irrefutable proof."

Salter dabbed at his lips with a napkin, holding one half of the sandwich in his other hand. "Is that when your partner knew, too? At the clinic?"

Pierce shook his head. "No. I think George knew much sooner than that."

***

After they ate, both men piled a few bills on top of the check the waitress brought. Pierce weighed them down with a few extra quarters. When Salter reached into his pocket to do the same, Pierce stopped him.

"It's enough," he said. "Tip well but don't be extravagant."

"Why not?"

"People will think you're on the take."

Salter looked alarmed.

They drove past Rags to Riches to find the alley still empty. It seemed that Singleton's intel about hustler hours of operation was accurate.

Pierce drifted northeast, finally pulling into a parking lot of a sprawling building on Lyons Avenue.

"Pleasant Autumns," Salter read from the sign. He glanced down at his list from the vice files. "What are we doing here?"

"Seeing someone I used to know," said Pierce, and got out of the car.

Salter scrambled to catch up to him. "So, this is like when we saw Amherst? This guy is going to help us?"

"No." Pierce reached for the door. "He's not going to help us."

***

"How are you tonight, Geno?" Pierce said, settling into the chair next to the bed. Salter hung back in the doorway to the room, which smelled strongly of Pine Sol and an undercurrent of urine.

Geno DiCarlo stared at Pierce, his expression confused. The man hadn't shrunk since his days on the job so much as he'd shriveled in on himself. He had wrinkles everywhere and he'd lost just enough weight for his skin to sag from his body like a battered thrift store jacket too large for his frame.

DiCarlo's mouth slowly opened, and his eyes betrayed a vacancy behind them.

Pierce held out his hand. "Walter Pierce. We used to work together."

"Walter Pierce." DiCarlo said slowly. They shook hands, but the old man's grip was weak. "I remember you." DiCarlo sounded almost triumphant, as if he'd passed an important test. "We used to work together."

It wasn't always this way. There were days when DiCarlo was lucid. Days he really did remember Pierce. On those days, they talked about the job. Mostly, though, they talked about the people they'd known. The ones who made them laugh. The ones who pissed them off. The ones they never quite figured out.

Pierce had learned a few things during those moments of clarity. Small secrets. Gossip, mostly. They were facts that had escaped his attention or knowledge all those years ago and reminded him of something important—his own fallibility.

"I remember you," DiCarlo repeated, and Pierce knew even Salter could hear the desperate lie in the old man's voice.

"We used to work together," Pierce repeated.

Days like this one were hard, but Pierce came anyway. He came out of loyalty. He came because he knew hardly anyone else did. And he came because of those few days when the old Geno DiCarlo shone through. Those days taught Pierce a valuable lesson.

All days like today did were to remind him how brutal the last few miles of road were on the journey of life.

Fuck *Jonathan Livingston Seagull*, he thought.

Chapter 24

"He used to be a cop, huh?" Salter asked.

Pierce had been quiet after they left Pleasant Autumns. So had Salter, though perhaps for different reasons.

"He was our sergeant," Pierce said. "Same job Fadelin has now."

"He was your friend?"

"That's going a bit far."

"You visit him, though. This wasn't the first time."

"No, it wasn't."

"If he's not your friend…?" Salter trailed off.

"You know how I told you not to ever let anyone own you?"

Salter nodded.

"That's important, but it doesn't mean you won't incur some debts along the way. A man pays his debts."

"You owe Mr. DiCarlo?"

"Not him exactly. He's just the one I can pay back."

Salter thought for a second, then he said, "Not pay it back. Pay it forward."

Pierce tilted his head. "I suppose so. Where'd you hear that?"

"It's an old idea. I read it in a science fiction book from the fifties. Heinlein, I think. I grew up on that stuff. Heinlein, Asimov, Bradbury."

"Pay it forward," mused Pierce. "That's what we do." He glanced at Salter. "Especially for the dead. They may be lying silent in their graves but that doesn't mean they don't want justice."

"Josephine Banfield," Salter said softly. "Shirley Jensen. Isaac Hermitage. Hudson Dorsey." He shook his head. "Their killer should be brought to justice, but the dead don't want anything. They're just dead."

"You really believe that?"

"Yes."

"Then why seek justice at all?"

"For the living," Salter said.

Pierce frowned. The rookie was wrong and right, all at the same time. He didn't feel like explaining that to Salter, so instead, he said, "Well, if it's the living you want to focus on, let's do that."

"Where are we going?"

"To follow up on your idea."

***

Jack Basil Pershing lived in the Manito neighborhood. His house might have been considered a mansion once upon a time. However, many of the houses being built further south dwarfed these 1920s models. Pierce thought the new ones lacked elegance.

"The guy must be rich," Salter commented as they cruised up the short drive to the front door.

Pierce remembered how smart Pershing was, getting into college at sixteen. "He had a head start."

The front door had a massive knocker on it and a push button doorbell to the side. Pierce chose the bell. He expected a housekeeper to answer, but when the door opened, he found himself face to face with Basil Pershing.

The last time Pierce had seen Pershing, the man had been a skinny seventeen-year-old with thick, sandy brown hair. At forty, the man's hair was lightly peppered with gray. Pershing remained just on the slender side of a medium build, but Pierce could see the wiry muscles in his arms and chest. He moved with a confidence not unlike what he'd shown in fifty-one, although back then, it seemed to Pierce it was mostly an act, like a boy trying on his father's clothes. It appeared far more natural now.

Surprise registered on Pershing's face. "Detective," he managed. He glanced at Salter. "Detectives," he clarified.

"Mr. Pershing," Pierce replied. "Do you have a few minutes?"

Pershing recovered and opened the door further. "Of course. Come in."

They entered.

"We can talk in the den," Pershing said as he closed the door and led them down the hall.

The den was more of a library. Bookshelves lined most of three walls from floor to ceiling. A large mahogany desk sat at one end. A wet bar was perched to the side. Four overstuffed chairs were situated in the center of the room, facing inward. Pershing beckoned toward these.

"Can I offer you gentlemen something to drink?"

"No, thanks," said Pierce. He heard the slightest tremor running underneath the surface of Pershing's voice. Uncertainty and dread.

Salter shook his head. "No, thank you."

Pershing sank into one of the chairs, motioning toward the others again. "Please, sit."

Pierce tended to stand during most interviews, but he decided to make an exception for Pershing because of his former partner's feelings toward the man. He settled into the chair directly opposite the man. Salter took the one to his right.

"I haven't seen you in a very long time, Detective," Pershing said quietly. "Over twenty years. I suspect this isn't a social call."

"No."

Pershing watched him, waiting for the penny to drop.

Pierce looked Pershing directly in the eye. "I have reason to believe Karl Etherton is back in Spokane."

Pershing had to be expecting the news, Pierce knew. Why else would he have come to the man's house, after all? Yet

Pershing's face still seemed to pale with shock. For a moment, he closed his eyes and balled his hands.

Pierce noticed Salter glancing at him, but he didn't return the look.

Pershing blinked twice and relaxed his hands. He wet his lips, then stood. "I think I need something to steady my nerves," he said, walking toward the wet bar. "Are you sure I can't make you one, too?"

"No," Pierce said.

Salter leaned forward and rested his elbows on his knees.

Pierce waited patiently while Pershing clinked some ice into a glass and poured himself a drink. He swallowed one while standing at the bar, then poured another. When he returned to where they were sitting, some color had returned to his face. He plopped down in the chair, sitting on the edge.

"Tell me," he said.

Pierce gave the bare details—two victims, both male, slightly different M.O. in their killings, but same fingers missing. Pershing listened, sipping from his tumbler until Pierce finished.

"The part about the ring fingers," Pershing said. "That was never in the papers."

"No," Pierce said. "We held it back. That's how I know it's him."

"Son of a bitch," Pershing breathed. He took another sip of his drink. "Do you know that, except for while I was overseas, I haven't slept a decent night since 1951?" He glanced up at Pierce. "I was always afraid he would find me again. Finish what he started."

Pierce eyed Salter. The rookie had thought Etherton might return to finish what he started, too. "We understand," Pierce said, feeling the need to include Salter.

Pershing scoffed. "I doubt that." There was no acrimony in his tone, only certainty. "Unless you've lived it, you can't know."

"You're right." Pierce waited a moment, then continued. "My partner came to see you a couple times, afterward."

"I remember," Pershing said. "It was before I shipped off to Korea."

"I have to admit, I was surprised to hear you went into the service."

"Why?"

Pierce hesitated. "The Army is… particular about certain issues."

Pershing seemed momentarily confused, then realization dawned. "Oh, that." He shook his head. "I'm not gay, Detective. I never was. Not really. I was just lost for a while."

"Lost, huh?"

"I was a young man whose father died in the war, being raised by a doting mother. Any armchair psychologist could predict that was going to result in one of two responses. Embrace my masculinity or… go the other direction." He shrugged. "I was confused is all, and I found projecting a particular persona made women want to be around me. I liked the attention. Looking back, it was all very foolish and misguided. Let's call it the folly of youth."

Pierce thought back to the events in 1951. Pershing may have assumed an identity to a degree, but he had admitted to following through with certain acts, at least with Etherton. Could those have been forced? He supposed so.

"After what happened, I knew I had to break free of that façade," Pershing continued. "So I joined the Army to…" He shrugged, searching for the right words. "To reassert my manhood, you could say. Besides, my father was a soldier, and he named me after a general. It seemed a natural path for me to take."

"You were in the war, right?" Pierce asked.

"Yes. I was wounded in the Battle of the Chosin Reservoir." He pointed to his left calf. "I took some lead running back to my foxhole."

Salter's expression registered surprise and he leaned back in his chair.

Pierce had some experience with foxholes. "What were you doing out of it in the first place?"

Pershing gave him a tight smile. "Earning a Bronze Star, apparently." He took another sip of his drink, nearly finishing it off. "Two of my friends—Billy and James—were wounded nearby. They were crawling toward the foxhole, but it didn't look like either of them were going to make it. I jumped out, ran to Billy, and dragged him into the foxhole. Then I ran out to get James. I was almost back with him when I got clipped."

"Heroic," Pierce said flatly.

"Yeah," Salter muttered, awe-struck.

Pershing waved a hand. "Plenty of people did far more. That time, there just happened to be a lieutenant in the next foxhole who saw it all."

Pierce said nothing. He knew Pershing spoke truthfully, though. He'd seen much the same in his war.

"The bullet shattered my fibula and tore up my calf muscle," said Pershing. "They sent me to a field hospital for treatment."

"Wait," interjected Salter. "You mean like *M*A*S*H*? The TV show?"

Pierce frowned. He noticed Pershing did the same.

"I don't care for the way they make light of what happened over there," Pershing said tersely. "Those doctors saved my leg."

"Sorry," murmured Salter. "I meant no offense."

Pershing waved his apology away. "I wasn't fit for front line duty after that. The Army wanted to send me home, but I talked the C.O. into having me transferred to the field hospital. I worked there for the rest of the war. It's what inspired me to become a doctor, in fact."

Pierce blinked in surprise. "You're a doctor?" he asked.

Pershing chuckled, his voice looser now. The booze was clearly working. "I know it seems a bit odd, after what happened to me. It wasn't my plan. The good Lord has a way of helping us find our way, though."

The religious pronouncement rang loudly in Pierce's ears. That was far less surprising than Pershing choosing a career in medicine. Many who suffered trauma found solace in religion.

Pershing stared off into the distance. "Before I left for the war, people looked at me as a victim. After I got back from Korea, they looked at me as a hero." He grunted and seemed to return to the present. "Those that remembered anything about the war, anyway." He drained the rest of his drink and set his tumbler on the small round table in front of him. "The truth is, I'm neither victim nor hero. None of us are. We're merely souls struggling to find our way."

"God helps with that?" Pierce asked, probing.

"At times. Perhaps not as much these days as when I first came home from the war, but he led me to my wife, who led me to the church."

Pierce glanced around. "Is she home?"

"No," Pershing said sadly. "I lost her in fifty-eight. Cancer."

"I'm sorry. That's very young to lose someone to cancer."

"The disease doesn't care about age, unfortunately. It took my mother the year before that. Made for a tough stretch. I almost stopped going to church after Regina passed. Out of respect for her, I stayed." An ironic smile touched his lips. "I'm still a deacon, in fact."

"You've had a rough road," Pierce said.

"I think we all have. That's life. The only way to respond is to be like water."

Pierce's brow knitted. Where had he heard that phrase recently? After a moment, he remembered. Brandon Treviling, the de facto leader at the sunflower hippie house where Kerry Chabot was staying.

"What's that mean, exactly?" Pierce asked.

"Be like water?" Pershing replied. "It's something Bruce Lee said."

"Who?"

Pershing smiled, clearly amused. "The martial artist?"

Pierce shook his head.

"Bruce Lee is far out," Salter said with an appreciative smile. "Enter the Dragon is amazing. That scene with the numchuks?"

Pierce glanced at Salter, then back to Pershing. "Kung fu movies, I'm guessing."

"That's what most people think of where he's concerned, I suppose," said Pershing. "It's certainly fair. I've been interested in martial arts ever since I returned from Korea. Exercising and learning to defend myself was how I coped with feeling vulnerable. Worrying that Dr. Etherton might come back at any moment."

"Makes sense," Pierce agreed.

Pershing motioned toward his wiry frame. "Thanks to my genetics, I was never going to be Jack LaLanne. Weightlifting helped me fill out some. I realized I could model myself after an ectomorph like Bruce Lee."

"So, you have a punching bag in the garage?" Pierce asked.

"A wooden kung fu dummy," Pershing said. "It amounts to the same thing."

Pierce had no idea what Pershing was talking about. "And the thing about being like water?"

"Water is shapeless," Pershing explained. "Pour it into a cup, it becomes the cup."

Pierce stared at him, wondering if this was going to turn into more *Jonathan Livingston Seagull* crap. "The point being…?"

"Whatever situation life puts you in, embrace it. Change form to learn and adapt, so you can stay at peace." Pershing took a deep breath and let it out. "At least, that's what I take from it."

Pierce contemplated his words for a few moments. Then he said, "Chop suey stuff aside, I can check with the sergeant to see about some police protection until we apprehend Etherton."

Pershing waved away his comment. "I'll hire private."

"Good luck finding any," Pierce said. "Most of it is already working at Expo."

"I'll figure out something." Pershing reached for his glass and spun the half-melted ice cube in it. "Will you catch him this time, Detective?"

"I'm going to do my best."

"It's not very Christian," said Pershing, "but I hope he burns in Hell. I really do. Until then, I'd like to know he's in a cage somewhere, not hurting anyone."

Pierce nodded in agreement. Then he said, "Listen, we came here for two reasons. One was to warn you. The other was to ask if you've remembered anything else in the years since this happened."

Pershing stared into his glass, still slowly spinning the cube inside. He took so long to answer that Pierce started to wonder if he was going to at all. Finally, Pershing said, "There's nothing I didn't share with you and your partner already. As often as I relive those moments, they are always the same. His charming presence. Those poor girls hanging from the wall. The clank of the manacles as he put them on me." He looked up at Pierce. "I can feel him out there, you know. I've always felt him out there. Yearning for me. Not in a sexual sense, or at least not primarily so. Mostly him yearning to finish what he started. I wonder if..." he trailed off, looking away and shaking his head.

"What is it?" Pierce asked.

Pershing swallowed and looked up again. He glanced at Salter, then returned his attention to Pierce. "You said both victims were men."

"That's right."

"No women?"

"No, not yet."

"I don't think you'll see any," Pershing said quietly. "Not while he's still trying to make up for me getting away."

Pierce took in his words. Finally, he stood slowly. "Thanks for your time," he said quietly. "We'll show ourselves out."

Pershing gave him a distracted nod, lowering his gaze to his glass again.

Pierce turned and led Salter from the den. Once they were out the front door and nearing the car, he heard the rookie let out a deep sigh.

"That was a lot," Salter said. "What he's been through, I mean."

Pierce climbed into the car and started it. Images of a naked, blood-streaked Basil Pershing in Karl Etherton's dungeon flashed through his mind. Him cutting away the manacle with a pair of bolt cutters while Amherst draped the young man in his own suit jacket. How crumpled Pershing looked wrapped in that jacket, huddled on a chair in Etherton's opulent living room.

Salter settled into the passenger seat. "What's next?"

"Time to go back to Queer Alley," Pierce said.

Chapter 25

Music thumped from inside Rags to Riches as Pierce and Salter walked up the alley.

Three men gathered under the hazy glow of a dim lightbulb which hung above the open back door. Regardless of their dress, the gestures of the three men were decidedly unmasculine. From how they held their cigarettes to the mincing steps they took when they walked, everything about them cried homosexual.

As the detectives approached, one of the men—the guy in white jeans and an untucked purple shirt—hummed the opening of the *Dragnet* theme. "Dum-de-dum-dum." He was tall and thin with shoulder-length wavy hair. He appeared to be about twenty-five years old.

The other two turned to face the approaching cops.

"Ladies and gentlemen," the second one crooned, picking up on his friend's theme music. "The story you're about to hear is true." He appeared to be around the same age. His hair was also shoulder length, but he wore shorts and a T-shirt. Pierce thought he looked like those lanky teenagers who rode skateboards around town.

"Fuck this," the third man muttered. He was young and black and disappeared through the club's back door.

Salter started to give chase, but Pierce grabbed his arm. The pursuit instinct was wrong, but a natural one for rookies. They hadn't yet learned how to prioritize their objectives. Pierce and Salter weren't there to bust anyone for prostitution or lewd conduct. They were there to solve a murder.

"Spokane Police," Pierce said.

"We didn't take you for the welcoming committee," Purple Shirt said. He inhaled on his cigarette, then turned to exhale.

"What's your name?"

Purple Shirt put his hand on his hip and pursed his lips. He flicked the ash from his cigarette. "You're not Vice. We know those pricks." His gaze drifted to Salter. "Ooh, this one's too adorable not to appreciate."

The guy in the T-shirt rubbed Salter's arm. "I think we went to school together."

Salter jerked away his arm. "No, we didn't."

"Shadle Park, right?"

Salter stepped back. The look on his face revealed the truth.

"Names," Pierce sighed.

Purple Shirt sighed. "Always the same, no matter the badge." He tapped his thumb against his chest. "The law knows me as Rick Clark, but down here, I'm the Purple People Eater." He winked.

"Clark," Pierce said. His gaze shifted to the guy in the T-shirt. "And you?"

"Danny Kerley."

Salter's eyes widened.

Kerley snapped his fingers. "See? What'd I tell you? We went to school together. You were on the baseball team, but you were a year behind, right?"

Salter's face slackened. "No."

Pierce cleared his throat. "You guys ever run across Hudson Dorsey or Isaac Hermitage?"

Clark angrily tossed his cigarette into the alley. "What about them?"

"They were murdered."

Kerley leaned toward Salter. "Auggie." He grinned. "Auggie Salter. Second base. You don't remember me? I played left field."

Salter's expression remained frozen.

Kerley shook his head in amazement. "Son of bitch, you're a cop."

Clark tapped Kerley on the arm. "Hey. Did you hear this?"

"What?"

"Huddie was murdered."

Kerley's eyes widened. "No shit?"

"That's what he said." Clark motioned toward Pierce. "Just like Isaac."

The two men stared at each other for a moment, then burst into laughter.

Pierce tilted his head. "What's so funny?"

Clark pulled at the tails of his shirt. "It's just that Huddie and Isaac came down here like they were God's gift. They said they were going to put us old hags out of business."

Kerley shrugged. "Guess that didn't work out so well for them, now did it?"

"Someone preyed on them," Pierce said. "I fail to see the humor in it."

"That's not going to happen to us," Clark said. He waved his cigarette around. "We're too smart for that to happen."

Kerley turned back to Salter. He pulled on the officer's jacket sleeve. "You need some help with your wardrobe."

"I've got a girlfriend."

"I didn't mean me," Kerley said. "I'm just saying you're out of style, unless you're itching to be a Republican booster or something."

Pierce's face warmed. "Have you heard about anyone creeping around?"

Clark laughed. "Are you serious? What world do you think this is, man? All anyone does down here is creep."

"Tell us about it."

"And you'll do what?" Clark pulled back. "You'll come down here and protect us? Right. Stonewall us twice, shame on us."

Salter stepped forward. "There's someone killing your kind, so why won't you help us?"

Kerley's eyes widened. "Our kind?"

"That's not what I meant."

"Hey, man. We played on the same team together. Hell, we even showered together. You and me, we're the same."

Salter glanced at Pierce. "We're not the same. I have a girlfriend and a kid."

Kerley cocked his head. "A kid but no wife? You're full of surprises, Auggie."

"Don't call me that. My name's Gus."

"Well, *Gus*, don't come down here with your hollow promises," Kerley said, his tone turning savage. "You're just like the rest of them, and here I thought maybe you'd be cool."

"You don't know me," Salter said. His face pinched with anger.

Pierce pushed the rookie back. "That's enough."

"I know you're one of Nixon's drug war thugs." Kerley flicked his cigarette into Salter's chest. "Just like the old Nazi with you."

Pierce should have stopped it, but the Nazi comment was a step too far. Salter stepped forward and slugged Kerley in the gut. Kerley let out a groan as he collapsed to his knees. Clark rushed to his friend and bent to help him.

Salter pointed down at Kerley. "I'm not one of Nixon's thugs!"

Clark looked up as he hugged Kerley. "You sure about that?"

Pierce pulled Salter's shoulder. "Let's go."

The rookie stumbled back. His gaze remained on the two gay men for several moments. Eventually, he turned. Pierce walked several paces behind Salter as they headed back to the car.

***

Pierce glanced over at Salter. The rookie stared out the passenger window on the way back to the Public Safety Building. Pierce believed the young man was struggling to hold back tears, so he didn't try to force the conversation. Instead, he let Salter sit with his feelings. This wasn't a therapy session. It was police work and the rookie needed to get used to the rollercoaster of emotions he'd experience throughout a shift.

Pierce rolled his window down and let the night air rush into the car. It was so cool at this speed he almost regretted lowering the window, but Salter followed suit and rolled his down too.

The drive back to the department wasn't typically long, especially at that time of night. With Expo running, the streets were more crowded than usual. Pierce took an alternate route, choosing not to go through downtown, which added a couple of extra minutes to their trip. They ran north on Napa Street, turning eventually onto Mission Avenue.

Pierce flicked on the emergency lights and gunned the engine. The heavy Chevy responded by leaping forward. The car fought against him, desperately wanting to wrestle control away from the detective. He kept a firm grip on the steering wheel and applied more pressure to the accelerator.

Soon, air howled through the speeding police car and blotted out the radio's traffic. The whirring red light flashed intermittently across the hood of the car.

They blew past Stop signs and through the red light at Division Street. The car bounced over uneven intersections, its engine roaring in protest. Pierce was alert for approaching cars or potential dangers.

Salter slid back and forth in the passenger seat, frantically grabbing at the dashboard and the inside of the passenger door. His face was alight with joy as they raced through the city.

When they neared the police department, Pierce slowed and quieted the flashing emergency light. The rookie eased in his seat and his smile faded into a look of regret. The threatened tears were now a thing of the past.

Pierce parked his car. The two men sat silently for a moment before getting out. They met at the back of the car.

Salter was the first to speak. "I shouldn't have lost my cool."

"Be back at seven-thirty," Pierce said. "We've got a lot of work to do."

The rookie stared at him. "Aren't we going to talk about what happened?"

"No." Pierce started to walk away.

"Why not?"

The detective stopped and looked back. "The brass sent you out without the proper training. What did they expect was going to happen?"

Salter looked down.

Pierce shook his head. "Look, kid. What you did wasn't anything that hasn't happened hundreds of times before. The question is, how do you want to conduct yourself going forward?"

"No. I swear." Salter swallowed, then licked his lips. "I never thought I'd do that."

"Then don't do it again."

Salter stepped forward, his eyes pleading. "Did it ever happen to you?"

"Once or twice." Pierce headed toward his car. He'd already said too much.

***

Pierce stepped into the lobby of his building and pulled the door quietly closed behind him. The door to the apartment on the left cracked open and Lois Macy stuck her head out. She held a folded newspaper and pen in her left hand. A pink sleeping bonnet sat cattywampus on her head. Strands of gray hair cascaded down past her eyebrows.

"Mr. Pierce," she whispered. "You're up at all hours."

"The job, Mrs. Macy. It can't be helped."

"People are sleeping." She waved the newspaper at the apartments above them. The crossword puzzle appeared to be half-completed.

"Yes, ma'am."

Her face pickled. "Don't let it happen again."

"I'll try, Mrs. Macy."

She glanced at the paper as if she wanted to ask his help with a question. Instead, she harrumphed and closed the door.

Pierce slowly trudged upstairs to his unit. Inside, he grabbed a can of Olympia and sat at the kitchen table. He shook a cigarette free from its pack and lit it. Pierce wanted to quiet his mind, but he couldn't. Every thought seemed to fold back in on the Etherton case.

For a moment, he thought about Connie, but that led him to thinking about her smoking those godforsaken Virginia Slims, which naturally brought him back to Vivian Kessler. Etherton hadn't contacted her in twenty-three years and why would he? Employers didn't usually keep in contact with former employees, so why did Pierce expect a serial killer to do such a thing?

Because he'd never worked a serial killer case before. No one in the department had.

Right now, Pierce believed Etherton had murdered four people and attempted to kill a fifth—Basil Pershing. There might be more victims they haven't found yet.

There might be more victims Etherton hasn't found, Pierce thought morosely.

He finished his cigarette then his beer.

Pierce replenished both and let his thoughts continue to spiral downward.

Chapter 26

Walter Pierce arrived at his desk at 7:30 a.m. It wasn't an easy feat. His head hurt from too many beers and a lack of quality sleep. It was going to be a lousy day. He'd taken two aspirin prior to leaving his apartment. They had yet to kick in.

He dropped into his chair and pulled himself closer to his desk. Pierce glanced around, but the rookie was nowhere in sight. Perhaps he quit after last night's encounter behind Rags to Riches. If it happened now rather than after the city spent more money to send Salter through the remainder of the academy, so much the better. Police work wasn't for everyone.

Pierce grabbed a notepad and started jotting down his thoughts from yesterday. He was so engrossed in his work he didn't hear the rookie arrive.

"Here you go," Salter said. He set a cup of coffee on the desk.

The rookie held another in his left hand. He wore the same suit as the previous day but had on a different tie.

Salter appeared surprisingly chipper for that early in the morning and it irritated Pierce. Not just that the rookie looked ready for a full day of work, but that Pierce was suffering from the self-inflicted wound of a hangover. He knew better.

Pierce grabbed the coffee and grumbled his thanks. He sipped. "You see your kid last night?" he asked.

Salter seemed surprised by the question. He shook his head. "I go up to Springdale most weekends."

"Last night, you said you had a girlfriend. Did you mean Frida?"

Salter's eyes widened slightly. "You remembered her name?"

"Is it her?"

"Yes. We're still… involved. Why?"

Pierce took another sip of the coffee. The pain in his head had begun to fade, but his memory of last night's ruminations remained. George Amherst's advice to him rang in his ears. He considered how to give it to Salter in a way the rookie might accept.

Finally, he simply said, "An old cop once told me not to let the job take the place of a good woman." He glanced up at Salter. "Same cop who taught me to always pay our debts. You follow?"

Salter nodded, though the rookie looked slightly confused as he did so.

Good enough, Pierce thought. The kid would need to work out the rest for himself.

Salter cleared his throat and asked, "What's our plan for the day?"

"Paperwork first."

"Then?"

Pierce waved a hand. The banging in his head blocked any formation of a plan beyond making notes. "Read the file and shut up."

"Yeah, sure." Salter grabbed the Etherton folder and sat in a nearby chair.

The next hour quietly passed. Other detectives filtered into the bullpen, but they mostly left Pierce alone. No one talked with the rookie.

Pierce eventually put the empty cup on the edge of his desk. "Refill."

Salter closed the file, grabbed the mug, and disappeared. Maybe there was value to the rookie after all.

"Pierce!" Sergeant Fadelin hollered. "My office."

He stood and smoothed his tie. Pierce delayed walking into the sergeant's office, hoping Salter would hurry back with the next cup of coffee. Not seeing the rookie, he exhaled and turned.

Pierce walked across the bullpen but didn't fully enter the sergeant's office. He remained in the doorway. "You rang?"

Fadelin looked up from some paperwork. "All right, let's have it. Where are you with the two homicides?"

Pierce shoved his hands into his pockets and leaned a shoulder against the door jamb. "Dorsey and Hermitage?"

"Don't play dumb, Pierce. On you, it's unbecoming."

He smirked. "I believe they're linked."

"How so?"

"Both men were homosexual, they were active in the sex trade, and each had his left ring finger severed."

"Christ." Fadelin put his pen down.

"It gets better. I believe there's a direct link to an old case."

Fadelin shrugged. "Are you going to make me guess?"

"Karl Etherton. He was the doctor who murdered two young women in fifty-one. Etherton also severed his victims' left ring fingers."

The sergeant's face whitened. "You gotta be shitting me."

"On the surface, it seems like a big jump—women to men—but Etherton attacked a young man in fifty-one, too. Tried to kill him, in fact, but Amherst and I got there in time."

Fadelin waved Pierce forward. "Shut the door."

Pierce stepped fully inside the office now. He made no move to close the door behind him.

"You were supposed to see me yesterday." The sergeant's face reddened.

"When?"

"We talked at Woody's party." Fadelin angrily tapped his desk with a finger. "I said see me tomorrow, which was yesterday."

Pierce nodded. There wasn't much else he could do since he'd forgotten.

"What were you doing instead?" Fadelin asked.

"Working the cases."

"Christ," Fadelin said again. He leaned and looked out his office window. "This is big. You need a different partner on this."

Pierce stiffened. "No."

"I'm gonna assign Barenz and Fletcher to help."

"The hell you are. Are you purposefully trying to sink this investigation?"

Fadelin jumped from his chair. "You want a punch in the mouth, Pierce?"

"I'm just saying, I'll take a half-trained rookie over the Bobbsey Twins."

"You don't understand, Pierce. The whole world is watching us. The President was just here. Media from all over the world is wandering around with their microphones stuck in the face of every dumbass itching to talk."

Pierce shoved his hands back in his pockets. "Reporters, huh?"

"Don't get any ideas."

"Maybe I should let one of them know how a serial killer is dumping gay boys around town."

Fadelin hammered the desk with his fist. "Don't get wise."

Pierce looked over his shoulder. Everyone in the bullpen was watching them, including Salter who had returned with the coffee.

"You're going to get me fired," the sergeant whispered. "My ass is on the line."

Pierce turned back to Fadelin. He kept his own voice low. "I'll tell you what. Let us work this for another week. If we can't shake anything loose in that time, you set Tweedledee and Tweedledumb on us."

The sergeant's gaze flitted about the bullpen. "I should put them on this now."

"More detectives mean more opportunities to talk with reporters."

Fadelin held up his fist. "Seventy-two hours, Pierce."

"Got it. Three days."

"No mention of a serial murderer, either. To anyone. I swear to God. If I hear one word of it anywhere beyond these walls, Barenz and Fletcher are getting the case. Then, I'm busting you down to meter maid."

Pierce settled into his desk chair and did his best to avoid the inquisitive glances of the other detectives. He grabbed the ceramic mug and sipped the lukewarm coffee. The pounding in his head had eased a bit, but it was going to be a long day.

"What was that about?" Salter whispered. He glanced furtively around the bullpen.

"Politics." He set the mug aside. "Now, let me think."

Pierce's mind whirred. Every homicide had a ticking clock associated with it. The further away an investigator got from the moment of murder, the harder it was to solve the crime. When the clock sped up like Sergeant Fadelin just did to him, it created additional pressure.

Unfortunately, whenever the brass inserted itself into an investigation, nothing good ever came of it. If Fadelin let the upper administration know about Pierce's concerns, they'd surely insert their noses into the ugly business. There would be no way for Pierce to leverage the entire department out of the investigation. He'd better hurry or the decision would be made for him.

Right now, he felt stuck. Where should he start?

The desk phone rang, and Pierce snatched the receiver, thankful for the interruption of his worrisome thoughts.

"Detective Pierce," he said.

"I heard you were looking for creepers." The male voice was breathy and low.

"Who is this?"

Salter looked up from the file and leaned toward the desk to eavesdrop on the conversation.

"No names," the caller said. "I don't want to be involved."

Pierce pulled his notepad closer. "Listen, Deep Throat—"

The man snickered. "This guy picked me up last night and—"

"Where did he pick you up?" Pierce interrupted. "What's your name?"

Salter closed the Etherton file. His brow furrowed with concentration.

"He took me to his motel," the caller continued. His voice remained heavy as if he might be excited to be talking with the police. "When he told me what he wanted to do, I split. I heard what happened to those other two guys."

Pierce gripped the phone tighter and pressed it harder to his ear. He hoped to hear something additional in the background. "What did he say he was going to do?"

"He said he wanted to tie me up."

"That it?" Pierce glanced at Salter.

"Isn't that enough? I mean, by the look in his eye, I knew something wasn't right. I probably would have gone with him if I hadn't heard about you asking around."

"What'd you hear?" Pierce asked. "Who told you this?"

"That's not the question you should be asking. Don't you want to know where this went down?"

Pierce rubbed the bridge of his nose. The caller had controlled the conversation. He hadn't answered a single question. Usually, Pierce would consider this a crank call and hang up. He'd had a handful of them in his career. However, the caller said a man picked him up, implying the caller was a male prostitute. Also, he stated the john wanted to tie him up. The two recent homicides had been bound before their deaths. Those two facts suggested Pierce should believe this informant.

Salter shifted in his seat as he studied the detective.

"You still there?" the man asked.

"What motel?" Pierce asked.

"The Spotlight. Room one-oh-seven."

"What'd he look like?"

"Good luck," the caller said, and the line went dead.

Pierce lowered the phone and stared at it.

"Who was that?" Salter asked.

"Might be a crank." Pierce hung up the phone.

He then jotted down as much information from the call as he could remember.

Salter stood slightly so he could see what Pierce was writing. "You don't think so."

"Let's check it out to be sure."

***

The Spotlight Motel sat at the corner of Washington and Second Avenue. It was a two-story affair with outside access. It was built in the late fifties when America's love affair with the automobile blossomed. Its convenient access to downtown made it an ideal destination for weary business travelers. Now that Interstate 90 finally opened after more than a decade of construction, the motel was attracting a different type of customer.

Pierce parked on the street. He and Salter walked to the office which was set apart from the hotel rooms.

The clerk looked up from his newspaper when they entered. A nameplate on the desk identified the clerk as Irving Marsh. A pegboard full of keys hung on the wall behind him. The small office smelled like burned coffee, stale cigarettes, and body odor.

Marsh was a skinny man with a balding pate. His white shirt was wrinkled, and the collar of his undershirt slouched around his neck. Marsh smiled politely at the two detectives. "Good morning, gentlemen. A room?"

Pierce swept his jacket back and revealed his badge and gun. Salter performed the same action and revealed the badge pinned to his belt. His gun still hung heavy in his jacket pocket.

Marsh's eyes widened, and his polite smile vanished. "I didn't mean nothing by it."

Pierce asked, "Is there a guy staying in one-oh-seven?"

The clerk peered through the large window at the neighboring hotel rooms, then consulted his ledger. "Yeah, there's a guest in there." Marsh stuck his finger on the ledger.

Pierce stared at the clerk, waiting for him to provide more.

The clerk smiled awkwardly before clearing his throat. "Right. Uh, John Smith rented the room for three days."

"Smith?" Pierce rested an elbow on the counter and looked at the ledger. "Looks like there are a few Smiths staying here. A couple of Joneses, too."

Marsh leaned back in his chair and spread his hands. "They pay in cash. What can I say?"

"Well, Irv," Pierce said, "you can tell us what this John Smith looks like."

"I don't know." Marsh shrugged. "Nothing really stood out."

Pierce's face hardened. "Try again."

"Yeah, yeah, sure." Marsh nodded several times. "Well, now that I think about it, he was polite, you know? And he had graying hair. A real nice-looking fella." His eyes darted to Salter, then came back to Pierce. "He came in alone. He wore this red tweed jacket." Marsh ran his hands down his wrinkled, white shirt. "It was a bit much, but ever since the Beatles did their Maharishi thing, everyone thinks they can dress like a weirdo and get away with it."

Pierce smirked. "So nothing stood out?"

Marsh shrugged a second time. "I guess not."

Salter rolled his eyes but remained silent.

"Let us in the room." Pierce thumbed over his shoulder.

The clerk slowly rose from his chair. "Shouldn't you guys have a warrant or something?"

"Do you really want us paying close attention to what you're doing here?"

"Good point." Marsh absently reached for the keyboard. "One-oh-seven, right?"

***

Marsh knocked several times on room 107. "Maybe he's asleep."

"Open it," Pierce said.

Salter stood off to the right. His hand was buried in his right jacket pocket, presumably around his gun.

The clerk inserted the key into the knob and turned it. He pushed the door open slightly. "Mr. Smith?"

Pierce slapped the door and pushed it open fully. The covers were pulled back on the bed and the pillow had a compression from where Smith had likely rested his head. The light on the nightstand was illuminated, so was the one in the bathroom.

"Smith," Pierce called. "Spokane Police."

There was no answer.

After a moment of silence, Pierce entered the room, and Salter followed. Irving Marsh remained in the doorway.

It was a small unit, so it didn't take long to search. In the bathroom, Pierce didn't find anything associated with a long-term stay. No toothbrush, paste, or razor. He returned to the main room.

"Check this out," Salter said. He dumped the contents of a brown paper bag onto the bed. Its contents included condoms, a cream-colored dildo, a male pin-up magazine, and a Screw newspaper. The rookie picked up the periodical. "You ever seen this?"

Pierce nodded. "It's for the freaks."

Salter flipped through it and his eyes widened. "Bondage. Gang bangs." He looked up. "They can sell this?"

"Welcome to the real world, kid." Something on the nightstand caught Pierce's eye. He stepped around the rookie and grabbed it. It was an open matchbook from The Liberty Tavern. There wasn't an ashtray. Perhaps Smith had smoked outside. Pierce slipped the matchbook into his pocket.

"I can't believe this," Salter muttered.

Pierce wrote his name and the telephone number to the police front desk in his notepad and tore the page out. He handed it to Marsh. "When Smith comes back, call this number and let me know."

The clerk nodded.

Salter continued flipping through the pervert newspaper, his eyes filled with a mixture of horror and wonder.

"Leave it," Pierce said. "We've got other places to be."

*****

The Liberty Tavern stood on East Sprague Avenue, clustered between a furniture shop and a shoe repair business. It had been there since before Pierce joined the Army. He'd had a few beers there when he first got home from the Pacific. When the area turned rougher, Pierce decided it wasn't a place he needed to frequent any longer.

He parked along the curb.

"I still can't believe people do that stuff," Salter said.

For the last five minutes, the rookie had blathered on about what he'd seen in Screw magazine. Pierce had forgotten what it was like to be so innocent. Years of seeing the worst in humanity had removed any pretense that mankind was filled with goodness.

Pierce yanked open the tavern's door and entered. Ricky Nelson's "Poor Little Fool" drifted from the jukebox. It had been a hit several years after Pierce returned stateside.

Two flags, an American and a P.O.W., hung above the bar. Pictures of Mickey Mantle, Marilyn Monroe, and General Patton were interspersed with advertisements for various beers.

Only a couple of older men drank in the tavern at that time of day. They sat alone at different ends of the bar. Neither bothered to look in Pierce's direction.

A sweaty bartender in a short-sleeved shirt and khaki pants washed a drinking glass. His silver hair was cut in a flat-top and a Marine Corps tattoo graced his right forearm. A cigarette burned in an ashtray.

Pierce approached the bar with Salter a step or two behind.

"What can I get you?" the bartender asked as he set down the tumbler.

"Need some help," Pierce said. He opened his coat to show his badge and gun. "Was a man in here last night? Gray hair. Red tweed jacket."

The bartender lifted the cigarette from the ashtray. "Kind of hard to miss that one."

"Was he sitting with someone?"

"Couldn't miss the other one either." The bartender inhaled on the cigarette. "Sitting together, they looked like a couple of Fruity Pebbles."

Pierce furrowed his brow.

Salter leaned toward him and whispered, "The breakfast cereal."

"His buddy had on a purple shirt." The bartender flicked his ash into the small tray. "Those two stood out like a sore thumb. Two sore thumbs, I guess."

Pierce glanced around. "Didn't know this was that type of place."

The bartender scowled. "It's not, and it never will be while I own the joint."

"What did the one in the red tweed look like?"

"Sorta average, outside of the weird get-up."

"If you saw his face again, would you recognize him?"

The bartender scratched his chin, thinking. "Actually, no, probably not. He sent his little friend over to the bar to buy the drinks, so I never went to their table. He wore a hat."

"What kind of hat?"

"The kind you cops used to wear all the time. Wider brim, though. Or maybe he just kept it low on his face, but you get the idea."

"He wore it the entire time?"

The bartender nodded. "There was a time when people removed their hats when they came in the place, you know?"

"What time did you see them?"

"Must've been around nine or so."

Pierce eyed Salter as he thought. So Rick Clark, the Purple People Eater, had met John Smith, who didn't care if he was seen but didn't want to be recognized. Their date happened before he and Salter interviewed Clark in the alley. If that was the case, why didn't he tell Pierce about Smith when they talked? Something wasn't adding up.

"How late do you stay open?" Pierce asked.

"Until midnight."

"You're in early this morning."

"Got to make hay while there's sunshine." The bartender set the cigarette down. "I don't have a lot of staff. With Expo running, I gotta put in long hours for the next six months to make some extra scratch. After that, I'll throttle back down."

"Got a phone book?" Pierce asked.

"Do I look like Ma Bell?"

Pierce raised an eyebrow. "Didn't know we were antagonizing you."

"Sorry." The bartender reached under the counter and pulled out the phone directory. He gently set it on the counter. "It's the standard response for customers."

Pierce flipped open the book. It only took a moment to find the address.

Richard Clark lived on Oak Street.

***

"Apartment E," Pierce said.

They stood on the porch of the large house. Many older homes in Spokane had been converted to apartment buildings. It was the same type of living situation Pierce found himself in now.

Five mailboxes hung on the outside wall, but only four apartments were inside the building.

"Maybe it's around back," Salter said. He bounded down the steps and disappeared around the side of the building. Pierce followed him.

Apartment E was, in fact, a basement apartment. Salter rang the doorbell before Pierce got there.

"Stand back," the detective said. "He's probably not your biggest fan after you smacked his pal."

Salter trudged up the stairs.

In a moment, the door opened and a sleepy-eyed Rick Clark opened the door. He wore only a pair of boxers. "Yeah?"

"Remember me?"

Clark blinked several times as he scratched himself inside his boxers. "Shit."

"Did you call me this morning?"

"Why would I do that?" Clark's face pinched with confusion. "I never want to see you again."

That's what Pierce thought. The whole scenario just got weirder.

Clark stood on his tiptoes and looked over Pierce's shoulder. "Is your friend going to come hit me?"

"He's not going to bother you."

"So you say." Clark dropped to his regular height and pulled his hand from his shorts. He reconsidered Pierce. "What's this about?"

"You met a man last night."

"I met a lot of men last night. You're gonna need to be more specific."

"You met this one at The Liberty. He wore a red jacket."

Clark smirked. "The doctor."

Pierce cocked his head. "He was a doctor?"

"He said he was, but I think he was trying to impress me, which is just a waste of time if you ask me. I'm only impressed by one thing." Clark rubbed his fingers together. "Moolah."

"How'd you meet?" Pierce asked.

"How do you think? He picked me up."

"Why'd you go to The Liberty?"

Clark sighed. "He suggested we get a drink first. I thought he meant we'd go inside Rags, but instead we went over to Liberty. Man, I never go there. That place is full of uptight true believers. They want no part of our scene. I thought the doctor was out of his mind taking us there, but I think he got off on tweaking those assholes."

"What happened with the doctor?" Pierce asked.

"He talked for a while, mostly about nothing. Where I grew up. What music do I like? That sort of thing. In the end, he wouldn't pay to play so I split."

"How good a look did you get at him?"

"Other than meeting in the alley, I sat across from him for thirty minutes while we had a drink."

"Can you describe him?"

Clark opened his mouth, then paused. His expression became mildly confused. "Not really," he admitted. "He was… average. His clothes stood out, but not the man."

"Would you recognize him if you saw him again?"

"I could try," he said.

"So, why didn't you tell us about this when we met last night?"

Clark shrugged. "What was there to tell? Nothing happened, as Nixon says." His face widened. "Why? Do you think this doctor had something to do with what happened to Isaac and Huddie?"

"I don't know. Maybe."

"Shit." Clark rubbed his bare chest. "You mean, I escaped his clutches?" He grinned. "See, I told you I was too smart for anything to happen to me."

Chapter 27

"Where are we going?" Salter asked.

Pierce side-eyed the rookie while he drove. "You ask a lot of questions."

"Sorry."

Pierce was quiet for several seconds. Then he said, "Don't apologize. It's a good trait for a cop." In his peripheral vision, he saw a self-satisfied smile appear on Salter's lips. "Just not for a rookie," he added.

Salter's smile faltered.

That bought Pierce a few minutes of silence, long enough to reach his destination.

Sumner Avenue was a twisting street, dotted with wealthy homes. Unlike the cookie-cutter designs of many of the new developments going in on the north side of Spokane, the houses Pierce passed were each a unique design. The styles drifted toward old English manor with some Victorians for good measure, but other nations and architectural styles were represented, as well.

He stopped mid-block in front of a two-story that was among the most modern, even though Pierce guessed it was built in the 1940s. When he'd seen it last, it had been painted white with black accents. Today, the colors were nearly reversed. The house itself was a faded charcoal, punctuated by dirty white trim. Only the house numbers were bright white, arranged vertically on a porch pillar. A two-car garage seemed to sag wearily off to the side of the house. The lawn, which Pierce remembered as perfectly cut and maintained before, grew raggedly now. Someone appeared to have cut the grass a couple of weeks ago.

He shut off the engine and got out, standing at the curb. Silently, Salter joined him there.

Pierce pulled out a cigarette and lit it. As he drew in the smoke, he enjoyed the twisting bite in his lungs. Then he exhaled as he stared at the house. Through the large first-story windows, he could see the interior was sparsely furnished. Similar windows adorned the second floor. Pierce imagined the house caught the light well most of the year.

However, it would always be a dark place.

"Whose house is this?" Salter asked.

Pierce ignored the question. He glanced down near his feet and saw a hole about four inches square cut into the lawn. He pointed to it. "What do you make of that?"

Salter glanced at the hole, then shrugged. "Gophers?"

"Are you kidding?" he asked, incredulous. "These gophers of yours have a degree in geometry? That hole is perfectly square."

Salter peered more closely at it, his eyes squinted in thought. Then realization dawned on him. "A real estate sign." He looked to Pierce for confirmation. "This house was for sale."

"And now it's not." Pierce wasn't surprised. No one he knew could afford to buy a home right now. Inflation was horrible and interest rates ridiculously high. If he and Connie hadn't bought when they did…

Goddamn it.

The whole situation with his wife still caught him by surprise at times, especially when he was focused on work. Like a George Foreman left hook, out of nowhere.

"You okay?" Salter asked.

"I'm fine. Does the address look familiar?"

Salter turned toward the house, searching out the numbers. Finding them only took a moment. Pierce waited while the rookie recited the address to himself. Once, then twice. Midway through his third recitation, his lips stopped moving suddenly and turned to Pierce. "This is Karl Etherton's house. Where you and Detective Amherst—"

"That's right."

Salter licked his lips nervously. "You don't think—"

"That he's hiding here?" Pierce shook his head. "I think he's too busy being someone else to go anywhere near his old identity." He waved toward the house. "I just wanted to see the place again. Help get back the scent."

"Are we going inside?"

Pierce stared at the smaller basement windows, now fringed with sheer white curtains. Twenty-three years ago, those curtains had been thick and black, to keep out prying eyes and block the sounds of violence. When he'd remembered those basement windows in the years since, they always seemed like feral black eyes, glaring at him with malevolence. Now, they appeared hollow and benign.

Strangely, he thought of the expression he saw on DiCarlo's face when he visited the man. Perhaps this house was like that. A broken shadow of its formerly evil self. The dungeon was surely gone. The space could be a den now, complete with a wet bar and billiards table.

That may be so, but Pierce still sensed it. Still felt what happened all those years ago.

"No," Pierce said. "We're not going in."

***

They ate a late lunch at Dick's Hamburgers. The fast-food joint was walk-up only. The customers were an eclectic mix of office people, blue-collar workers, students, and downtown denizens. Most of them ignored the officers or at least pretended to. A trio of college girls stood in line ahead of them, casting shy glances back at Salter. The rookie responded with a smile that evoked whispers and giggles.

When it came down to it, Pierce thought, college kids weren't much different than high school kids. The training wheels were removed, that's all. Though he was fighting in the Pacific at their age, he knew some of them weren't ready for the safety device to come off yet.

Had that been the case with Josephine Banfield and Shirley Jensen back in fifty-one? Josephine had been sexually adventurous for the time, he recalled. Perhaps her engine had outrun her tires in that regard. Just because someone thinks they're ready for something doesn't mean they can handle it.

Basil Pershing was a good example of that. He'd presented himself as a confident, suave prodigy, but he wasn't prepared for someone like Etherton. Neither were Hermitage or Dorsey.

Neither were we, Pierce thought.

The line shuffled forward. Ahead of them, the college girls got their orders and flounced away with smiling glances back to Salter. Pierce ordered a Double Whammy, fries, and a coffee. The rookie did the same.

They moved to stand in the waiting area. Pierce glanced at the young man. His features were handsome enough, though no one would ever call his looks rugged. He still had some of the roundness in his face Pierce equated with baby fat. His eyes were sharp, though. Wide-eyed, but sharp.

"Tell me what you think our next move should be," Pierce said.

Salter looked around. "Here?"

"We're waiting for our food. What better time?"

Salter bobbed his head in agreement. He raised his fist to his mouth and cleared his throat. "I've actually been contemplating this. You said Etherton was probably using a false identity—"

"Not probably," Pierce corrected. "He is."

"Right. Sorry. I was thinking, what's that paperwork do?" He watched Pierce as if waiting for an answer, but Pierce only stared back wordlessly. He wasn't going to do the rookie's work for him. "It's a mask, isn't it? It lets him pretend to be something else."

Pierce was mildly disappointed. The kid acted like he was spouting some great truth when he was pointing out a basic fact. He was about to say so when the fast-food attendant called out their number. Pierce walked to the window. He held out a five, but the man taking the order lifted a hand in refusal. "No charge, Officers. Manager's orders."

Pierce extended the bill further. "I appreciate the thought, but I don't work for him. We pay."

The man hesitated. "You might not work for him, sir, but I do. He says the cops eat for free."

Pierce moved his hand closer toward the man. "We pay," he repeated.

After a moment, the man relented and took the money. He rang up the sale with a scowl and gave Pierce his change.

Pierce grabbed the two bags. He made his way toward an empty picnic table and sat, handing one of the bags to Salter.

"Careful you don't spill the coffee," he said.

Salter fished the cup out of his bag and set it on the tabletop. He didn't reach for his food, however. "I thought we were going Dutch."

"Eat," Pierce urged.

Salter didn't reach for his bag, though. Instead, his expression grew contemplative again. He leaned forward. In a hushed whisper, he said, "How much does anyone ever really change?"

Pierce took the lid off his coffee cup and sipped. The brew was fresh and robust. "How long did you sit in a dark room with your lava lamp running to come up with that startling revelation?"

Salter looked hurt, but he forged ahead. "This guy, John Smith. If he's actually Etherton—"

"You're making a jump there."

Confusion registered on the rookie's face. "Are you saying you haven't considered that? We're chasing a guy that might have killed Hermitage and Dorsey. You believe Etherton killed them. Doesn't that mean Smith might be Etherton?"

"It could," admitted Pierce. He withdrew his burger from the bag and opened the Styrofoam container. He dumped his fries into the top half and balled up the paper sleeve, dropping it back into the bag. Salter was still staring at him, so he said, "Eat. You don't want this to get cold."

Reluctantly, Salter pulled his own food from the bag. He mirrored Pierce's action, dumping his fries into the top of the container, but didn't eat right away.

Pierce took a bite of the burger and chewed. When he'd swallowed, he said, "All right. Say Smith and Etherton are the same person. We don't know who Smith is. Finding him is priority one."

"I know."

"That wasn't the point you were working toward?"

Salter shook his head.

"Then what?" Pierce asked.

"Clark said Smith was a doctor."

"I'm a doctor."

Salter cocked his head.

"People lie, remember? Plus, Clark said he thought Smith lied to impress him."

"But Etherton *was* a doctor," Salter said. He gave Pierce a meaningful look. "How much do people really change?"

Pierce lifted his burger and resumed eating. "Are you proposing we background check every doctor in the city? Because we did a version of that back in fifty-one." He waved his burger at the rookie. "Let me tell you, that didn't play well with the administration, and it didn't get us anywhere."

Salter shrugged. "We could start with those doctors we got from the Vice files, and I think there's a quicker way to narrow the pool."

Pierce chewed thoughtfully, realizing now where Salter was going. He'd been considering it himself. He let the rookie have his moment, though. "How?" he asked.

"We go to the person most likely to recognize the man, even after all these years," Salter pronounced proudly.

Pierce nodded. "Okay, kid. We'll run that down. Now, eat your burger. They taste like hell cold. Oh, and you owe me two dollars."

***

Ideally, Pierce would have returned to the station and gathered photos to show the witness. However, he decided to first make sure Basil Pershing would agree to cooperate.

When he answered the door, Pershing looked haggard, like he hadn't been sleeping well. He invited the detectives back into his den once more and they followed wordlessly. Once they'd settled into the same seating arrangement as the previous visit, Pierce wasted no time getting to the point.

Pershing listened carefully. Pierce could tell he was uncomfortable with the topic, which was expected.

"I didn't ask you this before," Pierce said, "but do you think you'd recognize him today?"

"Absolutely," Pershing said, without hesitation.

"Twenty-three years is a long time."

"It hasn't erased my memory of him, Detective. If you put Karl Etherton in front of me, I'd know him in an instant."

"Good. We'll come back later today or tomorrow with some photos for you to look at."

Pershing nodded absently, his expression odd.

"What is it?" Pierce asked.

Pershing shook his head. "No, I'm probably being paranoid."

"Paranoia can be healthy in my profession."

A tight smile creased Pershing's lips. "I imagine so. I didn't think much about this on your last visit. Honestly, I was in a bit of shock, but I've thought of little else since." He stared down at his palms and ran them over the tops of his thighs nervously. "He'd have to use some other identity, wouldn't he? He couldn't still be Dr. Karl Etherton."

"No, he couldn't."

"A false identity means fake paperwork, but I doubt that would be an obstacle for him. Money can solve most problems." He looked at Pierce. "Paperwork might change who the world thinks you are, but you know what it doesn't change? Your face."

Pierce cocked his head. "His face?"

"It's a big risk, isn't it?" Pershing said. "Coming back to Spokane. Even after all this time, someone might recognize him."

"He'd be careful about that," Pierce agreed. He thought of how Smith—or possibly Etherton—kept people from getting a good look at his face. He wore flashy clothes so that's what people would remember. The bartender at The Liberty Tavern said he never took off his hat. The behavior was consistent.

"I wonder if he'd be more than careful. I wonder if he'd make some permanent changes."

Pierce's brow knitted. "Are you talking plastic surgery?" he asked, skeptical. "A face change?"

Pershing nodded slowly.

Pierce drew in a deep breath. He considered taking out a cigarette but knew some people who didn't smoke were getting finicky about having it in their homes. Instead, he eyed Pershing and thought about what he'd said. "Pardon me for saying so, but that sounds farfetched."

"Like *Mission Impossible*," Salter added.

"It did to me, too," Pershing said. "At first, anyway. After all, he's not a Bond villain." He fell silent, rubbing his palms against his pant legs again. Then he whispered, "Only, he is. No, he's worse, actually. Because he's real."

Pierce sat in silence, mulling over the thought. In his long experience, most cases never progressed past what he would call simple. Some of the criminal puzzles he'd solved over the years seemed complex while investigating because of the missing pieces. Once they were all put together, however, the explanation was simple. Jealous husband kills wife's lover. Greedy son kills parent for inheritance. Businessman murders partner because he wants to be sole owner.

Money, sex, power. The three things Amherst swore made up ninety-nine percent of people's motivations to commit crimes. Over the years, Pierce added revenge to the mix, and he'd found the four to be an inclusive list. Etherton's likely motivations involved several of them.

Since these were such base motivations, the crimes were simple. Rarely did they end up being anything more, once he'd solved them. No cases of identical twins, secret codes, or supernatural elements. They certainly didn't include someone getting a face change.

"Your expression is dubious, Detective."

"It's my job to be skeptical. Someone getting a face change sounds a little outlandish."

"We live in outlandish times," Pershing said. "I've thought this over and it isn't as crazy as it might sound. I'm not suggesting a radical change. He's not going from Spencer Tracy to Charles Bronson. However, a plastic surgeon could make significant alterations to his nose. Rhinoplasty has seen great strides in the last decade. Subtle work on the jawline or cheeks would only increase the difference."

"He could change his hair style, too," Salter interjected thoughtfully. "Grow a beard or add some glasses."

"Exactly." Pershing nodded at Salter, then he looked questioningly at Pierce. "Combined with the age difference, wouldn't that be enough to throw off any recognition?"

"Maybe," Pierce allowed. His mind was humming with the possibility. He glanced over at Salter, whose expression was contemplative. He turned back to Pershing. "How would someone go about getting that done?"

"I don't know exactly," Pershing admitted. "I do know it would cost money, which Etherton had. As a doctor, he knew doctors who knew other doctors. It probably wouldn't be difficult for him to find someone willing to do what he needed done."

"That doesn't speak too well of your profession," Pierce noted.

Pershing looked momentarily amused. "I was down at Riverfront Park for the Expo opening ceremony, Detective. Do you know what some of your colleagues did to the protestors who were present?”

“No.”

“Let’s just say it didn’t speak too well of your profession, either. There are people making bad decisions across every walk of life.”

“That’s fair.”

Pershing rose and held out his hand. “I’ll do whatever I can to assist you, Detective.”

Pierce stood and shook his hand. When he took hold, he noticed the man’s palms were bone dry.

***

On the way back to the station, Salter said, “He’s right, isn’t he?”

“I don’t know.”

“It makes sense. A false identity still doesn’t hide his face. If he’s going to return to Spokane, he needs a new look.”

“It’s a stretch,” Pierce argued, wondering how much he was trying to convince himself rather than Salter. Pershing’s words had worked their way into his head. More than that, they almost sounded plausible.

“For someone like you or me, it would be,” Salter argued. “But Etherton had the money and the access—”

“It still sounds like something you’d see on *The Twilight Zone*.”

“I love that show,” Salter said distractedly. “You ever see the one on the plane with—”

“*The Twilight Zone* isn’t real life,” interrupted Pierce again.

“No,” agreed Salter. “It isn’t.”

They rode in silence for a few blocks. Pierce took a route that swung wide of the park and Expo to avoid the worst of the traffic.

Next to him, Salter spoke quietly. “Etherton’s not very real life, either, if you think about it.”

Pierce didn't answer.

The kid had a point.

When else had anything like what Etherton had done happened in Spokane? Never. He hoped it never would again. If the event itself was unique, it only followed he should treat the suspect as also unique.

At his desk, Pierce instructed Salter to drag a chair over to join him. Slowly, they went through their list of perverts. First, they separated out the four doctors. Then, to be safe, Pierce created a secondary list of all the remaining men whose stature and age generally resembled Etherton or Smith. His gut told him the man masquerading as Smith was really Etherton. He was even beginning to buy the idea Etherton could have had his face altered to avoid detection. That didn't mean Pierce was going to rule out other possibilities. He'd seen too many detectives blow cases because of tunnel vision to fall prey to their mistake himself. He'd focus on the most promising theory the evidence pointed to, but not to the exclusion of other possibilities. In his long experience, doing otherwise was a good way to allow a suspect to slip past undetected.

At the same time, this was a different sort of case. Maybe the danger in this one lay in adhering too closely to standard procedures and regular ways of thinking. He had to be willing to adapt if the case demanded it. Approach the case differently. Use different tools. Even ask for help.

Pierce let out a long sigh.

"What?" Salter asked.

"Nothing," he said. "I just need to make a phone call."

***

The call was routed twice before he reached his destination. The first stop was the main switchboard. After a transfer and a long wait, a unit secretary answered. It was an even longer wait after that before a male voice came on the line.

"Special Agent Wilsky, Behavioral Sciences Unit," the man said briskly.

Pierce could hear the self-importance leaking through the telephone lines. Nevertheless, he introduced himself and said, "We could possibly use your help with a case."

"Give me the broad strokes," Wilsky said.

Pierce laid it out for him. He kept to established facts for the most part, only sharing theory when it came to Etherton's false identity.

When he'd finished, the agent remained silent on the other end of the line. Finally, he said, "I don't believe we can help you, Detective."

"Why not?"

"We aren't in a position to do much in the way of consulting, for starters. Our work is focused almost exclusively on Bureau cases. But that isn't the only reason."

Pierce heard something in the agent's voice he didn't like. His jaw flexed. "No?"

"Your case doesn't fall under our criteria for exceptional involvement. There is no interstate element to it."

"He could have fled the state back in fifty-one."

"Or he could have hidden in a cabin in the woods," countered Wilsky. "Point is, you don't know. We need affirmative evidence of interstate flight to justify our involvement. Frankly, Detective, even if your case met our criteria, I don't believe the Bureau would authorize it."

Pierce almost hung up then, but his curiosity won out. "Why's that?"

"Your theory is implausible. You've got a suspect renewing his activity after a twenty-three year hiatus. Outside of someone being incarcerated, which we know this man wasn't, that's unheard of. Serial killers do not operate that way."

"Maybe he was incarcerated under his assumed name or in another country," Pierce said. "Or maybe he was killing people somewhere else while living that identity."

"Or maybe you're simply desperate to catch a man that slipped through your fingers twenty-three years ago," Wilsky said. "We can't help you."

"You're the guy who makes that decision?"

"Well… no."

"I'll send a formal request, then."

"You can if you want, but my Agent-in-Charge listens to my counsel. I'll advise him not to waste our time with your case."

"Agent… Wilsky, was it?"

"That's correct."

"Fuck you, Agent Wilsky."

Pierce hung up.

***

He tried to send Salter home, but the rookie refused. Pierce almost suggested it would be good for him to have a meal with his family. Then he recalled Salter saying he only saw his girlfriend and son on the weekends, so he didn't push the issue. The two of them went to Reed's Diner again for dinner. They ate silently for the most part. Pierce ordered apple pie and coffee after his meal. Salter asked for the same, except he got the pecan pie.

Halfway through dessert, Salter said, "We don't have pictures for most of the people on the list who weren't arrested."

"We don't," agreed Pierce.

"So, are we going to talk to those people on our list tonight? Get a photo of each of them?"

"No," Pierce said. "I've been thinking about that. Say Etherton has a new face. He's going around town calling himself Smith. Maybe we've already talked to him. He'd be plugged into the gay scene, and he'd know we were casting a wide net. Our visit might have made him more cautious, but he's too arrogant to think we've caught him. If we show up a

293

second time and start snapping pics?" Pierce shrugged. "Might spook him."

"What, then?"

"What would you do?"

Salter's face scrunched in thought. He poked at the remains of his pie crust with a fork. Then his expression brightened. "Bring them in for a line up. Let Basil Pershing pick out Etherton."

"No," Pierce said. He took a drink of coffee to wash down the last of his pie. "Some of them are doctors. They have status and are used to being treated a certain way. We can't haul them downtown for a lineup. It'd never fly. Someone would call the brass and we'd be working crowd control at Expo by tomorrow."

Salter looked disappointed. "I still think having Basil Pershing look at them is the best option."

"You're right."

"I am?"

Pierce nodded. "So, if we can't bring them together in one place for Pershing to see…?"

Salter clapped his hands. In the next booth, a family of four stopped suddenly and gaped at him. "We bring Pershing along with us," Salter pronounced. "We go to their houses and do the lineup one at a time."

"That's the plan," Pierce said. He finished his coffee and stood. "Let's go sell our witness on it."

***

"It'll be perfectly safe?" Pershing asked hesitantly.

"Yes," Pierce assured him. "The two of us will be with you the entire time."

Pershing glanced at Salter. "I know you're experienced, but he seems rather… green."

"He's well-trained," Pierce lied. "Besides, I thought you knew how to judo chop people."

Pershing frowned. "I've never actually… I mean, outside of the war, I've never been in a physical confrontation. I don't think I want to be."

Pierce didn't entirely understand the thinking behind training to fight but never wanting to. He chalked it up to the hippie, new age, be-like-water mindset. "You won't have to," he said. "We'll be there the entire time. You'll be behind us. Your role is strictly to observe and identify."

Pershing's expression remained uncomfortable. "Forgive me, Detective. I know my experience with law enforcement is minimal, but this seems a bit… unorthodox."

"It is," Pierce admitted, "but we're trying to catch an unorthodox killer."

That seemed to convince Pershing. His mien became resolute, and he nodded. "All right," he said. "I'll do it."

***

They took the suspects in geographic order, going from the nearest to the next closest and onward from there. In each instance, Pierce knocked on the door with Salter beside him. Pershing stood a full stride behind them, with instructions to observe and say nothing unless he recognized Etherton.

"If you know it's him, just say so," Pierce told Pershing in the car before the first stop. "We'll grab him, but only if you're certain. Otherwise, if you're only suspicious, or you think it's possible it could be him, then say it's chilly and you wish you'd brought a jacket. We'll know to push the guy a little harder. Keep watching him while we do."

"I understand," said Pershing.

They stopped at Butch Kelso's first. Pierce asked innocuous questions for a few minutes while the quartet stood in the doorway. Pershing said nothing. In the car, he shook his head.

"Not even close," he told Pierce.

Dr. Lynch was next, with the same result. Parr and Armstrong followed, all with Pershing saying nothing during the interview and affirming after that he didn't believe the man to be Etherton in disguise.

"Even if his face has been radically changed, I'd know him by his eyes in an instant," Pershing said. "I still see those eyes in my dreams some nights."

They contacted Dr. Andrews next. He eyed them coolly from the open doorway, his previous charm much more reserved.

"I thought we'd reached an understanding, Detective," he said, his voice just barely above a growl.

"I have a job to do," Pierce said in a neutral tone. "I'm sorry if that inconveniences you."

"Sorry is what you'll be if I were to pick up the phone and make a couple of calls."

Pierce attempted to ask another standard question, but Andrews held up his hand to stop him.

"Assisting the police is one thing," he snapped. "Being drawn into something that has nothing whatsoever to do with me is another." Andrews grabbed onto the door handle and stepped back. "Good evening, gentlemen." He bit off every word as if it were a profanity and slammed the door in Pierce's face.

"Way to stick it to the man," Salter muttered.

Pierce ignored his commentary and glanced wordlessly at Pershing. Pershing hesitated, then gave a small shake of his head. Pierce suppressed a sigh and headed back to the car with Salter and Pershing in tow.

Despite his own belief there was no way he was their man, Pierce still took them to see Dr. Carlson, who had been Hudson Dorsey's physician. Pershing confirmed his belief.

"Not a chance," he told Pierce. "He's a kind person. Etherton could never pull that off. He could do charming, but never kind."

The final stop was Dr. Townsend. The skeletal man gave out the same arrogant vibe as the first time Pierce and Salter spoke with him. Pierce kept expecting Pershing to say something about wishing he had brought a jacket, but the witness remained silent. Nonetheless, Pierce pressed Townsend further than some of the others. If he was going to believe in the possibility of a face change, he couldn't dismiss a radical shift in weight and build, either.

"I believe I've answered each of these questions previously, Detective," Townsend snapped. "All without you having advised me of my rights, I might add. At this point, you asking them again almost constitutes harassment. How would your chief feel about you harassing professionals like me?"

"I'd like to think he'd be focused on me solving this case."

"I'm sure that is exactly what you'd like to think." Townsend drew himself up, standing perfectly erect. "This conversation is over. For any future interactions, I shall require my lawyer present."

The doctor closed the door with a thud.

On the way back to the car, Pierce looked sideways at Pershing. "Nothing?"

Pershing shook his head. "I almost felt like I needed a jacket for real, though. I think he and Etherton would have gotten along."

Pierce had the same feeling the first time they'd interviewed Townsend.

"He didn't have anyone working with him?" Salter asked. "Etherton, I mean."

Pierce stopped. "Why do you ask?"

"It just popped into my head." He nodded toward Pershing. "Because of what Basil said."

Pierce frowned. He didn't like the rookie using Pershing's first name. It was unprofessional. He pushed aside his irritation, though, and ran the idea through his mind. Etherton with an accomplice? He had to admit the thought had never occurred to him. He stood at the curb near the car, re-thinking the case. The more he did, the less likely it seemed, though. "There were no signs of an accomplice," he said. He turned to Pershing. "Was there anyone else?"

Pershing looked pale in the moonlight. He shook his head. "I would have told you."

"I know," said Pierce. "I don't mean it as something you withheld from us back then. I'm asking you now, though—do you remember anything that could point to an accomplice?"

"No," said Pershing. "There was only him."

Pierce nodded. He looked at Salter and shrugged. "I like that you're thinking about possibilities, kid, but that one doesn't fly."

Salter didn't appear bothered. "Just a crazy thought."

"This whole case is crazy," Pierce said.

After interviewing Townsend, it was nearly ten p.m. They decided to call it a night. Pierce drove Pershing back to his home.

As they pulled into the doctor's driveway, Salter blurted out, "Are you sure about Andrews?"

Both Pierce and Pershing turned to look at him.

"Excuse me?" Pershing asked.

"Doctor Michael Andrews. He was the one—"

"I remember him." Pershing's voice sounded strange.

"He didn't seem hinky to you?"

"He did," Pershing allowed, his tone hesitant. "So did that other doctor. Townsend, was it?"

"Andrews is a much better match," Salter said. "Are you sure it wasn't him?"

"I'm… pretty sure." Pershing sounded doubtful.

"If he—"

"I think we've done enough work tonight," Pierce interrupted forcefully. He gave Pershing a respectful nod. "Doctor, thank you for your help. We'll be in touch."

"I'm glad to be of assistance," Pershing murmured. He opened the car door and exited the car. Pierce watched in silence as Pershing walked to the front door and went inside the house.

"It's brave," Salter said. "What he did tonight."

"We all have to face our demons eventually," Pierce said. He turned to glare at Salter. "What the fuck was that, rookie?"

Salter's eyes flew open in surprise. "What did I do?"

"You haven't earned the right to talk to witnesses," Pierce barked. "So don't say anything."

Salter held up his hands. "What did I say? I thought we were trying—"

"We're trying to find a killer. A *killer*, you get that? It's not playtime. This isn't Mister Rogers and his neighborhood."

The confusion on Salter's face was genuine. His expression cut through Pierce's ire, lessening it.

"Look," he said, his jaw still tight. "You can't lead witnesses like that. It's suggestive. They might make an ID because of what you said instead of what they saw. Or make the ID in order to please you, whether on purpose or subconsciously. Your suggestions can taint the witness."

He watched as Salter processed the information. Confusion fell away, replaced by shame.

Pierce didn't relent. Shame wasn't a bad thing. Often, it was how people learned. "A tainted witness can destroy a case once it gets to trial," he continued. "Worse yet, it might result in arresting the wrong guy, leaving the real suspect still out there."

Salter swallowed. "I'm sorry," he murmured.

"I don't want to catch some man," Pierce said. "I want to catch the *right* man."

"I'm sorry," Salter repeated.

"You said that already. It doesn't unring the bell."

Pierce put the car into gear and headed toward the station.

***

An hour later, Pierce sat at his wobbly dining room table, clutching his second can of Olympia beer and staring down at the notes he'd made. All of them consisted of thoughts he'd gone over a hundred times and observations he'd examined and re-examined without anything new emerging. It struck him that the words were like a shopping list he'd made for a trip to the store that had already happened. The food was in the pantry, but he was still studying the list.

Only, it never changed.

It was maddening.

He let his thoughts drift to Connie.

The night grew much darker after that.

Chapter 28

Pierce arrived at the station at almost eight in the morning. The tang of vomit still lingered in the back of his throat from earlier that morning. Coffee and dry toast failed to completely wash away the acidic aftertaste.

Salter was already present, milling around in the same gray suit. The floppy bulge of his .38 in his pocket shifted heavily every time the rookie moved.

"You need to get a holster for that," Pierce told Salter as he sat down at his desk.

"They won't give me one."

Pierce didn't answer. If the kid was going to be with him until the end of Expo, he didn't want him wearing the same suit every day or walking around like he had a fist-sized rock in his pocket. Not for another five months. He reached into his desk and wrote down the name of a reliable haberdashery. Below that, a gun shop he knew cops frequented. He tore off the paper and handed it to Salter.

"Next payday, you go to both these places. Get a simple holster for your belt. You don't need to waste money on a shoulder rig since you're going back to patrol soon."

Salter took the slip of paper, frowning. "I had my heart set on the shoulder holster."

"Settle down, Steve McQueen." Pierce pointed at the note. "Get a suit at the haberdashery so you have two. Then get a third the following payday. Rotate through them during the week. Three should be enough, even when you have to take one of them to the dry cleaners."

"Okay," Salter said, still sulking. "Thanks for the advice."

"Can't have you looking like a mope."

Pierce withdrew the Hermitage and Dorsey files and flipped them open. Salter wandered away. When he returned, he had two coffees in small paper cups. He set one on the desk next to Pierce.

"You don't look so great," Salter said. "Catching a bug?"

Pierce's gaze slid to Salter, his eyes hard. "Let's worry about finding a killer."

Salter held up a hand in surrender. "Just asking. Sylvia has aspirin in her desk if you need it."

Pierce squinted at him. "How the hell do you know?"

"She told me."

"Why are you talking to Sylvia?"

"Why not?"

"This isn't a college campus," Pierce said. "We're not here to chase skirts."

Salter's brow knitted. "Could have fooled me," he muttered.

"What's that?"

Salter glanced at Pierce, his expression non-threatening. "I said, you could have fooled me. From what I've seen, you're one of the few people around here not on the make."

"I don't care what you think you know. You're *my* trainee, so you follow *my* rules."

Salter sighed. "I wasn't putting moves on her. I told you, I have a girlfriend. Sylvia and I were just talking. I've been getting here at seven and the last couple of days, you haven't."

That stopped Pierce cold. He realized Salter was right. Sergeant Fadelin gave his detectives a fair amount of latitude in managing their own workday, much like DiCarlo had before him. His only expectation was a hard day's work. Since being assigned this case, they'd given that effort and more. Pierce hadn't put in for a single minute of overtime. The department was well ahead in terms of work hours versus pay.

However, Salter had a point. Pierce should be setting a better example. Coming in at almost eight—and hungover—when his rookie was there at seven wasn't acceptable.

"Just be careful with that," Pierce said, his tone turning conciliatory. "People can get the wrong idea."

Salter nodded. He motioned toward the open case files. "What now?"

"Today, we read and research," Pierce said. "Until one, at least. Then we resume the tour with Basil Pershing."

***

Pierce pored over both case files, then passed them off to Salter to review. He began work on prioritizing the remaining names on their pervert list. Around eleven, he was considering a break for lunch when his phone rang.

"Pierce."

"Sergeant Berg, at the front desk. I've got three anonymous tips for you here."

Anonymous tips rarely panned out. However, the recent lead on John Smith had been from a nameless source. "I'll be right over."

He set the phone's receiver back into place and rose from his desk. When Salter started to do likewise, he held up his hand. "Stay here. I'll be back in a few minutes." Salter returned to studying the case files. Pierce had to grudgingly admire the rookie's work ethic and ability to focus. He didn't regret being hard on him, though. Without military experience, the kid needed a firm hand.

The walk to the front desk took him past either Records or Mahogany Row, where all the brass had their offices. None of them had those fancy desks anymore, though. After the move to the Public Safety Building, everybody got new desks, metal and utilitarian. Only the chief had one of the mahogany monstrosities that gave Mahogany Row its name. As much as he didn't want to deal with Hazel at the moment, risking a run-in with her was better than talking to any of the bosses. He strode briskly down the hall and past the Records division with his eyes straight forward. He didn't see Hazel.

Sergeant Berg was a jowly man who had recently lost about forty pounds. His uniform hung off him as if it belonged to his dad. Pierce thought about slipping him the name of a good tailor but knew the sergeant was too cheap to spend money on alterations, or he would have done so already. Perhaps he expected to eventually be fat again.

Without preamble, Berg extended a handful of messages toward Pierce. "I took the last one about ten minutes ago. Almost sent it to Vice but I heard you were working a homo murder, so here you go. Male caller, low voice. Kinda creepy. Refused to identify himself."

Pierce took the messages. "Why didn't you tell me about the other two? I've been here all morning?"

"Graveyard sergeant took those. They ended up under the logbook, so I didn't see them until half an hour ago. I set them aside to call you but then I had a woman come in to report a missing kid."

Pierce's ears pricked up. "Kid? How old?"

"She's seven, but patrol already located her at her friend's house."

"Oh."

"Don't look so disappointed, Detective," Berg said, his tone sarcastic.

Pierce frowned. "Only thing I'm disappointed in is how long it took to get these first two messages."

Berg leaned forward. "Excuse me?"

"I'm working a pair of homicides," Pierce said. "Tips are important."

Berg's craggy face dissolved into a scowl. He held up three fingers. "Know what these are, Detective?"

Pierce stared back at him, not answering.

"Three reasons for you to fuck off," Sergeant Berg said, turning his fingers around and slapping the three chevron stripes on his sleeve. He glowered at Pierce.

Not a battle I'll win, Pierce told himself. He turned and headed back toward his desk. While he walked, he reviewed the messages. The listed time on the one Berg took was 2246 hours. The "To:" box had "Dix/Vice" written next to it. After

Berg's terse description of the voice, the text read, "Caller claims man tried to pick him up near R-to-R last night. Promised money if he was 'into some kinky fun.'"

On any normal day, Pierce would have wadded that tip and tossed the paper into the trash. Today, he simply moved it aside and read the next one. It was marked as having been called in at 0116 hours.

"Male caller, refused to ID. Femmy voice. Claims he was engaged in consensual sex w/ a man named Andrew in the alley behind Rags to Riches. Turned rough. Man refused to stop until he finished. Complainant declined again when asked for ID or to make official report." It was signed with an indecipherable scrawl that Pierce knew belonged to Orrie Hatcher, the graveyard desk sergeant.

Andrew, Pierce thought. Doctor Andrews, perhaps? Or a coincidence?

He flipped to the third message, which came in at just after three in the morning. It was from Irving Marsh at the Spotlight Motel. "John Smith came back to his room" was all it said.

Pierce quickened his pace.

***

"I had just shut out the light when I saw him," Irving Marsh told them. The motel clerk was bleary eyed, as if he'd only recently woken. "I never close down entirely for the night, but at three, I dump the lights, so I can get some sleep in the back room. I don't get much traffic after that, and the bell wakes me if anyone comes in."

"You saw Smith," Pierce prompted.

"I saw lots of Smiths and Joneses," Marsh said, giving him a dark look, "like you pointed out before. But, yeah, I saw your Smith. Room one-oh-seven."

"Is he still there?"

Marsh shook his head. "He was here less than five minutes."

"Take me through it," Pierce demanded. "Moment by moment."

"I shut out the lights," Marsh told him. "I was getting the desk ready, locking the drawers and such, so I could crash. That's when I saw him go into his room. I knew you wanted to talk to him, so I called. I talked to some sleepy cop, who said he'd get you the message. About a minute after I hung up, Smith left his room and walked away."

"What was he wearing?"

"It was dark, but I think it was the same coat as before. or something like it."

"Was he carrying anything?"

"Not on the way in, but it looked like he had something in his hands when he left."

Pierce waved at him. "Let's see the room."

Marsh didn't argue. He grabbed the key and led them to 107. He unlocked the door and stepped aside. Pierce and Salter entered and looked around. The bed was untouched, looking the same as it had the last time they were there.

"No magazine," Salter said, "or the other stuff."

Pierce pressed his lips together. "He's cleaning up after himself."

***

Pierce shook a cigarette free from the pack and pulled it out with his lips.

"What do we do now?" Salter asked.

Pierce flicked the lighter and inhaled. The smoke bit into his lungs as he stared at the now vacant unit 107. He dropped back against his car and stared at the motel.

The rookie shifted in his stance. His eyes darted around, seemingly anxious to run after a killer he had no bead on. Pierce knew the feeling. He'd felt the same emotion many times in his life—in the war, on patrol, and as a new detective.

Pierce exhaled. He rolled the cigarette between his thumb and forefinger. "We must have gotten close."

Salter's brow furrowed. "You mean we found Smith?"

"Maybe."

"I bet it was Dr. Andrews." He smiled as he nodded. "He's got criminal written all over that smug face of his."

Pierce frowned. "Don't do that."

"Do what?"

"Presuppose."

"You saw how he acted." Salter excitedly waved his hands, like a kid trying to convince his parents to let him have an extra piece of cake. "He looked guilty."

"That's different than being guilty."

The rookie's shoulders slumped. "I guess."

Pierce thought about the anonymous call that mentioned someone named Andrew. Could it have been Andrews? He frowned as he smoked. Even if he took the unknown caller at face value, what did it prove? He already knew Andrews frequented the hustlers, even though he denied it. Going back at him with nothing more than an unidentified accuser was a losing proposition. Pierce wasn't interested in making things worse for himself.

He looked up to room 107 again. "Maybe Smith wasn't even someone we interviewed. Perhaps Smith was a friend of theirs—a confidant." As an afterthought, the detective added, "Or a relative."

Salter stared at him. "If that's true, then we're nowhere."

Pierce inhaled on the cigarette. "That's not true. We're close. Real close."

***

Pierce had three folders open on his desk—the thick 1951 Etherton file, the Hermitage case he'd taken from Barenz and Fletcher, and the Dorsey file which had started this recent mess. Salter sat in the side chair with his notebook open.

"May I see the Hermitage file?" Salter asked.

Pierce closed the folder and handed it to him. "Something come to mind?"

The rookie shook his head. "Not really." He spread the folder across his lap. "Just want a better look at it."

Pierce moved the remaining folders closer together on the desk and stared at them.

He felt stuck. In a different situation, he'd close all the files and work on another one of his cases. He had a couple that could use his attention. Pierce had found throughout his career as a detective that taking his mind off one case, even for a short period, would allow his unconscious mind to work on the one bothering him. Even if it didn't, when he returned to it, he saw the case with fresh eyes.

Unfortunately, he'd written a check Sergeant Fadelin would cash in two days—putting Barenz and Fletcher on the Dorsey and Hermitage cases with him. Pierce didn't trust taking his attention away from the recent homosexual murders. He didn't want to work with SPD's version of Abbott and Costello for a variety of reasons, the least of which was their attitude toward the victims. Pierce had a sinking suspicion those two would have let the Hermitage case languish until it was pronounced as unsolvable and been fine with it. If they got hold of the Dorsey file, they'd likely do the same. Working with those two would drive Pierce nuts.

"How many times do you read this stuff before it blurs together?" Salter asked.

Pierce eyed him.

The rookie waved his hand over the Hermitage file. "We've read these multiple times."

"Me more than you, so shut up, and read it again."

They fell silent once more as both returned to studying their respective files. Pierce wasn't sure how much the rookie was getting out of the Hermitage case after his display of attitude. Salter should be able to recite every piece of witness testimony and list the few pieces of evidence they had.

It was the same for Pierce. Sitting at the desk was more an act of discipline than anything else. He could get up and run around, but the wasted energy would serve no purpose.

The desk phone rang, and Pierce answered. It was Gloria Amherst.

"George is hoping you'll come by," she said.

"Is everything okay?"

"Everything's fine. He'd like to hear more about you know what."

Pierce didn't feel like rehashing the case right then, especially with his old partner. Things felt at a standstill and giving air to the words would make his hopelessness feel more real. "I'll stop by tomorrow. Is that okay?"

"Oh, sure, Walter," Gloria said. "That'll be swell. We'll see you then."

They ended the call.

Salter watched him. "Was that a lead?"

Pierce stood. "Keep reading."

"Where are you going?"

"You're not my mother."

***

Pierce left the Public Safety Building. He wandered aimlessly around its exterior with his hands shoved into his pockets. His thoughts drifted as he walked. They touched the Etherton/Smith case then bounced away to Amherst. His friend's health had declined significantly over the years since he'd left the department, but he seemed to have stabilized the past couple.

Was that the future awaiting Pierce—his body failing him after a career spent chasing criminals? Should he have chosen a different vocation—one that would have let him come home happy every night? Would that have made him a better husband?

Pierce found a bench near the sidewalk and sat. He rested an arm along its back.

A blond woman in a miniskirt walked by. Pierce guessed her to be in her early twenties with the easy gait of someone who didn't have a care in the world. He politely smiled, but she didn't pay any attention to him. Instead, her gaze remained focused ahead. Her hips swayed rhythmically as she continued down the block.

His thoughts went to Connie. He didn't need to wonder how she'd found so much success with new lovers. Women always had it easier than men—it was a truth he'd learned quickly once he got on the job. The recent liberation movement only put it on the front page of magazines. Men liked to believe they were the more promiscuous of the species, but women controlled the access. They were also better at hiding their indiscretions.

He wondered if Connie had stepped out on him during their marriage. There would have been plenty of opportunities with his late hours.

Pierce's attitude soured further. Perhaps leaving the department to clear his head wasn't a good idea.

He stood, brushed his slacks, and returned to the detectives' bullpen.

***

When he arrived at his desk, Pierce said, "Shut it down."

Salter looked up from the Dorsey file. He'd switched the cases at some point while Pierce was outside. "What?"

"Go home."

The rookie checked his watch. "It's not even five."

"You've worked plenty of overtime the last couple of days. Consider this making you even."

"But…"

"Spend some extra time with your kid," Pierce said, his tone firm.

Salter slowly closed the file. "What're you going to do?"

"I'm going home, too. See you in the morning."

Pierce turned and left the department.

***

Walter Pierce rested his forearms against the steering wheel and set his chin on the back of his hands. He'd watched Rags to Riches for the past three hours. It was shortly after ten and the joint was hopping. For an underground bar, it was much livelier than Pierce would have expected.

Perhaps the size of the crowd had something to do with the visitors to the World's Fair. Yet, how would those attending the Expo even know an underground club like this existed? It was something Pierce would have to chat about with The Vice King someday.

He didn't have a reason to observe the bar other than he felt lost in the Dorsey and Hermitage investigations. Rags to Riches was an actual location both victims had frequented. It made sense Smith went there, too. Perhaps the killer would be back. All Pierce had was a basic description of the man and the fact he sometimes wore flamboyant clothing. Would it be enough for him to find a needle in a haystack?

Probably not, but Pierce needed to do something. Even spinning his wheels in the shadows felt better than sitting home alone. Yet he didn't need to remain in the shadows.

Pierce climbed out of the car. He walked down the block and approached the entrance to Rags to Riches. A thumping bass line emanated from the building. He opened the door and stepped inside.

The club was dark but flashing colorful lights provided enough illumination for Pierce to see. The bar was full of men and women, although everyone seemed paired up with the same sex.

"You're in the wrong place, Jack," a heavy male voice off to his right said.

A large Negro with a bodybuilder's physique stepped out of a pocket of darkness. His black T-shirt was tight around his chest and biceps. His nose was flat, and his afro was large.

Pierce pulled his suit jacket to the side to reveal his gun and badge.

"Nothing illegal here," the bouncer said.

"Didn't say there was."

The bouncer's face tightened. "Your face says otherwise."

Pierce cocked his head.

"In case you forgot, homosexuality ain't illegal."

Technically, the man was right. Homosexuality wasn't illegal, but sodomy still was. Yet with how the country was changing, Pierce wondered how long that law would stand.

"You're misreading me," Pierce said. "I'm looking for someone."

"Aren't we all?" The Negro smiled without joy. "Who you looking for?"

"Dr. Smith."

"Doesn't ring a bell."

"Gray hair. Red tweed jacket."

The bouncer shrugged. "Like I said."

"Mind if I look around?"

"Can I stop you?"

"No."

The Negro smirked. "Then have at it." He waved his hand toward the club. "Play nice."

Pierce didn't take offense to the threat. He could have, but it wouldn't have gotten him anywhere. The detective nodded once before wandering deeper into the establishment. The music was turned up too loud and the female singer sang much too fast. It seemed the chorus was in French but none of it made sense to Pierce.

On the dance floor, men wriggled with men while women swayed with women. Lights flashed and pulsed to the sound of the music. The scene seemed all wrong to Pierce. He turned away and studied the tables.

Clusters of men gathered at various tables while women did the same. It seemed like a playground, where boys and girls naturally separated by their sexes. Only this playground came with grown-up ramifications.

There were three gray-haired men in the establishment, but none wore a red tweed jacket. However, that was a garment that could be easily abandoned. None of the older men even glanced his way, they were too involved with their male counterparts, all of whom were significantly younger.

Pierce could make a scene and ask them for identification. Instead, he studied them closely.

None of them looked remotely like Etherton. Two were quickly dismissed as being a close fit to the man described as Smith—one was rather short, and the other was fat. The third, however, fit the stature, but he was rather ugly. He couldn't imagine the Spotlight Motel's clerk calling this man handsome.

The music changed to some other irritating song. All the laughing and dancing by the club's patrons annoyed Pierce.

Everyone seemed to be happy except him.

***

Mrs. Macy didn't greet Pierce when he entered the lobby of his apartment building. He quietly closed the door and went up to his unit. He considered having a beer and something to eat, but his foul mood negated either. He simply took off his clothes and went to bed. Maybe a good night's rest would equal a better day's output tomorrow.

Pierce lay in the darkness. Any time a thought or worry came to him, he mentally batted it away. It took some time, but eventually the sweet caress of fatigue enveloped Pierce. Sleep wouldn't be far off.

A gunshot brought him awake, and Pierce realized immediately where he was.

He was back in Okinawa, pinned down by the Japanese. Pierce and his squad had gotten separated from their platoon during a firefight. He and his men had begun to claw their way back, one bloody gun battle at a time, but most of the squad had been wiped out—only Pierce and Claude Beetner remained.

Tanks fired rounds off in the distance. Warships sitting off the coast added to the barrage. The sound of deadly small arms fire seemed like annoying flies in comparison.

A single Jap soldier snuck up behind them, using a nearby tree for concealment. Had the Jap soldier had any rounds left in his rifle, both Pierce and Claude likely would have died. However, the enemy combatant was down to only his bayonet.

Pierce heard the man too late, but Claude hadn't. He jumped between Pierce and the Jap soldier just as the enemy thrust his bayonet. Pierce turned in time to hear Claude squeal.

The Jap yelled something guttural as he tried to yank his rifle loose from Claude's torso. However, Claude held onto the enemy's weapon, not letting the bayonet slide out of his chest. Pierce shot the enemy twice—once in the heart, a second time in the throat. The Jap flopped backward, gurgling his last breaths as he drowned in his own blood.

Pierce turned his attention to his friend. Claude was stabbed in the lung, and there wasn't anything he could do about the wound. Both he and Claude had used the bandages they carried on other squad mates who were now dead.

Claude needed help. The two of them were three hundred yards from the rest of the unit and the medic. A choice had to be made. For Pierce, it was an easy one. He slung his rifle over his shoulder and lifted his friend.

"Leave me," Claude said. Blood spilled from his lips as he spoke.

Gunfire erupted as Pierce stood with his friend cradled in his arms. Pierce didn't pray as he ran. Instead, he counted steps. *One. Two. Three.* He fell at seventy-two and Claude cried out in anguish.

Tank cannons continued to fire as did those from the warships. Explosions erupted in the distance. The annoying buzz of small arms gunfire lingered.

Pierce reached for Claude.

"No," his friend whispered and weakly pushed away Pierce's hands. He coughed dark blood.

"Stop it," Pierce said. He hefted Claude once more into his arms.

Pierce returned to counting as he ran. *One. Two. Three.*

Rounds whizzed by them until Pierce's foot caught on a tree branch and he tumbled onto Claude.

"Hang in there," Pierce said, but his friend didn't answer.

They only had fifty yards to go.

Pierce once again lifted his friend. Claude felt heavier than before, but Pierce couldn't worry about that now. His legs churned, and he didn't bother counting the steps. He could see the unit up ahead.

American GIs were engaged in a heavy firefight as Imperial Japanese soldiers attacked with their bayonets out. Several men stumbled around in apparent confusion, like childlike zombies. Pierce had seen that behavior before, and it meant one of two things. Either a man had reached his emotional limits and had snapped—battle fatigue, they called it—or an artillery shell had landed near enough to concuss the soldier. Either event brought on the same result. Confusion. Slow wits. Both were death sentences on the battlefield. He'd seen men wander into the line of fire with that identical expression on their faces. He couldn't worry about them now. Only Claude was his concern.

If any of the enemy soldiers noticed Pierce running, they could divert toward him. He ran as if two lives depended on it. When Pierce made it all the way back to behind his unit's line, he screamed, "Medic! Medic!"

He set his friend down and stared at him in horror.

Basil Pershing, clothed in the uniform of a Korean War GI, clutched at his bloody chest. A chunk of his head was missing, and his eyes were wide in shock. "Pierce!" Pershing cried.

He reached for the wounded man. "I'm here."

Pershing stared intently at Pierce. "Why didn't you save me?" He grabbed Pierce by the shirt. "Why?"

Pierce snapped awake, bathed in a cold sweat. He stared into the darkness for a moment, then left the bed and went into the kitchen.

It was a stupid idea to try to go to sleep without having a beer.

Chapter 29

Pierce sipped coffee as he flipped through the Etherton file. His head hurt and an unlit cigarette shook between the fingers holding the mug. He was waiting for the aspirin to kick in.

Salter dropped into the chair next to him. "You beat me."

"Uh-huh." His gaze cut to the rookie. "Can't you borrow a suit from anyone else?"

Salter rubbed his hands down the lapels. "It's the only one I've got."

Pierce grunted. "Probably bought it for church."

"Mostly, yeah. At least, I'm getting my money's worth out of it now. I've worn it more this week than the whole year."

"Christ."

Pierce forgot what it was like to be a rookie. To have little cash available and struggle to make ends meet. Plus, Salter had a kid to worry about. He and Connie didn't have any children but that didn't stop Pierce from knowing how expensive it could be.

"If we're going to do this for the whole of Expo," Pierce said, "you need a couple more suits."

"I know," said Salter. "You told me already."

Pierce rubbed his eyes, wishing the aspirin's effect would hurry. He recalled the conversation now. His head was fuzzy from the hangover, was all. "I remember. I'm reminding you."

"You don't have to. I plan on going to the haberdashery right after I have some bread."

"Don't wait that long. You can't be tramping around in the same suit until then. Go after work tonight."

"Where do I get the money for that?"

"Borrow from someone or put it on a credit card."

Salter nodded.

"Be conservative. None of that polyester bullshit like Barenz and Fletcher, and nothing denim either."

The rookie appeared disappointed.

"I'm serious. You need to look professional out there. Not like some bozo on The Sonny & Cher Show."

"Yeah, okay." Salter stood. "Mind if I get some coffee?"

Pierce handed the rookie his mug. "Top mine off while you're at it."

The rookie was only gone a minute when the phone rang. Pierce let it ring twice before lifting the receiver.

"Detective Pierce," he said.

"Hi, yes. This is Basil Pershing. I hope I'm not bothering you."

The image of a wounded and bloody Pershing on his nightmare battlefield came back to Pierce. "Not a bother. No."

"Well, this is a bit embarrassing."

Why didn't you save me?

Pierce leaned forward. "Go ahead."

Pershing cleared his throat. "I think I might have been hasty yesterday."

"About what?"

"About Michael Andrews. You see, I've been giving it some thought. A lot of thought, actually."

Pierce looked at the ceiling. His stomach roiled. He'd drank too much after the nightmare.

Pershing continued. "I'm thinking it might be him—Dr. Etherton."

Salter came into Pierce's peripheral vision. The rookie set the mug on the desk in front of Pierce.

Pierce pulled the coffee closer. "Maybe you're mixed up, Doctor."

"You're thinking it was because your junior suggested it, aren't you?"

"That crossed my mind."

The rookie's brow furrowed as he watched Pierce.

Pershing chuckled lightly on the other end of the telephone. "That crossed my mind, too. Believe me. I spent most of the night worried about it. Could I be pointing the finger at an innocent man? I don't think so."

Pierce stared into his coffee. "You think Andrews is Etherton."

"I do, but I'd love to be proven wrong. I can't get one thought out of my head."

"Which is what?"

"He's seen me. If Andrews is Dr. Etherton like I think he is, he's going to come after me."

Why didn't you save me?

Pierce sighed. "We'll look into him."

"Will you?" Pershing sighed with relief. "I can't thank you enough."

***

Hazel Thompson leaned over the Records counter. "What can I help you with today, Walter?"

She wore a simple one-piece red dress with a white belt around her waist. The white buttons should have run all the way up to her neck, but one remained undone, revealing more cleavage than was appropriate for the workplace.

Pierce did his best not to look. Salter, on the other hand, stared unabashedly.

"We need anything and everything you can find on Dr. Michael Andrews."

"Who's he?"

"A person of interest in a homicide. It's important."

Hazel casually reached for a Records Request form, but she never took her eyes from Pierce. "You know who else is a person of interest?"

Pierce glanced at Salter. The rookie continued to stare at Hazel's chest. Pierce handed the form to the rookie. "Go over there and fill it out. Bring it back when you're done."

Salter looked up, surprised to be given an assignment. "Yeah?" He hurried away from the counter.

When it was just the two of them, Pierce said, "Now, Hazel…"

She frowned. "Don't start, Walter."

"All I was going to say is I'm unavailable."

"That's what you were going to say?"

"Yes."

"So, when your divorce is final…?" Her question hung in the air.

Pierce scratched his chin. "I guess I won't have an excuse any longer."

Hazel smiled. "You play hard to get better than any man I've ever met."

"I imagine most men don't play hard to get with you."

"Ain't that the truth."

Salter returned with the form. He handed it to Pierce who gave it a quick once over before passing it on to Hazel.

"Give us a holler if you find anything," he said.

"It'll be my pleasure."

***

Pierce and Salter returned to the bullpen.

Salter dropped into the chair next to Pierce's desk, but Pierce remained standing. His gaze darted to Sergeant Fadelin's office. The sergeant was hunkered over his desk, hastily scribbling on something. Pierce next checked out Barenz and Fletcher. Those two monkeys were huddled together, snickering over something like a couple of rejected cast members from Laugh In.

The clock was ticking, Pierce thought. He didn't want to sit at his desk, waiting for something to happen. He wanted to shake a tree and see if anything came loose. Right now, the only tree he had to shake was Dr. Michael Andrews.

"Let's go," Pierce whispered. He spun on his heel and left the Detectives' Office.

***

"This is police harassment!" Dr. Andrews yelled.

Pierce hadn't even finished his third knock before the man opened the door and began shouting.

He and Salter stood together on the front porch of the Andrews home.

The doctor stood in the doorway. His hair was wet and shaving cream covered half his face. He wore a thigh-length bathrobe and leather slippers. He held a black telephone in his left hand while the receiver was tucked between his chin and shoulder. A cord ran to the nearby wall.

"Sir," Pierce said. "We'd like to follow-up on a couple of things."

Andrews angrily spun the rotary dial on the phone while he hollered. "I know my rights, you sons of bitches!"

Another spin of the dial.

"My taxes pay your salaries!"

Salter glanced around, clearly worried by the implications of a doctor screaming harassment.

"My attorney will have your fucking badges!" One more spin. "When he gets done with you, you'll shit blood!"

"We'd like to know where you were—"

"Get off my property!" Andrews screamed. "You see they're on my property, don't you?"

Pierce glanced over his shoulder. Neighbors exited their homes to see what was happening.

"It's the gestapo!" the doctor yelled as he spun the dial again. "Don't trust the cops!"

Salter's hand slipped into the right pocket of his suit jacket.

Pierce reached out and lightly touched the rookie. He shook his head.

Dr. Andrews jerked his head toward the telephone receiver. "Hello? Yes. This is Doctor Andrews. I need to speak with Charles. Because the fucking cops are here, that's why. Yes, I'll hold." Andrews pointed the receiver at Pierce. "You've had it now, buddy. Your ass is grass."

Pierce pulled his business card from his pocket and extended it to the doctor. "Just so he spells my name right."

***

Pierce slammed the door and started the engine. Salter dropped into the passenger seat. The car lurched forward before the rookie could shut his door. Salter reached for it and pulled it closed.

"Andrews got under your skin?" the rookie asked.

"No," Pierce lied. His hands tightened around the steering wheel.

Salter turned in his seat. He held onto the dashboard to stabilize himself as Pierce weaved the car through the neighborhood. "It's him, right? He's Smith. He's the killer."

"We don't know that." Pierce's face warmed.

"If he's not Smith, why's he acting like that?"

Pierce strangled the steering wheel. "People are assholes."

Salter stared at him.

They came to a Stop sign and Pierce halted the car. He eyed the rookie.

"Listen, kid. There are a lot of reasons people do the things they do. Not all of them have to do with them being guilty of a crime. Maybe Andrews had some run in with the law when he was younger. Perhaps his father was a cop who smacked him around, so he hates anyone with a badge."

A car pulled up behind them and Salter turned to check it out.

Pierce continued. "Andrews might not be Smith. He could just be an asshole. We've got to be careful in our assumptions."

322

Salter flopped in his seat. "There's a car behind us."

"I know. I heard." Pierce stomped on the accelerator and the Chevy zoomed through the intersection.

"All that bluster could be a smokescreen," Salter said.

Pierce nodded slowly. "Could be."

The rookie turned hopefully to the detective. "So it might be him?"

"We've got to be sure."

"How do we do that? Set up a stakeout or something?"

"Maybe."

The in-car radio crackled, and a female dispatcher called for Pierce. He lifted the microphone and said, "Go ahead."

"*Please call your supervisor as soon as possible,*" the dispatcher said. "*Subject matter related to your current investigation.*"

"Copy." He returned the microphone to the dashboard.

"That was fast," Salter said.

"What is?"

"The doctor's lawyer calling Sergeant Fadelin."

Pierce hadn't thought of that.

The nearest call box was mid-block near Grand Boulevard and Eighteenth Street near Manito Park. Basil Pershing didn't live too far from this location. Pierce pulled into the parking lot and got out. He lifted the receiver and paused, steeling himself for an ass-chewing from Fadelin. Pierce called the department and was routed to the sergeant's desk.

"Where you at?" Fadelin asked.

"The South Hill."

"Doing what?"

Pierce rested his hand on the call box's cover. Maybe this wasn't about his dust-up with Andrews. "We're following up on the Dorsey and Hermitage murders."

"How's it going?"

"We're making headway."

"Tick-tock," said Fadelin. "If you don't solve it by tomorrow, I'm bringing in Barenz and Fletcher to help."

"Threats."

"Not a threat. A promise."

Pierce glanced back to check on the car. Salter watched him with curiosity. Pierce turned back to the phone and pinched the bridge of his nose. "Is this why you called?"

"No. I can kick you in the testes anytime. A lead on the homo killings came in."

"How'd you get it?"

"He asked for you by name. Said you already interviewed him. Since you're out of the bullpen, the desk sergeant sent it to me."

Pierce straightened. "This caller give you a name?"

"Sure did," the sergeant said. "Danny Kerley. He sounded like a real fruit."

***

Danny Kerley lived in a studio apartment on East Trent Avenue, just outside of downtown. He answered the door after the second knock. Kerley stood in the doorway. He wore a pair of faded blue jeans and nothing else. He was a thin man with pale skin. Several bruises covered his torso.

The stench of marijuana drifted out of the apartment along with some screechy guitar music.

Kerley's eyelids drooped as he considered Salter who stood slightly behind Pierce. "Spokane's Finest."

Pierce also detected an odor of beer emanating from the man. He frowned. This already seemed like a waste of time. "You called?"

"I was assaulted," Kerley said.

"By who?"

"Him." Kerley lifted his chin toward Salter while his finger pointed to a fist-sized bruise in his abdomen. "He hit me here."

"That was two days ago," Pierce said.

"So? He still hit me." Kerley glared at Salter. "That's police brutality."

"File a complaint. We're not here for games." Pierce turned and pushed Salter down the hall. The rookie hung his head and allowed himself to be guided from the building.

"Wait," Kerley called.

"You had your chance," Pierce said over his shoulder.

"Dr. Andrews," Kerley shouted. "He's the other one who hit me."

Pierce stopped and turned. Salter moved closer to his shoulder.

Kerley stepped into the hallway. "Two nights ago. The bastard took it too far."

"Where did you meet?" Pierce asked as he walked back down the hall.

"Rags to Riches. In the alley."

"He picked you up?"

Kerley nodded.

"Where did you go?" Pierce asked.

"Some motel on Sunset Highway, I think."

"You think? Did you get the name?"

Kerley's face scrunched. "The Twilight?"

Pierce knew the business. It was a motor lodge at the edge of town on the old highway. It had fallen into disrepair over the years and now rented rooms by the hour.

"You don't sound so sure," Pierce said.

"I'm sure."

"What happened?"

Kerley crossed his arms over his bare chest. "He wanted to get it on, and I said I wanted to get paid first. That's when he started hitting me."

"You're admitting to prostitution?" Pierce asked.

"I'm admitting to getting my ass kicked." Kerley ran his fingers through his hair, then his eyes cut away toward his apartment.

"How'd you learn his name?"

Kerley nodded twice. "He put his wallet down when he went to the bathroom."

Pierce stared at him in disbelief. "He just plopped his wallet on the table and went to the can?" He shook his head. "No one does that."

Kerley froze momentarily. Pierce could see the gears moving behind the hustler's eyes.

"Okay," he admitted. "We were already naked. His pants were hung over the chair. The wallet was in the back pocket. He went to the bathroom—"

"You got naked before getting paid?" Pierce interrupted.

Kerley crossed his arms. "Are you going to let me tell this story?"

"I don't want a story. I want the truth."

"Fine." Kerley shifted on his feet and looked away. "The truth is, we got inside the room and had a few nice moments, if you follow. I let him get naked before I insisted on getting paid. I do that because most guys could care less about money at that point. They just want to get off. He said he had to use the bathroom first. While he was in there, I fished out his wallet and that's when I saw his driver's license." He brought his gaze back to Pierce. "It said Dr. Michael Andrews."

"You saw doctor on his license?"

Kerley swallowed with some difficulty. "No."

"Then how did you know he was a doctor?"

"He said to call him that."

"Just doctor?"

Kerley rolled his eyes. "No. He wanted me to call him, Dr. Mike. You know, like Dr. John, the Night Tripper?"

Pierce had no idea what the man was talking about. He eyed Salter who nodded his understanding.

"I thought he was cool," Kerley said, "until he hit me."

Pierce asked, "When did he start hitting you?"

Kerley's eyes narrowed.

"Before or after you tried to rip him off?"

"I didn't try to rip him off." Kerley's lips pursed. "What kind of question is that?"

"When did he hit you?" Pierce repeated.

"After he came out of the bathroom. I said pay me and he hit me instead."

Pierce studied the bruises on Kerley's torso. They were consistent with the bruising on the Dorsey and Hermitage corpses. "Did he try to hit your face?"

Kerley shook his head. "Not really."

Salter leaned against the wall and folded his arms over his chest.

"Did you hit him?" Pierce asked. "Did you leave any marks?"

Kerley nodded. "I hit him once."

"Where?"

"On the back. With a lamp. He fell to the ground. That's when I grabbed my pants and took off."

"Why didn't you call the police right then?" Pierce asked.

"And admit to prostitution?" Kerley smirked. "No, I called in and told some cop about it but didn't give my name."

Pierce thought back to the anonymous tip Sergeant Hatcher took. He chalked up the differences between that message and Kerley's account to the desk sergeant's poor note-taking. "No one is going to arrest an assault victim for prostitution," he said.

Kerley eyed him doubtfully. "Yeah, right. Even you brought it up. Not every cop in your department is as understanding as you." His eyes cut to Salter, and he tapped the bruise on his abdomen.

Salter looked away.

Pierce asked, "If you see this man again, could you pick him out of lineup?"

Kerley licked his lips. "Yeah, sure."

"You're confident?"

"Oh, yeah."

Pierce cocked his head. "Because you don't seem so."

"Hey, man," Kerley said. "The guy just beat me up. I'm not in a hurry to be in the same room with him again."

"All right." Pierce scratched his chin. "We're gonna have a photographer come around and get some pictures of your bruises. Don't go anywhere for a while."

"Where am I gonna go?" He waved a hand in front of his bruised chest. "Who's gonna wanna pay for this now?"

***

They sat in the car outside Kerley's apartment. Pierce put the key in the ignition but didn't start it. He let his mind work through the problem.

"What do you think?" Salter asked, interrupting his thoughts. "Should we go see Andrews again?"

Pierce stared straight ahead. "If he has an injury on his back consistent with the strike that Kerley described, then we can arrest him and get a search warrant for his house."

"Do you think he'll just show us his back?"

His eyes slid to the rookie. "Not a chance in hell."

"So how do we—"

"Let me worry about that." Pierce turned the ignition key and the engine rumbled to life. He grabbed the microphone and called for dispatch.

The operator repeated his call sign and said, "*Go ahead.*"

"We need photographs of Danny Kerley, an assault victim." Pierce provided the man's address.

"Copy," the dispatcher said.

"What's the ETA on that?" Pierce asked.

There was a pause before the dispatcher responded. "*Might be a while. Photographer is en route to a collision scene up north. Also, please contact your supervisor on a personal matter.*"

Now what? Pierce thought. He closed his eyes. Why couldn't they just broadcast some of this stuff over the air? It would make life so much easier for cops in the cars. He pressed the transmit button. "Copy."

The nearest call box was a mile away. They drove to it in silence. Pierce's initial thought was that Andrews's lawyer had finally called the department. But the dispatcher said it was a personal matter. That had ominous tones to it. His parents were long gone, and he didn't have any siblings. That left Connie. Did something happen to her? Even though they were getting divorced, she was still his wife and he loved her.

Pierce parked the car and got out. Salter watched him with concerned eyes. He dialed the department and asked for Sergeant Fadelin. When his supervisor answered, Pierce tried to play off his concerns by saying, "Twice in one day. Some sort of record."

"It's Amherst," Fadelin said. "His wife called."

"What happened?"

"He had another stroke. He's at Sacred Heart right now. He's not supposed to make it through the night."

Pierce stared at the whiskey bottle in the corner of the call box. Memories of George Amherst flooded back to him.

"I'm sorry, Walter," Fadelin said. "I know he's your friend."

Pierce hung up without responding.

***

Walter Pierce stepped into the hospital room with Gus Salter on his heels.

George Amherst lay motionless on the only bed in the room. Various tubes ran from his nose, mouth, and arms. Machines beeped nearby, monitoring his heart.

The window shades were up, and the sun shone across George's pale, haggard face.

Gloria Amherst hunched over the bed with her cheek pressed into her husband's hand. She opened her eyes when she heard Pierce enter. She stood and wiped the tears away from her face.

"Walter," she said.

"I just heard."

He held out a hand, but she ignored it and hugged him instead. Gloria shook as she wept silently. Pierce didn't utter any words of encouragement. He wasn't sure of the proper decorum in this situation. She wasn't his wife.

Behind him, Salter shifted about. Pierce wanted to tell the rookie to stand still but figured that would be worse than the idiot moving aimlessly around.

Gloria sniffled and pushed back. She pulled a Kleenex from the pocket of her dress and wiped her nose. "Thank you for coming."

"I'm sorry I didn't come by yesterday."

"It's okay." Her lips twisted as she seemingly struggled to hold back more tears.

"Had I known…" His thought hung in the air.

"Had we known," Gloria said, "I would have insisted."

Pierce gently rubbed her upper arms. "Is there anything I can do?"

"Just being here is enough. George always said he enjoyed working with you the most."

"He did?"

She nodded. "He used to tell me he learned so much from you."

Pierce furrowed his brow. "He was the senior detective. I learned from him."

"Not in his eyes." She squeezed Pierce's hand. "The way he told it, you saved his career. He could never thank you enough."

Pierce flexed his jaw.

"He wouldn't tell you that, of course." Gloria slid her arm around Pierce's waist and rested her head against his chest. "Ol' hardheaded George."

"Ain't that the truth."

"Will you stay with us awhile, Walter?" She looked up at him.

"Sure. We got nowhere to be." His gaze slid to Salter. "You can take off if you want."

The rookie settled into a chair. "It's okay. I'm your partner. That's what we do, right?"

Pierce nodded, then faced George. "That's what we do."

***

It was almost seven o'clock. The sun hung just above the horizon and a light on the bedside table illuminated the room. The television hanging from the ceiling silently ran an episode of *Movin' On,* some show about a trucker that Salter seemed interested in.

Gloria sat in a chair next to George's bed, her eyes rarely leaving her husband. The heart monitor continued its slow methodic beep near her head. Pierce thought the sound would have driven him mad had he been so close to it.

Nurses occasionally stopped in and checked on George. After doing so, they would make a note in his chart, probably that they visited the patient. Everyone needed a paper trail these days.

Pierce leaned forward and rested his forearms on his knees. He lowered his head. Exhaustion began to overwhelm him. It had been a long few days.

The door opened and Hazel Thompson entered. She was dressed differently than she had been at the department. She now wore a blue blouse with long white slacks. She clutched a manilla folder to her chest.

Salter stood and smiled. "Ma'am," he said.

Pierce slowly rose. "Hazel."

"I'm sorry to interrupt," she whispered. Her eyes landed on Gloria. "Really sorry." Hazel's attention returned to Pierce. "You asked for this information, and said it was important, so I wanted to get it to you right away."

"We'll step outside," Pierce said.

"No," Gloria said. "Whatever it is, George would like to hear it."

Pierce held out his hand to Hazel and she gave him the folder. He opened it and found several pages of printouts regarding Dr. Michael Andrews. There were also photocopies of three newspaper clippings.

"What's all this?" Pierce asked.

Hazel tapped the small articles. "I called a friend of mine at the *Chronicle* and asked a favor."

"A friend?"

"Yes, and you're gonna owe *her* dinner for what *she* found."

Pierce spread the clippings apart and scanned them. Salter peered over his shoulder.

"They're write-ups about Andrews," Hazel said. "You know, human interest stuff. Back when they did the new-boy-in-town fluff pieces."

"Look at this." Pierce pointed at a paragraph in the first clipping. "It says here that Andrews grew up in an orphanage in Athol."

"Idaho?" Salter asked.

"Massachusetts."

"Well, check this out," the rookie said. He tapped another clipping. "He earned his doctoral degree from Brandeis University. Where the hell is that?"

Pierce shrugged.

Hazel shook her head.

"Isn't that where Eleanor Roosevelt went to college?" Gloria asked. "I don't know where it is, but I think that's where she went."

"Was your friend a reporter?" Pierce asked. "Did she confirm this stuff?"

"She works in their Archives section." She smiled. "Sort of like me." Her eyes cut to Gloria and her expression melted.

Pierce mumbled to himself. An orphan from the other side of the country would be perfect cover for Etherton posing as

Andrews. Valid orphan and graduation records would certainly go a long way in proving that impersonation or Andrews's authenticity. Anyone could claim to be something when building a new identity. It was the proper credentials that established one's validity.

They'd need to verify Andrews's attendance at medical school, Pierce thought. Get hold of the orphanage records. He squinted.

"What is it?" Salter asked.

"Death certificates," he said. "We'll need to search for those, too. Make sure Etherton didn't take some dead kid's name."

Salter's mouth hung open momentarily, then he nodded in understanding.

"I can help with that," Hazel said.

"Okay," Pierce muttered distractedly. He checked the printouts she brought. Michael Edward Andrews was roughly the same height and age as Dr. Karl Etherton. He had no local law enforcement history prior to 1953 but he suddenly began appearing frequently after that. Andrews's record was extensive as a complainant, a victim, and a suspect.

There were complaints filed against his neighbors, clients, and business owners. He was listed as a victim in three assaults and two fraud cases. He was a suspect in two harassment cases, one malicious mischief incident, an assault, and the lewd conduct that landed him on Pierce's radar in the first place. However, he'd never been convicted of any charge.

Andrews also was cited for speeding seven times and had received thirteen parking infractions.

Pierce tapped the list of incidents. If Andrews was Etherton in disguise, wouldn't he go out of his way to keep a low profile?

Maybe he couldn't, Pierce decided. He certainly read like a man unhinged.

Pierce closed the file and handed it to Salter. The rookie took it and returned to his seat, the TV show forgotten.

"Thank you," Pierce said to Hazel.

"You're welcome."

She pulled a folded note from the pocket of her dress and handed it discreetly to Pierce. He opened it. On it was her phone number.

"In case you want to talk," she whispered. "No pressure."

He slipped the paper into his pocket. Pierce was about to say thank you, but the telephone on the stand next to the bed rang loudly.

Gloria jumped, but she didn't move to answer it. The phone rang again.

"I'll get it," Pierce said.

He stepped around the bed and reached for the phone just as it rattled a third time. He snatched the receiver off the base.

"Hello?" he whispered.

"Detective Pierce?"

He straightened. "Yes."

"Orrie Hatcher here." The graveyard desk sergeant, Pierce thought. "I heard you were up there with Amherst. How's the old goat doing?"

"Not too well."

"Yeah, I guess we all got to punch the ticket some time."

Pierce grimaced and glanced at Gloria. He wondered if she could hear the stupid bastard on the other end of the line.

"Anyhoo, Sergeant Berg said you gave him some grief about peter puffer tips coming in slow."

"Now's not the time, Orrie."

"Hey, don't bite my head off, Walter. If you don't care about some pole jockey claiming a doctor's about to kill him then you can find out about it tomorrow."

Pierce pressed the receiver harder into his ear. "What are you talking about?"

Hatcher chuckled. "It's your usual weirdo stuff. Some homo-sounding fella just called in. Said a doctor was going all schizo and losing his mind. Talking all Charlie Manson like. Devil this and Satan that. Said he was going to kill himself and take all the fags to hell with him. It sounded sorta bonkers, but I was gonna send a patrol unit to check it out anyway. Then I remember you bitching about tips, so— "

"What's the address?"

The sergeant read it to him. "If I remember my coordinates correctly, it's just above Cannon Hill Park."

Pierce didn't need directions. He knew the house. "We're on our way." He hung up. "Let's go, kid."

Salter stood.

Pierce patted his former partner on the arm. "I'm sorry, pal. We gotta go catch a killer." To Gloria, he smiled kindly. "I'm sorry."

He took a step toward the door then stopped to face Hazel. "Thank you for bringing the papers."

"Anytime."

Pierce nodded, then he and the rookie ran toward the exit.

Chapter 30

The Chevy rounded the corner hard, and Pierce accelerated. Next to him, Salter clutched the door handle to avoid sliding across the seat. Neither man wore a seat belt.

"I don't get it," Salter said, readjusting his position. Pierce had just finished relaying the sergeant's message to him.

"What's to get? Andrews is going for number three. His victim managed to get to a phone."

"But all that devil talk? That's never come up before."

Pierce tapped the brakes as he neared a stop sign. His head snapped left and right. Seeing no oncoming traffic, he blasted through the intersection without stopping. "We've never heard from any of his victims before," he reminded Salter. "We've only seen their bodies. We have no idea what he talked about before he killed them."

"So… he's crazy like Manson?" Salter somehow sounded both dubious and worried at the same time.

"I don't know." Pierce drove around a slow Oldsmobile Starfire, gunning the engine and whipping into the left lane. The woman behind the wheel of the Olds glared at him. "But we're going to find out."

Salter didn't reply. His hand dropped to his right jacket pocket.

Less than a minute later, Pierce brought the Chevy to a stop at the curb. Salter glanced out the window and pointed. "It's not this one," he said. "It's the next house over."

"This is safer," Pierce said. There was no time to lecture the rookie about officer safety when responding to a dangerous situation. He'd get all that in the police academy soon enough.

Pierce reached for the radio mic and raised dispatch. "Send a uniform to my location," he said tersely and recited the address.

"*Copy*," came the dispatcher's reply.

Before she could call a patrol car for the task, Pierce shut off the engine and the radio died with it. He got out of the car. By the time Salter did the same, Pierce was already around the front of the vehicle and to the sidewalk. As he cut across the neighbor's grass toward Andrews's house, tactical considerations ran through his mind like second nature.

Should he wait for a patrol unit?

No, he decided. No time. Sergeant Hatcher should have followed his instinct and sent uniforms when the call first came in. They were on the way now, at least.

He debated sending Salter around to watch the back of the house but rejected that plan. Leaving the rookie alone was a bad idea.

Pierce neared the house, listening for any signs of struggle inside. Out of habit, he reached for his gun. Without breaking stride, he slid his .38 from its holster and held it to his side.

Soft entry or hard?

Years ago, there would have been no consideration given to knocking. An old-school cop like Amherst would have bulldozed right through the front door without knocking or having a second thought about it. However, the world had changed since 1951. Greater considerations were given toward individual freedoms. Sometimes those became obstacles to good police work.

Pierce mounted the steps to Andrews's house. Salter scrambled behind him. In his peripheral vision, Pierce saw the rookie had mirrored his own tactic, drawing his gun and holding it pointed toward the ground.

Good. If Salter followed his lead, they'd be fine.

At the door, Pierce paused. Given the phone call Sergeant Hatcher described, knocking now seemed absurd. He had enough information to justify going in without an invitation. If all of this was a hoax or a trap set by Andrews, Pierce was ready to face down the results later.

An image of Basil Pershing, uniform-clad and bleeding in his arms, flashed through Pierce's mind.

Why didn't you save me?

Josephine Banfield and Shirley Jensen could very well shout the same question at him. In his dreams, they sometimes did.

"Not this time," muttered Pierce. He tensed to kick in the door, then stopped to try the handle first. Surprisingly, the heavy lever dropped. Pierce gently pushed and the front door swung open a crack.

"Can we go in?" Salter asked in a whisper from behind him. "Don't we need a warrant?"

Another image struck Pierce—the horrific dungeon in Etherton's old house.

"I hear someone calling for help," Pierce said, his voice low.

"I don't hear anything," Salter said, sounding confused.

"Sure, you do." Pierce pushed the door the rest of the way open. The heavy wood made no sound as it swung on its hinges. Inside was a carpeted foyer with spare furnishings, all modern in style. A large, minimalistic clock hung on the wall. The black and silver monstrosity looked like something that belonged at a train station in a science fiction movie. The wide staircase in the center of the room went upstairs. Pierce saw a doorway to his left and another to the right. A hallway next to the stairs led deeper into the house.

"Keep your eyes peeled," he instructed Salter and stepped over the threshold.

Pierce scanned the foyer. The door to the right was closed but the left one was open. It led to a sitting room. He carefully leaned through the doorway to examine the entire space. It was empty, but something else caught his eye.

Tossed casually over the back of a chair was a red tweed jacket.

Pierce's pulse quickened.

The man in the red tweed jacket was seen with both Hermitage and Dorsey. He was probably the one who killed him. Now, the red tweed was here in Andrews's home. It was his jacket.

Andrews *was* Smith. Too much of a coincidence, him having that same jacket and being part of the gay scene.

Which meant Andrews murdered those two young men.

Pierce stepped back into the foyer. He made for the closed door on the right. As he crossed the carpeted floor, he heard movement near the rear of the house. He wheeled around and leveled his gun in that direction but saw nothing.

Another memory struck him, this one a fact. Etherton ran out the back of his house in 1951.

That wasn't going to happen again, Pierce resolved.

He ignored the closed door, which probably led to the kitchen. He focused on the direction he'd heard the noise. With Salter trailing several feet behind him, Pierce crept down the hallway. He strained his ears for any sound. All he could hear was the ticking of the clock in the foyer and Salter's excited breathing.

Three quarters of the way down the hall, Pierce stopped at a door, which stood open a crack. He motioned for Salter to stand on the other side of the entryway. Then he pushed the door inward and stepped through.

The room resembled a studio apartment, not unlike his own. A bed in the corner. Armoire nearby. A small dining table with two chairs. Nearest the door, a single overstuffed chair and loveseat sat beside a coffee table. A paper bag sat on the table.

Servant's quarters, Pierce thought in a flash.

All these details flooded past him and then washed away in a moment when he saw the bodies.

On the floor next to the chair lay a white male on his stomach, his face turned away from them. Blood pooled around his middle. A likewise bloody knife lay a foot away.

Seated in the chair, his face bruised and battered, was Dr. Michael Andrews. He looked at Pierce with a hollow expression. No recognition registered in his eyes.

Pierce knew the look immediately. He'd seen it scores of times in the Pacific. He saw it in his dream last night.

Battle fatigue.

Or a concussion.

Pierce glanced down at the doctor's hands. His right was empty but splattered with blood.

In his left, a gun dangled loosely in his fingers.

"Doctor," Pierce said in a quiet, firm tone. He tightened the grip on his own .38. "I need you to listen to me."

Andrews cocked his head, the focus in his eyes shifting. It seemed to Pierce the man was only just now seeing him. Whether from shock or a concussion, his disconnect was severe.

"Doctor…" Pierce began, but Andrews suddenly lurched awkwardly to his feet. His arms stayed at his side.

"He's got a gun!" Salter screamed from behind him, his voice high-pitched and reedy.

Even as the words registered in Pierce's ears, the pistol tumbled out of Andrews's slack fingers and fell to the carpeted floor. In the same moment, gunshots erupted from behind Pierce. Three sharp barking explosions came from Salter's weapon. At least one struck Andrews in the chest. The doctor stumbled backward a half-step, bumped the edge of the chair, and collapsed into it. Blood streamed down his chest, drenching the man's white T-shirt.

Pierce had seen that in the war, too.

Heart shot.

Slowly, Pierce holstered his own pistol and turned toward Salter. The rookie still held the gun out at an arm's length. His hands shook as he stared down the barrel at the now-sitting dead man.

"Finger off the trigger," Pierce said in the same tone he'd used moments ago with Andrews.

Salter's quivering index finger slowly withdrew from the trigger and came to rest alongside the guard. Pierce reached out and took the gun from him. Salter's arms dropped heavily to his sides.

"I… I got him," he said.

Pierce looked over at the still form of Andrews. "You got him," he said.

Salter's already pale expression whitened further. "Where's the gun? He had a gun in his hand. I saw it."

"He dropped it," said Pierce.

Salter shifted his gaze to Pierce. "When?" he asked shakily.

"Before you shot him."

"Befo…" Salter shook his head. "But… he was going to shoot you."

"I don't think he would have." He motioned toward Andrews. "He either had a mental breakdown or a concussion."

Salter appeared stricken. He looked back and forth between Pierce and Andrews, his mouth moving long before any words spilled out. "I… I…."

Watching the rookie struggle to process what had occurred, Pierce's ire with the department's recent hiring choices, especially those with no prior military service, flared. He shifted Salter's gun into his left hand and put it into his jacket pocket. He rested his right hand onto Salter's shoulder and caught the rookie's gaze with a hard stare. When he spoke, though, his voice carried as much compassion as he could muster.

"You did good," he said softly. "How could you know he wouldn't shoot me?"

Salter's eyes misted over.

Pierce squeezed Salter's shoulder. Then he turned and moved closer to the two bodies. Andrews lay still, his seated position making it appear he had fallen asleep while watching Johnny Carson. His bloody hands sat in his lap. Pierce noticed they were both uninjured. He stopped scrutinizing Andrews and focused on the other body. He stepped around the knife, noting its blood-smeared blade.

The victim on the floor was clad only in his underwear. His torso was freshly battered from blunt force blows that would have left significant bruises had he lived. Pierce looked closer at his left hand, but all his fingers were intact.

As soon as he saw the man's profile, he recognized Richard Clark, the Purple People Eater, one of the hustlers from Queer Alley. Squatting down, Pierce checked for a pulse at Clark's neck. He held his fingers there for five long seconds and felt nothing.

Pierce stood and walked to the table. He lifted the paper bag and dumped it. Several condoms spilled out, along with a cream-colored dildo. Pierce's jaw set. He looked over at Andrews, still slumped in the chair. The bleeding had ceased. The entire front of his torso was now painted red.

"I…" Salter began, then stopped. "Oh, no," he whimpered.

Pierce returned to the rookie, who was staring at the dead man he'd shot. Pierce put an edge into his voice, one he'd heard from his platoon sergeant time and again during the war. "Listen to me," he said.

When Salter didn't tear his gaze away from Andrews, Pierce reached up and slapped him sharply. The rookie's eyes came into focus and met Pierce's.

"Listen to me," Pierce repeated. "I'm going to tell you how this happened."

****

Patrol officers arrived two minutes later. First one pair, then several. The third pair emerged from the back of the house, having entered through the unlocked back door. At Pierce's direction, the officers secured the premises, then hunted for anyone else inside. After planting Salter in the front seat of his car, Pierce joined the searching officers. He felt like he was holding his breath the entire time they moved through the house. Each door they opened, Pierce expected to find another dungeon, another body. Only when the last room was revealed to be empty of people did he feel like he could exhale again.

Sergeant Fadelin arrived next. True to form, he sought out Pierce, the senior detective, and left Salter seated in the car, staring out the windshield.

"Is this the guy?" Fadelin asked. "The homo killer?"

Pierce looked him straight in the eye. "That's a complex question, Sergeant."

"Then break it down for me."

Pierce reached for his cigarettes and offered Fadelin one. The sergeant took it and both men lit up. Once he'd inhaled and blew out the first breath of smoke, Pierce said, "I'll start with what we know is almost certainly true. Michael Andrews is the man who killed Richard Clark."

"Clark's the one on the floor inside?"

Pierce nodded. "I can also say it's most likely that Andrews is the man who has been masquerading around the gay underground as Dr. Smith. He had a room at the Spotlight Motel and he took one of the hustlers from Queer Alley to the Liberty Tavern."

"So, Andrews is Smith," Fadelin said. He drew in smoke, nodding at the revelation. "Did he kill your other two homos?"

"They're not homos," Pierce said with a quiet fierceness. "They're victims."

"Sure, but did he kill them?"

"It looks that way. M.O. is similar. Same kind of victim, same injuries to the torso. Circumstantial evidence points to him, too." Pierce tapped his ring finger, where he still wore a simple gold band. "No mutilation on this one, though."

"Sounds like you interrupted him before he could get to that."

"Maybe."

"So, you got your man." Fadelin blew out a cloud of smoke and appraised Pierce. "Is he your guy from fifty-one, though? Etherton?"

"I don't know."

"What's your gut say?"

Pierce stood still for a few moments, taking another drag while he thought. Finally, he said, "There are too many similarities for it to not be connected. Beyond that?" He shook his head. "We'll have to sift through the evidence and figure it out."

Fadelin motioned toward the car where Salter sat. "How's the kid?"

"In shock, I think." Pierce knew Fadelin had served in Korea, so he didn't need to elaborate further.

"What happened?"

Pierce took the final pull from his cigarette, then dropped it to the sidewalk and crushed it beneath his heel. "We heard sounds of distress, so we went inside. It only took a few seconds to figure out where they were, down the hall. As soon as we came through the door, Andrews saw us and raised the gun. Gus shot him."

"That's it?"

"That's it."

Fadelin eyed Pierce carefully. "Rookie beat you on the draw?"

Pierce shrugged. "Young reflexes. Besides, I was distracted, looking at the body on the floor. It all happened in a split-second."

"Split-second, huh?" Fadelin considered Pierce's words. Then he finished off his own cigarette and stepped on it, grinding it into the pavement. "Sounds to me like a righteous shoot," he said. "One less piece of shit in the world."

Pierce nodded. He couldn't argue with that.

***

After, Pierce remained next to Salter, shepherding him through Fadelin's eventual questions. Salter leaned against the closed passenger door, his hands in his pockets, shoulders slumped. He answered woodenly but his words echoed those Pierce had already spoken. For his part, Fadelin framed the questions to guide Salter's replies in that direction. Any small inconsistencies were knocked aside or ignored by the sergeant, though Pierce made mental note of them. He'd need to coach Salter better for subsequent interviews.

"I think that's enough for tonight," Fadelin finally said. He reached out and slid his hand behind Salter's neck, his thumb resting on the rookie's cheek. "You did good, Gus," he said, with a comforting squeeze.

Salter looked as if he'd been struck, but he nodded without reply.

Fadelin turned to Pierce. "His gun?"

Pierce removed the weapon from where he'd been storing it in his own left jacket pocket since the shooting. He handed it to Fadelin. "Who've we got on this?" he asked. "Not Barenz and Fletcher?"

Fadelin shook his head. "Don't worry about it, Walter. This is a varsity game. I've got it handled." He motioned toward Salter. "You'll see he gets home?"

"I will."

Fadelin walked away, already barking orders to the nearby patrol officers who were drifting around, seemingly without purpose.

"Let's go," Pierce said evenly. He started to walk around to the driver's side of the car, but Salter didn't move. Pierce stopped. "Gus," he called, a little louder. "Come on. I'll take you home."

It took another few moments before Salter roused himself. He popped open the door and lowered himself into the passenger seat.

Pierce got behind the wheel, started the engine, and pulled away from the house. He had to pick his way along slowly, avoiding police vehicles and personnel on foot, until they reached the police line stretched across the street. A sullen veteran patrol officer lifted the tape to let them pass, barely looking their way.

Once past the barrier, Pierce realized he didn't know where he was going next. He didn't know where Salter's home was.

"Where do you live?" he asked.

Salter recited an address near the Wandermere development, north of the Spokane city limits. His voice was robotic and small.

"Is your car at the station?"

Salter nodded.

"I'll get someone to ferry it out to you tomorrow, okay?'

"Sure."

"Sounds like a good job for Barenz and Fletcher," Pierce added. "If you don't mind the stench of their matching Brut cologne hanging around the interior for a month or so."

Salter didn't react to the joke.

Pierce kept driving. He cut through downtown, careful to avoid coming within view of Rags to Riches and turned north on Division. He usually wished there was a north-south freeway but, at the moment, Pierce preferred surface streets. He could think better at thirty-five miles per hour than at fifty-five.

He drove in silence. He'd already passed Francis Avenue before Salter finally spoke.

"I messed up," the rookie said, his words thick. "I messed up and I killed him."

"No," Pierce said.

"You said so, and you were right. I shot him dead as shit." He turned to look at Pierce. "I fucked up."

"No," Pierce repeated. "He was a killer. There was a dead man at his feet and a gun in his hand."

"He dropped the gun when he stood up."

"No, he didn't."

"You told me."

"It doesn't matter. Gus, you've got to keep this straight."

"Lie, you mean."

Pierce drove several blocks without speaking. Then he said, "Michael Andrews was a sadistic monster who killed three people. He didn't do it in self-defense or in war. He did it for his own sick pleasure. That makes him worse than a piece of shit. It makes him evil. You hear me, Gus? He was an evil man."

"He was an evil man with empty hands," Salter said softly.

"His hands weren't empty," insisted Pierce. "They were bloody, and he held a gun. You responded appropriately and probably saved my life. You definitely put down a murderer and there's no one who won't say good riddance to him."

Salter shook his head. He choked up as he spoke. "I never thought it'd be like this."

"Have you ever heard anyone say the end justifies the means?" Pierce asked.

"Of course. In college. Intro to Philosophy, but—"

"There is no but. He was a killer. He's dead. His victims got some measure of justice. How does you getting fired serve any good purpose? It doesn't. It just makes you another one of his victims."

Salter was quiet for a few moments. Then he murmured, "It can't be this way. It can't."

"You're shook up, that's all," Pierce told him. "It happens to everyone. You'll get a good night's sleep and feel better tomorrow."

"No," Salter said. "I don't think I'll ever feel better about this."

***

Salter's apartment was a tiny, one bedroom. Pierce walked him inside and told him to sit down on the small, ratty couch. The rookie obeyed without argument. Pierce found a six-pack of Miller High Life beer in the fridge with only one bottle missing. He grabbed one for each of them, then pulled open a couple of drawers until he found a bottle opener. After popping both tops, he returned to the living room, taking a seat at the other end of the couch. He handed one of the beers to Salter.

His partner made no move to accept it.

"Come on, Gus," Pierce urged lightly. "If there was ever a Miller Time, it's now."

"I don't want to celebrate."

"Celebrate?" He shook his head. "This isn't celebrating. It's commiserating. Now, take the goddamn beer."

After a moment, Salter reached out and took the High Life. The two men drank in silence for a while. Pierce noticed a framed photo of a woman in a tie-dyed dress, seated on porch steps, holding a toddler on her lap. He picked it up. "Is this Frida and…" He realized he didn't know Salter's son's name.

The rookie didn't answer.

Pierce examined the photo for a few moments longer. "Your boy favors his mother, but he's got your chin."

Without looking at Pierce, Salter said, "I think maybe I should tell the truth. Accept the consequences."

Pierce replaced the photo, adjusting it to the same angle as before. "You can't. You already told Fadelin what happened."

"That isn't what really happened."

"It is now. Once the lie starts, it can't be undone."

Salter shook his head in disgust. He took a swig of beer. "I could say I was confused. In shock."

"You'll still come off as a liar."

"I *am* a liar. *We're* liars."

Pierce leaned forward, letting his beer bottle dangle between his legs from his fingers. "Listen to me. Let's say you could backtrack, which you can't, but let's say you could. You're not thinking this through."

"How so?"

"Everything anyone needs to know about this case has been resolved or will be. Andrews is the killer. We stopped him. Clark will be his very last victim unless you decide to throw yourself on your sword here."

"We don't know everything," Salter argued. "What about Etherton? Is that who Andrews really is? We don't know that."

"Not yet. We'll know in a day or two when I finish the follow up. But you're missing my point, Gus. Right now, justice was served. You're a hero. If you start saying the wrong things and people start looking too closely, it all unravels. That's how a good shoot becomes a bad shoot. How a hero becomes a criminal. How a closed case becomes an open wound that never heals. One with no finality for the families of the victims. Not for you, either. And not for the department."

"Is this really how it is?" Salter asked, still sounding as if he didn't believe the events he'd just been part of.

"This is how it is," Pierce told him.

"And Andrews... or Etherton... whoever he is, do you really believe he deserved to be shot like that? Unarmed and—"

"Bloody?" Pierce asked. "With a gun in his hand, a knife on the floor, and a dead body at his feet?"

Salter soaked in his words. "He deserved it," he said, as if trying on the words for size.

"He deserved it," Pierce confirmed and tapped the neck of his bottle against the rookie's. The clink of glass on glass reverberated through the tiny apartment.

Salter didn't answer. He took another drink of beer, leaned back, and closed his eyes. "He deserved it," he whispered again, now almost like a mantra.

"He did." Pierce sipped the High Life, remembering something he'd heard only days ago, though it now had new meaning to him. "You dance with bears," he said quietly, "you get mauled."

***

Later that night, Pierce lay in his single bed, staring up at the myriad cracks in the ceiling that were barely illuminated by the moonlight spilling through the window. His body was still and anyone who saw him would be forgiven for thinking he was asleep. His mind, though, was racing.

He turned over every fact he knew, every conclusion he'd drawn, every theory he'd thought of or heard. Images flickered through his head like some kind of poorly edited "Coming Attractions" trailer shown at the movie theater.

Etherton's dungeon. Andrews in his chair, Clark at his feet. Dorsey on the banks of the river. Basil Pershing from his dreams.

Why didn't you save me?

Maybe I did, Pierce thought. Maybe Andrews was Etherton in disguise. The crazy theory could be true.

Pierce shifted his hands behind his head, underneath the pillow where it was still cool. The last thing he'd wanted was to be alone tonight. The solitude of his apartment was loud. It battered him with the reality of his own failures. Not even Mrs. Macy had been at her door to admonish him when he came home, robbing him of that welcome respite.

He couldn't call Connie. They were too far past that now. For all he knew, she wasn't alone.

He couldn't call Hazel, either. Not yet.

The near anonymity of a bar stool didn't appeal to him. Plus it was too late—all the joints were closed. He could hit one of the quiet after-hours places he knew of, but that opened up too many risks. He knew about them because they were illegal. Showing up for a drink there was no better than accepting free meals, something he'd always refused to do.

That left a return to his own kitchen table for more bottles of Olympia, or nothing.

Pierce chose nothing.

He stared at the ceiling, working out what tomorrow would look like. Now that the fire of the moment had passed, he saw the way things might go with cold clarity. Fadelin's comment about this being a varsity case wouldn't stop him from assigning Barenz and Fletcher. In fact, the way this case needed to shake out was exactly why he'd give it to them. It's what Pierce would do in his place. He wouldn't like it, but he'd hold his nose and do it anyway.

The Bobbsey Twins would buy the story he and Salter told them like it was on sale. They'd do it because it was the easiest route to finishing the work. Salter would become the hero Pierce predicted. A bad man would be dead. The public and the Expo visitors could go on with their lives without worry. All the important questions had been answered.

Except he didn't think they were.

Andrews's true identity, for one. He could still be Etherton, couldn't he?

His hands bothered Pierce, too. How he was able to pummel Clark's body without so much as a scrape to his knuckles? He tried to remember if he'd seen any injuries during their previous contacts but couldn't recall any.

Another fact clanged in his head. Why was that goddamn back door unlocked? Maybe it was nothing, but it bothered Pierce. There were still neighborhoods where people didn't lock their doors, but he knew the rich never failed to guard what was theirs. So why wasn't it secure?

Pierce lay in bed, his eyes fixed above, until he dropped off for a couple hours of broken sleep. The dreams that found him were the worst yet.

Chapter 31

Barenz and Fletcher looked even worse than Pierce felt.

The two detectives, along with Pierce, were crammed into Sergeant Fadelin's small office. With the door closed, the temperature in the room seemed to climb several degrees from the heat of their bodies. Brut cologne, body odor, and coffee breath filled Pierce's nostrils. He sipped his own coffee to mask the smell.

Fletcher was the only one who spoke besides Fadelin. Barenz sat silently, his eyes red and bleary, his chin and cheeks already covered in thick stubble. He cradled his coffee in front of him like it was the cure for cancer.

Fletcher's tired voice croaked while he spoke. He started outlining all they'd done since the shooting yesterday. Fadelin interjected occasionally to get clarification but, for the most part, Fletcher's report was uninterrupted.

There weren't any surprises at first. Even though he hadn't worked the scene himself, Pierce had experienced so many in his career that hearing Fletcher detail what he and Barenz did was like watching a movie he'd already seen, only with different actors.

The comparison stuck in his tired mind. He'd thought about movies last night, too. The disjointed Coming Attractions playing in his head. When was the last time he'd been to a movie? Done anything besides pine over Connie and grieve their lost marriage?

"Patrol found the back door open," Fletcher said, which was the first surprise of the morning, and it caught Pierce's attention.

"You're sure about that?" Pierce asked. "It was open, not unlocked?"

"I'm sure that's what they told me," Fletcher said.

Pierce thought about the sounds of movement he'd heard near the back of the house. He'd dismissed them as coming from the room where Andrews and Clark were. Now, he wondered.

"What's it matter?" Fletcher asked.

In 1951, Etherton escaped out the back door minutes before he and Amherst arrived. The approaching sirens warned him and he fled. Now, the back door was used again.

"I don't know if it matters," Pierce said, not wanting to rehash the old case with Fletcher. "I'm just confirming. Carry on."

"Carry on?" Fletcher smirked and cocked his head. "Why, thank you, your highness." He waited several seconds out of spite, and then continued.

Nothing else Fletcher said about the shooting scene surprised Pierce in the slightest. He ticked off the facts in his mind as Fletcher reported them, but it was a rote exercise.

Until the next unexpected revelation.

"By the way, when the photographer showed up to take pictures of your other victim, Kerley," Fletcher said, "he was too late."

"Too late?"

"Guy killed himself."

Pierce's eyes narrowed. "How?"

"Slit his wrists."

"That doesn't make sense," Pierce muttered.

"Sure, it does," Fletcher told him. "All these queers, they're a bunch of basket cases. This wouldn't be the first time one of them decided to check out over some emotional bullshit. Their suicide rates are like double normal guys."

Pierce ground his teeth together and said nothing. He waved for Fletcher to continue. The detective renewed his recitation, bringing events up to the present.

Then came the final surprise. Fadelin took over and explained how everything was going to be handled. Pierce listened in silence, not bothering to protest. It was clear

Fadelin had been in consultation with the brass, probably even the chief himself. Nothing Pierce said would matter.

At the end of the briefing, Fadelin asked, "Are we all understood?"

Barenz and Fletcher nodded in unison. Pierce didn't. Instead, he asked, "Who made the notification to Clark's next of kin?"

Both detectives stared at him resentfully. Only Fadelin had the decency to look embarrassed at the oversight.

"I'll handle it," Pierce said.

"Figures," muttered Barenz. It was his only contribution so far.

Pierce didn't bother to reply.

***

Richard Clark's father remained stoic while Pierce told them what little he could. Seated next to him, Clark's mother trembled and wept silently. Pierce finished and asked if they had any questions. Mrs. Clark didn't speak, only continued to cry without making a sound. Mr. Clark asked a couple of logistical questions about claiming their son's body. Pierce gave them the timeline and details.

Then he left.

He'd made many death notifications in his career. Short and to the point was best. Out the door soon after was also key. Let people grieve in their own way and without an outsider's gawking.

Pierce stopped at a pay phone and called Salter. The rookie's voice sounded stronger today, though it still cracked with tiredness.

"No harm in getting some extra rest today," Pierce told him.

"I will."

"Stick to what we talked about, Gus."

"I will. I understand now."

He was a rookie who didn't understand much, Pierce knew. Yet he believed Salter when he said he'd keep to the plan. Any sane man would.

"Have you got family with you?" Pierce asked.

"My parents came by this morning."

"That's good."

"Frida's bringing William over later today."

"That's even better." Pierce opened his mouth to say goodbye but Salter spoke again before he could.

"Sorry I'm not there to help you," Salter said.

"I was working alone before you came along. I'm used to it."

"Don't get too used to it. I'm coming to work tomorrow."

"You can take a few more days."

"I want to work," Salter said adamantly.

"All right." Pierce shifted the phone from one ear to the other. "Make sure you eat something today. I'll see you in the morning."

He hung up.

Back at the station, he spent several hours grinding away on Andrews's identity. He checked with Hazel, who added a few more details to the mix. During their short conversation, her usual forward flirtation was muted. When they'd finished, though, she asked him if he wanted to go get lunch.

"I can't," he said. Then he added, "Not today, anyway."

There was one other person he needed to check on.

***

Basil Pershing didn't seem surprised to see him. Instead of leading him into the library like the previous visits, the doctor closed the door behind him and stood in the foyer. He looked at Pierce expectantly.

"Was it him?" Pershing asked. "Was I right?"

Pierce glanced down at Pershing's hands. The man's knuckles were raw on both. Pierce nodded slowly, one of his nighttime suspicions confirmed. He raised his eyes to meet Pershing's. "Michael Andrews is dead," he said.

"Dead? How?"

"My partner shot him."

"Was he… *him*?" Pershing trailed off. He looked at Pierce beseechingly.

"You tell me," said Pierce.

Pershing stared back at him. "I don't think he was."

"You sound sure of it," Pierce said flatly.

"Even if Andrews isn't Doctor Etherton, he's still a killer, isn't he?"

"At least three times over."

"Sometimes things work out, I suppose," said Pershing.

Pierce pointed to the man's battered knuckles. "What happened there?"

Pershing lifted his hands to look at the injuries. "I was a bit too zealous in my training yesterday. The wooden kung fu dummy is less than forgiving."

"Do you want to hear a story?" Pierce said.

"I'm not much for stories, Detective."

"You'll like this one. In it, a boy is nearly murdered by an evil man. Many years later, after the boy has grown, he thinks he may have discovered that same evil man, living in disguise. He goes to the man's house and confronts him. Beats the truth out of him, in fact. Only to discover he wasn't the same evil man, after all."

Pershing stared at him. "It sounds like, if that were true, the hero of this story would be a suspect of some kind."

"That would depend on when the confrontation happened, I suppose."

"I'm not familiar with this tale," said Pershing. "But I'm sure the man and this evil person would have been alone when they had their conversation. If they had one at all." He took a deep breath and let it out in a long sigh. "In any event, in this real world we live in, Doctor Karl Etherton is still out there. Which means I'm still in danger."

Why didn't you save me?

Pierce winced slightly at the words and the dream memory. Then he said, "I have a feeling you're capable of protecting yourself these days."

"Let me show you something," Pershing said. "Perhaps set your mind at ease." He turned and walked away.

Pierce followed. As he walked, he brushed his jacket aside to expose his gun.

Pershing led him down a hallway and through a door to a garage that was almost as large as the entire house Pierce used to live in with his wife. A pair of cars were parked just inside the roll up doors, leaving a massive open area near the back half. Woodcuts of Japanese characters hung from the back wall next to a poster of a shirtless Oriental man in a karate pose. The man had an intensely focused snarl on his face.

"This is where I practice," Pershing said. "My sifu comes by once a week for private lessons, as well."

Pierce didn't bother asking what sifu meant. It was obviously some Oriental word for teacher. Instead, he pointed toward a device that reminded him of a fat coat rack. The thick pole rose up from a wooden stand to about five and a half feet high. Several pegs about a foot and a half long extended out at odd angles from the pole.

Without a word, Pershing stepped up to the device. He slapped one peg with a sharp movement, which caused it to spin. Deftly, he blocked the oncoming peg with his other hand, then struck the center pole with his fist.

The brief demonstration over, Pershing stepped away. Pierce looked closer. He saw brown streaks of dried blood in multiple places along the pole and on some of the outcroppings. The wood was untreated and nearly white, so the blemishes stood out.

"I've been at it more often than usual," Pershing explained. "Ever since you came to visit with the news he might be back."

"I can see that."

Pershing held out his hands again so that Pierce could see his raw knuckles. "This is the price you pay when you train hard, Detective. This is how I hurt my knuckles."

Pierce nodded slowly to himself and chose to let that be the truth.

***

"You're a stubborn son of a bitch," Pierce said. "I'll give you that."

He sat next to George Amherst's bed. His old partner lay absolutely still, other than to draw shallow, ragged breaths that almost resembled a snore. The two of them were alone. Now that Amherst had somehow defied his doctor's expectation and lived through the night, Pierce convinced Gloria to go home and get some rest.

"The doctor says he's stable," Pierce assured her. "I'll call you right away if anything changes."

Gloria reluctantly agreed, then thanked him with a wordless hug before leaving. Pierce was glad to see her go. Not just because the poor woman desperately needed sleep, but because he wanted to be alone with Amherst.

"Some things never change," said Pierce. He sat leaning forward, holding his hat in his hands. "In more ways than one, I suppose. You're too stubborn to die, and Etherton's still out there somewhere."

Pierce set his hat on the small table near the bedside.

"Andrews wasn't Etherton," he told Amherst. "His background checked out as completely legit. Orphanage records, medical school, his residency, all of it. I even talked to someone who knew him personally. Called him a smooth, arrogant asshole with a hot temper underneath. Couldn't get a more accurate description of the man."

Pierce frowned at his own words.

"All that Etherton noise was just that—noise. I let the fifty-one case get into my head, all because of the mutilated ring finger. I thought it was unique enough that it could only be Etherton. But I was wrong, partner. Maybe Andrews heard about our case somehow. I think the symbolism of that finger is universal, is all."

He stared down at the simple golden circle on his own finger.

"Andrews was a cute fucker," he said. "Probably thought he was making some grand statement about society and marriage or something. None of that matters, though. The important part was he was killing innocent people."

Pierce let a tight grin crease his lips.

"Maybe not so innocent in some people's eyes, but you know what I mean. Hermitage, Dorsey, Clark… they never did anything to deserve what happened. No more than Banfield or Jensen did back in fifty-one. Or Pershing."

Pierce's grin faded.

"Pershing," he repeated. "I think that one paid a visit to Andrews before the doctor's final party with Clark. Tuned him up some. The thing is, George, I don't know if he did it earlier in the day or if he showed up shortly before us. See, Clark somehow got to the phone. He called it in to the police. Andrews would never have allowed him that opportunity. He was too smart, too controlling. If Pershing showed up and started beating Andrews, that would give Clark time to make the call. Or it could be Clark was still a willing participant at that point. He seemed like he had guts—maybe he jumped into the fight and it was Pershing who gave him those bruises. Andrews didn't have any markings on his hands, after all. Then again, I don't think he had any when we talked to him before, either. The injuries to Clark were all in soft-tissue areas."

Pierce sighed.

"You see? So many unknowns. As for the rest of what happened, I can't say for certain. Pershing might have fled because Andrews pulled the gun. Maybe Clark tried to leave, too, and that's what got him knifed. Or something else entirely. Maybe Pershing came earlier or was never there at all. I just… don't know."

Pierce stood and slowly paced in the small hospital room.

"I don't have the heart to push Pershing on it. Neither would you, given your soft spot for the guy. His presence at the scene—whenever it happened—unravels everything. It'd be worse than Salter telling the truth about how the shooting went down. And, just like the shooting, it doesn't matter in the end. Andrews still killed Clark. If Pershing was able to exorcise some demons in the process… well, maybe he deserves that opportunity, doesn't he?"

Pierce shook his head. "I don't know. The world has changed, George. Nothing's what it used to be. Not even the truth."

Amherst's heart monitor beeped a steady rhythm.

"I don't think I'll ever know the whole of it," Pierce continued. "Everything is getting shut down, just like back in fifty-one. Even though it's all related, they're making each of the cases out to be separate events. Easier to keep four small cases quiet than one big one, I suppose. No one wants to hear the word serial killer. Not with Expo going on."

Pierce turned sharply on his heel, continuing to pace the small area next to Amherst's bed. Amherst's ragged breathing and Pierce's own steps were the only other sounds in the room.

"So, Andrews and Clark are going down as singular events. 'Homosexual murder,' they're calling it. A violent lover's quarrel. No connection to anything else. The doctor was a pervert, and he killed his lover. Salter will come out a hero. End of story."

Pierce paused in his pacing, shaking his head.

"Hudson Dorsey is being reclassified as an accidental drowning. His injuries will be attributed to the time his body was in the water." Pierce looked at Amherst's haggard face. "I guess some fish in the Spokane River have sharp teeth, huh, partner? Bunch of razor-toothed finger eaters."

In the old days, Amherst would have acknowledged Pierce's joke with a knowing grunt. Today, he only continued breathing, his eyes closed, his mouth slightly open.

"The Isaac Hermitage case is getting reassigned back to those idiots, Barenz and Fletcher. Those two will sit on it for a while and dump it in the unsolved bin. I'm sure the brass won't even have to order them to do it, just give them the file and let nature take its course. They caught the Kerley suicide, too, and have already wrapped it up—coincidences, be damned."

Pierce shook his head again.

"There's more there, partner. I know it. There's more to Andrews I still haven't found and…" He took a deep breath before speaking. Then he let it out and said, "I still think Etherton's out there, George. I know it sounds crazy but… I can feel something. The fifty-one case is connected. I know it."

He glanced down at his old partner. The stubble on Amherst's slack cheeks was dark against his pasty skin. He lay like a corpse, perfectly still except for his breathing.

"I don't have the strength anymore," Pierce whispered to him, surprised at how his voice caught in his throat. "I've resisted the bad parts of the system my whole career. You know I have. I've kept my head down and worked my cases. I've spoken for the dead, but I'm no Serpico, George. Never wanted to be. I can't take this on. Besides, any loose string I pull will only cause everything to unravel for Salter. The kid doesn't deserve that. Hell, this city doesn't deserve it, either."

Pierce listened to machines beep. He glanced at his watch. Then he turned back to his unconscious partner.

"I'm just too tired," Pierce repeated to him, his tone pleading.

Amherst said nothing.

Pierce accepted that as agreement. He patted his friend's hand, then squeezed it. Then he rose to go to the cafeteria for some coffee. Gloria wasn't coming back until morning, so he'd remain at George's bedside until then.

It was going to be a long night.

Interlude II

2023

"She's checking up on you," Wardell Clint said.

The early afternoon sun washed over him and former Chief Robert Baumgartner. After wordlessly eating sandwiches at the patio table an hour ago, they moved to a pair of wicker chairs that faced the lake, taking only the water pitcher and glasses with them. Baumgartner put those on the small table between the two chairs.

On the lake, Darla drifted past on a boat. She waved and kept going.

Baumgartner waved back. "It's what people do, Ward. They look out for those they care about."

"Then Walter Pierce must have absolutely loved young Augustus Salter. Taking care of him like he did."

"You disagree with the man's logic?"

"No," Clint admitted. "His logic is sound, but I disapprove of his actions. They were corrupt."

"It's easy to attack the dead," Baumgartner said. "They can't defend themselves."

"Neither Pierce nor Amherst need to defend themselves. They've got you doing it for them."

Baumgartner kept his eyes toward the lake. His face was more serene than Clint remembered it. He supposed the constant parade of crises, large and small, that Baumgartner dealt with as chief was the reason he'd always looked focused and intense back then.

More lines in his face, too, Clint thought. *Man is getting old.*

"I'm doing what you asked, Ward. Giving you the truth you wanted. It isn't my fault if you don't like what you hear. I warned you about that earlier, didn't I?"

Clint scoffed. It had been a hollow warning, one designed to brush away the less diligent.

"A legend was born out of that shooting," Clint said. "The start of a Spokane Police family dynasty. The entire department loved Lieutenant Gus Salter."

"The *entire* department?" Baumgartner asked. "You, too?"

"I never thought much about the man," Clint said, with a shrug. "He was just part of the brass when I came on. Now I know the truth."

"What's the truth?"

"He was as dirty as Pierce and Amherst."

Baumgartner reached for his water glass and took a drink, still not bothering to look at Clint. "What are you going to do, Ward? Open an IA case against them? They're all dead."

"Internal Affairs? Me?" Clint shook his head. "IA is just another cog in the machine."

"Then, what?"

"I'm going to find the truth. That's what I do."

Baumgartner grunted but said nothing.

Clint glanced down at the notes he'd brought along. "At least Salter had an excuse back then. He was a rookie. Pierce was a shit detective, though."

Baumgartner didn't react. "I never knew the man, but Gus had great respect for him."

"Puts his intelligence in question, too, then."

"What are you on about?"

"Both of these investigations," Clint said. "They're riddled with errors."

"*Riddled* with them?" Baumgartner set down his glass and finally looked at Clint. "It was a different time, remember? They didn't have DNA and all the other fancy tools at their disposal that you have today."

"I'm not talking about technology. I'm talking about basic police work." He eyed Baumgartner disparagingly. "Maybe you forgot about all that in the years you spent in the ivory tower, playing pattycake with politicians."

Baumgartner wasn't baited by his comment. "What errors are you talking about?"

"Facts they overlooked. Angles they didn't consider. Places they should have dug deeper."

"Easy to criticize without offering specifics."

"You want specifics? Here's one: Pierce stopped searching for Etherton once they found Andrews, even though he knew Etherton was still out there."

"He didn't know that for certain. Not then."

"He should have. Serial killers don't stop being killers. Andrews sure as hell didn't kill Isaac Hermitage or Hudson Dorsey. He didn't kill Daniel Kerley, the informant, either."

"No, he didn't," Baumgartner agreed. "You already know the official outcome of those cases."

"Oh, I do. Hermitage? Unsolved, thanks to Barenz and Fletcher, a couple of detectives even worse at their jobs than Pierce. Dorsey? Accidental drowning, which is an absolute joke that doesn't hold up to any scrutiny. And Kerley? A very suspicious suicide."

"Crimes against homosexuals weren't vigorously pursued back in those days," Baumgartner said. "It was wrong, and it was something I watched for during my time as chief."

"Don't play the politician with me," Clint snapped. "You just told me the truth about those cases, even though I'd already worked some of it out for myself. I'm not here so you can crow about your legacy. I'm here to get the rest of the story."

"Is that really what you want, Ward? Facts? Or just to feed whatever conspiracy theory you've got on the front burner?"

Clint tapped his case notes. "This is real. Pierce should have dug deeper. Maybe he'd have seen more clearly if he had."

"Like you?"

Clint scowled. "Let me ask you something. When they found young Basil Pershing in Etherton's dungeon, he was chained to the wall, right?"

Baumgartner nodded.

Clint held up his left hand in a fist. Then he encircled the wrist with the forefinger and thumb of his right. He stared at Baumgartner. "Why only one shackle? Why not both?"

Baumgartner shrugged. "Etherton was interrupted by the approaching sirens. Maybe he heard them right in the middle of the process. What's your point?"

Clint ignored him, pressing onward. "What about the twenty-three years between the cases? What was the killer up to during that time?"

"I don't know. No one does."

"What about between seventy-four and your victim in oh-five? That's twenty-nine years."

Baumgartner turned over his hands. "As I said, we don't know."

"I might." Clint flipped through his notes, though it was mostly for show. He had this case memorized backward and forward. "I found eleven supposedly unrelated assaults and three murders during that second gap. All of them have similar elements to them."

"Similar how?"

"You really need me to break this down for you? Didn't you work homicide once upon a time?"

"That's exactly why I need you to be more specific."

"Fine." Clint bit off the word. "Victim profile is consistent throughout. All three deaths had severe bruising to the torso."

"What else?"

"There are other commonalities between the different cases, but those are the only two that exist across all of them."

Baumgartner smirked. "You're telling me… what exactly? That in thirty years, three gay men were murdered? In a region of a half million people?"

"Wasn't half a million back then, and it was only twenty-nine years, not thirty."

"Still nearly three decades, Ward."

"Be that as it may, there were eleven assaults, too, with injuries consistent with the homicide victims."

Baumgartner held up his hands. "Oh, well that's different." His tone was laced with sarcasm. "Because a bruised torso is such an uncommon event."

"One was probably a prostitute," Clint added.

"Probably? Your theory is already showing cracks, Ward."

"I'm trying to solve a case decades down the road," Clint said. "These cases were evidence of someone either ramping up or continuing his work. If Pierce had done his job when the trail was still fresh—"

Baumgartner waved a hand to cut him off. "Now you're playing Monday-morning quarterback. The scholarship on serial killers was in its infancy back then. That's another one of the tools you have that they didn't."

"The FBI report was available," Clint countered. "The information was there if someone competent were paying attention."

"According to you, no one else in the world is competent."

Clint cocked his head. "You *do* know how serial killers work, don't you? They don't stop voluntarily. It's a compulsion, not a hobby."

"I *actually* do know some of the reasons they stop." Baumgartner lifted his finger and began counting off possibilities. "Incarceration. Moved out of the area. Died."

"That doesn't explain these assaults and killings."

"Did any of these homicide victims have a missing ring finger?" Baumgartner demanded.

Clint didn't answer right away. Then he admitted, "No, they did not."

"They did not," Baumgartner repeated. "That's because they weren't related. You're making connections that aren't there."

Clint leaned back and folded his hands. "There's something here. We both know it."

"And you're determined to know what it is, aren't you?"

"I am."

"Why? Why not let the dead lay in peace?"

"Because the truth matters," Clint insisted. "People in power don't get to make the truth be what they need it to be."

"They do it all the time," Baumgartner said. "It's called history."

Clint scoffed. "History is the biggest conspiracy there is, but don't think you'll distract me. There's a series of conspiracies wrapped up in these cases. You admitted as much yourself."

Baumgartner regarded him for a long moment. Then he asked, "Did it ever occur to you that, sometimes, a conspiracy might actually exist for the good of the people?"

"How can that be?"

"It's a chaotic world," Baumgartner said. "People need to believe some order can be imposed upon it. They don't want to know how a supposedly upstanding member of their town has actually been an active serial killer for five decades. They need to believe it's impossible that the police wouldn't find him and bring him to justice. That we can protect them from bad men." He stared hard at Clint. "People need their illusions, Ward. The right ones make it possible for our world to function."

"I'm sure that's what those conspiring motherfuckers tell themselves so they can sleep at night, but it's bullshit."

"Maybe everything we've talked about today is bullshit," Baumgartner said quietly.

Clint smiled coldly. "Nice try. I'm going to shine a light on this."

"What proof do you have?"

"The official record, and I have your testimony."

"Maybe I made it all up."

"You're telling me you're lying?" Clint scowled. "I don't believe it. It all lines up too nicely."

"That," Baumgartner said pointedly, "is exactly how people describe crazy conspiracies."

"You're saying this whole conversation is a sham?"

Baumgartner turned over his hands. "I asked what proof you had."

The two men stared at each other for a long minute. Clint could hear the slosh of water against the dock below and the call of loons in the distance. A small boat with a tiny motor putted past. He didn't bother looking to see if it was Darla, checking on her man again. Instead, he tried to decipher Baumgartner's expression. The former chief's countenance was flat and unreadable.

Have I been wasting my time?

No, he decided. He'd already filled in gaps he only suspected before today and learned new information. Even if he stood and walked away now, this trip was a success. Yet there was more he wanted to know.

Needed to know.

"Let's talk about your case," Clint said in a low voice, "and don't leave anything out."

Part III

2005

"No good decision was ever made in a swivel chair."

- George S. Patton,
U.S. Army General

Chapter 33

Detective Robert Baumgartner paused between two heavy steel doors. He held a thin manila folder in his left hand. An electronic buzz sounded and the door behind him locked. Baumgartner's hand tightened around the folder, bending it. A second later, the door ahead of him unlocked and Baumgartner's grip relaxed. He stepped into the visitor's section of the Spokane County Jail.

Heads turned in his direction. Women that Baumgartner suspected were wives or girlfriends of inmates eyed him with cool hostility. In a jail lobby, it was an us-versus-them mentality, and Baumgartner fit squarely into the latter category.

Baumgartner ignored the various glares until he reached the exit door. His forearm pressed the push bar, and he stepped out into the late morning sunlight. He breathed easier whenever he was out of the concrete monolith.

His gaze swept the landscaped area between where he stood and the Public Safety Building, the home of the Spokane Police Department. Baumgartner remained vigilant whenever he left the jail.

A couple of years prior, a gang member attacked another detective in this same vicinity. When that detective left the jail, he failed to pay attention to his surroundings. Instead, the man decided to text his girlfriend. The detective's head was down when the gang member approached and hit him. The detective was knocked unconscious. Luckily, the man's life was saved by citizens who were visiting a relative in the jail.

Baumgartner walked along the pathway and noticed his image reflected in the north windows of the PSB. He watched himself a moment too long and felt stupid. Anyone inside the offices would know what he was doing and call him out for it. He rounded the corner and entered through the west doors.

Fluorescent lights bounced off recently waxed linoleum floors. The Public Safety Building showed its age in its outdated design, though the city did its best to operate the facility in a clean and efficient manner.

Baumgartner strode down the hallway until he reached the Detectives' Division. He passed by various cubicles as he entered the Major Crimes section. He tossed the file onto his desk. He hung his suit jacket on a hook attached to his cubicle. Baumgartner dropped heavily into his chair, slapped the space bar on his keyboard, and called his computer to life.

"Well?" a woman asked. "How'd it go with Jones?"

Baumgartner looked over his shoulder.

Dusty Maragas stood next to him. She wore a black pantsuit with a red shirt. She held a large binder in her left hand. Her bangs fell into her eyes.

"He denied everything."

"The son of a bitch busted his wife's jaw."

Baumgartner shrugged. "I know."

"You told him we got witnesses?"

"It's not my first rodeo."

Maragas shifted the binder to her other hand. "I'm just asking."

"Yeah, I told him."

"He still denied?" Maragas clicked her tongue against the back of her teeth. "Some people."

"My thoughts exactly. What're you working on?"

"The Henderson case." Maragas blew air up the front of her face to move the hair out of her eyes. It didn't work so she swept them away with her hand. "Before you ask, I didn't get anywhere either."

Baumgartner's desk phone rang. He leaned forward and checked the caller ID screen. "Lieutenant Salter," he said.

Maragas frowned. "What's he want?"

"Do I look like a mind reader?"

"You barely look like a detective."

Baumgartner faked a laugh.

The phone rang a third time before he could lift the receiver. "Hey, Lieutenant." He tried to put as much levity in his voice as he could. It was best to be cordial when dealing with Augustus Salter.

"My office," the lieutenant said. "Bring your partner."

The line went dead.

Baumgartner stared at the receiver.

"That went well," Maragas said.

"What'd we expect? It's Salter."

***

Baumgartner smoothed the lapels of his suit jacket before stepping into Lieutenant Salter's office. He noticed his partner doing the same. Maragas also took time to futz with her hair.

The door to the lieutenant's office was open but neither detective entered. Instead, they waited just outside where Salter could see them.

Inside, Augustus Salter leaned on his desk, both elbows supporting his weight. His eyes drifted over a file. Several pages were folded over as if he were reading something older in the report.

The lieutenant surely heard the detectives but hadn't invited them inside yet. It was a power play and it pissed off Baumgartner. He cleared his throat.

Maragas eyed him, and Baumgartner shrugged a single shoulder.

Salter continued to read.

Baumgartner checked his watch. Only a handful of seconds had passed by, but this kind of bullshit was why he hated the brass. It seemed they took every opportunity to remind their subordinates about the power structure. Those opportunities had become more frequent since the Major Crimes sergeant went out for shoulder surgery and the lieutenant was temporarily covering her duties.

"Sir," Baumgartner said.

Maragas frowned.

Salter pulled the rolled pages back into the file and closed the folder. He looked up at Baumgartner and Maragas, flatly taking in their presence. "Enter."

Baumgartner paused so Maragas could step into the office first. She took the chair on the left. Baumgartner gently lowered himself into the one on the right.

Lieutenant Salter was a serious man in his mid-fifties. Despite the lieutenant's reputation as a boss who cared about his people, Baumgartner hadn't seen much of that over the past year. In fact, he couldn't recall a time when the man cracked a smile. His silver hair was flecked with dark speckles and cut in a businessman's style. He wore a gray suit, white shirt, and red tie. Even though he was seated in his own office, Salter still wore the suit jacket. Baumgartner spied the leather holster from the lieutenant's shoulder rig peeking through the parted front of the jacket.

"James Lockett." Salter set his hand on the file. "Ever hear the name?"

Maragas said, "Sounds familiar."

Baumgartner nodded, but he couldn't place where he'd heard it.

"Lockett was found murdered a couple years back in High Bridge Park," Salter said. His hand rubbed the file in circular motions. "Investigated by Barenz."

Baumgartner and Maragas exchanged glances.

Joe Barenz had been a dinosaur by the time he retired—a fat, sluggish dinosaur. His clearance rate was atrocious, and no one wanted to work with him. Barenz became known as The Wasteland because any cases assigned to him withered and died.

The conspiracy bandied about the department was that Barenz stayed around for exactly that reason. The administration took advantage of his natural affinity to drag his feet on cases not easily solved. When they didn't want better detectives saddled with unsolvable ones, they assigned them to Barenz.

Baumgartner believed it to be nonsense, since he'd already had a few unsolvable cases during his short time in Major Crimes. However, Barenz had reached his mid-sixties. Baumgartner hadn't heard of anyone else hanging around the department that long, let alone a homicide detective with a horrible clearance rate.

Salter continued. "The case went nowhere under Barenz."

"Little surprise," Maragas muttered.

"Sins of the previous lieutenant."

"Sir?" she asked.

Salter gently patted the file. "We all age out eventually." The lieutenant's eyes took on a distant stare. "SWAT guys can't run and gun forever. We retire the dogs for their safety and that of their handlers. The administration moves patrol officers away from the street if we think they're liable to get hurt. Yet we let detectives hang around long after they've lost their efficiency because we don't think they're a danger to themselves or society."

Baumgartner grabbed the handles of his chair but held his tongue. He was all for removing dead weight like Joe Barenz, but he didn't like the idea of an administrator telling him he had to stop being a detective. Baumgartner enjoyed the job and had no intention of ever leaving it.

"Lockett's parents carry some weight in their community. They're Mormon—" The lieutenant paused and eyed both detectives. "Not that their religious affiliation should make any difference."

Baumgartner shrugged. Maragas did the same.

"Anyway, they reached out to Councilman Dennis Hahn."

"He's Mormon?" Baumgartner asked, genuinely surprised.

"Presbyterian, I believe. But Hahn gave a campaign speech at the Locketts' church." Salter furrowed his brow. "Parish?"

His gaze bounced between the detectives. Not getting any help, he said, "You get the point. They called him and—" Salter abruptly lifted his hand from the file and snapped his fingers. "Ward. The Mormons call it a ward."

Voices came from down the hall. Someone laughed as they approached.

Salter paused, waiting for the noisy group to pass. When it was quiet again, the lieutenant said, "Anyway, Hahn called the mayor and asked for a favor. It rolled downhill to the chief and now to us." He lifted the file and extended it toward Maragas. She leaned forward and took the folder from him.

"You want us to look into it?" Maragas asked.

"I want you to do more than that," Salter said. "I want you to rework it from the beginning." His words carried a heaviness to them. "Treat it like Joe Barenz never put his grubby paws on it."

Maragas narrowed her eyes. "Is there something you're not telling us, sir?"

Salter flopped back into his chair. He waggled a finger at the Lockett file. "Make that a priority."

***

Maragas walked ahead of Baumgartner as they headed down the hallway. She repeatedly glanced over her shoulder. Baumgartner expected her to take the back way toward their cubicles, but she didn't. Her pace quickened.

"Where you going?" he asked.

She raised the file. He interpreted that as a signal for him to be quiet.

Maragas turned at the entrance to the Detectives' Division. The receptionist looked up from her computer. The woman was about to say something, but noticed the path Maragas was on. The receptionist returned her attention to her work.

Several small interview rooms sat off to the right. Maragas pulled open the first door. "After you."

Baumgartner stepped inside. He'd had plenty of private conversations inside the interview rooms. In a department fueled by gossip, it was one of the few places to avoid eavesdropping.

A small table was attached to the north wall. Two plastic chairs sat on either side. A metal rail ran the length of the wall which allowed handcuffed prisoners to sit comfortably during an interview.

Maragas pulled the door behind them and locked it. When she turned around, she dropped the file onto the table. "The fuck was that?" she whispered.

"Salter?"

Maragas pointed in the direction of his office. "What's he dragging us into?"

"I don't know. Sounds like a cold case."

"Two years old isn't a cold case. It's still lukewarm." Maragas settled into a chair and turned the file toward her. "Did you hear what he said?"

"I was there."

"*Make it a priority.*" Her face pinched as she imitated Salter's gruff voice. "Like we don't have other cases. Everything we've got is a goddamned priority."

"It's probably because of the heat he's getting."

Maragas flipped the file open. "From some upstart councilman? Hardly." She shook her head. "That's like getting heat from a piece of white bread. Guy's not going anywhere in this town."

"You never know." Baumgartner rested his shoulders against the wall. "Maybe Salter saw something in the file."

"What do you mean?"

"I don't know." He waved a hand. "Maybe Barenz screwed up the case and exposed the department to some liability. I don't know."

"Stop saying that."

"What?"

"You said I don't know three times since we've been here. You're sounding like a broken record and that's not going to help us."

Baumgartner's face warmed and he pushed off the wall. "All I'm saying is maybe Salter saw something in the file."

"Like what? He was never a detective, much less Major Crimes." Maragas flipped to the back of the file so she could read the initial report. Before she reviewed it, she eyed Baumgartner. "Or maybe what you're really trying to say is the lieutenant saw something, but he kept his mouth shut so he wouldn't pollute our investigation?"

That wasn't what Baumgartner thought, but he nodded anyway.

She smirked. "You're smarter than you look."

"That's my secret weapon."

"Looking like a knuckle dragger but having a fully developed brain?"

"The ladies seem to like it."

Maragas rolled her eyes. "There you go, proving me wrong." She lifted her chin toward the other chair. "Now, sit down and shut up. Let's figure out this hot potato."

Chapter 34

After leaving the interview room, Baumgartner ran James Henry Lockett through the NCIC database. The National Crime Information Center was the central database utilized by all United States law enforcement agencies.

It appeared Joe Barenz had performed this check previously as well, but Lieutenant Salter had requested Baumgartner and Maragas conduct the investigation as if it landed on their desk that day, so he did it again.

The only difference between the report Baumgartner ran and the one in the case file was Lockett was listed as dead. The rest of the man's history read the same. Lockett had been arrested once for Indecent Exposure, which was pleaded down in court to Urinating in Public. He'd also been arrested and charged twice for Possession of a Controlled Substance— Marijuana. Both times he'd been ordered to attend a drug counseling program.

There was also a single Field Interview report with Lockett listed as a contact. In 2002, Officer Wardell Clint contacted Lockett during a directed enforcement patrol. Lockett had been walking through High Bridge Park during the evening. Though he was not engaged in illegal activity, his proximity to an area known for criminal acts prompted Clint to identify the man.

The resulting Field Interview report was not in the original case file. Baumgartner printed it and added it.

Maragas appeared at his cubicle. "I've got us an interview with the parents. Not until later, though."

The case file contained the phone numbers and addresses for the parents as well as some friends. The brief narrative described what Barenz had learned from each of these potential witnesses. In terms of solving the case, the information provided little insight. A second, handwritten list of potential witnesses was loose inside the file. Barenz had drawn a line through several and labeled them as deceased. Others were marked as M/A which Baumgartner guessed meant moved away. The ones marked N/I were easier—not interviewed. Only a couple were check-marked. Baumgartner figured those were the ones the detective had actually interviewed in addition to those on the other list.

Maragas continued. "I'm thinking we should check out the crime scene now. Maybe grab some lunch after."

"What about the guy who found the body? Maybe we could talk with him and get a better read on the scene."

Maragas shook her head. "That's a scratch. He died last year."

Baumgartner leaned back in his chair. "Anything suspicious?"

"He fell from a cliff in Glacier National Park."

"It's suspicious in my book."

She rolled her eyes. "I talked with his wife."

"Already? That was fast."

"That's the name of the game. Act boldly. Anyway, they were hiking and he got too close to the cliff. He tripped over a tree root and went over the edge."

"Unlucky for him."

"Unlucky for us, too."

***

High Bridge Park sat in a valley west of downtown. To the south, Interstate 90 rumbled by along with an elevated train trestle. Latah Creek ran lazily along the eastern edge of the park before it connected with the Spokane River.

Maragas drove along West Riverside Avenue while Baumgartner sat in the passenger seat. They headed toward the location where James Lockett's body was found. Maragas had her window cracked while she smoked. She held the cigarette near the opening. Whenever she exhaled smoke, she directed it out the window as well. Even so, her car reeked of cigarettes. The vanilla-scented air freshener—yellow and tree-shaped—that hung from one of the knobs on the dash, did little to alleviate the smell. To combat it, Baumgartner popped a piece of gum into his mouth.

"So we interview Barenz after lunch?" he asked.

Maragas stared straight ahead, but her faced soured.

"Something wrong?"

She shrugged a single shoulder. "Barenz."

"Everyone knows he did shitty work."

Her eyes cut to him. "In that case, I'll let you do the talking."

Baumgartner studied her. There was something unspoken in her words.

"Stop looking at me," she said without turning his way.

The car left Riverside Avenue and turned into High Bridge Park.

Large Ponderosa pine trees filled the park. Its unaltered landscape attracted many who enjoyed walking in that type of environment. Sometime in the late eighties, High Bridge Park became a gathering point for gay men. Some would sit in their cars until approached. Sex happened in vehicles, among the trees, and in the nearby restrooms. Neighbors and traditional park attendees often complained to the city. The department made token efforts to combat the activity, but it remained a low priority.

Maragas parked the car and the two detectives climbed out. She dropped her cigarette, ground it into the dirt, and reached inside the car for the file. Baumgartner carried a walking wheel tape.

James Lockett was found two years ago in a cluster of trees, one hundred feet southeast of the restrooms. The detectives headed toward the lavatories.

Maragas waved away irritating gnats.

Baumgartner walked alongside her, kicking up dirt and dust as he went. "It's likely the killer met Lockett here and convinced him to walk into the woods."

"Probably. You ever work enforcement down here?"

"Yeah."

While working patrol, Baumgartner had participated in several nights of directed enforcement at High Bridge Park. He ordered many men to leave the area after identifying them. Baumgartner hated that kind of enforcement. He didn't care what the men were doing, only that they were doing it in public.

"Someday," Maragas said, "nobody's going to give a damn about who fucks who."

Baumgartner grunted. "What fairy tale are you living in?"

She slapped his arm with the file. "Don't you want a better society?"

"Sure, I do, but people are people. Everyone thinks their way is better than their neighbor's."

When they arrived at the restrooms, Baumgartner extended the handle on the walking wheel tape. He set it on the ground.

"Ready?"

Maragas wiped the back of her hand across her forehead. "This heat."

Baumgartner stared at her.

She rolled her eyes. "Whatever. You know you're feeling it, too."

They walked in a southeasterly direction.

The detectives fell silent as they concentrated on the possible killing site up ahead. When the numbers on the wheel tape passed ninety, Baumgartner slowed his pace and read them off aloud. "Ninety-three, ninety-four, ninety-five."

They were in a thick cluster of trees now. Maragas turned around and walked backward. "I can barely see the restrooms."

"Ninety-six."

"At night," she said, "this would be optimal."

"Ninety-seven."

"You can stop." Maragas opened the file and removed an envelope. Inside were crime scene photos. As she reviewed them, Maragas passed them to Baumgartner.

James Lockett was found with his clothes on, but his pants were around his ankles.

Maragas said, "What if the killer had him push his pants down as a way to keep him from running?"

Baumgartner lifted an eyebrow. "So, Lockett thinks he's in for a good time, and then wham! The killer's on him?"

"As good an explanation as any. The autopsy found no anal tearing or semen."

"Maybe the killer wore a condom."

Maragas smirked. "That accounts for the semen, but it wouldn't necessarily stop the tearing."

Baumgartner dropped his eyes. He knew she was right, but he also knew his idea was worth considering.

"You're saying he controlled himself so as not to hurt Lockett before he killed him? Yeah, let's go with that." She didn't try to hide her sarcasm. "Besides, there was no evidence of saliva or other DNA found on Lockett's penis."

"Meaning what? Maybe Lockett gave the killer some oral, then the guy killed him?"

"Or this was never about sex." Maragas passed more autopsy photos to Baumgartner. "The bruising around the neck and on the chest, right?"

Baumgartner had seen the photos back at the station. He accepted them from Maragas but paid them little attention now. He shuffled them together and handed them back. "So, the killer lures Lockett into the woods and chokes him to death before beating him?"

"Why doesn't he beat him first?"

"Because if Lockett cries out, maybe someone comes to his rescue."

Maragas crossed her arms. "What if he didn't? What if the killer hit Lockett first and the victim cried out? It's dark and the park is full of trees. Unless someone had a flashlight it might be hard to find the attacker."

Baumgartner glanced around at the trees. Even in the middle of the day, the place was quiet and secluded. Only the distant hum of traffic on the bridge high above and the muffled sound of the river flowing over rocks could be heard. "Do we know if the moon was out?"

She shook her head. "Report doesn't say. Have to check an old Farmer's Almanac."

"Or the internet." Baumgartner smiled playfully. "Either way, moonlight would make a difference."

Maragas nodded. "Would it change if the killer beat the victim before or after his death?" She grabbed the autopsy photos and pointed to the left ring finger. A slight cut ran around the circumference of the finger near where it connected to the hand. "What do you make of that?"

"Maybe the victim was wearing a ring and it cut him during the fight."

"Sharp ass ring. It wasn't on Lockett when he was found."

Baumgartner eyed the photo more closely. "No ring indentation on the finger, either."

"Lockett wasn't married."

"Kind of odd for him to wear a ring on that finger, isn't it?"

"Yet…" Maragas tapped the image of the cut. "This remains."

"Perhaps the killer took the ring as a trophy," Baumgartner said. "Or maybe the guy who discovered the body."

"If the hiker took it, we'll never know." Maragas flicked the photo with her finger. "You know what bothers me most?"

"What?"

"Almost no foreign DNA on the body. Most homicides, there's an overabundance."

"The killer was smart."

"Or at least careful. There's been no match in CODIS, so he's never been in the system, either. What's that tell you?"

Baumgartner pursed his lips. "He's sophisticated?"

Maragas nodded. "And knows how to stay out of trouble."

Baumgartner felt a small surge of pride at her acknowledgment.

"Come on," Maragas said. "Let's get some lunch."

***

Baumgartner scooped a handful of popcorn from the silver bowl. He shook it, then picked a couple of larger pieces to toss into his mouth. "You got plans this weekend?"

Maragas sipped her soda. "Why do you ask?"

"Just making conversation."

They were at Domini's, a sandwich shop in the heart of downtown. A waitress had already taken their orders. Behind the service counter, in the upper corner of the restaurant, an old television quietly ran a soap opera.

At this time of afternoon, the lunch rush was in the rearview mirror. The restaurant was almost deserted now. Across the street, several people loitered in front of the Spokane Transit Authority's bus plaza.

Maragas motioned her drink at Baumgartner. "You asking me on a date?"

Baumgartner's face pinched. "No."

"Am I too old for you or something?"

His brow furrowed further. "No."

"I'm only forty-five. Older women can still bring it."

"I know," he said. It sounded a little defensive, so he repeated it with a softer tone. "I know."

"Then what is it?"

"It's nothing." He swallowed. "I'm not asking you out. I was seriously just wondering what you were doing."

"I'm not doing anything." Maragas reached into the popcorn bowl and pulled a couple of pieces out. "You were wondering if I might already have a date with someone, weren't you?"

"No."

"Yes, you were." She flipped a piece of popcorn expertly into her mouth. "I'm not gay, by the way."

He shook his head. "I know you're not."

"I've heard the rumors. The way you guys talk when you think no one is listening."

Baumgartner glanced around. He wasn't sure why he did that. It wouldn't matter if anyone heard what he said. "Listen. I don't talk about you when you're not around. If anyone does, I shut it down."

She chewed on her popcorn. "If you say so."

"Let's change the subject," he said.

"To what?"

"Barenz."

Maragas rolled her eyes. "Why?"

"Because something bothers you about him, and I want to know what."

"It doesn't matter." She dusted the popcorn salt off her hands.

"We're partners," Baumgartner said. "You never mentioned him."

"He's dead to me."

"Obviously not."

Maragas crossed her arms and stared at Baumgartner. They stayed that way for several moments.

The waitress arrived. "Pastrami and Swiss." She set a tray in front of Baumgartner. It contained a massive sandwich. "And a turkey and cheddar, meat and cheese tray." The waitress set the second tray in front of Maragas. "Need anything else?"

Both detectives said, "no" and the waitress walked way.

Baumgartner leaned forward to examine the lunch Maragas ordered. "No bread. Who does that?"

She lifted several slices of turkey and stuffed them into her mouth. "Me."

He settled back into his chair and lifted the first half of his sandwich. "About Barenz?"

"You're not going to leave this alone?"

Baumgartner bit into his sandwich as he shrugged.

"Joe grabbed my ass on his last day."

"His last day?" Baumgartner asked after swallowing.

"The son of a bitch leaned into my ear and said he waited for years to do it. Offered to get us a hotel room and take me around the world, if you know what I mean."

Baumgartner knew exactly what she meant.

Maragas curled her lip. "I can still smell his coffee breath and Brut cologne."

"Brut?"

"My dad wore the same shit." Her nose crinkled.

"Why didn't you punch him?"

"Why do you think?"

Baumgartner bit into his sandwich again while he thought. She picked at her meat and cheese tray. When Baumgartner thought he had a reasonable explanation, he said, "Because it was his last day and not yours."

Maragas nodded. "What proof was there? He grabbed my ass and said something dirty. If I hit him, I would have left a mark. Maybe somebody would have seen me do it. The best I could do was leave it alone."

"Sorry."

"For what? He finally left and you got promoted."

That was two years ago. Baumgartner wasn't initially partnered with Maragas. However, after Salter came into the unit, the lieutenant decided to juggle the roster. Baumgartner and Maragas were assigned together. Many were unhappy with the realignment, but Baumgartner wasn't. He liked working with Maragas. He hoped she enjoyed working with him.

Maragas quit picking at her food and slid it to the side. "I'm done."

Baumgartner lowered the portion of the sandwich he was still eating. "You've hardly touched it."

"So? I'm done. Let's go."

"Seriously?"

She waved for the waitress.

"I'm still eating."

"You can eat while I drive."

Baumgartner shoved a larger bite than was advisable into his mouth and struggled to chew.

Maragas watched him with disgust. "That's why I'll never let you take me out."

"I didn't ask you," he said through a mouthful of food. "Besides, I thought you were gay."

Maragas smirked, trying unsuccessfully to hide a smile.

***

Nathan and Suzanne Lockett lived on Nora Avenue in the Logan neighborhood. St. Aloysius Gonzaga Catholic School sat across the alley to the south. Beyond that resided Gonzaga University. The unassuming home was old, built in the post-World War II craze. The yard was impeccably kept as were most homes along this street. Baumgartner imagined the residents took pride living in proximity to the famous university.

The Locketts welcomed the detectives in as if they were expecting them.

"Councilman Hahn's a good man," Nathan Lockett said after the four of them sat in the living room. Nathan looked like the father from the old *Family Ties* sitcom—tall and lean with salt and pepper hair and a full beard. He wore a blue plaid shirt and khaki pants.

"A good man," Suzanne parroted. She sat next to her husband with her hands tucked between her legs. Her brown hair was short and cut asymmetrical, a hairdo almost a decade out of style. Her burgundy dress fell below her knees even while seated. "We appreciate him talking with the mayor about our son."

"We're sorry for your loss," Maragas said.

While she continued the initial introductions, Baumgartner's gaze swept about the living room. It was a clean home with everything put in its place. A picture of Jesus holding a candle was displayed above the fireplace.

There was no television in the room. Instead, a bookshelf sat in the corner. The Holy Bible, Book of Mormon, and a dictionary were clustered together on the top shelf. The rest of the space was filled with fiction books by authors Baumgartner didn't recognize. It appeared the novels were a mixture of romance and mystery, but many had religious sounding words in them like grace, omen, and angel. Baumgartner wondered if they might be Christian fiction, maybe even Mormon.

A thought occurred to him then. How much conflict was there for a Mormon family living in the vicinity of a Catholic school and university? Baumgartner wasn't a religious man, so he wondered if it even mattered.

Pictures of children hung about the living room. Baumgartner attempted to count faces and settled on six. The Locketts had half a dozen children—two boys and four girls. He noticed James was among them but couldn't figure out his position among the brood.

"James was our youngest," Nathan said.

Baumgartner's gaze slid back to the father.

"I noticed you looking."

"Where do your other children live?" Baumgartner asked.

"All over," Nathan said. He glanced at his wife who confirmed his statement by nodding. Nathan added, "Salt Lake City, Boise, Mesa, and Seattle."

"Two of our daughters live in Boise," Suzanne said.

"None of them live in Spokane?"

"No," Nathan said. "Not anymore."

Maragas leaned forward. She balanced a notebook on her knee. "Was James involved in anything that might have gotten him hurt?"

Nathan glanced at his wife before saying, "Not that we know of. No."

Suzanne looked down at her hands. She pulled at her dress.

"Mrs. Lockett?" Maragas said.

"Hmm?" She didn't lift her eyes.

"Is there something your son was involved with?"

She shook her head.

"Our son was a good boy," Nathan said.

"He was arrested for Indecent Exposure," Maragas said.

Nathan's face took on an expression of piousness and he waggled a finger. "He urinated in public. That's hardly indecent exposure."

"He was also arrested twice for possessing marijuana."

"Youthful indiscretions. While I don't condone what he did, that doesn't make him a criminal. Besides, it was marijuana. It might be an intoxicating substance but at least it is one which the Good Lord grows naturally. It's not like that scourge, methamphetamine."

Baumgartner held his tongue. In the eyes of the law, it certainly made James Lockett a criminal.

Maragas tapped her pen against her notepad. "Mr. and Mrs. Lockett, you know where your son's body was found."

"We know," Nathan said.

"We know," Suzanne whispered.

A silence descended over the room. Outside, a dog barked somewhere in the neighborhood.

Nathan stared straight ahead as if he were sitting at an interrogation table and willing himself not to break.

Suzanne continued to pull at her dress. The hem was now above her knees.

Maragas scooted toward the edge of her chair, closing the distance between herself and the parents. It was a slight move, and a psychological ploy. "It's an area known as a meeting place for homosexuals."

Nathan stiffened. "James liked to hike."

"He liked to hike," Suzanne repeated softly.

"Your son was found with his pants around his ankles."

Nathan's expression hardened. "We know how he was found, Detective. His killer violated him in the eyes of God, and he will pay for that in the afterlife."

Suzanne balled her hand into a fist, clutching her dress and pulling it further up her legs.

"What we want," Nathan said, "is for you to find the monster who harmed our son and make him pay for his sins on this Earth."

Maragas set her pen down on her notepad. "To do that, we need to deal in the truth."

Nathan tugged his wife's dress free from her hand and smoothed it back in place. Suzanne looked up and forced a polite smile.

"We are telling the truth," Nathan said. "Our son liked to hike."

Suzanne set her jaw and blinked several times before saying, "He liked to hike."

Maragas glanced at Baumgartner before asking, "How about his friends? Who did James hang out with?"

For the next several minutes, Nathan and Suzanne listed a series of names. Maragas compared them to the list Joe Barenz had in his file. There were no matches.

"What about a few of these names?" she asked. Maragas ran down the separate, handwritten interview list from Barenz's notes.

Nathan eyed his wife. "None of those names ring a bell."

"Maybe they were friends of his we never met," Suzanne offered.

***

Baumgartner pressed the doorbell and waited. Maragas stood on the opposite side of the door, an officer safety habit even though this was expected to be a friendly contact.

They were in the Shadle Park neighborhood. When Baumgartner was a kid, this area was highly desirable. Now, it was starting to show its age. Younger and poorer families had moved in. Houses showed neglect with unkempt lawns and failing roofs.

The lock turned and the door opened. A heavyset man stood before them in a dirty white tank top and blue athletic shorts. Leather sandals covered his feet. He clutched a can of Rainier in his right hand.

He quickly appraised Baumgartner before letting his gaze linger on Maragas. "Hey ya, Dusty."

"Joe," she said.

"What brings you around?"

Baumgartner lifted the Lockett case file. "We've got some questions."

Joe Barenz sipped his beer, then rubbed his lips with the back of the hand holding the can. "Why didn't you call first?"

"We were in the neighborhood," Baumgartner said.

Barenz's eyes cut to Dusty. "Boy Wonder going to do all the talking?"

"As much as he can," she said.

"I said I was sorry for what happened."

"It wasn't something that happened. It was something you did. Sorry doesn't begin to cover it."

Barenz grunted. "That's what Sheila said, too." He turned and walked into the house.

Baumgartner followed the retired detective inside with Maragas behind. She closed the door.

Barenz shuffled into the living room, burping twice as he went.

The room appeared to have been decorated by a woman. Two bronze sconces were affixed at opposite ends of the longest wall; purple candles sat atop them. Artwork with violet-colored tones hung in between.

A picture of Jesus among a group of children stood atop a cabinet television. A dusty bible lay next to it.

The room smelled of body odor, stale beer, and even staler cigarette smoke.

A basket of clothes sat on the couch. Next to it was a pile of towels.

"Go ahead and move that," Barenz said. "They're clean."

Maragas picked up the towels and put them on the coffee table. Baumgartner put the basket on the floor. The detectives sat on the couch.

Barenz positioned himself in front of the larger recliner and dropped into it. The footrest snapped up into place. A full ashtray sat on the floor. He pulled a pack of cigarettes from the side pocket. "Now, what's this about?"

A gameshow played loudly on the television. The host asked a contestant to "Spin the wheel."

"Mind turning that off?" Baumgartner asked.

Barenz frowned as his attention swung toward the tube. He slowly reached for the remote and muted the sound. "Good enough?"

"We want to ask some questions about James Lockett."

"Who?"

Baumgartner opened the file and removed the envelope of photographs. As he searched for one with Lockett's face, Maragas shoved the towels to the furthest edge of the coffee table. Baumgartner set a picture down.

Barenz shook a cigarette loose from the pack, then lit it. After he exhaled a plume of smoke, he leaned sideways in the recliner. He lifted himself on an elbow to better see but quickly settled back into place. He held out the hand which held the cigarette. "Gimme that photo, darling."

"It's Detective Maragas."

"Not in my home." Barenz sucked on his cigarette before sipping his beer.

Maragas curled her lip and didn't move from her seat.

Baumgartner stood and handed the picture to the retired detective. Barenz accepted it without looking away from Maragas.

"Well?" she asked.

Barenz stuck the cigarette between his lips. The smoke drifted up to his eyes and he cocked his head to avoid it. "I remember this one."

"What do you remember?" Baumgartner asked.

"Whatever was in the file."

"There wasn't much in there." Baumgartner lifted the folder for emphasis.

Barenz spun the picture and it sailed onto the coffee table. "Well, there you go. Unsolvable." He inhaled on the cigarette, then exhaled forcefully. A plume of smoke floated over the room.

"Let's start at the beginning," Baumgartner said.

"Why bother?" Barenz leaned to the side and farted. "Sometimes fags die."

Baumgartner stiffened. He would expect a statement like that from the criminals he ran across daily, but never a retired detective. Baumgartner wasn't naïve. He knew some officers might feel that way, but to actually voice those feelings around someone not trusted seemed reckless.

His eyes cut to Maragas who remained calm. She studied Barenz.

"Don't get your panties in a bunch," Barenz said to Baumgartner. "What I'm saying is it was probably a crime of passion. A lover scorned. That type of thing." He waved his beer can. "We all understand that, right?"

Baumgartner canted his head. Was Barenz really dismissing murder as okay because it was a crime of passion?

Barenz tilted his beer back, discovered it empty, and shook it. "I mean, I've thought about killing Sheila plenty of times, but I've never done it."

Maragas looked down the hall. "Where is Sheila, Joe?"

"Her fucking sister's. Been there for a couple years now." Barenz twisted the beer can and it folded in on itself. "She won't divorce me because it's a sin." He threw the can at the picture of Jesus with his left hand. It missed, sailed over the television, and hit the wall. "Apparently living apart is still a blessing in the eyes of the Lord."

"So, James Lockett," Baumgartner said to bring the conversation back to the reason for their visit.

Barenz's face pinched. "What?"

"James Lockett?"

"You got the file." Barenz reached over the side of the recliner and crushed his cigarette in the full ashtray. Some old butts were knocked onto the carpet. "What more do you want from me?"

"Why didn't you go further with it?" Baumgartner asked.

"There was no evidence. Even the DNA came back unmatched." Barenz pushed on the footrest and brought the chair upright. He stood and wobbled. "What was I to do?"

"Interview friends and family," Baumgartner said.

"I did."

"There's hardly anything in here."

Barenz put his hands on his hips. He tilted his head back and looked down the bridge of his nose. "Why are you here?"

"We told you. We're looking into the murder of James Lockett."

"Bullshit." Barenz angrily waved his hand. "The case was filed. Dead. Who made you pull it out?"

"Salter," Baumgartner said.

"I heard he was running the show now." Barenz rubbed his stomach. "What's he doing? Some sort of audit on my cases or something?"

"He caught some heat from a councilman connected to the family."

"Connected how?" Barenz slid his hand inside his shorts and scratched his crotch. "What's the connection?"

"They're Mormons," Baumgartner said. "He made a campaign stop at their church."

"Ah." Barenz pointed repeatedly at Baumgartner. "Jesus freaks, like Sheila."

Maragas motioned toward the recliner. "Sit down, Joe. You're making me nervous."

"I need a beer."

"In a minute," Baumgartner said. "Just a couple more questions and we'll let you get back at it."

Barenz crossed his arms. "Then I'll stay standing." His eyes challenged Maragas.

Baumgartner pulled a photograph from the envelope and set it on the coffee table. "What did you make of the wound on his left ring finger?"

The retired detective leaned forward. "Didn't make nothing of it." Barenz's eyes told a different story, though.

"What aren't you telling us?" Baumgartner asked.

Barenz shook his head. "It's nothing. I got my hopes up is all."

"What do you mean?"

"I worked a case during the Expo. Another homo, but this one was missing his entire ring finger. The killer snipped it right off." Barenz mimed a pair of scissors with his fingers. "Snip, snip."

Baumgartner and Maragas shared a look.

"And?" Baumgartner asked.

"And nothing," Barenz said. Disappointment flashed through his eyes. "This other murder was almost thirty years old, and my lieutenant said I was fishing for connections. I made the mistake of telling him I thought I could catch Salter in a lie—"

"What lie?" Baumgartner interrupted.

"—but that was about the dumbest thing I could have done. Salter's been Teflon since he shot that perv doctor way back when."

"Nobody's Teflon," Dusty said.

"It's cute you think that." Barenz said. He again put his hand in his shorts and scratched himself. "I was ordered to let it go, that's exactly what I did. I know how to be a good soldier and follow orders."

"Tell us about these connections you were fishing for," Baumgartner said. "Tell us about the lie you thought Salter told."

"Ask your lieutenant," Barenz said. "He's at the center of it all."

Maragas leaned forward. "There was a list of names in your file we haven't accounted for. Potential witnesses."

"Which ones?"

Baumgartner flipped open his notepad and read the names, avoiding the ones marked as deceased or moved away. "Deborah Dorsey, Kerry Chabot, Doctor Scott Lynch, Doctor Ralph Townsend, Gerald Parr, and Basil Pershing."

"Pershing?" Barenz smirked. "Salter can tell you about him, too. It's all connected." He headed toward the kitchen. "Now, I'm done answering questions. I'm gonna get myself a beer. If you're still here when I get back, we're watching *Wheel of Fortune*."

Chapter 35

Baumgartner trailed Maragas as she marched confidently down the hallway of the Public Safety Building toward Major Crimes. He admired that about her. While the first "policewomen" hired by SPD served in a limited capacity, Maragas was part of the second wave of women to join. That group served as full-fledged cops, though Baumgartner suspected that Maragas and others were probably token hires at the time. However, she'd proven herself more than worthy in patrol before promoting to detective.

As far as Baumgartner was concerned, patrol was the true proving ground for cops. There were those who flourished, those who survived, and those who fled the division at the first opportunity. The lattermost group sought refuge from answering high priority calls that exposed them to danger. If they tested well, it meant becoming a detective. If they couldn't test out, they instead went into what he considered various soft positions associated with patrol—Neighborhood Resource Officers, Volunteer Services, and the like.

Cops like himself—and Maragas, he believed—who thrived in patrol weren't running from anything. Instead, they were running toward the next challenge. For Baumgartner, who had been a Field Training Officer and a SWAT operator, investigations was the next horizon.

Still, being the new guy again was jarring after being the big dog in patrol. He quickly learned the ropes, though, and, thanks to Salter, was reassigned to Major Crimes in what had to be record time. Now, he was the new guy all over again.

Maragas was a good partner. She trained him without coddling or condescension. He appreciated that, as well as her bias for action. It reminded him of a good SWAT officer in that respect. Right now, as she strode through the bullpen directly toward the lieutenant's office, he wondered if her tendency to "act boldly" wasn't about to bite her in the ass.

Not just her, he realized.

Us.

Baumgartner didn't voice any protest, however. He'd learned very early in his career to always back his partner's play. The middle of the fight wasn't the time to air out disagreements.

Maragas reached the open doorway to Salter's office. She rapped sharply on the frame with her knuckles. "We need to talk, Lieutenant."

Baumgartner couldn't see Salter's reaction, but when Maragas stepped into the office, he followed her inside. Without being told, he closed the door behind himself. When he turned around, Salter eyed him curiously but didn't comment.

The lieutenant slid his gaze to Maragas. "What is it, Detective?"

Maragas held up the Lockett case file. "I don't appreciate getting dry-gulched, sir."

Salter's eyes narrowed. "Dry-gulched? What the hell does that mean?"

She gave the folder a shake. "I thought at first you didn't want to pollute our thinking with this case. Admired the sentiment, in fact. Now I think you're just hiding things."

Baumgartner tried to keep his expression neutral while Maragas spoke. He'd sometimes heard patrol officers speak harshly to other officers or even to a sergeant on occasion if it was warranted. To hear Maragas tear into a lieutenant was another level entirely. Baumgartner imagined how angry it'd make him if he were the one sitting across from her.

Salter's reaction was cold, however. He didn't respond for several seconds. Then he said, "I told you what you needed to know. Don't think you know better than I do what that is."

"You're right," said Maragas. "I don't know your job, but I do know my job, Lieutenant. Believe it or not, I may even know how to do it better than you."

"I'm sure you do. I was never a detective."

"I recall." Maragas stared at him, her expression hard. "Before I wear out any more shoe leather on this, I need to know something. Do you want this case solved?"

"Yes." There was no hesitation in Salter's voice.

"Then I need to know what you're not telling me."

Salter turned over one hand and twitched a finger. "Ask away."

"Why did Barenz get shut down when this case was first worked?"

Salter frowned. "Worked? Barenz? That's a stretch."

"He made notes. Conducted interviews. He was a lazy bum most of the time, but he seemed engaged on this one." She peered more closely at Salter. "I think it had something to do with you."

"It did," Salter admitted. "He was looking to use this case as a cudgel to beat me with."

Baumgartner felt his pulse quicken. He wasn't naïve enough to believe vendettas between officers didn't work their way into official police work, but a detective gunning for a lieutenant? That had old grudge written all over it. He edged forward, listening carefully.

"Barenz wanted to connect Lockett to an old unsolved of his, a young man named Isaac Hermitage," Salter explained. "Hermitage may have actually been a victim from an incident I was involved with back then."

"Back when?" Maragas asked. "Which incident?"

"From seventy-four," Salter said.

Maragas leaned back in her chair. "Oh, *the* incident, huh? The one that made you."

Baumgartner knew the basics of the tale. It was department legend and he'd first heard about it at the academy. The story was repeated by patrol officers once he hit the street, including his own training officer. The details differed depending on who did the telling, but all of them recounted how young Gus Salter, who had not even been through the academy yet, saved a veteran detective's life in a fierce gun battle with an armed murderer named Michael Andrews. The event was held up as a heroic example for others to follow. Salter was even awarded the first-ever Silver Star when the department created the medal almost a decade later.

It was a high bar to be compared to, Baumgartner thought. Like a basketball player being asked to emulate Michael Jordan.

Salter gave Maragas a short nod. "Barenz wanted to discredit me."

"Why?"

"Bad blood from way back. He and his old partner never liked me, and they had no love for Pierce, either."

"Walter Pierce?" Baumgartner asked.

"The very same," Salter said. He cocked his head. "You knew him?"

"No, but I was in the training car when he died. My FTO took me to the funeral."

Salter glanced down at his desktop. "That was a sad day. Pierce was the last of a generation."

"What made Barenz think he could beat you up over this case?" Maragas pressed.

"I imagine he thought he could prove that Lockett's death was related to Hermitage somehow. Then he'd look to connect Hermitage to the suspect in my shooting, Dr. Andrews. Cast doubt on the official report somehow. Make a mess. That's what people like Barenz do. Hell, aside from being lazy, it's just about the *only* thing people like him do." Salter shrugged. "When his intent became clear, my predecessor shut him down. He wasn't trying to solve a case, he was trying to get revenge."

"Revenge for what?"

"All the slights the world has given him," said Salter, "some of which I'm sure he saw as coming directly from me."

Maragas didn't speak for several seconds. Her brows knitted in concentration. Baumgartner felt a tickle in his throat but resisted the urge to clear it.

Finally, Maragas asked, "What made Barenz think he could connect the cases?"

Salter didn't reply immediately. He glanced at the closed door, then reached for his coffee cup. He took a sip, his eyes thoughtful. Baumgartner grudgingly admired his self-control. If it'd been him in the lieutenant's place, he'd probably be roaring mad by now.

Next to him, Maragas waited as patient as Salter.

The lieutenant lowered the cup and deliberately placed it on the desk. "Barenz in his prime was a mediocre detective, at best. But he was onto something. True to his nature, though, he had that something wrong."

"You're speaking in riddles," Maragas said. Then she added, "Sir."

Salter reached for a notepad and pen. While he scrawled on the paper, he spoke. "The man I shot in seventy-four was a murderer, but he wasn't the only murderer we were looking for." He finished writing and put down the pen. "Pierce and I thought it was possible a man named Karl Etherton was responsible for the deaths of Isaac Hermitage and another man, Hudson Dorsey."

Baumgartner recognized the name Dorsey from the file.

"Etherton?" Maragas asked, tilting her head again. "The guy from the fifties? Doctor with the dungeon?"

"You know your history."

"History is all he probably is by now," she said. "Even if he were alive, he'd have to be in his eighties."

"That sounds right."

"Barenz liked an eighty-year-old man for the Lockett killing?" Maragas asked, incredulous.

Baumgartner's reaction mirrored hers. His own grandfather had lived into his eighties. He'd been a strapping man in his time, but Baumgartner couldn't imagine his grandfather capable of besting anyone in their twenties.

"Lockett was in an extremely vulnerable position, wasn't he?" Salter asked. "If the killer used a blunt-edged weapon to strike the head, how strong would he need to be for that blow to be effective?"

Maragas considered. "Not very strong," she admitted. "If placed correctly."

Salter pushed the paper across the desk toward her. Maragas made no move to accept it. "I'm not saying it was Etherton who killed Lockett," Salter said. "That's the theory Barenz intended to push. Even if he was wrong, it would have shined a light on the old Hermitage and Dorsey cases due to the similar victim profile and M.O.s. Barenz could also link them both to the Richard Clark case."

When neither Maragas nor Baumgartner reacted, Salter added, "Dr. Michael Andrews murdered Clark at his home. Pierce and I got there too late."

Maragas lifted a hand, palm up. "What's the connection?"

"Victim profile and the killer's methods, as I said." Salter was quiet a moment, before he said, "There was a time during the investigation that Pierce suspected Andrews was actually Etherton. He wasn't, but the idea that Etherton might return to Spokane remained."

"Etherton's name is nowhere in Barenz's file," Maragas said.

"It is if you know what you're looking for."

Maragas stared at the file for several seconds. She glanced at Baumgartner before saying, "That's why Barenz has a second witness list."

Salter dipped his chin in confirmation.

Maragas flipped it open and read several names. "Still alive and in Spokane, we've got Deborah Dorsey, Kerry Chabot, Doctor Scott Lynch, Doctor Ralph Townsend, Gerald Parr, and Basil Pershing." She looked up. "Barenz seemed particularly worked up over that last one."

"Pershing," Salter said quietly. "Aside from Etherton, he was the one commonality. A victim in fifty-one, a witness in seventy-four."

"What's the significance?"

"I'll let you decide."

Maragas leaned forward and picked up the paper slip from the desk. She cast a suspicious eye toward Salter. Baumgartner was glad he wasn't on the receiving end of that look. "Is this going to dirty us, Lieutenant? Because it sounds like there was some shady shit going on with these cases back in the day."

"It was a different time," Salter said. "A different era."

Baumgartner knew that was code for dismissing corrupt police behavior in the past, whether well-intentioned or outright dirty. Perhaps what Salter said about it being a different time was true but Baumgartner didn't like it. Just because dishonest actions were a part of the fabric back then didn't excuse the ethical lapse. Different era or not, wrong was wrong.

"Maybe so," Maragas said, "but there's a council member involved in this, too. The whole affair reeks of political bullshit on top of whatever problems there are with the case itself."

"Let me worry about the political bullshit," Salter told her. He pointed to what he'd written. "Read those files, then find who killed James Lockett and knock down this case."

"No matter the cost?" Maragas asked.

Salter's expression was resolute. "No matter the cost."

＊＊＊

When they returned to their desks, Baumgartner let out a long breath of relief. "Jesus," he said. "Warn me before you do that next time."

"Do what?"

"Wave a cape at a bull. Especially one wearing lieutenant's bars."

Maragas brushed his comment away with a sweep of her hand. "Would it have made a difference?"

Baumgartner wanted to say yes, but realized she was right. Instead of answering, he gestured toward the paper Maragas had collected from Salter's desk before they left the lieutenant's office. "What'd he write down?"

She peered down at the notes. "Victims and years. I'll need to pull the report numbers and get the case files from Records."

"Great," muttered Baumgartner. He dreaded trips to the Records Division, where Hazel Thompson was the Queen of Mean. He had never met anyone he classified as a crone until his first encounter with the records clerk, who had been a fixture in the police department for decades. Officers and detectives legitimately feared the wrath of Hazel, which could be provoked by something as simple as incorrectly completing a records request form or exceeding the policy on the timeframe for submitting reports. He wished the woman would finally decide to retire.

"I'll handle it," Maragas said. She handed the Lockett file to him. "You get good addresses on the local witnesses on Barenz's list."

The two detectives each sat down at their respective desks. Baumgartner began running the names on the witness list Barenz had compiled. Next to him, the clatter of keys came in bursts as Maragas looked up report numbers. She finished a few minutes before he did and pushed her chair away from the desk.

"Wait for me," Baumgartner said. "I'm almost done. We can go straight from Records to the car."

Maragas leaned over and examined his work. "You've got at least another ten minutes to go."

"Five, tops."

She grunted doubtfully and reached into her desk. "I'm going for a smoke."

To Baumgartner's chagrin, finishing the task took him closer to ten minutes than five. He slid his notes into the Lockett file and took it with him down the hall to the west doors of the building. The large public entrance was on the south side, directly across from the courthouse, but employees were allowed to use this side entry.

Through the double set of glass doors, Baumgartner saw Maragas standing ten feet away from the entrance. She leaned forward, her elbows resting on the concrete retaining wall that ran the length of the west side of the building's wide sidewalk. She stared off into the distance while a cigarette smoldered between her fingers.

When he stepped through the outside doors, Maragas glanced in his direction. She stood and took a final drag on her cigarette. "You get them all?" she asked, exhaling a plume of smoke.

Baumgartner nodded. "Except for the ones that were dead."

"Was that many?"

"More than I expected."

Maragas frowned. "Dead witnesses don't say much."

Baumgartner shrugged. The first lesson Maragas reinforced when they'd been partnered together was witnesses lie. Some did it on purpose; others were just unreliable. He already knew that from his earlier work in investigations and patrol, of course. What he learned anew was having fewer witnesses in a case wasn't necessarily good, but it did make for a simpler investigation.

Maragas stubbed out her cigarette and flicked it into the sand ashtray that ringed the top of the nearby garbage can. "Let's get these other files, huh?"

Baumgartner pressed his ID card against the reader. When it clicked, he held the door open for her and followed her inside. They headed to the Records Division. Baumgartner hoped Hazel Thompson was busy or at lunch so they wouldn't have to deal with her exacting nature. As they approached the officers' counter, he saw Hazel working nearby.

Hazel Thompson had probably been a tall woman at one time, but now she had a hunched posture. Her brown hair was cut into a bob and laced with gray. She wore a crème-colored shirt with large white buttons and a blue skirt. Pearl earrings hung from sagging earlobes. While her face was wrinkled and worn, sharp eyes caught everything that happened in or around her domain.

"Detectives," she said, cordial but distant. Her voice held the slight waver of age.

Maragas greeted her and reached for a request slip. "Okay if I put multiple report numbers on the same slip?" she asked. Maragas wrote down one number and looked up. "I know you don't usually like that, but it might be easier for this one."

"Why?"

"These are older cases. Physical files, probably stored in the archives."

Hazel's expression turned to one of disapproval. Baumgartner didn't blame her. He imagined going offsite to the archived records storage building was a pain. Then again, it was her job. "That might take a couple of days," she told them. "I'll need to send someone to retrieve the files."

Maragas glanced down and resumed writing. "This is a priority case," she said.

"Says who?"

Maragas finished filling out the form. "Well, right now, it's just me asking. I suppose it could be Lieutenant Salter, if it needs to be. Or the chief, if Salter won't do." She slid the request form across the counter. "Do you think maybe the overnight crew could scare them up? If we could have them in the morning, that'd be great."

Hazel glanced down at the slip of paper, then did a double take. "These are very old," she said, her voice softening. She looked up at Maragas. "I recognize these names. These were Walter's cases."

Baumgartner was impressed. Over her career of forty-plus years, how many reports had she processed and filed? How did she remember these?

"I wish he were still here to help," Maragas said, her own tone quieter, too. "We could use the assist."

"He would have liked that," said Hazel. Her eyes shone with tears. "He talked about them sometimes."

Baumgartner looked away awkwardly. Now he recalled Hazel was at Pierce's funeral. She wasn't officially his widow, since they'd never married, but they'd been together for a long time. He should have recalled that.

"You were in the honor guard that day," Hazel said to Maragas.

"I was."

"You all did a good job." Hazel's voice was raspy. "You sent him on his way right."

"We did our best. He deserved that."

"Yes, he did." Hazel cleared her throat. "I'll see if I can get one of those lazy interns from swing shift to pull these. The reports should be here in the morning."

"Thank you," Dusty told her. "See you then." She started to go, then stopped. "You still like poppy-seed?"

Hazel smiled. "Who doesn't?"

"Crazy people," said Maragas.

The two detectives turned away from the counter and headed out to the car.

***

"I don't think I've ever seen her smile," Baumgartner commented as Maragas pushed open the west doors. "Or get emotional at all. Except maybe being angry at some cop screwing up paperwork."

Maragas waited for him to step through. "Old people weren't always old," she said. "Everybody has a past."

"I know that."

Maragas ignored his protest. Instead of following Baumgartner, she returned to the retaining wall a few strides away. Baumgartner had already turned towards the north lot. He saw her change direction and pulled up short.

"What are you doing?"

Maragas tapped out a cigarette in reply and lit up.

Baumgartner sighed and shuffled over to join her. He held up the file. "You want to start with the closest?"

Maragas shook her head. "I want to read the files we get from Hazel before we talk to any of the witnesses. No sense flying blind when we can get all the background first."

"Then what's the plan?"

Maragas didn't answer right away. The silence was reminiscent of Salter's power play earlier when he assigned the case to them. Baumgartner set his jaw and waited.

"This case is going to go bad," Maragas said.

"For us, you mean?"

She inhaled deeply and lifted one shoulder in a mild shrug. "For somebody."

"You can't know that."

Maragas blew smoke out her nose. "I don't *know* it, but I can *feel* it. There's an ugliness to this one."

"We work murders. Every case is ugly."

"It's all relative," she said, "but this one feels fucked."

Her apprehension was curious to Baumgartner. Since being partnered with Maragas, he had yet to see anything rattle her. This was something less than being rattled but he could read the concern in her eyes while she smoked next to him.

They stood in silence for another minute before Maragas spoke again. "Call it a day," she said. "We'll attack this again tomorrow."

Baumgartner didn't argue. In a fresh case, they worked as long as they could go in order to accomplish as much as possible before the trail grew cold. But this case was already two years old. The other ones Salter mentioned were decades old. Any leads they might discover were not going to get any colder overnight. Besides, he had a date lined up with a nursing student. Darla might not be Miss Right, but she was looking pretty good as Miss Right Now.

"Whatever you've got planned," Maragas said, "make it an early night. Hazel gets to work at six, and we're going to be waiting for her."

Chapter 36

Baumgartner walked into the bullpen at 6:15 a.m. All the desks were dark except for the one belonging to Maragas. Light shone down from the long fluorescent bar underneath the top cabinet, illuminating the desktop, but her chair was empty.

He'd already stopped by records. Hazel was munching a poppyseed muffin and drinking Starbucks coffee when he arrived. When he asked if Maragas had been past yet, Hazel swallowed a bite and said, "Come and gone," before returning to her muffin.

Baumgartner turned on his own desk light and wandered around the unit. He spotted a sliver of light coming from underneath the interview room door. He walked over and knocked.

"You're late," Maragas called from inside.

Baumgartner entered the room. Maragas sat in one of the chairs with multiple files spread out across the table. Her hand curled around a Starbucks cup. An empty muffin paper was crumpled next to it. A second coffee cup sat nearby with a green plastic stopper still in the drinking spout.

He didn't bother to respond to her comment. Instead, he pulled the other chair close and sat down across from Maragas. "What do we have?"

"I'm only a few minutes into the seventy-four cases." She motioned toward a thick binder that was still closed. "Why don't you get after the fifty-one case?"

Baumgartner reached for the coffee first, murmuring his thanks. Maragas didn't acknowledge the nicety, already reading again. Once he had a couple of sips of the dark brew, Baumgartner slid over to create elbow and leg room and grabbed the binder from fifty-one. He flipped it open and started reading.

For the next several hours, the detectives studied the case files. When the coffee ran out, Baumgartner retrieved their ceramic cups from his desk and hers and refilled them at the Major Crimes coffee station, the first of several trips. Once he finished reviewing the fifty-one case, he started in on the seventy-four cases, following the same reading order Maragas took. Meanwhile, she looped back around to the fifty-one file.

By the time they were finished, it was nearing lunchtime. Baumgartner's stomach grumbled.

Maragas closed all the files and stacked them on top of each other. "Let's lock these up and get some food."

At his desk, Baumgartner slid open an unused file drawer on his desk. He had two drawers but had only been in the unit long enough to partially fill one. Maragas lowered the case files into the empty drawer and directed him to lock it. Baumgartner hadn't needed to lock his desk before and didn't have the key on his ring. He had to scrounge around in the center drawer until he found it.

Once Maragas was satisfied the files were secure, she tossed her car keys to Baumgartner. "Pull around to the west doors."

"What are you going to do?"

"Query regional agencies for unsolved sexual homicides with mutilation." She shrugged. "Maybe we're just one more stop on some serial killer's tour of the Pacific Northwest. We get a return on our query, maybe there's DNA on their case, too. We submit, could be we get a match."

Baumgartner wished he'd thought to do that. He nodded his agreement and headed out to get her car.

Once Maragas emerged from the west doors and took over driving duty, Baumgartner hoped for another trip to Domini's. Instead, Maragas took them through a Zip's drive-thru. The regional hamburger chain was a favorite among patrol cops.

When Maragas asked what he wanted, Baumgartner ordered his usual—two cheeseburgers, fries, and a cola.

"At least get diet cola," Maragas said, her tone disapproving. "You're not burning SWAT calories anymore."

"Diet tastes like shit. Get me some extra tartar sauce, though."

She wrinkled her nose. "*That* tastes like shit."

Baumgartner wondered how she could taste much of anything due to smoking so often but didn't say so.

Maragas sighed and recited his order, followed by her own. "Cheeseburger, no pickle, and a black coffee."

Baumgartner handed her a bill as they crept forward to the window. "On me," he said.

She shook her head. "We go Dutch."

"Don't worry," he said. "Just because I pay doesn't make it a date."

"That's not it."

"What, then?"

"Something Salter said to me when he was a sergeant on patrol. This was years ago, before I made detective."

"What'd he say? Don't date your co-workers?" It was a piece of advice Baumgartner's mentors had given him. He hadn't followed it initially, but it only took one soured relationship with a dispatcher to convince Baumgartner of the wisdom in those words.

"He didn't need to tell me that," Maragas said. "No one needed to." She took some cash from her pocket and peeled off several bills. "What he said was to always pay your own way. Never let anybody own you. He said it should be a priority."

***

They ate in the car, parked under a tree alongside Corbin Park. The park was only a block wide north to south but ran several blocks east to west. City streets looped around it, reminding Baumgartner of the Playfair horse racing track that no longer existed out on the eastern fringe of the city. Citizens meandered through the park with dogs while a foursome of young men played two-on-two at the half-court basketball slab. Everyone from joggers to power walkers to parents with strollers circled the park on the asphalt trail that ran along the outside edge.

Baumgartner jammed his first burger into his mouth, eating quickly. It was a habit he'd picked up on patrol and hadn't yet shed since his promotion. Next to him, Maragas watched disdainfully.

"Don't choke," she cautioned.

"I've got a system," he said.

He did, actually. One burger to curb the hunger, then enjoy the fries and second burger at a leisurely pace. Maragas seemed to sense his method, because she ate quietly and didn't say anything until he'd finished the first burger and taken a drink of soda.

"Didn't I tell you this was a mess?" she said.

"I think you said it was fucked."

"It *is* fucked."

"Ask you something?" Baumgartner slid his second burger from the bag. "What made you decide to send out the query to other departments?"

"You wouldn't have?"

"I might have," Baumgartner hedged, though he knew it wouldn't have been high on his list of actions to take in a case like this. "This seems like a pretty local case."

"Could be it is." Maragas took a small bite of her burger. Baumgartner waited impatiently for her to finish chewing before she continued. "Just covering my bases."

"In case it's that guy Etherton?" Baumgartner had a hard time keeping the skepticism out of his voice.

"You don't give the idea much credence?"

"No," said Baumgartner.

"That sounds close-minded."

"It's not. I'm being realistic."

"Share this realism with me, then." Maragas took another bite of her burger and stared at him, waiting.

Baumgartner sipped his Coke while he organized his thoughts. "It all hinges on believing the man is still alive and has successfully assumed a new identity. It's what Pierce and Salter thought back in seventy-four and look how wrong they were."

"He definitely assumed a new identity," Maragas said.

"How do you know?"

"He escaped, didn't he? He kept on living. The only way to do that and avoid detection was to be someone else. So, logically, he was successful at that."

Baumgartner grabbed several fries and stuffed them in his mouth. "Fine," he said, still chewing. "But the idea of him coming back to Spokane and committing the same crimes again while in disguise? I just don't see it."

"That's because you lack imagination."

"Good thing I'm a detective, then, and not a comic book writer."

Maragas smirked, but Baumgartner saw amusement in her expression, too.

He forged ahead, encouraged. "In the end, most cases are straightforward. There's no grand conspiracy of the elite, no surgery to get new faces, no crooked cops covering up secrets, or whatever. It's just run-of-the-mill human darkness."

"Most of the time," Maragas agreed. "Either way, you're right about seventy-four. Doctor Michael Andrews was his own brand of shithead, but he wasn't Karl Etherton in disguise."

"Exactly."

"The question is, did Andrews kill Isaac Hermitage and Hudson Dorsey? Official reports aside, of course."

Baumgartner narrowed his eyes. "Simplest answer is yes."

"The right answer isn't always simple."

"Okay," said Baumgartner. "Say Pierce and Salter were right about Etherton getting a new name or even plastic surgery. He comes back to Spokane and kills Hermitage, Dorsey, and maybe Kerley, too. How does that link him to James Lockett?"

Maragas lifted her hand and tapped her ring finger.

Baumgartner sighed. "Those killings were almost thirty years ago. Unless Etherton is immune to the aging curve..."

"Look," Maragas said, "the idea of an eighty-something-year old man still active as a serial killer strikes me as unlikely, but *unlikely* doesn't mean *implausible*. It's a far cry from impossible."

Baumgartner took a moment to consider the proposition. His thoughts drifted back to his own grandfather again. He tried to imagine the man being physically capable enough to overwhelm a twenty-year-old. The man had remained tough as nails, sure, but that was different than winning a fight against a much younger opponent. It was difficult to see.

"I don't think someone that old would be strong enough," he said.

She dipped her chin in agreement. "Eighty is getting up there," she said. "Seventy would be easier to believe, but it isn't strength that worries me. In a man, strength is the last thing to go. Think about old boxers, like George Foreman. He still had all of his punch, even during his comeback."

"Foreman wasn't eighty. He *still* isn't."

"I realize that. It was an analogy. My point is coordination and agility deteriorate much earlier than strength. If you're going to protest that an eighty-year-old man couldn't have killed Lockett, that's a better argument than lack of strength."

"Strength, coordination, reflexes... take your pick," Baumgartner shrugged. "Regardless, I seriously doubt it."

"You're not wrong," said Maragas. She bit into her burger and chewed, staring out through the windshield. "I was thinking about how we tend to look at people when they get older. We infantilize them. Assume they are frail and weak. Because of this, we assume they're harmless."

"Most are."

"Are they?" She shook her head. "I think what happens with most people that age is we forget about them. We see them but barely notice them. They're no longer relevant to much of what is happening in the world, at least in our eyes. But what if…" She trailed off, pursing her lips while she thought.

"What if what?" Baumgartner prodded.

Maragas glanced over at him. "Look at it this way—how much do people really change over time? If someone is a jerk at thirty or forty, is there any reason he wouldn't still be a jerk at eighty?"

"Probably. Maybe more so. Old people get grumpy."

"How about a sexual deviant? He's not going to undergo a fundamental psychological change just because the years pass. If anything, his nature would become more firmly embedded in who he is."

"At eighty, I don't know if sex is a priority."

"Acting on it might not be, but I'll bet the thoughts and wishes are still there."

Baumgartner shrugged. He couldn't imagine his grandfather chasing skirts while in his eighties but there was no way he could argue what the man may have thought about or longed for.

"Why should it be any different with a serial killer?" Maragas asked. "His nature won't have changed. The compulsion is still there. He'd want—no, he'd *need* to act on it. If he's smart, he could find ways to level the playing field with his victims."

"How?"

"Subterfuge. Weapons." Maragas waved her half-eaten burger. "There's a big difference between winning a wrestling match and a well-placed stab with a sharp knife."

"Lockett wasn't stabbed."

"You're missing my broader point."

Baumgartner took a deep breath and let it out. Then he picked up his soda and wrapped his lips around the straw. While he drank, he thought about her theory.

It sounded crazy.

"You think I'm off my rocker," Maragas said.

"No," Baumgartner replied automatically. He could hear the way he involuntarily elongated the word and inwardly cringed. He might as well have yelled yes.

"It's all right," she said. "We can disagree. This is a good process."

Baumgartner eyed her closely. "Do *you* believe Etherton is our guy?"

"Not really." Maragas gave him a tight grin. "I'm just not willing to completely discount it yet. Even if I was, if we bust this case open and arrest someone else, any good defense attorney would throw up this theory as an alternative at trial. It only takes one juror who believes in conspiracies to hang a jury. So we have to run it down as best we can, if only to disprove it."

Baumgartner nodded slowly. That much he understood and agreed with.

They shifted back to the Lockett case, bouncing the facts back and forth, ensuring both saw them in the same way. A couple of minor points resulted in some debate, but in the end, their respective viewpoints were similar. Then they volleyed the details of the fifty-one and seventy-four cases to ensure the same. Baumgartner found the attention to detail displayed by Maragas to be both admirable and disheartening at the same time—would he ever reach that same level, he wondered? The result was they saw and understood the fact pattern in much the same way. Both detectives now had the same baseline understanding, which made moving forward much easier.

"What's next?" Baumgartner asked.

It was a legitimate question. Most cases had obvious avenues when it came to investigating. This one might, if it weren't for the additions Salter threw at them. Now, it seemed too sprawling, and Baumgartner was uncertain which aspect to explore first.

"In a normal case," Maragas said, "I'd be in favor of redoing those early interviews Barenz conducted. Talk to anyone connected with Lockett. This feels different, though."

Baumgartner nodded while he chewed. "I don't think it was someone Lockett knew. Not with where it happened or how he was found."

"I tend to agree. So, instead, we most likely have a stranger-to-stranger case, which is exponentially harder."

"Not to mention we've got no match on the DNA." Baumgartner reached for a fry and dipped it into the tartar sauce.

"Which still bothers me," Maragas grumbled. "So does this bombshell from the lieutenant. I don't know if any of these other cases are remotely connected but since our suspect pool is currently a large percentage of the male population in Spokane, these old cases seem like a good place to start." She took a bite and stared thoughtfully out the window. When she'd swallowed, she added, "Who knows? Maybe that handsy slob Barenz was onto something."

"I doubt it," Baumgartner said, and reached for another fry.

* * *

The first witness was Doctor Scott Lynch. He answered the door and stared at them coldly. Sunlight shone through his thin white hair and reflected off his scalp. A pair of glasses perched on his nose. He wore tan casual slacks and a blue short-sleeved shirt with all but the top button done. To Baumgartner, he looked ready for the golf course.

"Why are you here?" he snapped at Maragas as soon as she showed her badge.

"We're doing some follow-up on a cold case," she explained. "Can we come in and ask you a few questions?"

"No, you may not come in," Lynch said imperiously, "and if I agree to answer any questions at all, they had better be *few*."

Maragas smiled. "Have I done something to offend you, sir?"

"It's *Doctor*," Lynch said. "Don't try to establish rapport with me. Just get on with your questions."

"All right," Maragas said easily. "Detectives spoke to you back in 1974 about a case that—"

As soon as she mentioned the year, Lynch's features hardened further. He stepped back through the entryway and swung the door shut with a slam.

Baumgartner looked at Maragas. "I'll take that as a *declined to be interviewed*?"

Maragas frowned and headed for the car.

***

The next stop was another doctor, this one Doctor Ralph Townsend. The man's flat countenance and skeletal physique immediately creeped out Baumgartner. He didn't invite them inside, but instead closed the door behind himself and led them around the side of the house toward the backyard. Despite the man's age, which Baumgartner estimated to be early seventies, Townsend moved gracefully. Once in the backyard, he gestured to a table on the patio, and they all sat.

"Do you remember talking to detectives years ago?" Maragas asked him. "This would have been in seventy-four."

"I do," said Townsend. His voice had a smooth, urbane quality that reminded Baumgartner of the actor Peter Cushing. "What about it?"

"We're conducting some follow up."

Townsend raised his brow. "If I recall, that was resolved. One of your officers shot the man responsible, did he not?"

"He did," Maragas said.

"A doctor," Baumgartner added, wanting to put the self-assured Townsend off balance.

Townsend seemed unfazed. "Every profession has its bad apples," he said.

The sliding glass door behind Townsend opened. A young Filipino man in a loose-fitting salmon-pink shirt and white shorts leaned his head out. "Should I bring some refreshments, Doctor?"

Townsend tilted his head slightly. "Detectives? Some iced tea, perhaps?"

Maragas shook her head. "No, but thanks for the offer."

"That will be all, Crisanto," Townsend said, without turning his head.

The young man smiled solicitously and slid the door closed.

"Who's that?" Baumgartner asked.

"My companion," Townsend said.

Baumgartner's eyes narrowed. A number of comments and questions occurred to him, none of which would help their current investigation. He clenched his jaw and remained silent.

Townsend showed no discomfort at the exchange. He folded his hands. "How exactly can I help you, Detective?"

"When Detective Pierce spoke to you before," Maragas said, "he confirmed you frequented male prostitutes downtown."

Townsend stared at her, unblinking. When she didn't say anything else, he said, "Is that a question?"

"More me asking for confirmation, but yes."

"I see. Then, yes, that is true."

"You saw male prostitutes."

"Often," Townsend said. "In those days, much of the trade was behind a bar called Rags to Riches. They called it Queer Alley, though I suppose that moniker might not be so acceptable today."

"Did you ever see Isaac Hermitage?" Maragas asked. "Or Hudson Dorsey?"

"I may have. I liked variety."

"How about Daniel Kerley? Or Rick Clark?"

Townsend eyed her coldly. "Detective, I can't say for certain if I used the services of those men or not. I never asked their names. My interactions were purely transactional and purposefully anonymous."

"I could show you their pictures."

"I'd rather not."

"Why?"

"I assume they were victims of some kind. I'd prefer not to see that. It's distasteful. For your purposes, it is safe to assume if they were working in that alley in 1974, then in all likelihood, I may have had consensual sex with them."

Maragas smiled tightly, no humor in her eyes. "I'm surprised you're squeamish about that. You were a doctor, after all."

"I *am* a doctor," he corrected. "However, my specialty was as a podiatrist, not a forensic pathologist."

Maragas walked through the remainder of the interview carefully while Baumgartner took notes. Out of habit, he jotted down a few facts, but in his opinion, Townsend said nothing of consequence.

While the man spoke, Baumgartner reviewed his biographical details from the file. Aside from the ancient entries in the system regarding patronizing a prostitute, Townsend had no criminal record. He was retired from a long practice. There was no reason to consider him a suspect.

When Crisanto returned near the end of the interview to check again about refreshments, Baumgartner's jaw tightened once more. He wanted to ask how old Crisanto was, though his own honest estimate put the man in his twenties. Maybe the living situation was entirely consensual, but he couldn't shake the idea that Townsend was somehow exploiting Crisanto.

When the interview was complete, Townsend escorted them politely back to the front walkway. Baumgartner caught a glance of Crisanto watching them through a slight part in the front curtains.

As soon as they were in the car, Maragas let out a long sigh. "That guy made my skin crawl."

"Mine, too," Baumgartner agreed. "If this were a movie, he'd be our guy."

Maragas started the car. "Hundred percent. I get the feeling he's somebody's guy for some unsolved case somewhere."

"You think Crisanto is there voluntarily?"

"Probably."

Baumgartner frowned. "Is that racist? To ask, I mean. Or homophobic?"

"Maybe, but would you think any differently if it was a young white woman who was waiting on him like that?"

He considered. "No, about the same," he said.

"Me, too. Anyway, I think we both get a pass on this one."

"Why's that?"

"Because Doctor Ralph Townsend is a creepy fuck."

Baumgartner laughed.

Maragas smiled slightly. "It goes to my earlier point, though. He's someone I could see being physically capable of a crime like Lockett's murder."

"He's, what…?" Baumgartner consulted his notes to find Townsend's birthdate. He did some quick math. "Seventy-three. Not mid-eighties."

Maragas shrugged. "I'm just sayin'."

***

Deborah Dorsey couldn't have been more different than Townsend. A thin woman in her mid-seventies, she sat on a loveseat and smiled placidly at both detectives. A severe hooked nose that gave her a witch-like appearance wasn't enough to change Baumgartner's impression she was a kindly person. Her light gray hair was pulled into a tight bun. Her caregiver, a thirty-something red-headed woman who introduced herself as Rosalind, stood nearby, hovering protectively.

Maragas asked Deborah a few questions, but Baumgartner could tell she'd assessed the situation in much the same way he had upon meeting the woman. She wasn't a suspect. After a couple of exchanges, it became clear she had little to offer in terms of new information.

"Do either of you have children?" she asked the detectives. She focused most of her attention on Baumgartner.

He shook his head in unison with Maragas.

"If you ever do, I pray you don't experience losing them like I lost my Hudson." Tears brimmed the old woman's eyes. "A piece of me died right there with him. It was like some of the light went out of the world, never to return."

A stab of guilt hit Baumgartner. He felt bad for reminding the woman of what he was sure had been the most terrible event in her life.

"But we go on," Deborah said. "We have to. What other choice is there?"

She gave them a plaintive look, as if the question weren't rhetorical and he or Maragas might have an actual alternative to offer. He knew there were several, of course, but he wasn't about to offer those thoughts to her.

Maragas thanked her and the two of them left.

"This job is depressing sometimes," Baumgartner grumbled. "First, a dirty old man and then a sad old woman."

"That could be us in a few decades."

"I might get old, but I'll never be dirty."

Maragas let out a bark of laughter. "You already are."

Baumgartner narrowed his eyes. "I'm no pervert."

"I didn't say that but you've got a reputation as a bit of a dog."

"That's different."

Maragas shrugged.

Baumgartner let out a long sigh. "I need a vacation."

Gerald Parr was a name Baumgartner had been tempted to cross off the list. Pierce's original report noted he had been a john who frequented male prostitutes. He'd been ill when Pierce and Salter conducted their initial interview. The notes also stated Parr's wife had been present.

It was this last fact that convinced Baumgartner to leave him on the list. He imagined Parr had been less than forthcoming about his activities. That must have occurred to Pierce and Salter yet he remained essentially a footnote in the investigation. He mentioned this to Maragas as they drove to Parr's home in northeast Spokane.

"Probably a gut feeling," she said, blowing smoke out the open driver's window. "It's the kind of question that would be nice to ask one of them, but since Pierce is gone…"

"We could ask Salter."

"You want to ask him?"

Baumgartner looked away. He was grateful to Salter for selecting him for Major Crimes, but he still regarded the man with a strange mixture of fear, respect, and mystery. Running a case with Salter appealed to him about as much as going to a nudist beach with his parents.

Regardless of the reasons Pierce and Salter may have discounted Parr as a suspect, he and Maragas found a new one. The man answered the door in a wheelchair, and they soon learned he had multiple sclerosis.

"Hit me at fifty-seven years old," he told them. "It's a slow burn. I was able to use a cane up until about four years ago."

Maragas walked through her questions with him. While they spoke, Baumgartner noticed the photos on the wall and nearby shelf. They showed a woman he assumed was Parr's wife. None of the pictures were recent. He waited for an opening in the interview to ask about it.

"I lost her in ninety-nine. A crash on New Year's Eve." He shook his head. "Everyone was all freaked out about Y2K, but not us. We should have listened and stayed home that night."

"I'm sorry," Baumgartner said reflexively.

Maragas was respectfully quiet for a moment, then asked, "Back in the seventies, when you were around the hustling scene, did you come across anyone suspicious?"

Parr shifted slightly in his chair. "Looking back, suspicious was all I saw. I suppose that had more to do with me than anyone else. I shouldn't have been down there. I shouldn't have done what I did."

"Anybody stand out to you more than the rest?"

"I didn't have much to do with anyone except the men I… the ones I met."

"No other johns?"

Parr winced slightly at the word. "Not really. At least, not directly. We saw each other in the bar or the alley, that's all."

"No one stood out?"

"There were a few that seemed more… sharklike? I'd say predatory, but that has a different connotation than the meaning I'm trying to convey." He paused. "Or maybe it doesn't entirely."

"These men seemed dangerous to you?"

"That's a good way to put it."

Baumgartner made a note on his pad.

"Do you remember who any of these dangerous men were?" Maragas asked.

"No," said Parr, "but a couple of them were doctors. Or so I heard."

"Doctors," Maragas repeated. She glanced at Baumgartner. He suspected the image of Townsend's ghoulish features was going through her mind. It was certainly flitting through his.

"One of them was caught, wasn't he?" Parr asked. "A detective shot him. It was in the newspaper."

"What about the other doctor?"

Parr turned over a tremulous hand. "I don't know."

"Would you recognize him if you saw him again?"

"I don't think so. It was a long time ago." He looked from Maragas to Baumgartner and back. "I'm sorry."

Maragas asked a few more questions. They thanked him and left.

As they walked toward the car, Baumgartner asked, "Doesn't MS usually hit people when they're young?"

"Usually," Maragas said. "Apparently not always. Who's next?"

***

After Baumgartner gave her an address, Maragas headed across town and into the Shadle neighborhood. She guided the car through a residential neighborhood and stopped in front of an expensive brick home easily the most ornate house on the block.

"Nice digs," Maragas muttered.

Baumgartner reached for the case file. He flipped it open and read. "This is the Chabot residence. Kerry Chabot and his father, Frederic, were both interviewed back in seventy-four." He snapped the folder shut. "Frederic's dead now."

"Looks like Kerry found his way home," said Maragas.

They walked up the stone pathway, which cut through the perfectly formed lawn. Baumgartner rang the bell. A few moments later, a man in his late forties answered. He was barefoot and wore an Adidas T-shirt and loose-fitting black trunks. Several days' growth of scraggly beard spotted his pudgy face. He stared at them for a full second, then said, "You're not the cable guy."

"No," said Maragas. She lifted her badge. "Are you Kerry Chabot?"

He rolled his eyes. "Oh, my *God*," he said in frustration. He turned and walked away from the door, hollering as he went. "Kerry! Door!"

Baumgartner stood waiting outside the open doorway with Maragas. In his patrol days, if this had been an active call, he would have interpreted the man's actions as an invitation to enter and resolve whatever situation he'd been called to. Learning to resist such inclinations had been part of his transition to detective. Having almost none of his interactions being emergency in nature was one of the most difficult adjustments to make.

A second man appeared in the hallway wearing casual, light blue slacks with the cuffs rolled and a matching collared shirt with several buttons undone. The man walked toward them. He resembled the first man, though he was considerably thinner and slightly effeminate. "May I help you?" he asked as he drew near. His voice had the same affect as his physicality.

"Kerry Chabot?"

"Yes. What's this about?"

Maragas showed her badge. "I was hoping we could chat with you."

Kerry's eyes widened with concern. "Has something happened to Paul?"

"Paul?"

"My partner. He's at work right now. Is he all right?"

Maragas held up her hands. "I'm sure he's fine. That's not why we're here."

"Oh." Kerry rested a hand on his chest. "Well, thank heavens."

"Could we come in to talk?"

"Certainly." Kerry opened the door wide to allow them entry. Once he closed it behind him, he led them down the hallway. "Sorry about my brother," he said. "He's a little abrasive. Especially towards authority figures."

"No problem," Maragas said. "We get that a lot."

Kerry stopped at an entrance. A pair of interior French doors stood open to reveal a well-lit sitting room. He waved them inside. Baumgartner noticed a glass of wine on the end table, as well as an open paperback sitting face-down next to it.

Kerry motioned for them to sit. Once they were settled, he said, "You're not investigating my father, are you?"

Maragas tilted her head in confusion. "I thought your father had passed away."

"Oh, he has, but I imagine his financial chicanery has long outlasted him." He waved his hand at the surrounding home. "Although, I suppose I shouldn't be too critical, since I'm living in a house he bought and paid for."

"Actually," said Maragas, "we wanted to talk about something else." She paused a beat, then added, "Hudson Dorsey?"

Kerry's eyes flared open in surprise. "Oh, my." His hand came to rest on his chest again. "I haven't thought about Huddie in… many years."

"We're working on some older cases," Maragas explained. "Including his."

Kerry's expression shifted and his eyes hardened. "You mean, he didn't drown? That was the official story, you know."

"He may have. We're looking into it."

Kerry pressed his lips together. "Please. When those detectives came and talked to me, they said it was murder. They may not have gotten much else right back then, but they were right about that."

"Why do you think so?"

Kerry hesitated. "I'm embarrassed to admit it now, but I suppose you already know, don't you? Huddie and I were dabbling in the hustler scene. It was the Expo and the city was flooded with people. Some of them were men willing to pay nicely for sex. We were young and it seemed like a good way to make some money, getting paid to do what we would have done for free." He hesitated. "In some cases, anyway."

"What makes you think Hudson was murdered?"

"Aside from the detectives saying so, you mean?" Kerry's tone took on some harshness. "How about the fact Huddie was a strong swimmer? Or that he refused to swim anywhere except a pool? He thought lakes and rivers were too dirty."

Baumgartner didn't remember seeing that in Pierce's original report. He jotted it down.

"What's too dirty?" came a voice from the entryway.

Baumgartner turned to see a slender, attractive blond woman in her early sixties. Her hair hung to her shoulders in a stylish cut. She wore a billowy white shirt with a rose-colored, lace-like scarf. The shirt ran into a flowing skirt of the same color, making it difficult to see where one garment ended and the other began. Her attire reminded Baumgartner of the rock singer, Stevie Nicks.

"Lake water," Kerry said. "The river."

"The river?" The woman cocked her head. "I'm afraid I'm lost, dear."

"That's because this isn't a conversation for you, Amelia." Exasperation seeped into Kerry's voice. He motioned toward the open doorway. "Do you mind?"

Amelia's gaze swept over the two visitors. "You're the police," she said, a statement rather than a question.

Kerry sighed. "Yes, Amelia. Bravo. Now, please give us some privacy?"

Amelia made no move to leave. She considered Maragas briefly before her eyes lit on Baumgartner. Her expression blossomed into a smile. She stepped forward and extended her hand to him, palm down.

"Amelia Chabot," she cooed. "Welcome to my home."

Out of habit, Baumgartner took her hand. She kept her palm down and lifted it slightly toward his face, smiling at him. His neck grew warm.

"*My home*?" Kerry repeated, his tone vexed. "Is that what Dad's will said? I seem to recall a more equitable arrangement."

Amelia ignored him momentarily, her attention remaining on Baumgartner. He found himself unusually flummoxed. He squeezed her hand briefly and let go. She let it drop slowly, as if allowing the remnants of their touch to trail behind her hand. "I apologize for my son's rudeness. He and his brother are more alike than he cares to admit."

Kerry made a sharp meow sound. "Put your claws away, *step*-mother, and please, let us have the room."

"*Let us have the room.*" Amelia's broad smile grew even wider. "You learned that phrase from your father. How nice to hear an echo of his voice in this house again. It's been so many years."

"Yes, yes," Kerry said, "and you're so terribly lonely. I think the detective here skews a little young, *n'est-ce pas*?"

"You're using that phrase wrong," Amelia said, her smile never wavering. "But I can take a hint." Her eyes bore into Baumgartner's. "A hint is all I need."

Baumgartner swallowed and smiled weakly.

Without another word, Amelia Chabot twirled around and glided from the room. Baumgartner watched her go with some relief and a tinge of regret.

Kerry let out a long sigh. "I am *so* sorry. I'd love to say she's getting horrible in her old age, but the truth is, she's always been that way."

"Not a problem," Maragas said, glancing side-eye at Baumgartner. "You were saying you didn't agree with the official cause of death?"

"It never made sense," Kerry said. "The detective would say murder when they talked to me but, in the end, they called it a drowning. Plus, the last time I saw Huddie was in the alley while we were hustling. I came back from a date, and he was gone."

"You don't know where he went?"

"No, but I assumed he got a date of his own. It's not like he suddenly decided to go for a swim at ten or eleven at night."

"Any idea who he left with?"

"Yes." Kerry nodded slowly. "I'm sure he left with the man who killed him and threw him in the river." His jaw flexed and his eyes shone. "Unfortunately, I have no idea who that man is. Those detectives never found him. I hope you'll fare better, but given the amount of time that's passed, I'm afraid you'll do about as well."

***

Basil Pershing was the last name on Barenz's list who wasn't either deceased or moved out of the area. Baumgartner wasn't looking forward to the phone interviews with the latter group. In-person interviews were difficult enough when it came to reading someone. Doing so over the phone was exponentially harder.

Since Maragas had left the list order up to him, he'd purposefully saved Pershing for last. He was intrigued by the man's history as a survivor in fifty-one, barely escaping the same fate as the other two victims. This was more than enough to pique Baumgartner's interest. That Pershing cropped up again during the seventy-four case only increased his curiosity.

"It's that one." He pointed to one of the older homes in the Manito neighborhood they'd arrived in.

Maragas turned into the short drive. The house looked almost a century old, though it was clearly well maintained. Baumgartner had occasionally come into contact with wealthy people during the course of his job, but seeing up close how the rich lived still made him shake his head in awe.

Baumgartner reached for the massive knocker, but Maragas stopped him. She motioned to a push-button doorbell on the side. "Seems more polite, don't you think?"

Baumgartner lifted a shoulder dismissively. On patrol, the louder and more authoritative the knock, the better. It was yet another difference he had to adjust to over the past few years.

They stood waiting for a long while. Baumgartner wanted to reach for the doorbell to ring it again, but Maragas seemed to want to wait. He shifted from foot to foot and looked around at the lawn and flower beds, all looking like something out of *Home & Gardens* magazine.

Finally, there was a loud click as the lock disengaged and the door swung open. A man in his early seventies greeted them. His iron gray hair had specks of black in it. He had a medium build and appeared fit. He wore dark green slacks and a light tan collared shirt that had the look of casual elegance. His eyes were contemplative as he took in their presence. When he spoke, his voice was hesitant.

"Can… can I help you?"

Maragas slid her badge from her belt and held it up. "Spokane Police, sir. Are you Basil Pershing?"

He paused before nodding. "I am."

"Can we come in and talk to you?"

"Certainly." Pershing stood aside and let them in. "Let's go into the den. It's more comfortable than standing in the foyer."

"Lead the way," said Maragas.

Pershing led them down the hallway. His gait was steady and sure. Maragas followed him and Baumgartner fell in behind her. He glanced around at the design on the tile floor and ornate woodwork on the trim. He thought of the house he lived in, which he'd always thought of as nice. Compared to this place, he lived in a cardboard box.

The den was lined with bookshelves on three walls that ran from the floor all the way to the ceiling. Outside of a library, Baumgartner had never seen such a collection. There was a wet bar at one end of the room, next to a large desk.

Mahogany, I bet, he thought. Just like in the chief's office.

Pershing gestured toward four overstuffed chairs in the center of the room, like some sort of furniture huddle. The three of them settled into them. Baumgartner had to admit it was one of the most comfortable chairs he'd ever sat in.

Pershing folded his hands and waited, watching Maragas. She wasted no time telling him the reason for their visit. When she mentioned Etherton, Pershing leaned back slightly. His expression turned somber.

"I… I'd have imagined he was long gone by now," he said quietly.

"He may be. We don't know if there is any connection, but we have to run down every possibility."

"He must be eighty-four or eighty-five," Pershing said. "Do you really think a man that age capable of such a crime?"

"The murder happened two years ago," Maragas said, but Baumgartner could hear in her voice that she knew it was a weak objection.

Pershing didn't bother to argue the point. His gaze seemed far away as he stared up at the bookshelves. Maragas paused before speaking again. Baumgartner looked around the den. Aside from the books, there were a few items hanging on the wall behind the desk. He couldn't make out all of them but they appeared to be typical vanity wall fare—diplomas and awards. A Japanese sword. No personal photos, however.

"You may be the last person we know of who saw Karl Etherton," Maragas said. "If he were still out there, do you have any idea why he'd come back to Spokane?"

Pershing drew in a ragged breath. "Your predecessors asked me that almost thirty years ago. At the time, I was egocentric enough to think it was me. That he wanted to finish what he started." He paused. "I wanted that to be true. I had prepared for him. Trained. I wanted to exorcise him from my life."

He glanced at Baumgartner then looked directly at Maragas.

"I think the detectives wanted to believe it, too. We all convinced ourselves of this absurd idea he was here in Spokane, living in disguise. Killing young men. Working his way back to me." He shook his head. "We were all wrong. It was someone else. Another monster, as if we needed any reminders that such men are commonplace in the world. Making that one go away didn't help them, or me, or those young men."

It certainly helped Salter, Baumgartner thought, recalling stories of how that shooting had launched his career.

"Monsters like Etherton are more common than we want to admit," said Pershing, his tone distracted as he glanced down at his hands. "You've certainly heard about the one who killed that man and his girlfriend in Coeur d'Alene and kidnapped her two children."

Baumgartner had. In spring of that year, Joseph Edward Duncan kidnapped Shasta and Dylan Groene from their Coeur d'Alene home, just over the Washington-Idaho border. Duncan killed Brenda Groene, her boyfriend, and her thirteen-year-old son. A manhunt lasted for seven weeks. Eventually, authorities rescued Shasta but discovered her brother had been murdered weeks prior.

"Your point?" Maragas asked.

Pershing nodded knowingly like a professor might. "Killers are also common when we consider their ordinary nature. It renders them human. Small. Then it dawns on you that they are every bit as fallible as the next man. Just as susceptible to the ravages of time, of nostalgia, of regret."

Baumgartner shifted in his seat. He'd thought hearing from Pershing might illuminate some aspect of the earlier cases, but all they were getting was a lecture. He cleared his throat. Neither Maragas nor Pershing looked his way. Pershing was still staring down at his hands, his expression odd. Maragas watched him intently as the silence unfolded.

"Karl Etherton no longer haunts me like he once did," Pershing finally said. "Not after I realized how small he was. *If* he's back in Spokane, I'm certain it is for some mundane, disappointing reason."

"Such as?"

Pershing spread his hands. "I have no idea."

"Do you still think he might come after you?"

"I hardly fit the victim profile any longer." Pershing lowered his hands and smiled darkly. "Though, perhaps he might do so strictly because I represent unfinished business."

Maragas asked a few more standard questions, getting no more information than was already in the case files. Baumgartner felt antsy. He'd anticipated the conversation with Pershing and now it was a disappointment. He wanted to move on.

Finally, Maragas thanked Pershing and rose from her chair. Baumgartner did likewise. At the front door, he exited first and started toward the car. When he glanced over his shoulder, he saw Maragas had stopped in the doorway. She said something to Pershing and he replied, but Baumgartner couldn't make out the words.

He stood at the passenger side door, waiting for Maragas. She arrived, popped the lock and they got inside. As she started the car, he asked, "Back to the station to do phone follow-up on the rest of the list?"

She nodded. "You do that. I'll see what else I can scare up on background."

"Whose background?"

"Etherton's."

Baumgartner smirked but didn't argue. He wasn't looking forward to having a telephone receiver plastered to his ear for the next several hours, interviewing witnesses. It was better than doing meticulous research. Besides, Maragas was far more skilled at that than he was.

"What'd you ask him?" Baumgartner asked. "At the door, when we were leaving."

Maragas pulled out of the driveway and headed toward the nearest arterial. "I asked if he wanted me to recommend a security service."

"What'd he say?"

"He declined."

"That's it?"

"No. He said just because he was no longer haunted by the man didn't mean he wouldn't welcome a visit." She turned onto South Grand Boulevard and accelerated north. "I got the feeling he wasn't as over it as he wants to believe." Maragas glanced at him, then back to the roadway. "Or us."

<h1 align="center">Chapter 37</h1>

Robert Baumgartner never wanted to be a salesman. An academy instructor insisted that cops sold their services to the citizenry daily. They did it through their uniforms, their actions, and their words. As such, they needed to learn the skills associated with sales. Baumgartner and most of his classmates thought it bullshit. It was barely better than the new age mumbo-jumbo the department's counselors espoused to normalize their services.

Baumgartner sat at his desk with a telephone receiver pressed to his ear. He was on hold with a local nursing home. A Muzak version of a popular eighties song dribbled in his ear. He couldn't recall the artist and didn't want to try. His thoughts drifted back to his early days of training.

Boiled down to its basic core, Baumgartner believed most recruits went to the police academy to learn about the law and how to fight. Getting sunshine blown up their collective asses about the need for sales training made little sense to them.

However, some of the sales training Baumgartner ignored began to rear its head during his first year in patrol. He struggled to talk suspects into handcuffs while other officers seemed to have a gift of gab for such situations. Too often, Baumgartner found himself going "hands on." That led to a disproportionate number of complaints regarding his use of force. It enhanced his reputation with other officers but made his life difficult when it came to the brass and Internal Affairs.

When the cruddy Muzak ended, a male voice said, "I'm sorry for the wait. We're finding her. Won't be long."

Baumgartner forced a smile, knowing it would change how he sounded. "That's okay. I appreciate the help."

The music resumed, and Baumgartner returned to his thoughts.

A sergeant pulled Baumgartner aside one night for some roadside counseling. The two men sat in their cars, facing in opposite directions. Each had their window down. The sergeant wanted to check in on his second-year officer.

"Fighters don't have a long career in the department, Bob," the sergeant said. "They tend to wash out young. Sooner or later, they make a mistake. Take things too far. The ones who make law enforcement a profession, learn how to talk themselves out of a problem. My point is it works at any level—patrol to the upper administration."

The music ended. "We found her," the man said. "Hold on."

A moment later, a woman came on the line. Her voice was strong and confident. "Hello?"

Baumgartner forced a smile. "Denise Carter?"

"Yes. Who is this?"

"Detective Robert Baumgartner, Spokane Police Department."

There was a pause on the line. "What's this about?"

"Your husband, ma'am. I'm following up on the murder of James Lockett."

"Who?"

"The man your husband found dead in High Bridge Park."

"My husband is dead, Detective." Carter sounded irritated by the call. "If you didn't know, he died in a hiking accident."

"Yes, ma'am." Baumgartner lowered his head. "I'm sorry for bothering you at work. It's the only working number we had for you in the file, and you changed your address."

"The house was too big for me alone."

"I can see you after work if that's better."

Carter clicked her tongue against the back of her teeth. "What is it you want?"

Baumgartner had a question he wanted to ask but figured leading with it would be bad form. He needed to work up to it. "Mrs. Carter, did your husband ever talk with you about what he saw that day?"

"He talked to me about it, yes."

Baumgartner patted the Lockett file. "Did he happen to mention anything about an injury to Mr. Lockett's hand?"

"No."

"He didn't say anything about an injury to a certain finger?"

"What? No." Carter's voice moved away from the phone. "I'll be right there. I'm almost done." She returned to the phone. "I really need to wrap this up, Detective. I'm needed back on the floor."

"Okay," Baumgartner said. "We're almost done. Did he mention a ring?"

"A ring?"

"Like a wedding ring."

"Wait a minute," Denise Carter said. "Is this ring missing?" Her voice rose sharply. "You wouldn't call me if the ring was there."

Baumgartner cringed. He hated not being able to see her. So much was lost without facial expressions.

"You think my husband stole it," Carter said.

"I'm calling to find out if he said anything about it."

She huffed. "That's not a denial. You cops are all the same. Listen, if you need anything else, don't call me."

The line went dead.

Baumgartner pulled the phone away from his ear and stared at it briefly. He set the receiver in place, then scratched through Denise Carter's name.

The follow-ups by phone had been an exercise in futility. He'd called eleven people since they'd returned from their interview with the doctors.

Two numbers were disconnected.

Six went to voicemail. This high number wasn't an anomaly in Baumgartner's experience. Since the department blocked their number, anyone with Caller ID would likely ignore the incoming call until they checked their voicemail. Baumgartner left messages requesting a call back. Most people never did.

Three calls were answered. The first two told Baumgartner he had the wrong number.

Only Denise Carter's work number proved to be true, and he crapped out on the call because of how he went about his inquiry.

Maragas peaked her head around the corner of his cubicle. "How's it going?"

"Fantastic," Baumgartner said.

"That good?"

He leaned back in his chair. "I feel like I'm banging my head on the wall."

"It's a good thing you're partnered with me."

"So you can teach me humility?"

Maragas rolled her eyes. "You're not getting that from me. Let's go."

She headed for the exit.

Baumgartner jumped from his chair. It slid backward and banged against his desk. He hurried to catch up to her. "Where we going?"

"I've found Etherton's kid."

***

Maragas sat in the driver's seat with her knee pressed against the steering wheel. She cupped her left hand around her cigarette while she lit it with her right. A breeze from the open window fought to snuff out the flame. She blew out a plume of smoke.

They headed up Monroe Street. The traffic was always thick on the arterial, but at the end of the workday it became incredibly slow.

"I'll tell you this," Maragas said. She paused to puff on her cigarette. "Amherst and Pierce documented everything."

"What are you talking about?"

"Didn't you read the file?"

"I read it." Baumgartner lowered his window. "They never put in the kid's name."

"They put in the wife's."

"Verdna. So you found the mother?"

"Ah." Maragas held up the hand holding the cigarette. "I found Verdna Daugherty."

"Verdna Daugherty. That's her name now?"

Maragas twisted her lips and shook her head in disapproval. "You didn't read the Etherton file."

"I was there with you. I read it."

Maragas inhaled on the cigarette. "What was written on the inside cover?"

Baumgartner twisted to face her. "What?"

"Exactly." She passed a slow-moving Toyota. "You didn't read the file."

"So what'd I miss?"

"One of them, I'm guessing Pierce because the penmanship was orderly, wrote Etherton nee Daugherty."

"What the hell is nee?"

"Refers to a woman's maiden name."

"So Verdna Daugherty married Karl Etherton?"

"Can't get anything by you." Maragas smiled before inhaling from her cigarette.

Her sarcasm burned. Baumgartner resolved to focus more on smaller details. He couldn't rely on Maragas to always be the one to do so. "Where's Verdna living now?" he asked.

She turned toward the window and exhaled a plume of smoke. "Verdna's dead."

"How'd she die?"

"Old age. Heart attack."

Their car raced up the Monroe Street S-curve.

Baumgartner snapped his fingers. "That's how you found the son. Her obituary."

"Found it online, courtesy of the *Lewiston Morning Tribune*."

"She lived in Idaho?"

"Seems so. They were nice enough to print that Verdna was survived by her son, Vincent Daugherty of Spokane, Washington."

"You're right," Baumgartner said as he settled back into his seat. "That was nice of them."

***

Vincent Daugherty lived on Glass Avenue with an unobstructed view over the southern part of town.

Maragas parked a couple houses away and the two detectives got out.

"Does he know we're coming?" Baumgartner asked.

"No. We're approaching him cold."

"You run his name?"

She smirked. "He's clean. No entries. Not even a parking ticket."

Baumgartner pointed at Maragas. "Brush yourself off." Cigarette ashes covered her jacket.

"Bah." She flicked the ash away. "One of these days I'm going to give these things up."

"They've got warnings on the packs for a reason."

"The fuck do I care? I'm not pregnant."

She led the way to the Daugherty residence, a two-story white house. Baumgartner cast a final glance toward the south to appreciate the view.

A red Hyundai Elantra was in the driveway.

Maragas rang the doorbell.

"Just a minute," a voice hollered from inside the house.

The door opened and a white male in his early sixties stood there. He wore a blue polo shirt, khaki shorts, and leather sandals. His legs were extremely tan as if he spent a lot of time on the golf course.

He looked vaguely familiar to Baumgartner. It took him several moments to realize it was the resemblance to the old black-and-white photo of Karl Etherton in the case file. The man in the doorway wasn't a spitting image but there was no mistaking his relation.

His gaze bounced between Maragas and Baumgartner. "Yes?"

Maragas swept her coat to the side and revealed her badge and gun. "Detectives Maragas and Baumgartner, sir. Are you Vincent Daugherty?"

"Vince. Yes. That's me." His face pinched with concern and his shoulders hunched. "What's going on? Did something happen to Pam? The kids?"

Maragas held up her hand. "Your family is fine, sir. We're here on an unrelated matter."

Daugherty breathed a sigh of relief and his body relaxed. "What's this about?"

"May we come in, sir?" Maragas asked. "We'd like to talk with you about your father."

***

It was a peaceful living room. Two couches faced each other while two wingback chairs bookended the sitting area. Framed photographs of family members were scattered about the room, some on the walls, others placed on pieces of furniture. It appeared as if the Daughertys had many grandchildren.

A white ceramic bowl sat in the middle of the coffee table and held a mound of pine cones. A powerful cinnamon aroma wafted from the bowl.

Baumgartner and Maragas settled onto one of the couches.

Vince Daugherty sat across from them. His brow furrowed as he waited for the detectives to speak. No one had spoken since they entered the house.

"Is anyone home with you, sir?" Maragas asked.

"My wife is out with our daughters and granddaughters." Daugherty waved a hand. "It's Princess Day. No boys allowed." His face remained tight, but something flashed in his eyes—a brief happiness. Talking about Princess Day probably brought Vince Daugherty joy on a normal day.

However, two detectives sitting in his living room was anything but normal.

"We're sorry to trouble you," Maragas said.

Daugherty's lips tightened. "It's no trouble." It was a lie. Baumgartner could see he didn't want to be troubled with questions about Karl Etherton.

"When's the last time you've heard from your father?"

"I haven't heard from him—ever."

Baumgartner leaned in and studied Daugherty. The aroma of cinnamon was stronger near the table.

"According to the case notes," Maragas said, but Daugherty interrupted her.

"Excuse me, Detective. I don't mean to be rude, but my life isn't in any case file."

Maragas cocked her head.

"I understand my father did some horrendous things, but I was too young to understand what was happening back then. My mother kept the couple of clippings that made it into the Boise paper. When I was finally old enough to comprehend his actions, she told me. I must have been fourteen, maybe fifteen. All I knew growing up was I didn't have a father."

Daugherty bent forward and removed a pine cone from the ceramic bowl. He held it the way a boy might hold a baseball. "The older I got the more faded my father's memory became. I was so young when they split apart that those memories I do have aren't even of a person but of a symbol. A symbol I never saw." Daugherty turned the pine cone in his hand. "When my mother read the news of my father's activities—." He looked up. "She destroyed every connection she had to him. No picture of my father survived her purge. No letters. Nothing with his signature. My mother wiped Karl Etherton from our existence."

"You have nothing from your father?" Maragas asked.

"Nothing." Daugherty leaned forward and returned the pine cone to the bowl. "And I want nothing. In fact, I don't even know what Karl Etherton looks like. You could show me ten photos and I couldn't pick my father out of them."

Maragas asked, "When did your mother change your last name to hers?"

Vincent Daugherty's shoulders relaxed, and he nodded. "My mother told me later in her life she sensed something wasn't right with my father. He'd stay out late and make feeble excuses about what he'd been doing. His cool demeanor toward her, which she'd initially taken to be suave and charming, became clinical and distant." Daugherty changed his position. "She had no inkling he might be doing something nefarious. As you can imagine, we had these discussions when I was an adult. After my teen years."

Both Maragas and Baumgartner nodded.

Daugherty continued. "Anyway, she had enough of his odd behavior and filed for divorce. According to my mother, he didn't contest it. Supposedly, my father said, 'It's probably for the best.' He agreed to the divorce and sent support payments every month. Like clockwork, my mother said. Until the discovery."

The discovery, Baumgartner thought. The basement dungeon where two young women were killed, and Basil Pershing was found manacled to the wall.

Daugherty rubbed his hands across his pants. "When the reports of my father's activities became newspaper fodder, my mother filed with the court to have our last names changed to her maiden name."

Maragas glanced at Baumgartner before asking, "No one in the press noticed the connection?"

Daugherty shrugged. "It was the early fifties, Detective. People didn't have the internet. Besides, we were living in Boise by then, not Spokane. A woman petitioning the court for name changes wouldn't likely raise a lot of interest. Besides, my mother found a sympathetic clerk in the county court system. A friendly ear if you will. That woman understood the trauma my mother and I would suffer if the press discovered where we lived. It's my understanding the requisite paperwork worked its way through the court system without ever abiding by the public disclosure requirement. Once our last names were officially changed, we quietly packed up and moved to Lewiston where we didn't know anyone, and no one knew us."

Maragas scooted toward the edge of the couch. "Your father never found you?"

"No."

"You've never searched for him?"

"Why would I? My father was a killer, a rapist, and a sadist." Daugherty looked away. He grabbed a picture from a nearby table and stared at it. "My wife knows my history. My bloodline." He looked up. "But my kids? They don't know the horrible truth. I've never told them about their grandfather. As far as they know, my father is long dead. They're Daughertys, untainted by Etherton blood."

"Why'd you move to Spokane?" Maragas asked. "If you weren't looking for your father and you never searched for him."

"My children," Daugherty said. "Our oldest son attended Whitworth on scholarship. Our youngest daughter attended Eastern Washington. The oldest daughter skipped college all together and moved to Spokane with her friends."

He handed Maragas the photo and she took it. The picture was of a happy family gathering.

"Our kids were in the Spokane area while my wife and I were living in Lewiston. It only made sense for us to move up here. In ninety-two, that's what we did. I worked as a civil engineer, therefore I found employment fairly easily when we relocated." Daugherty crossed one leg over the other. "So, I must know. Why are you asking about my father?"

Maragas passed the photo to Baumgartner. She said, "There's been a murder. The signature at the crime scene is similar to that of your father's."

"Signature?"

"Certain marks on the victim."

Daugherty inhaled deeply. "If he's still alive, he'd be old. Very old. How could he even commit such a crime?"

"That's what we're trying to determine," Maragas said.

Baumgartner studied the happy family in the photograph before setting it on the coffee table.

"I wish you luck in finding my father," Vincent Daugherty said, "but my hope is he's been dead for many years."

Maragas pulled out a business card and set it on the coffee table. "If your father tries to contact you…" She left the thought unfinished.

"You'll be my first call," Daugherty said. "He's not anyone I want around my family."

***

It was after five when Baumgartner and Maragas returned to the station.

"Let's call it a day," Maragas said.

Baumgartner didn't argue. He'd been there since shortly after six. She had arrived earlier than him.

He climbed out of her car and headed toward his own.

Baumgartner had no plans with Darla that night. It wasn't too late to call and see about getting together, but he didn't want to seem desperate. They'd just been together last night. Besides, she hadn't called him yet.

He should go to the gym. His workouts became sporadic after the promotion to detective. Since the step up into Major Crimes, the workouts were almost not existent. He'd make the gym three days in a row, then not go for two weeks. He couldn't bench press nearly the weight he once could, and he knew he'd fail the SWAT run if he attempted it today.

To make matters worse, his pants were squeezing him around the waist.

He passed a McDonald's, and the idea of grabbing a Big Mac came to him. Maybe he'd get some fries with it. Perhaps add a refreshing Coke to wash it all down.

What a moron, he thought. He'd just been telling himself how much he needed to go to the gym and here he was thinking about eating something guaranteed to be loaded with a million bad calories.

Baumgartner frowned. Maybe he should just call Darla and see what she was doing later. They could go out and get something decent to eat. If he called her though, he'd seem too eager. He didn't want that.

Jesus, my head's a tennis match tonight.

He turned his attention to the Lockett case. Thoughts of murder and torture taunted him. Visions of an aging Karl Etherton banged around his skull. An idea percolated at the edge of his brain. Etherton may not be physically capable of committing the Lockett murder, but what if he had help? A younger man who provided the muscle.

He frowned while he drove. The idea didn't seem illogical exactly, but improbable. It solved the problem of Etherton's advanced age, but was that just him looking for a solution to fit his own take on the case? Why would a young man be involved with someone Etherton's age, anyway?

An image of Townsend and his companion, Crisanto, popped into his head.

Baumgartner tapped his fist against the steering wheel. If he didn't push those wandering thoughts aside, they'd plague him for the rest of the night.

A jingle entered his consciousness now. *Two all-beef patties, special sauce—*

Baumgartner frowned. The gym or food? Or hunker down and work some more on the Etherton problem?

If he continued on this familiar route home, there was another McDonald's up ahead. Maybe if he skipped the Coke, the calories wouldn't be so bad. It was a lie he told himself, but there was no way he'd skip the fries.

Baumgartner should turn soon to take a different route.
He stayed the course, though.
Two all-beef patties, special sauce—

Baumgartner shuffled into the Major Crimes bullpen at ten minutes before seven. He'd slept poorly, waking frequently throughout the night. When the alarm went off, he slapped his snooze button several times, eventually leaving him pressed for time once he finally got out of bed. As a matter of convenience, for breakfast, he went through the same McDonald's that had provided his dinner the night before. While he drove to the station, he scarfed down an egg and sausage sandwich, potato patty, and slurped coffee. After he parked, he stuffed the fast-food bag into a garbage can while walking into the station.

Despite everything, he somehow managed to be early, which gave him a mild, grudging sense of pride.

Maragas looked up at him from her desk as he approached. "You look like someone threw ten pounds of dog shit into a five-pound burlap sack and beat it with a rake," she said. "You get drunk last night?"

He shook his head. "Bad sleep, is all."

Three files lay open on her desk. She held a pen and rested her hand on a yellow legal pad. Several pages were folded over. The current page was half full of her scribblings.

"What's this?" Baumgartner asked.

"Funny you should ask." She handed him a piece of paper. "I saved these for you."

Baumgartner scanned the page, which contained a list of names with dates of birth and nothing else. He looked at Maragas questioningly.

Maragas held out her coffee cup and waggled it. "Fill me up and I'll tell you everything."

Baumgartner didn't argue. He accepted her cup, dropped the paper on his desk, and grabbed his own cup. At the coffee station, he glanced toward Salter's office. The door was open, and the light was on. He admired that about the lieutenant—he might be brass, but he kept long hours. It may not be street work, but at least the man wasn't lazy.

Back at the bullpen, he plunked the mug onto his partner's desk. She was busy writing and reached for it without looking his way. It occurred to him that, as detectives, they often offered water or soft drinks to witnesses or suspects in order to elicit trust and, eventually, testimony. It seemed like the tactic worked on detectives, too.

When Maragas finished writing, she leaned back in her chair and sipped her coffee. Her appraising gaze lighted onto Baumgartner's shirt.

"What?" he asked. "You don't like the color?"

"Color's fine. It's the grease spot I find questionable."

Baumgartner frowned. He looked down and examined his shirt. Maragas was right; a nickel-sized circle of grease had stained his shirt. He cursed lightly.

"Baking soda," said Maragas. "It'll get that out. Now, listen up."

Baumgartner resisted the urge to brush at the blemish on his shirt. He sat in his chair and faced Maragas. "Enlighten me."

"You know the request I put out for similar cases? We got multiple hits."

Baumgartner leaned forward, his interest piqued. "From where?"

"Several places. Seattle. Portland. Boise." She paused, then added, "Moscow."

Baumgartner raised his brows. "Moscow is about half an hour from Lewiston," he said.

Maragas nodded knowingly. "Just a short drive away from Verdna Daugherty and her son. Yet still a big enough town to easily hide in."

"You don't think…?"

"What I think is it might all be a coincidence, or it might be something. It's more likely he hid in a bigger city like Seattle or Portland, but that's why we're doing the follow-up." She motioned toward the list on his desk. "I gave you the suspect names from Seattle and Portland. I took the ones from Idaho cases."

"Wait, these are *suspects*?"

"Of one kind or another, yes. I reached out to the lead detectives on the cases to get some of them. Some had strong suspicions, others just a gut feeling. No probable cause in any, though. That's why the cases are still unsolved. Right now, we're looking for possible connections to either Lockett or Etherton. Hopefully one with some DNA evidence, waiting to be matched."

"All right." Baumgartner turned to get started, then stopped. "Hold on a second. When did you get all of this?"

"Some this morning," Maragas said. Then she shrugged. "A little last night. I made the mistake of coming inside to use the upstairs gym. Afterwards, I checked my email before I went home. Ended up spending a couple of hours here at my desk in sweaty workout clothes, but I got the info."

Baumgartner thought of his lack of success with phone interviews the previous day. "I'm surprised you were able to talk to the detectives without playing phone tag for a week."

Maragas smiled grimly. "If there's anything a homicide detective is willing to talk about any time, day or night, it's an unsolved case." She motioned toward the list on his desk. "I forwarded the relevant case reports to your email for reference, but remember, we're not trying to solve their case. We're trolling for connections."

"I got it."

"Good. Now, get cracking."

Baumgartner got to work. He ran the first name on this list, Benjamin Pilar, through all the databases he had easy access to—the local system, statewide criminal records and warrants, national records for convictions and warrants, and relevant departments of licensing. All of it started to build a picture of Pilar. Petty sex crimes, misdemeanor assaults, but always a valid driver's license.

He turned to other systems the department subscribed to at considerable expense for Major Crimes investigators to use – ones that accessed credit scores, insurance claims, property listings, and court records. His progress was slow. On patrol, he'd resisted the switch to typed reports, preferring to write his by hand. As a result, his typing prowess left something to be desired. Coupled with the fact he only used these programs sporadically, he stumbled around the interface, typing slowly, as he tried to elicit the information.

Pilar's basic profile didn't change as he gathered more information. He didn't appear very mobile, as all his known addresses were in the greater Seattle metropolitan area. He saw no connection to Lockett. As for possibly being Etherton in disguise, his age was fifteen years too young to fit. The age difference alone made him want to move onto the next name on the list, but then he realized Etherton could have chosen that birthdate purposefully to throw off the scent.

Baumgartner switched over to his email and opened the case file Seattle PD had shared. As he read through the report, he saw some similarities to Lockett. The Seattle victim suffered multiple bruises on his torso. The man's nipples had been cut off, which was no doubt the mutilation that caused the detectives to respond to the request Maragas sent. The nature of the torture seemed dissimilar to him, but Baumgartner didn't consider himself an expert on serial killers. Perhaps the psychology at play made the location of the injury less important than the intent behind it.

He sipped his coffee and continued reviewing the Seattle case file. It took some time looking through the document for Baumgartner to confirm the victim's sexuality, but when he did, the man fit the profile in that respect, too. Then Baumgartner muttered that since Etherton had both male and female victims, this last point didn't matter much at all.

Pilar's current address was in Everett, Washington. That was roughly a five-hour drive to Spokane. Or longer, given traffic on most days. Could he have traveled all the way to Spokane just for sex? While Baumgartner knew some people still had hangups regarding gays, he didn't think it was severe enough to merit that much effort to hide an affair, homosexual or otherwise. Especially not since the Seattle area was gay friendly.

His brows knitted while he considered the thought. Pilar wouldn't be coming to hide his sexual activities, he realized. His sexuality had nothing to do with it. He'd be coming to hide his predatory activities. That seemed much more likely to be worth the effort of a long drive.

It meant Baumgartner couldn't eliminate Pilar as a suspect. He placed a plus sign next to the name, tracing over the marking several times while he reviewed his logic. In the end, it seemed sound to him. There might not be enough to talk Salter into letting him and Maragas drive across the state to interview Pilar, but that was tomorrow's problem.

Today, he had the remaining names on the list.

***

They broke at eleven for lunch, slipping across the small plaza between the Public Safety Building and the courthouse to the High Nooner. The café served sandwiches and salads and was a favorite among many on the criminal justice campus. Judges, prosecutors, public defenders, and private attorneys of every stripe sat at tables next to cops, support staff, and anyone who had the ill fortune of having business at the courthouse that day.

Baumgartner ordered a three-meat Italian sub, loaded with cheese, onions, and peppers, and sprinkled with vinegar and oil. He skipped a Coke. Maragas opted for tomato basil soup and coffee. Baumgartner thought they might get the food to go and eat while working at their desks, but Maragas sat at one of the empty tables in a corner.

"We need a brain break from all the smaller details," she explained. "Take a look at the big picture again, so we don't lose sight of it."

Baumgartner unwrapped his sandwich and tore into it. After a few bites, he stopped. "I was thinking about this case last night," he said. "I had an idea."

"Is that why you couldn't sleep?" Maragas asked.

"Part of the reason. What if..." Baumgartner paused, suddenly feeling foolish. He forged ahead anyhow. "Etherton's age is a problem, but what if he had someone younger helping him?"

"An acolyte?"

Baumgartner was unfamiliar with the word. "A junior partner," he clarified.

Maragas thought about it while she ate several spoonfuls of soup. Then she said, "It solves the physicality issue."

Baumgartner nodded, feeling a small burst of pride.

"Problem is," Maragas said, "serial killer partnerships are rare."

His pride immediately deflated.

"It's happened, though" Maragas continued. "Karla Homolka and Paul Bernardo, for example."

Baumgartner shook his head, not recognizing the names.

"The Ken and Barbie Killers?"

Baumgartner's head shake became a nod. He remembered that case from the late eighties.

"Then there's Faye and Ray Copeland," said Maragas.

Baumgartner looked at her, waiting. He didn't know who the Copelands were, either.

"They killed their farm hands, as many as a dozen of them," Maragas explained absently. She ate some soup, her gaze faraway. Then she said, "They were elderly, too. Seventy, seventy-five when they were caught, but I think most of their killings happened when they were in their fifties." She smiled wryly. "Then, of course, there was Bonnie and Clyde."

"I was thinking more like The Hillside Strangler," said Baumgartner.

She nodded. "That's a better comparison. Not only did the police think it was just one suspect well into the investigation, but the age difference and power dynamic between Bianchi and Buono fits your theory, too."

"It's not a theory," he hedged. "It's just a thought."

"That's how all good theories start." Maragas paused to sip her coffee. "Problem is, it's rare, like I said."

"We just rattled off multiple examples," Baumgartner protested, feeling protective of his idea despite his own doubts.

Maragas smiled patiently. "We *cherry picked* multiple examples. Historically, less than ten percent of serial killers involve any kind of accomplice whatsoever."

"Ten percent isn't rare. It's uncommon."

Maragas picked up her spoon. "If you had a ten percent chance of winning a million bucks, would you bet your house?"

"Only if I was feeling lucky."

She pointed the spoon at him. "Exactly, but a ninety percent chance? You'd bet your house and your pension."

"I see your point."

"How about this wrinkle? Serial killers account for point oh one percent of all murders in the United States. How about now? Still willing to bet?"

Baumgartner's shoulders slumped. *0.01%*? Multiplied by ten percent for the probability of an accomplice made the results infinitesimally smaller.

"It's good that you're thinking, though," said Maragas, in an obvious attempt to bolster his confidence. "I did some thinking, too. I wondered if we're missing the boat by suspecting Etherton at all."

"I said that before," Baumgartner pointed out. "Is it because of the false identity part or the age issue?"

"Neither. The potential for a copycat."

Baumgartner took a bite of his sandwich and chewed thoughtfully. In his mind, it was either related to Etherton or not. He leaned heavily toward not. An attempted copycat wasn't something that occurred to him.

"Problem is," Maragas said, "how does a copycat know about the signature injury?" She lifted her left hand and wiggled her ring finger. "That fact was always a hold back in both cases. Back in fifty-one, I imagine it was to spare the delicate sensibilities of the public. In seventy-four, it was more likely to weed out bad tips and false confessions. Either way, no civilians knew about the missing finger."

"Information gets out," Baumgartner said.

"I don't think this did. I think they were actually very careful to make sure it didn't. So, if Lockett is a copycat… and only cops had access to the prior cases…" She gave him a knowing look.

"No way," Baumgartner said, shaking his head vigorously. "There's no chance this is a cop."

"No chance?"

"None," he said firmly.

"Cops do bad things sometimes," Maragas said.

"Not like this."

"What about DiBartolo?"

Baumgartner's jaw tightened. He still remembered that night in 1997 when the Spokane County Sheriff's deputy reported an attack in Lincoln Park on him and his wife, Patty. Baumgartner and his fellow patrol officers had flooded the streets, looking for suspects that matched the description the deputy gave. Later, DiBartolo fell under suspicion and was eventually convicted for murdering his wife. The entire incident left a profound impact on the community and law enforcement alike.

"That's different," he said through clenched teeth. He put down his sandwich, his appetite suddenly gone.

"Sure, it is. I'm only pointing it out to illustrate we can't rule something out just because we don't like the implications."

"You really think Lockett was murdered by a police officer?"

"No," Maragas admitted. "I don't think this is a copycat or a duo at work. We're following possible theories here, right?"

"It wasn't a cop," Baumgartner reiterated.

Maragas held up her hands in mock surrender. "Ease up, big guy. I agree with you. We're just talking here."

"As long as we're just talking, there's something else that bothers me."

"What's that?"

"Lockett's ring finger. It's still there."

Maragas took a spoonful of soup and motioned with her free hand for him to continue.

"We're looking at it as a match to the signature injuries from the fifty-one case and the ones in seventy-four," Baumgartner explained. "It's not a match, though. It's only similar."

"You're right. The injury might be unrelated."

"We could be chasing our tails with all of this Etherton bullshit just because The Wasteland saw something that would allow him to go after Salter again."

"Regardless of what Barenz thought," Maragas said, "Salter saw the similarities, too. Don't forget that."

Baumgartner shrugged a single shoulder.

Maragas leaned forward. "The victim profiles from seventy-four match our case. Age, gender, sexuality, and the surreptitious hookup scene."

"Not the signature injury," Baumgartner emphasized. "Whoever killed James Lockett didn't take his finger."

"No, he did not."

"So, it was someone else. Not Etherton."

"Or maybe Etherton changed his M.O.," Maragas said. "Maybe some of these other cases we're sifting through were his work. He wouldn't be able to stop himself from killing, but he might have been able to resist the compulsion to take the finger. With Lockett, that resistance may have wavered. Instead of amputating it, he merely cut around it but stopped himself. That's how we ended up with the similar injury to the finger."

"That's a whole lot of mights and maybes."

Maragas gathered up her trash and stood. "Let's go knock some of them down, then."

***

Another two hours of work had Baumgartner jumping out of his skin. As a patrol officer, he craved action. When he became a detective, he accepted the fact real investigative work wasn't like television. His days of adrenaline-fueled chases and fighting with suspects were largely over. Even in the slower paced environment of investigations, he still preferred the more active tasks—going to crime scenes, finding suspects and witnesses, conducting interviews out in the field, or interrogating a suspect in the interview room.

The meticulous research work today made him feel more like a bookkeeper than a cop.

He'd been staring blankly at the screen for a while, thinking of calling Darla even though she hadn't even texted him yet today, when he heard Maragas let out a long exhale. Somewhere in that sigh, he thought he detected astonishment rather than exasperation. He glanced over to find Maragas staring at him.

"I might have something," she said. "If nothing else, it'll get us out of the office." She stood, notepad in hand and waved to him. "Come on, let's go."

***

In the car, Maragas explained.

"Lawrence Howson," she said, while she drove and smoked. "He was a suspect in a Moscow murder in eighty-nine. The victim's name was Peter Isserling. The detective who worked the case has since retired, but he was plenty helpful when I called. He liked Howson for the homicide but had no physical or circumstantial evidence, so there was no arrest."

"No physical or..." Baumgartner trailed off, shaking his head. "That sounds like no evidence, period. Why was he even a suspect?"

"Same reason Doctor Townsend was. Or Gary Parr. Howson was contacted as a suspicious person frequenting prostitutes."

"Male ones?"

"No," admitted Maragas. "The female variety."

"Well, that doesn't fit."

"It doesn't fit Lockett," Maragas said, "but it fits the fifty-one case Pierce and Amherst worked."

"Etherton, you mean." Baumgartner pursed his lips, dubious. "Is that all?"

"Evidence-wise, yes, but this detective I talked to said he had a wrong feeling about Howson from the very beginning. That's why he stayed on the suspect list."

"That was a risk," Baumgartner said, his voice full of doubt. The retired Idaho detective was lucky Howson didn't sue for defamation. A gut feeling wasn't recognized by the courts as valid criteria to list someone as a suspect in a crime.

"Whatever his reason, it's a lucky break for us," said Maragas. "When I worked up Howson's background, it shows he lived in Boise from fifty-nine to sixty-seven. His history is lean before that, hard to pin down. He's solidly in Boise until sixty-seven, though, and then he moved to Moscow. Remember how you pointed out that it's only a thirty-minute drive from Moscow to Lewiston, where Vince and his mother lived?"

Baumgartner nodded.

"I think you were onto something with that. When did Vince move to Spokane to be with his kids and grandkids?" she asked.

Baumgartner thought for a moment. "Ninety-two, wasn't it?"

"Bullseye. Guess when Lawrence Howson moved from Moscow to Spokane."

"Ninety-two?"

"Close. It was early ninety-three." Maragas got onto the freeway and headed east. "He's been living here ever since."

Baumgartner looked out the window. He thought this was unlikely, to say the least. Barely a coincidence, but he was reluctant to dampen Maragas's enthusiasm.

"You're still not buying it," she said. "The chance he might be Etherton in disguise."

"Seems like a stretch."

"Hell, yes, it's a stretch," Maragas agreed. She took a deep drag and spoke as she exhaled. "But it's the first one on the list we can go see in person without leaving the Lilac City."

That made sense to Baumgartner. Regardless, he was glad to get out of the office, even if it meant interviewing another old creep like Townsend.

A couple of minutes later, Maragas left the freeway at the Thor/Freya exit and turned southbound. As the Impala climbed the steep grade up Ray Street toward Thirty-fifth Avenue, Baumgartner asked where they were going.

"Avalon Adult Care," Maragas told him.

"The old folks' home?" Baumgartner asked, and she nodded.

Avalon Adult Care was located on Thirty-Sixth Avenue, just off the main commercial thoroughfare. Baumgartner had never been there before, but he was friends with another police officer, Tom Farrell, whose mother lived there for a few years before she passed away. Farrell said it was a quality operation that handled everything from assisted living in one wing to full-time care in another, as well as hospice services. As he recalled, Farrell's mother had gone through all three phases during her time at the facility.

Maragas parked and they walked to the reception desk. The receptionist directed them to E-Wing. Glancing at a map, Baumgartner saw that wings A and B were assisted living, while C and D were marked as for complete care. E-Wing was the hospice center.

"Is this guy Howson dying?" Baumgartner whispered to Maragas.

She turned over her hands while they walked. "Context clues say probably so."

Baumgartner frowned. Howson was becoming a less likely suspect by the moment. The idea that someone this old could go from potentially murdering James Lockett two years ago to hospice care seemed absurd. After the points Maragas made at lunch about percentages, his own notion about a younger accomplice appeared equally ridiculous. This trip was looking like a waste of time, even if it succeeded in getting them out of the office for a while.

At the hospice center, an employee was stationed at a standing desk, watching the two of them approach. The man was slightly pudgy, in his late thirties with short blond hair and glasses in a thick black frame. He wore a pale blue nurse's uniform. His nametag read "Corey." When he spoke, his tone was low and respectful.

"May I help you?"

Maragas showed her badge. "We're here to interview Mr. Howson."

Corey frowned slightly and reached for the nearby keyboard. "I'm not aware of any appointments," he said.

"We didn't call ahead," Maragas explained.

Corey's expression turned to disappointment. "Then I'm sorry, Officer, but Mr. Howson is in palliative care. We don't generally allow anyone other than family—"

"Corey?"

The nurse pursed his lips at her interruption. "Yes?"

"We're investigating a murder. Mr. Howson may have the solution."

"That hardly seems likely," Corey said. "He's been in our care for almost two years now."

Baumgartner raised a brow at the news. Howson having anything to do with Lockett's murder was looking thinner and thinner.

"Even so," said Maragas. "The information he can share with us predates his time here."

"I don't think he's in any condition—"

"Corey?"

The nurse crossed his arms, dipped his chin, and cocked his head in irritation. "Yes?"

"We just want to talk to him for a few minutes. Is he capable of that?"

"Capable? That depends on the day, but—"

Maragas spread her hands benevolently. "Then lead the way. We'll talk to him for a minute or two and then be out of your hair."

Corey stood his ground for a few seconds, then took a deep breath and exhaled heavily. "All right, but our number one concern is the well-being of our patients during the short time they have left. I urge you not to do anything to upset that."

"We won't," Maragas said.

Baumgartner could hear the lie in her voice. He imagined Corey could, too, but the nurse had already made his decision. He led them down a hallway until they reached room twenty-three. A whiteboard outside the room had the name HOWSON, LAWRENCE written in black marker strokes.

Corey rapped lightly on the door, paused a moment, then stepped inside. "Mr. Howson? You have a couple of visitors."

Maragas followed Corey inside, and Baumgartner slipped in after her.

Lawrence Howson sat almost upright in a hospital bed with the back raised. An oxygen tube sat below his nostrils and was cradled by his ears, like a pair of glasses might. A monitor was connected to him with several wires, but Baumgartner noted it was less than he'd seen in the average emergency room patient.

Howson looked every bit of his eight-plus decades. His hair was thin, white, and appeared brittle. Age spots dotted his forehead and cheeks. Those cheeks hung loosely, almost as if he had shrunk inside his own skin and now had too much of it. The skin itself had a sallow look to it.

From Baumgartner's vantage point, it appeared the man's frame had wasted away to leave a skinny core with spindly limbs. He may have been tall at one time, but he now seemed small and withered.

An aroma of decay hung in the room. It was as if the old man were rotting from the inside while his heart fought stubbornly to keep him alive.

"These are police officers, Mr. Howson." Corey spoke like a parent talking to a child. "They want to ask you a couple of questions. Is that all right?"

Howson didn't look at Corey while the nurse spoke. Instead, he stared at Maragas. As decrepit as the rest of him was, the man's eyes were sharp. "That's fine," he said, his voice wavering with age.

"Are you feeling well today, Mr. Howson?" Corey asked.

"I'm feeling fine. Don't talk to me like I'm an imbecile."

"Okay," said Corey. Embarrassment flashed across the nurse's face. He folded his hands and looked at Maragas, as if granting her permission to proceed.

Maragas hesitated.

Baumgartner knew why. Interrogating a suspect with a guardian angel present was never a good idea. The suspect might feel safer and therefore even be more open, at least about what they considered mundane details, but the odds that the protector would jump in and call a premature halt to the discussion were too great. And an outright confession with a third party watching was unlikely.

He considered asking Corey to help him with something outside the room. Perhaps back at the desk. Some information on his computer, maybe? While Baumgartner was concocting a plausible ruse, Howson spoke up.

"You can go, Corey," the old man said. His voice sounded stronger.

Corey looked slightly annoyed at the dismissal. He glanced at Maragas, then Baumgartner, and finally Howson. Then he drew himself up and said, "Of course." He turned and strode quickly from the room.

At least that's solved, Baumgartner mused.

Maragas stepped closer to Howson, showing him her badge. "I'm Detective Maragas," she said. "Spokane Police Department. I know this is kind of awkward, Mr. Howson, but since you aren't able to get up and leave this interview, the law says I need to read you your rights before we talk. Is that okay with you?"

Howson flicked a few fingers without raising his hand. "Get on with it."

Maragas recited the constitutional rights, reading from a card even though Baumgartner was certain she could do it from memory. While she read, he moved deeper into the room. The furnishings were spare—just a chair on each side of the bed and a single bedside table. Nothing adorned the plain walls, which were painted a soft, warm shade of tan. Baumgartner imagined it was a very bland place to die.

Maragas finished her recitation and asked if Howson understood his rights.

"Of course, I do," he said.

"Will you waive your rights and speak to me?"

"Why not?"

"I need a definitive yes or no, sir."

Howson sighed with exasperation. He flicked his fingers again dismissively. "Yes, then. Now, what's this about?"

"We're investigating a homicide," Maragas explained. "Your name came up."

"Came up, did it?" Howson's gravelly tone dripped with sarcasm. "Does that mean I'm some kind of suspect?"

"Not exactly," said Maragas. "Person of interest might be more accurate."

Baumgartner wandered to the opposite side of the bed from Maragas. Howson didn't look his way, but he could tell the old man was watching in his peripheral vision.

"What kind of interest?" Howson asked.

"You had some trouble in Moscow?" Maragas replied, avoiding the question. "Years ago?"

"If you mean a detective with an axe to grind, then yes, I did."

"An axe to grind, how?"

"As I recall, his parents had a late-in-life divorce," said Howson. "His mother and I had a dalliance or two. He was less than thrilled about it."

Baumgartner suppressed a smile. If that was true, it explained the detective's so-called gut feeling about Howson.

"If I spoke to the detective again, would he confirm what you're telling me?" Maragas asked.

"How would I know? I imagine he'd lie about it, though. That's what police officers do."

Baumgartner's inclination to smile faded. People's predisposal to think ill of the police irritated him. He looked away from Howson to mask any expression, glancing around the room. He noticed a slender photo album on top of the bedside table and stepped closer.

Howson's head snapped to face him. "Are you trying to intimidate me?" he growled, his glare intense. "Is that what you're up to? Looming over me like that?"

Baumgartner lifted his hands peacefully. "I'm just standing here." He motioned toward Maragas. "Talk to her."

Howson continued to glower at Baumgartner for several moments. Then he said, "Mind your business, son." He turned back to Maragas. "What else do you want to know?"

"How long have you lived in Spokane?" Maragas asked.

"About twelve years," snapped Howson. "I'm not doing much living in case you didn't notice. I'm doing a whole lot of dying, though."

"You seem spry."

"Spry?" Howson let out a dry, cackling laugh. "Ha! You aren't much of a detective, are you?"

"I have my good days and bad."

"Mostly bad, I'll bet."

"You might win that bet," said Maragas.

Baumgartner wondered how long she would spar with the old man. He only half-listened as she asked him questions about his reason for moving to Spokane and how he spent his time prior to coming to reside at Avalon. His mind wandered. He'd already decided to risk a call to Darla tonight. There was a new restaurant on Northwest Boulevard he wanted to try and he thought she'd like it. Absently, his hand drifted down to the slim photo album on the table. He flipped open the cover and glanced casually at the first photo.

"Leave that alone," barked Howson. "That's my private property. You don't have a warrant."

Baumgartner almost closed the album just to avoid listening to any more of Howson's braying. Then a spark of recognition hit him. He glanced up in surprise to see Howson staring at him with naked hatred.

"What is it?" Maragas asked.

Baumgartner dropped his eyes back down to the open page of the album. There were multiple photographs arranged in an orderly row. Baumgartner didn't know the woman or the children in the photos, but he immediately recognized the man smiling amongst them.

Vince Daugherty.

Chapter 39

"You're him," Baumgartner said, surprise resonating in his voice. "You're Karl Etherton."

Howson's glare radiated rage. "I don't know what you're talking about," he said. Despite his anger, the words lacked sincerity. Instead, they sounded rote, as if he was speaking lines from a play. "My name is Lawrence Howson."

Baumgartner glanced over at Maragas, who was watching the exchange intently. He grabbed the photo album and held it up. "All of these pictures are of Vince Daugherty's family. His kids. His grandkids."

Howson said nothing. His face trembled with fury.

"Let me see that," Maragas said.

Baumgartner handed it across the bed to her. He half-expected Howson to lash out with one of his skeletal hands to stop him, but the man remained still.

Maragas opened the photo album and studied its contents. Realization flooded her features, then hardened into certainty. Her eyes narrowed as she flipped through the pages.

"None of these are posed," she noted. "Most are from a distance." She looked up at Howson, then to Baumgartner. "They look more like surveillance photos than family shots."

Howson grunted but said nothing.

Maragas turned back to him. "How long have you been stalking these people?"

Howson's jaw flexed. His eyes smoldered as they flicked back and forth between the two detectives.

"Well?" Maragas asked.

Howson stared at her, his upper lip twitching. "You had no right to look at those photos."

"Tell us the truth." She held up the photo album. "You're him. You're Karl Etherton."

"Please call Corey back in." Howson laid his head back on his pillow and looked at the ceiling. "I'm not feeling well."

"Is that how you're going to play this?" Maragas asked. "You want to cower behind Corey now?"

Howson looked down his nose at Maragas.

"You don't want to talk with us? That's fine. Here's what's going to happen. I'm going to hold on to this." She held up the photo album.

Howson lifted his head. "You can't. That's mine."

"Don't worry," Maragas said. "I won't leave with it. Yet." She jerked her head toward Baumgartner. "Not until my partner writes a warrant for it." Her expression hardened. "Then we'll take it as evidence."

Howson's upper lip curled. "You bitch."

"Want to talk with us now?"

The old man's gaze cut to Baumgartner. "She's got you on a short leash, doesn't she?"

Baumgartner held his tongue.

Howson turned back to Maragas. His lips twisted as he seemed to make a decision. He lifted his chin and calmly said, "I wasn't stalking them as you say. I was getting to know them."

"By spying and taking photos without their permission?" Maragas asked.

Howson stared at her, unrepentant. "I had every right to do so," he said. "They're my family."

"My partner was right," Maragas said. "You're Karl Etherton."

Howson's reply was immediate. "I am."

The shock of the revelation reverberated through Baumgartner. He hadn't expected this to be true at all. Now they stood at the bedside of a killer who'd escaped justice for over fifty years. The enormity of the fact struck Baumgartner speechless. Then another consideration invaded his thoughts: Howson—*Etherton!*—still seemed an unlikely suspect in

Lockett's murder. Baumgartner stood in silence, contemplating the turn of events.

Maragas, however, didn't miss a beat. "I have some different questions for you," she said.

"Oh, I'm sure you do."

"Will you answer them?"

"Yes." Etherton seemed to sit straighter as he spoke. "Yes, I will. What does it matter now? People should know the truth, even if they won't understand."

"I want to understand," said Maragas.

"No, you don't. You want to convict me. Unfortunately, you're too late. Whatever gods may be have already passed sentence. I'll be gone long before your court process plays out."

"Then consider this setting the record straight," said Maragas.

Etherton flicked his fingers at her. "Ask your questions."

"Let's start with these photos." Maragas lifted the album. "Why take them?"

"Simple. It's the only way I could be part of their lives."

"You followed them from Lewiston to Spokane?"

"Of course. While they were in Lewiston, I had a place in Moscow. It was close enough but not too close."

"How'd you find them after they left Boise? Verdna changed her name."

Etherton scoffed. "Back to her maiden name. I didn't even need a private detective to find her." He shook his head. "Stupid, unfaithful bitch."

Maragas tilted her head questioningly. "Unfaithful?"

Baumgartner understood her confusion. There were no notes in the Etherton case files about marital infidelity. Perhaps because the doctor was divorced before the murder investigations began.

Etherton nodded, sneering. "She fooled around with some singer while we were married. A crooner, whose ridiculous style was already obsolete by fifty-one. I guess I wasn't paying enough attention to her, so he did." He glanced at the photo album Maragas still held. "Truth be told, I thought the kid was his. Was convinced of it. When she ran off with him, I figured good riddance. It left me alone to pursue my own interests. They didn't last long as a couple, by the way." He chuckled. "Imagine that."

"That's why the finger," Maragas said, more to herself than either Etherton or Baumgartner.

Etherton answered anyway. "Women are faithless by nature."

"If you didn't think Vince was yours, why stalk them?"

"I got curious," Etherton said. "Found them in Boise. As soon as I got a look at the boy, I knew he was mine. I should have known. That crooner was weak. My bloodline is strong."

"Vince seems like a good man."

"Don't try to work me," Etherton said. "You didn't come here to learn about my familial relationships. Get to the questions you really want to ask."

"I think it was about family all along," Maragas said, "and revenge. You couldn't risk taking it out on Verdna, so all the others were her by proxy."

Etherton cackled. "Don't think you can fit me into one of your convenient textbook explanations, missy. I'm far more sophisticated than that."

"Why the ring finger, then?"

He pressed his lips together, hesitating. Then he said, "You're right in that respect. Taking the wedding finger was for Verdna. Besides, those bitches were never going to need it."

"Did you kill James Lockett?"

Etherton's brow knitted in confusion. "Who?"

"James Lockett. He was murdered two years ago, in High Bridge Park."

Etherton's lip curled. "I have no interest in fags."

Baumgartner cocked his head. Maragas's eyes cut to his before returning to Etherton.

"How did you know he was gay?"

"You said High Bridge Park. Did something change and it stopped being a magnet for the queers?"

"You're saying you had nothing to do with the death of James Lockett?"

"Did you not hear what I said? Let me repeat it for you: I have no interest in fags."

Maragas paused, then opened her notebook and read from her list. "How about Tav Sterner? Portland, in ninety-six?"

"Is that a man? No."

"Keith Rollins in Seattle? Ninety-one?"

"No." Etherton sounded exasperated. "Definitely not."

"Peter Isserling in Moscow, 1979."

Etherton shook his head. "Do you think I'd be stupid enough to play in my own backyard? I learned my lesson. Why are you asking me about men?"

Maragas's eyes flicked to Baumgartner again. Then she asked, "How about Stephanie Pedin? Boise, eighty-six?"

A cruel smile formed on Etherton's lips. "Ah. That one was mine. She was a beauty. She lasted a while."

A chill crawled across Baumgartner's shoulders.

Maragas listed three other names, all female. Etherton shook his head, almost sadly, as if mourning lost opportunities.

"Are there others?" she asked him, flipping closed her notebook.

"Of course."

"Who?"

Etherton shook his head. "That's not the game. You ask me a name and I'll tell you the truth. I'm not ready to take you on a grand tour just yet."

"Why not?"

"You haven't earned it."

"All right. Let's go back to the beginning. Did you kill Josephine Banfield in 1951?"

"Of course. First, I fucked that little minx three ways to Sunday. Then the real fun began. Once the play started to get a little stale, I brought in the other one."

"Shirley Jensen?"

"Just so. She was delicious in another way."

"What way?"

Etherton eyed her shrewdly. "She was a little shy. That was a nice change of pace from Jo. That one was Little Miss Adventure. In the beginning, at least."

Baumgartner's hands hung uselessly at his sides. His right hand began to curl into a fist. His jaw grew tighter. Etherton noticed his tensing and the old man smiled.

"Why did you kill them?" Maragas asked.

Etherton's smile deepened. "Do you mean why were they destined to die for my pleasure? Or why it happened when it did?"

"Both."

He shook his head. "I could try to explain the former to you, but it would be like explaining how a television works to an ant. You could never understand such things. They are beyond your grasp."

"That's rather grandiose."

"It is," he agreed, "and it is also true. Now, as for the timing?" He shrugged dismissively. "The police were on the way. I heard their sirens. My time was up."

"Is that why you left Basil Pershing alive? You ran out of time?"

Etherton shook his head again, looking disappointed in her. "Left him alive? That poser? He was right there with me the entire time. He hurt those girls at least as much as I did."

A sick warmth flooded Baumgartner. He listened to Etherton's words in dull shock.

"He didn't care much about the sex," Etherton continued. His voice was laced with nostalgia. "He was at least half a fag, but he knew better than to come onto me. Finding a kindred spirit when it came to the other parts, though—the pain, the process…? Well, that's rare. I haven't found it since, not that I was looking."

"Basil Pershing was your accomplice?" Maragas said, her voice slightly shaken.

Acolyte, Baumgartner thought.

"I let him join in, yes. He earned his spot, though. Lured those girls right into my den."

Maragas stared at him, looking almost as stunned as Baumgartner felt. Finally, she sputtered, "Isaac Hermitage in seventy-four. Was that you?"

Etherton's lip curled. "I don't kill men."

"Hudson Dorsey. Daniel Kerley. They were also murdered that year."

"Not by my hand, they weren't."

"Hermitage and Dorsey had their ring fingers cut off," Maragas said.

An appreciative smile creased Etherton's lips. "Clever," he said. "Basil always was a clever lad."

***

Baumgartner and Maragas huddled together in the hall outside Etherton's room.

"Let's get a uniform up here to stand guard," Maragas said. "There's no use booking him."

"Why post a patrol officer, then?"

"Can you imagine just walking away from a confessed serial killer? We need to keep him secure while we figure out what's next."

"Pershing is next," Baumgartner said.

"I agree, but first, we have to update Salter." She pursed her lips. "Maybe we can get Etherton to swear out a statement against Pershing."

"Maybe."

"You call dispatch. I'll finish up with Etherton."

Baumgartner called in their request, outlining that the custody detail was ongoing. Then he waited for the patrol officer near the reception station. From behind the tall desk, Corey eyed him suspiciously. Baumgartner knew he'd have to explain the situation to the nurse before he left but decided to wait until the uniformed officer arrived.

Maragas returned first.

"What'd he say?" Baumgartner asked.

"He'll do it. He demanded immunity from the prosecutor, but he'll do it."

"That's all he said? You were gone a while."

Maragas patted her jacket pocket for her cigarettes. "I need a smoke."

"Dusty? What else did he say?"

She looked at him. "He said a lot. He's a sick-minded man. But about testifying against Pershing, he said he had no issue with it. He was adamant about it, in fact. He said he didn't want people thinking he was responsible for a bunch of, and I quote, fag killings."

Baumgartner nodded slowly.

"I'll be out front," Maragas said, pulling her cigarette pack from her pocket. "You got this?"

"I got it."

Twenty minutes later, Officer Dan Flowers arrived. Baumgartner only knew the young officer in passing, but he seemed eager to please. After giving instructions while Corey looked on with increasing agitation, Baumgartner sent Flowers down the hall.

"Where's he going?" Corey demanded.

"The man you know as Lawrence Howson is now in police custody," Baumgartner explained.

"The man I know as...?" Corey shook his head in confusion, as if to clear it. "I don't understand."

"You don't need to. Just cooperate with Officer Flowers."

"He can't stay here. This is a private facility."

"He is staying here," said Baumgartner, his voice firm. "You can cooperate and allow it voluntarily, or I can go get a search warrant."

"Get a warrant, then."

"I will, but while I'm writing it and getting it signed by a judge, that officer will remain posted outside room twenty-three. Nothing will change except some paperwork." Baumgartner took a moment and forced himself to embrace his inner salesman. "Now, I know you're concerned about the welfare of your patients, Corey. That's why you take control and sometimes challenge authority. I know it's not because you're petty." He gave him a knowing look. "Forcing me to waste the time to get a search warrant that isn't going to change a thing would be petty. Especially since it would be taking me away from an active homicide investigation."

Corey stared back at him, processing. Finally, he said, "Fine. He can stay, just as long as he doesn't disturb any of the other patients."

Baumgartner glanced down the hall where Officer Flowers stood guard. "He won't. Look at him—he's the most agreeable cop on the planet."

***

They rode to the station in silence. Maragas chain-smoked the entire way. Baumgartner's stomach rumbled and he almost asked if they could swing through a drive-thru. He didn't want to face Salter while hungry. Asking Maragas to divert from their course was something he wanted to do even less, so he sat quietly.

When they were parked and walking inside the station, Maragas said, "We need to get this son of a bitch."

"Agreed."

"Let me do the talking, then."

Baumgartner shrugged. That wasn't much different than their usual routine.

They found the lieutenant's door open. Inside, Salter sat at his desk. His jacket hung from a nearby rack and his sleeve cuffs were rolled up. He seemed to sense something foreboding in their arrival and asked, "What is it?"

Maragas immediately sat. Baumgartner closed the door and sat beside her.

"We found him," she said. "We found Etherton."

Salter leaned back slowly. The gun in his shoulder holster shifted when his back came to rest against the chair. He said nothing, only gestured for her to continue.

Maragas told him everything.

As she outlined their actions, Salter listened attentively. He didn't interrupt but occasionally nodded with approval. When she detailed Etherton's confession, Baumgartner thought he saw some eager satisfaction seep into the lieutenant's features. He expected the revelation regarding Pershing would elicit a shocked reaction, but when Maragas shared it, Salter's expression simply turned grimmer. There was no surprise, at all.

"That's why the one manacle," he muttered. "He did it himself. To pose as a victim."

"It would appear so."

Salter looked up at them. "Then the mutilations to his victims were a misdirection. To point us at Etherton, so we'd chase our tail." Salter reached up and pinched his nose between his thumb and forefinger, closing his eyes. "We knew it, I think. All along, in our hearts."

"You and Pierce?" Baumgartner asked, breaking his silence since they'd entered the office.

Salter nodded slowly. "We never said the words, but the thought hung heavy between us, always unspoken."

Maragas leaned forward. "You never followed up on it, sir?"

"I was never a detective." A rueful smile touched his lips. "That case was why I never took the exam, in fact."

"It was that bad, huh?" asked Baumgartner.

"It haunted me. Pierce, too, right up until the end. If you ask Hazel, she'll tell you. It was never far from his thoughts. I spoke to him just a week before he passed, and he brought it up."

Salter cleared his throat, then reached into a desk drawer and withdrew a lozenge. "Summer colds," he muttered to himself. Salter unwrapped the lozenge and popped it into his mouth. After he tossed away the wrapper, he stared down at his hands.

"I told myself I never wanted to experience a case like that again, so I stayed in patrol until I was eligible to test for sergeant. I realized something the last time Pierce and I spoke." He looked up at the two detectives. "There was another, equally compelling reason I never became a detective. Sure, I never wanted to face another case like that first one. It was that horrible. But a part of me was also *afraid* I never would."

He gazed plaintively at them, especially focused on Maragas. "Isn't that the strangest thing?"

"No," Maragas said. "It's not strange at all."

Salter swallowed, then he cleared his throat again. "In a perfect world, we should have re-opened all three cases—Hermitage, Dorsey, and Kerley. Unfortunately, the official story had become the truth and over time, it's hard to battle against. Once the lie is told, it never stops." Salter paused, as if mulling over the words. Then he continued, "Still, the more we thought about it, the more we felt we had missed something. That we'd been fooled and somehow got the wrong guy. All along, there was this unspoken, crazy thought of who that might be."

"Pershing," said Maragas.

"Pershing," agreed Salter. "All those feelings didn't change one important point—the evidence."

"We have new evidence," Maragas said. "Etherton's testimony. Now is the time to act boldly. We can link him to the fifty-one cases, re-open the seventy-four—"

Salter coughed. He covered his mouth with one hand and held up the other for Maragas to stop talking. When he got control of himself, he said, "Slow down. Let's focus on the Lockett case first."

"The earlier cases are leverage in that one," Maragas explained. "They add weight when we go at him."

Baumgartner nodded enthusiastically in agreement.

"Do you remember when you told me there was political bullshit surrounding these cases?" Salter asked Maragas.

"I do."

"That bullshit still exists. That's my area of expertise—handling it. We need to proceed cautiously."

Maragas crossed her arms.

Baumgartner said nothing, but doubt regarding Salter was creeping in. The lieutenant had asked them to solve the Lockett murder, regardless of cost. Was he balking now at the price?

"Let's start with Etherton's testimony." He lifted the phone and punched a number from memory. Baumgartner sat and waited while Salter spoke with someone named Art. After a short while, he pieced together it was Arthur Tuck, a young prosecutor he had occasionally worked with on some of his own cases.

After some explanation, Salter put the call on speaker. "I'll let the detectives fill you in on the details."

Maragas recounted their investigation a second time. Baumgartner sat impatiently, occasionally shifting in his chair. His stomach rumbled, but he ignored the hunger. Going to get Pershing was the most pressing desire. He didn't like having to wait and over-strategize like this.

When Maragas finished, Tuck asked, "What is it you're asking for?"

"Will your office grant immunity to Etherton in exchange for his testimony against Pershing?" Salter asked.

"I'd have to get my boss to okay that," Tuck said. "That's the kind of deal only the Chief Prosecutor can make."

"Will he?"

"I can almost guarantee his answer will be no. No immunity. He's way too hardcore to even consider it. Maybe he'd entertain taking the death penalty off the table, but no more. Although, that sounds like a moot point, since your guy is dying. He'll be dead before trial."

"Maybe, maybe not," said Salter.

"You said he was in hospice. That's a days and weeks proposition, not months."

"Doctors aren't always right. Why not take a chance?"

"I would, but my boss won't."

"Why?"

"Because, from his perspective, there's simply no profit in making this deal," said Tuck. "Not in terms of legal strategy, certainly. Do you have any other evidence against Pershing to corroborate Etherton's statement?"

Salter glanced at Maragas.

"No," she admitted, "but we might find some if we search his house."

"That search warrant would be predicated on Etherton's statement and nothing else, making it extremely vulnerable to suppression at trial. We all know a bad search warrant can kill a case."

Maragas frowned but said nothing.

"Even so, that's not the biggest issue I see," Tuck continued. "The largest problem is political. Can you imagine the backlash if my boss gave a deal like this to a serial killer? Someone who has been murdering people for, what? Fifty years?"

"If what he says is true, Pershing has been doing the same for just as long."

"What about the families?" Salter asked. "Don't they deserve some closure?"

"They do. If it was my call, I'd take a hard look at it. Sometimes, difficult decisions have to be made, even if they're unpopular with the public. We owe it to the victims and their families."

"Exactly our thoughts," Salter said.

"I'm glad we all agree, but I can't go to my boss with this deal," Tuck said. "He has a completely different outlook. Bring him Etherton and I believe he'll gladly take the case, even if it means securing a posthumous conviction. He won't deal, though. His is an elected position. Anyone running against him would beat him up over an immunity deal, and much of the public would agree. He's too smart a politician to risk that."

Salter took a deep breath and let it out. He glanced questioningly toward Maragas and Baumgartner to see if they had any other questions. Baumgartner shook his head. Next to him, Maragas did the same.

"All right, Art," said Salter. "I appreciate your honesty. Do me a favor?"

"What's that?"

"Forget this conversation."

There was silence for a few moments on the other end of the line. Then Tuck said, "I'll look forward to seeing whatever case you send over, Gus. That's the case we'll examine."

"Thanks," said Salter, and ended the call.

The three of them sat quietly for several seconds. Baumgartner felt coiled up, like a boxer ready to spring from his corner. He knew better than to be the one who broke the silence.

Finally, Maragas asked, "What do you want us to do, boss?"

Baumgartner heard the resentment in her voice. She must have the same worries he did regarding Salter's conviction to see this case through to the end.

"Will Etherton still give you a sworn statement without immunity?" he asked.

Maragas thought about it. "I can probably convince him. I got the sense the immunity piece was more of a symbolic demand on his part. He wants to tell his side."

Salter glanced at his wristwatch, an ancient analog piece with a leather strap. A small cough started that turned into a bigger one. "Damn cold." He shook his head. "Go up there in the morning and get Etherton's statement. Keep working your case."

Maragas checked her phone. "It's not quite quitting time yet. Why don't we pay Pershing a visit and see what we can get from him?"

Salter turned over his hands. "Whatever you think is best. You're the detectives."

Chapter 40

"I need something to eat," Baumgartner said.

Maragas rolled her eyes. "All you ever do is eat."

"All you ever do is smoke."

She waved her hand as if to dismiss his comment, but the cigarette between her fingers only reenforced Baumgartner's argument. Maragas stuck the cigarette between her lips. "Fine," she said. "Where do you want to go?"

They stopped at Dick's and he ordered a couple of Whammys while Maragas ordered a fish sandwich. They got a large order of fries to share.

A flock of squawking seagulls gathered in the parking lot while the detectives ate at one of the picnic tables. Some patrons tossed bread and fries in the direction of the birds, which only encouraged their racket. Meanwhile, three shirtless, homeless men stood at the corner, drunkenly serenading the drivers stuck at the traffic light. Their rendition of "Silent Night" was as out of key as it was out of season.

"I thought being a detective would be a lot more glamorous," Baumgartner said before biting into his burger.

"We're about to interview a serial killer," Maragas said. "What's more glamorous than that?" She shoved a ketchup-covered fry into her mouth.

"Yeah. I guess."

A car honked at the three homeless men, and they shouted in return. Several more cars honked.

"Gonna be a long night," Maragas said, "regardless of how our interview with Pershing turns out."

Baumgartner grunted before taking another bite from his burger. He knew what she was talking about. They still had to write their initial reports concerning Karl Etherton. One of them, likely Baumgartner since he was the junior detective, would have to log Etherton's photo album into evidence at the property room.

The follow-up interview with Etherton would wait until tomorrow morning. Afterward, the detectives would notify Vincent Daugherty they located his father.

Maragas picked up several fries and swished them through a splotch of ketchup. She held them up for intense study. "Not many get to say they broke a serial killer case."

"Let alone two."

"Let alone two," Maragas parroted. "Yeah." She dropped the fries onto the wrapper of her sandwich. "Maybe we should wait. Call Pershing down to the station. Interview him on our terms, not his."

The idea immediately struck Baumgartner as wrong. He was chewing when she spoke, so he shook his head demonstratively until he finished and swallowed. "If he gets wind he's a suspect, you know he'll lawyer up. Then anything he says is inadmissible." Baumgartner thought it far more likely someone like Pershing would simply refuse to talk, but from a legal standpoint, the result was the same.

"He'll know as soon as I read him his rights," said Maragas. "It won't matter if we're in an interview room or at his house. As soon as he realizes the spotlight's on him, he'll ask for a lawyer. But if we don't do it..." She paused, reaching for her fries but not picking them up.

"What is it?" Baumgartner asked.

Maragas met his gaze, then glanced around to see if anyone was close enough to hear. "What if we don't trigger Miranda?" she asked.

Baumgartner's brow knitted. "How do we get around that?"

"Oh, come on, Bob," Maragas chided. "You've never cut the custody prong out of the equation?"

Baumgartner knew what she meant. The requirement of police officers to advise suspects of their Constitutional Rights specific to Miranda had two conditions: the suspect was in custody, and the officer was asking guilt-seeking questions.

Both conditions had to be met before the Miranda warning was triggered.

"Sure," said Baumgartner. "When I worked property crimes. Meet someone on their turf or neutral ground, tell them you're leaving when the conversation is over…" He shrugged. "No custody, no Miranda."

"Exactly, and whatever they say is admissible."

"As long as you actually leave and don't arrest them."

Maragas gave him a knowing look.

Baumgartner considered her strategy. "If we show our cards and then don't arrest him, he might run," he said. "It's risky."

Maragas turned over her hand. "Act boldly," she said.

Baumgartner took a deep breath and let it out. To buy time, he took another bite of his hamburger and chewed methodically, thinking it over. Maragas picked up her fries again and absently twirled them in ketchup, watching him.

Finally, he said, "If we believe there's no way he doesn't lawyer up…"

"You know he will. He's too smart."

"Then an ambush interview is the only way to get something." He hesitated. "Maybe get something," he added, then tore off a bite of his burger.

"So, it's settled," said Maragas.

"Settled," Baumgartner agreed through a mouthful of hamburger.

"Okay, then." She laid down her mostly uneaten fish sandwich. "Let's go."

Baumgartner still had half of his first sandwich to go. His second remained untouched in its wrapper. "What, now?"

"There's still another killer out there." Maragas wrapped up her food and stuffed it into the bag. "You can eat while I drive."

***

They parked several houses down the street from Basil Pershing's home. The two detectives silently climbed out of the car and quietly closed the doors as if they were working a graveyard shift.

A Honda Accord zoomed by with four teenagers inside. Its loud stereo boomed as it passed. The driver honked twice, and the kid in the passenger seat whooped.

"What is it with people honking?" Maragas asked.

"So much for a stealthy approach."

When they stepped onto the sidewalk, Maragas appraised Baumgartner.

"How bad is it?" he asked.

"Button your jacket. No one will notice."

While on the drive, ketchup had squirted out of Baumgartner's second burger and landed on his shirt, right above the grease spot she noticed earlier in the morning. He wiped it off but only succeeded in smearing its remnants across the bottom of the garment.

Baumgartner decided not to button the jacket since it would hinder his ability to get to his holster cleanly. It was better to be alive and considered a slob with a quick draw, than to be dead and tidy.

They approached the house. Baumgartner stepped to the left side of the door. Maragas moved to the opposite. Before she could ring the bell, Baumgartner grabbed the large brass knocker and slammed it against the door several times.

Maragas lifted an eyebrow, and Baumgartner shrugged.

Several moments passed before Basil Pershing opened the door. He still looked impeccable as before, but his nose was red and slightly chaffed. He clutched a tissue in his left hand. A wool scarf looped around his neck.

"Detectives…?" he said. His voice sounded scratchy. "I'm sorry, I don't recall your names."

"Maragas and Baumgartner," Maragas said, waggling her finger between the two of them.

"Of course. I'm sorry."

"May we come in?" Maragas said.

"Is everything all right?"

"We have some follow-up questions from our last interview."

Pershing forced a smile. "I'm not feeling well."

"The flu?" Baumgartner asked.

"Summer cold."

"It's going around," he said.

"We'll only take a few minutes of your time," Maragas said. "Then we'll be on our way. You can go back to recuperating."

Pershing lowered his head as if considering his options. He stepped back and made room for the detectives to enter. The three of them returned to the den where they had been earlier.

"Would you like some tea?" Pershing asked. "I was about to make some."

"No," Maragas said. "Thank you."

Baumgartner shook his head.

The three of them sat in the same positions as before. A box of tissues rested on the table next to Pershing. He dropped the tissue he'd been holding and pulled another from the box. After wiping his nose, Pershing asked, "What's this about?"

"We've located Dr. Etherton," Maragas said.

Pershing cocked his head. "Where?"

"It's okay," she said, deftly avoiding his question. "He can't hurt you anymore."

"Is he dead?"

"Oh no, Dr. Etherton's very much alive."

Pershing straightened. His gaze bounced from her to Baumgartner and back again. "Where is he?"

"I'm afraid we can't tell you that."

Pershing pinched his lips together and lowered his eyes. He blew his nose, wadded the tissue, then set it on the table next to the other. "You said you had follow-up questions."

"We do," Maragas said. "About Josephine Banfield and Shirley Jensen. Do you remember them?"

"Of course, I do. Memory is a curse, Detective, and a spiteful one. I may walk into a room on occasion and forget why, but unfortunately, every terrible moment of the experience alongside those two poor girls is branded into me." Pershing set his hands on the armrests and crossed his legs. "Why do you ask about them?"

"You were there with them in fifty-one. In that dungeon. Isn't that correct?"

"You know it is. There was an official report."

"And you saw Dr. Etherton kill them?"

"Do we really have to do this now?" Pershing bounced his foot. "This is ground well-covered, and I'm not feeling well."

"Just a few more questions," Maragas said, "and my partner and I will leave."

Pershing motioned for her to continue.

"It's strange for a sexual sadist to cross his orientation lines," she said.

Pershing stared at her, and his foot stopped bouncing. "Was there supposed to be a question in there?"

"Dr. Etherton admitted to killing Josephine and Shirley."

"Well, there you go. That's wonderful news."

Maragas nodded. "He also admitted to killing a number of other girls in Washington and Idaho."

Pershing furrowed his brow. "Well, I assume that's enough to put him away for a long time."

"More than enough," Maragas said.

"I'm confused." Pershing reached for another tissue. "Are you here to ask for my cooperation in testifying against him? Because I would."

Maragas narrowed her eyes. "You're not the least bit worried about what he might say once we get him on the stand?"

Pershing wiped his nose, then clutched the tissue. "I'm not following."

"He didn't kill men."

"Fags," Baumgartner said.

Pershing blinked as if slapped but retained his composure.

Baumgartner raised an apologetic hand. "His word. Not mine."

"He was very adamant about that," Maragas said. "He had no interest in men."

"What are you saying?" Pershing asked.

"It puts into doubt your alibi from fifty-one."

"My *alibi*?" Pershing touched his chest. "I was a victim. He attacked me."

"He's saying otherwise."

Anger flared in Pershing's eyes and his jaw flexed twice. A calm quickly returned to the man, though. He blew his nose and casually wiped its tip. Pershing crumpled the tissue and put it on the table with the others. He slowly pulled out several clean tissues. "You don't have Etherton, do you? You're here on what they call a fishing expedition."

"He called you clever boy," Maragas said, "for cutting off your victims' ring fingers."

Baumgartner rested his elbows on his knees. "Etherton seemed truly impressed by what you did. Master and student type of deal."

Pershing stood. "I don't think I like your accusations. It's time you leave."

Dismay struck Baumgartner. Their ambush wasn't working. He resisted the urge to glance at Maragas.

"He's laying a lot of bodies on your doorstep," his partner said. "Don't you want the chance to say something about that?"

"I just said everything I have to say on the matter," Pershing replied acidly. "You need to leave."

A brief silence hung in the air. Baumgartner could feel their chance to trap Pershing in a lie slipping away.

"Now," the doctor said.

Next to him, Maragas shifted in her seat, as if preparing to stand.

Act boldly.

"We have your DNA," Baumgartner said as he stood.

Maragas froze but did well by not looking surprised at his bluff. She continued to watch Pershing as she rose to her feet.

Pershing smirked. "Don't be ridiculous."

"You run around in that community," Baumgartner said, "you're bound to leave some DNA."

Pershing balled his fists and appeared to have difficulty swallowing. Baumgartner had struck a nerve.

"I'm a respected man in this community," Pershing said.

"Which community are we talking about?" Baumgartner asked.

"*This* community," Pershing said. He repeatedly pointed at the ground as he spoke. "I'm a goddamned veteran. A war hero." Pershing's voice strained and grew raspy. "You've no right to talk to me in that manner!"

It didn't seem like true anger, rather that of a stage actor, someone who had rehearsed their lines to pitch-perfect precision. Regardless, it excited Baumgartner like the lumbering boxer who finally cornered his faster and cagier opponent. Baumgartner swung a metaphorical haymaker, looking to knock out Pershing.

"Your DNA was found on James Lockett's body." As soon as the words left Baumgartner's mouth, he regretted them. The accusation was too specific. There was no wiggle room for him to work with now.

Pershing's blinked several times before peace returned to his face. "As I suspected," he said. "A fishing expedition. You've got nothing."

"We know you killed him," Baumgartner said.

A smile hinted at the corner of Pershing's mouth. "You'll talk with my lawyer."

"Hudson Dorsey and Daniel Kerley," Maragas said. "You killed them, too."

"I have no idea who you're talking about." Pershing stepped toward the edge of the room. "I want you out of my house."

Maragas and Baumgartner exchanged a look. It was one of missed opportunity, and Baumgartner felt the ultimate responsibility for it.

"Now," Pershing said. He pointed toward the front door.

Baumgartner stepped around the coffee table. Maragas moved in the opposite direction. For a second, she blocked Pershing's view of Baumgartner. He snatched a couple of used tissues from the table and shoved them into his jacket pocket. In his haste, Baumgartner knocked another tissue to the floor.

It was a rash decision, and one Baumgartner might not have made if he had not felt so stupid for blurting out the accusation about DNA.

As the detectives neared the edge of the room, Pershing stared at the tissue on the floor. He canted his head.

"You can't take them," Pershing said.

"Take what?" Baumgartner said.

"My tissues." Pershing pointed at the floor. "You've taken my tissues."

"Don't be gross."

"That's illegal," Pershing said flatly. "You can't do that."

Baumgartner passed Pershing on the way to the door. "I don't know what you're talking about."

***

Baumgartner revealed what he'd taken on the drive back to the station.

"The fuck?" Maragas said. "You took his snot rags?"

He nodded. "It was dumb, right?"

"You bet it was dumb. You can lose your job over some bullshit like that."

Baumgartner rested his head against the seat. "Act boldly," he said weakly.

"You mean the tissues or the DNA bluff you tried with him?"

"I was too specific," said Baumgartner. "I should have kept the details vague."

"You blasted right past your exit on that one, yeah," said Maragas, but her voice held no accusation. "In the end, though, I don't think it matters. We took a swing at him and missed. We might never have gotten a statement from him, and we sure won't now. We'll have to build our case on the evidence."

She glanced over at Baumgartner, her eyes dropping to the pocket of his jacket.

"Dumb," Baumgartner repeated. "I know."

"If you were going to do it, you should have been smart about it. Wear some gloves or something so as to not cross-contaminate it. Not to mention, maybe you'll catch his cold now." Her face pinched. "Fucking gross."

He glanced at her.

"Put that shit in a bag. Who knows what kind of crap you've had in your pocket?"

"You thinking I should keep them now?"

Maragas scoffed. "You already broke the law. No reason to throw it away now. Who knows if it'll come in handy later?"

"What should I do it with it?"

"Whatever you do, definitely wash your hands and put on some gloves before you pull them out of your pockets." She shivered. "God, I wouldn't want that freak's germs in my body."

***

When Baumgartner got home that night, it was nearly eleven. He and Maragas had stayed late to finish their reports. Lieutenant Salter wasn't there so Baumgartner hadn't revealed his lapse in judgement about stealing the tissues. He wasn't sure if he ever would.

Baumgartner tossed his car keys onto the kitchen table. He also set down a brown evidence bag and some latex gloves that he'd taken from the trunk of his car.

For a while, he stood in the kitchen, unmoving. He stared at nothing, re-running the interview with Pershing in his mind, seeing himself grab the tissues over and over again. Regret clung to him, reminding him of the stench that remained in the back seat of his patrol car when he'd transported a homeless person.

Taking the tissues had been stupid.

But what was done was done.

He shook himself free of his reverie, pulled an aluminum pan from the cupboard, and set it on the counter. Next, he tugged on the snug-fitting latex gloves. As he did so, he considered the pan. He'd washed it a couple of weeks back after baking a frozen pizza on it. It was clean, but was it clean enough for what he wanted to do now?

Baumgartner walked into his home office. Next to his computer was a printer. He opened the paper drawer and removed four sheets. He returned to the kitchen and laid the sheets across the pan.

He then gently pulled several tissues from his jacket pocket. Baumgartner laid them on the pan and spread them out. The process was thwarted in places because Pershing's mucus had long ago dried. Even so, he carefully set the pan in the oven and closed the door.

Baumgartner would let the tissues continue to air dry in the safety of the oven, just to be sure. In the morning, he'd put them in the paper bag and secure it somewhere.

What he would do with them afterward was still undecided.

Chapter 41

Maragas beat him to the station the next morning.

"You're late," she said, clearly irritated. She wore a black suit and a blue shirt. Her hair appeared washed and was pulled back with a clip.

Baumgartner checked the clock. "It's quarter after seven."

She stood, then collected a notepad and pen. "I've been here since six-thirty."

"Were we supposed to meet that early?"

Maragas brushed past Baumgartner as she headed for the exit. "I hope you ate already. We're not stopping for breakfast."

He hurried to catch up. "Are we heading up to the old folks' home?"

"The assisted living facility? Yeah. That's where we're headed."

Maragas strode quickly down the hall. Baumgartner was nearly a foot taller than her, and he had trouble keeping up. She glanced back at him. "Aren't you excited?"

"Yeah."

"You don't look it."

He shrugged. "I slept like shit last night."

"Me, too. It's like the night before a state championship."

"That's not why I slept bad," Baumgartner said.

They pushed through the west doors and exited outside.

Maragas asked, "What's got you twisted up?"

"The tissues." Baumgartner waved a hand. "I shouldn't have taken them."

"Flush them down the toilet."

His face pinched. "You said not to throw them away."

"If you're going to have a cow about it, get rid of them."

"But I could still get in trouble."

"Only if Pershing complains. So far, there hasn't been a peep from him or his lawyer. And so what if he does complain? He's a scumbag, and what can he prove, anyway?"

Baumgartner fell silent the rest of the way to the car. The implications of lying about his actions sat like a lead weight in his gut.

When Maragas settled behind the steering wheel, she said, "Listen. When we get Etherton's confession, none of it will matter. The stolen Kleenex will be a non-issue. You can pretend it never happened. Okay?"

***

They were driving up Monroe Street when Maragas's phone rang. She pulled it from her jacket pocket. "The department," she muttered.

Baumgartner frowned. Maybe they'd been counting their chickens too early when it came to Pershing and his lawyer calling the brass.

"Hey, Lieutenant." Maragas tilted the phone away from her mouth and eyed Baumgartner. "It's Salter," she said softly.

"I got that." He pointed ahead. "Pay attention to the road."

Maragas adjusted the phone and spoke. "Yeah. He's with me. We're headed up to interview Etherton now. Early bird gets the worm. You know what they say." She smiled at Baumgartner.

Her grin quickly melted.

"What's that? When?" Maragas shook her head. "Yeah. Yeah. Thanks for the heads up. No, we're gonna continue up there. Thanks for the call." When Maragas hung up, she squeezed her phone. "Motherfucker."

"He's dead," Baumgartner said.

She nodded. "Thirty minutes ago."

Baumgartner dropped his head back against the seat. "I didn't know you were coming in earlier. I would have stepped it up."

500

"There's no way you could have known."

Even though she said that, her eyes told him a different story. Dusty Maragas was angry she'd missed an opportunity to reinterview Karl Etherton because Baumgartner only came in forty-five minutes early that morning.

***

Patrol Officer Ray Zielinski stood outside the Avalon Adult Care Home. His brown hair was combed to the side and his dark blue uniform looked sharp. Worry creased his face as Baumgartner and Maragas questioned him.

"Why are you out here?" Maragas asked. "You should still be at your post. It's a crime scene."

Zielinski frowned at her. "On a natural?"

Maragas matched his frown. "Every death is a homicide until proven otherwise."

Zielinski glanced at Baumgartner, then back to Maragas. "I... I didn't think of it that way. It's an old man in hospice, so..."

"Forget it. When did you get here?"

"Our sergeant assigned us shifts. Mine started at four. I was supposed to be there until I was relieved by a day shifter."

"Which would be what? Six?"

Zielinski shrugged. "They've got roll call and what not. I'd get a few minutes of overtime, which is okay by me."

"Why are you still up here and not the day shifter?" Maragas asked.

Zielinski looked down at his shoes. "We stood around for a bit, shooting the breeze. You know how it is. When we were making the guard change, we peeked in on Etherton and he was dead. I figured the day shifter shouldn't get stuck watching this dead guy right out of the gate."

"Plus, the overtime," Baumgartner said.

Zielinski shrugged a second time.

Maragas sighed. "No one went into his room while you were there?"

"No one."

She eyed the rookie. "You never left your post?"

"No, ma'am."

"Not even to take a leak?"

"No, ma'am."

Maragas squinted. "You weren't flirting with one of the nurses?"

Zielinski smirked. "Not if you paid me extra."

"Tell me no one has picked up the body yet," Maragas said.

"Not yet." He thumbed over his shoulder. "It's still in there."

Maragas nodded. "All right. You can leave. Before you go home, though, write a report."

"About standing guard?"

"Consider it a CYA report."

Zielinski's eyes widened. "What do I have to cover my ass for? I didn't do nothing wrong."

"Then you'll have no problem with a report."

***

Corey the nurse stood at a computer located on a mobile workstation outside Etherton's room. He looked up as Baumgartner and Maragas approached.

"Detectives," he said.

"Waiting for the body to be picked up?" Maragas asked.

"The funeral home will be here within the hour."

"What's happening with his remains?"

"Mr. Howson—"

"Etherton," Maragas interrupted. "Dr. Karl Etherton. That's his real name."

The nurse stared at her for a moment. "Well, I don't know about that. Mr. Howson is set to be cremated."

"Does he have a headstone and site picked out?"

Corey waved at his computer. "Doesn't say in here. That's information you'll have to get from the funeral home."

Maragas motioned toward Etherton's room. "Mind if we step inside?" She didn't wait for an answer.

Baumgartner followed her in.

Lying on the bed, staring at the ceiling with his mouth open, Dr. Karl Etherton's visage was forever frozen in a scream. The stench of death was worse today.

Maragas whispered, "Jesus."

"He's not saving Etherton," Baumgartner said.

"Please, Detectives," Corey said, poking his head through the door. "Can we step outside?"

They ignored the nurse and hovered over the body.

"Were you here when they found him?" Maragas asked.

"No," Corey said. "He died right before I came on shift."

"Strange, him dying like this. Right after talking with us." Maragas leaned closer to Etherton's face. "He seemed sharp yesterday. Seemed like he had a while left in him."

"I probably should have sensed it," Corey said.

Both detectives turned his way.

The nurse shrugged. "It happens. It's called terminal lucidity. Patients get mental clarity right before they die. Some believe it's God's way of giving them a chance to say a proper goodbye. Anyway, he seemed more with it yesterday than I'd seen him in a while." Corey glanced at Etherton. "He was really someone else the entire time, huh?"

When neither detective answered, Corey shrugged and left the room.

Maragas shook her head. "I don't buy it."

"Buy what?" Baumgartner asked. "That this was a natural?"

She waved at Etherton. "The son of a bitch suddenly gets a burst of clarity and spills his guts right before he dies? Come on."

"You heard the nurse. Terminal lucidness or whatever."

Maragas pursed her lips in thought. "You think getting it off his chest…" She scowled and shook her head. "No. The man was evil. There's no way."

"We found him," Baumgartner said, "and he confessed to his crimes before he died. Let's consider ourselves lucky."

"We didn't get lucky." She pointed at the dead man. "He got away with it. He got away with them all. That's the opposite of luck."

Dusty Maragas turned and left the room.

Baumgartner took one final look at Karl Etherton, then followed her.

***

"It's hearsay now," Lieutenant Salter said, his voice scratchy. "All of it. Everything Etherton told you about Pershing is inadmissible."

Baumgartner and Maragas sat in front of Salter's desk. They had gone directly there after leaving the Avalon Adult Care Home.

"What about the hearsay exception?" Baumgartner asked.

"The statements he made against his own interest," Salter said, "those will fly. He's still on the hook for his confession, not that it matters." He grabbed a tissue from the box on his desk and blew his nose. "However, there's nothing solid to corroborate his statement regarding Pershing. Can you imagine any judge allowing the second-hand account of a known serial killer as the sole evidence to indict an upstanding member of our community?"

"A doctor," Maragas said, disdain in her voice.

"War hero," added Baumgartner.

Salter opened a lozenge and stuck it in his mouth. "It would never happen."

"So what do we do?" Maragas asked. "All I'm seeing are bad choices."

"There are bad choices and then there are bad choices." Salter interlaced his fingers. "The art of leadership is understanding which are the ones you can live with." The lozenge clicked against his teeth as it moved around his mouth. "The way I see it, we've got two viable options."

"We?" Maragas asked.

"We're in this together now," Salter said. "The three of us."

Baumgartner slid down in his chair. "Like Amherst and Pierce."

Maragas waved at the lieutenant. "And you and Pierce."

Salter nodded. "The chain is linked again. It only stays connected by its weakest link, though. That's why there are different types of bad choices."

Baumgartner glanced at Maragas. She stared ahead.

"What are these two choices?" she asked.

"You two can push the Basil Pershing matter and risk a shit storm," Salter said, "or you can be smart and take a win."

"A win doesn't sound like a bad choice," Baumgartner said.

"It does when you have to ignore Basil Pershing."

"The fuck?" Maragas said.

Salter held up his hand. "Hold on. Announcing you found Karl Etherton will be big news. You'll solve a fifty-four-year-old case. A notorious one. At the same time, you'll also solve a number of murders across Washington and Idaho." He paused, then added, "Including rolling in the ones you believe Pershing killed."

"What?" Baumgartner asked, stunned.

"You can't undo the old, settled cases," Salter said. "As for the newer ones, we put those on Etherton. In the process, you'll give some closure to the families left behind."

"It's not closure," snapped Maragas. "Etherton didn't kill any of the male victims."

"The families won't know that. To them, a long journey of not knowing will be over. They will finally have the name of the person who took their loved one from them. They can move on, if they're able." He waggled his hand between the two detectives. "Not only that, it'll rocket both of your careers. So what if Etherton takes the hit? He's dead."

"So are his victims," Maragas said. She didn't bother to hide the righteousness in her voice.

"They're silent now. Just like Etherton. This is the way. The families get closure. The public will see you doing your job and they'll make themselves known. Trust me. I've been there."

"When is a win not a win?" Baumgartner muttered, still shaking off the shock of Salter's proposal.

"We're going to ignore the truth of James Lockett's murder?" Maragas asked. "Or those other guys Basil Pershing murdered back in seventy-four?"

"You're not ignoring anything," Salter said. "As I said, those cases in seventy-four have been officially handled. The Lockett murder will go down as Etherton's."

"That's bullshit," Maragas said.

"As far as the city's concerned, those old cases are done. Leave it alone."

Maragas crossed her arms. She clearly didn't want to leave anything alone. "What if we can get Pershing today?"

Salter furrowed his brow. "How do you recommend we do that?"

A spike of cold zipped up Baumgartner's spine. He reached out to touch Maragas's arm. "Don't."

She ignored him. "We've got his DNA."

"You what?" Salter's gaze bounced from Maragas to Baumgartner, then back to Maragas. "How?"

"We took some Kleenex from his house. He's got the same summer cold you do."

Salter's eyes lowered to the collection of tissues gathering on his desk.

Maragas continued. "All I've got to do is put a couple on evidence with Lockett's stuff. We run them through the system, then get a warrant for a DNA sample from Pershing.

They match up and we get him." Maragas snapped her fingers. "Just like that."

"No." Salter's expression hardened. "We won't do that. You won't do that."

"He's a killer, Lieutenant."

"Once you compromise yourself like that, you can't take it back."

"I don't see how planting evidence on a heinous man we know is guilty is any different than pushing a lie that someone else did the killing."

"It isn't different," Salter admitted. He held up his first two fingers. The gesture reminded Baumgartner of the hippie peace sign. "Except for these two points. Letting Etherton take the hit for all of the murders is the least disruptive option. It doesn't destroy any of the work that has gone before nor does it revictimize the families."

Maragas opened her mouth to argue but Salter dropped a finger before she could speak.

"What you're suggesting isn't for the families," he said. "It'd be for our own benefit. So we can see justice done in the exact way we want it to happen." He shook his head. "That isn't always the best way."

"It should be," Maragas asserted.

"It should," Salter agreed.

Maragas ground her teeth together. Baumgartner watched the corner of her jaw flex and heard the strained control in her voice. "Then let's do it that way," she pleaded. "I'll admit I took the tissues from his house. He threw them away. They were trash."

"She didn't take them," Baumgartner interjected. "It was me. I took them."

Salter eyed the two of them for a long moment. Then he motioned toward the tissues on his desk. "He threw them away like I did?"

"Yeah." Baumgartner nodded.

"It won't stand up in court. A defense attorney will jump on it like O.J.'s bloody glove. It'll be ruled an illegal seizure. You want your names tied to that type of shit? Sketchy decisions follow you through your days." Disappointment crossed Salter's face. "Don't let this moment make you question who you are. Putting a thumb on the scale might have worked back in the fifties, maybe even the seventies, but it's not going to work now."

"You're telling us to play politics with our cases," Maragas said. "I'm still not seeing the difference."

"That's why you're not a lieutenant."

Silence descended over the room. The only noise was the hum of the air-conditioning unit.

After a few seconds, Salter lifted the small garbage pail from under his desk and held it out towards them. "Give me the tissues. I'll dispose of them."

"I don't have them here," Baumgartner replied.

Salter watched him, as if trying to gauge his sincerity. Then he replaced the trash container and folded his hands. "Is this your plan, too, Bob? The both of you want to plant evidence to make this case?"

Baumgartner shifted slightly in his seat. "I…"

"It's my call," Maragas interrupted. "I'm lead."

"You're talking about something unethical and illegal," said Salter. "I don't think rank or position really come into play here."

"Good," said Maragas. "Then I guess you won't stop us."

Salter's eyes narrowed. "Tread carefully, Detective. There's a lot at stake here."

"I realize that. We're trying to catch a serial killer who's been dropping bodies for fifty-plus years."

Salter remained quiet for several seconds. "Okay, let's say you plant this evidence in with Lockett's. Say you even get away with it. You still don't have any legally obtained DNA from Pershing to compare. You've got no probable cause for a warrant and he's already refused."

"There are ways to get some. Off-book."

"Call it what it is," Salter said. "Dirty. Corrupt."

Maragas shrugged. "I don't see a problem with making sure a monster like him goes down any way possible. I'll sleep fine afterward."

"No, you won't," said Salter. "Trust me."

Baumgartner tilted his head, wondering what the lieutenant meant. Before he could ask, Salter continued.

"You're not the only one here." Salter twirled his finger. "There's three of us. Now, I'm going to do you a favor and forget you ever mentioned anything about this plant job." He took a moment to give her a hard stare. "That's done, you hear me? Not happening. Now, tell me what else do you have to support a case against Pershing?"

Maragas glared at Salter. Baumgartner could almost feel the heat coming off her.

"We've got M.O.," he blurted, trying to come to his partner's aid.

"M.O. can be copied," Salter said evenly, not taking his eyes from Maragas. "Hell, it was—Pershing emulated Etherton's M.O. to send the investigation that direction."

"Victimology," Maragas said evenly. "Etherton killed women, Pershing killed men. That differentiates them."

"That's academic. It's not probable cause."

"He had opportunity," she said. "He lives here."

"I've lived here my whole life. Does that make me a suspect?"

"Is that a confession, Lieutenant?"

"Oh, fuck off, *Detective*. I'm trying to help you. Both of you."

"Then help us put this piece of human garbage away." Maragas leaned forward. "You said you wanted us to clear Lockett's murder *no matter the cost*. Well, this is the cost."

"No, it isn't." Salter shook his head. "You try this, and you won't get the result you think. Best case, a halfway decent defense attorney rips your DNA evidence apart, leaving you with no case at all. Worst case, *you* go to prison instead of Pershing. Is that what you want?"

The lieutenant's words chilled Baumgartner. He knew cops sometimes lost their jobs and, in some rare instances, were incarcerated for their deeds. Those individuals and their acts always seemed distant from him. He never imagined he might end up in a situation where he could be the one facing such repercussions. He wiped his sweaty hands on his pant legs, regretting his actions more than ever now.

"We've got Etherton's word," said Maragas. "That counts for something."

"You heard what Artie said about that." Salter's tone brooked no disagreement. "Besides, he might be lying. He could be taking a last shot at the one who got away."

"Funny," said Maragas. "Pershing said something similar."

Salter leaned back in his chair, letting out a long sigh. "We've got nothing on Pershing, and the only way to get anything is not acceptable."

"I don't think it's—" Maragas began.

"It's unacceptable," said Salter, his tone hard. "We're not doing it. Not when there's another way."

"Putting all of the murders on Etherton?" Maragas asked, her voice riddled with contempt. "We've got the same exact evidence for Etherton as we do for Pershing—M.O., opportunity of location, and the hearsay of a dying man. It's all circumstantial."

"The difference is you've got probable cause to get Etherton's DNA. It'll match some of the cases you know he's responsible for. Those will be ironclad. With that foundation, the rest can be tied in by circumstantial evidence—the killer's M.O., his proximity to the murders, and his confession to you."

"He didn't confess to all of them," Baumgartner said, remembering. "Just to the two in fifty-one and another, more recent one. Stephanie Pedin."

"I'm sure he said more than that." Salter gave him a meaningful look. "And a detailed confession to all those murders is against his own interest, so it isn't hearsay like what he said about Pershing. His confession will carry weight."

"You want us to lie?" Baumgartner asked. "A minute ago, you said—"

"I want you to help me do what is best for the public good," said Salter. "We can't get to Pershing, but we can give the families of the victims closure. They deserve that. They deserve justice."

"It's not justice," Maragas argued. "It's a lie."

"The two aren't necessarily mutually exclusive," Salter said quietly.

"How is this any different than handling Pershing my way?" she demanded. "You're still framing a man for murders he didn't commit. It's a lie."

"And once it's told, it can't be undone," agreed Salter. "The difference is, this plan will work. It's clean. It's better for everyone involved. You'll see that in time. When you're not angry anymore."

"I'll never not be angry about this, Lieutenant."

Salter spread his hands and said nothing.

Maragas glanced over at Baumgartner, her jaw continuing to flex. He saw indecision in her eyes as she looked at him. After a few moments, cold calculation settled in. She let out a sigh of surrender.

"We'll do it your way," Maragas said, resigned.

Salter blew his nose in a tissue. "Good. It'll be fine, trust me." His eyes cut between the two detectives. "It's not over where Pershing is concerned, either."

"It sounds like it." Baumgartner eyed him. "What if he's not done killing?"

"He's seventy-one," Salter said. "How much more trouble can he cause? Let him think he outsmarted us. We'll catch him eventually."

"You really believe that?" Baumgartner asked. "Because the son of a bitch has already gotten away with it for over fifty years, and he's still getting away with it."

"For now," Salter said.

"Only for now," echoed Maragas. She stood and left the office without a word.

Baumgartner rose to follow her. Salter held up a hand to stop him.

"This is done," the lieutenant said. He sounded worn out to Baumgartner. "If anything goes sideways, it's on me. I ordered this. I made it happen. You understand?"

Baumgartner nodded slightly. Salter looked as if he wanted more from him, so he added, "I understand, sir."

"I'm not sure you do," Salter said, his voice gravelly. "Maybe you won't ever have to."

Baumgartner didn't know what to make of that comment. Should he be insulted, or did Salter mean something else?

"As shitty as this situation is," Salter said, "at least it'll do some good for someone like you."

"Someone like me?" Baumgartner asked.

"Major Crimes isn't your final stopping point, Bob. For Dusty, I don't think she wants to go anywhere else. She's at the end of the road and she'll stay there until retirement. You've got more ladder to climb. Who knows? Someday, you might even be a captain. Playing it smart right now will be a big boost for you."

Baumgartner shrugged. He didn't see himself that way, though the truth was he'd never thought much beyond wherever he was at any given moment in his career.

Salter leaned forward, his sharp eyes piercing Baumgartner. "This is important. When it's your turn, you have to do better. You hear me? You have to do better."

Baumgartner opened his mouth to say that didn't seem like a very high bar to clear, then snapped it shut. Instead, he said, "All right. I will."

Salter nodded his approval.

Baumgartner stood and went to find his partner.

***

Maragas wasn't at her desk. He found her outside the west doors, lighting what he was pretty certain was her second cigarette since leaving the meeting.

She looked up at him as he drew close. Her expression was twisted with anger.

"He's a fucking murderer," she said.

"I know."

"I want to nail him."

"Me, too."

"Then give me those tissues."

Baumgartner shook his head. "No. Salter's right."

"Oh, fuck Salter. He didn't have to listen to Etherton crowing, did he? Remember how he talked about killing those girls?"

Baumgartner nodded. "It was disgusting."

"What about that piece of shit Pershing? He deserves to die in prison."

"He does."

"Then give me those tissues," Maragas repeated.

"No. You'll use them."

"*You're goddamn right I will!*" The volume of her voice remained low, but her words crackled with fury. She stared so intensely at him that Baumgartner was forced to glance away. When he looked back, Maragas put her cigarette between her lips and took a hard drag from it.

"No," he repeated, but he heard the indecision in his own voice.

Maragas watched him for a long while, smoking. He waited, remaining silent. Finally, she stubbed out her cigarette and pointed at him. "This isn't over. I don't care how long it takes. Meanwhile, you better hang onto those goddamn tissues. Keep them somewhere safe."

Baumgartner didn't answer. After a few seconds, Maragas brushed past him and headed back inside.

***

That evening, Baumgarter stood once again in his kitchen. He didn't feel hungry. In fact, his greasy lunch sat like a ball of lead in his gut. He got a bottle of beer from the fridge and took several sips while he stared at his stove. The events of the past two days whirred through his mind's eye like one of the avant-garde films a woman he'd briefly dated insisted upon attending. The dissonance he experienced watching those movies annoyed him. He understood and recognized the individual images but knew he was missing something in the way they were presented, the way they went together.

This case was like that.

Two killers, both deserving justice.

What did that word mean?

Or closure, for that matter?

He stood, sipping the beer, torn between what Salter presented and what Maragas wanted. He felt he understood both. But, just like the confusing flicker of those films he never wanted to watch in the first place, he wasn't sure what to make of it all.

You don't have to decide today.

You can be loyal to both of them, today.

Baumgartner wrestled with that thought while he finished his beer. Then, he plunked the empty bottle on the counter. He fished a pair of latex gloves out of his pocket and pulled them on. Methodically, he opened the stove, removed the pan with the now certainly dried tissues on it, and set the pan on the counter. He shook open the paper evidence bag he'd brought home with him and carefully transferred the tissues inside the bag. Once finished, he creased the top of the bag and folded it over several times, running his fingertips along each fold. He would have preferred some tape to seal it, but once he flattened the bag, it should be fine.

With little effort, he managed to clear a space near the back of his freezer. He rested the bag there, then stacked several frozen pizza boxes in front of it. The edges of the brown paper bag extended beyond the corners of the pizza boxes, seeming to frame them. He stared at the smooth brown slip of exposed paper for a moment, then nudged the stack of boxes off kilter to cover it. After that, he closed the freezer door.

Detective Robert Baumgartner opened the refrigerator and reached for another beer. He had a feeling it would be second of many more that night.

Interlude III

2023

"You went along with it, didn't you?" Detective Wardell Clint asked. "The official story?"

Baumgartner nodded slowly without looking Clint's way. The late afternoon sun bathed his face as he stared out at the lake with unfocused eyes. The way the light struck Baumgartner's features accentuated their craggy, aged quality. Clint realized Baumgartner was roughly as old as Salter had been at the time of the 2005 investigation.

Clint reached for his water glass. It was almost empty. So was the pitcher between them. He took a final swallow. Before he could speak, Baumgartner beat him to it.

"Are you going to call me dirty, too?" he asked. "Or just incompetent?"

Clint hesitated. What the former chief had told him was dirty as hell in his estimation. However, saying so now might derail this process, and it wasn't over yet. They were almost finished, but there was still more he needed to know.

As for incompetent, that went without saying. An insult, though, was just as dangerous as an accusation. Either one might end the interview prematurely.

So, Clint ground his teeth together, and said, "The lieutenant told you to make that choice. He bears the responsibility."

"Gus Salter is in his grave. I don't think he feels the weight of that decision anymore."

"Just like Karl Etherton didn't have to face his own reckoning," said Clint.

Baumgartner's eyes narrowed. "Don't compare the two of them."

"I'm not. Just the fact they both escaped the consequences of their actions."

"Gus didn't escape anything. Were you listening? He bore that burden for over thirty years." Baumgartner's voice sounded both sad and reverent. Then his expression hardened. "As for Etherton, you're right. He got away clean. Only a damaged reputation."

"Or an enhanced one, depending on who you ask," Clint said, reluctantly agreeing with him. "True crime buffs wouldn't shut up about him for a while afterward. Then when podcasts became a thing…"

"It wasn't exactly justice," Baumgartner said. "But Salter was right about closure for the families."

Clint didn't argue the value of a solved case on those left behind. His issue here was with its veracity. "Hanging all those murders on him didn't do anything else except clear cases for homicide detectives across the region."

"The bar wasn't high to attach a case to him," Baumgartner agreed. "Even if the case couldn't be linked solidly enough to close, it was left open with a caveat." Baumgartner swept his hand in front of him like a headline. "Likely victim of infamous serial killer, Karl Etherton."

"More notoriety for him," Clint said, disapprovingly, "and still no punishment."

"Unless you believe in Hell."

"I don't go in much for mythology," said Clint, dismissing the idea. He eyed Baumgartner closely. "Lockett's case was classified as solved, with Etherton listed as the unprosecuted killer, cleared due to exceptional circumstances—he was deceased. There's no mention of Basil Pershing anywhere in the file. Why not?"

Baumgartner frowned. "What evidence did we have?"

"You had Etherton's statement."

"That was problematic, at best."

"Even so, it is still evidence. Why keep the part about Pershing out of the file?"

Baumgartner turned to face Clint, his eyes intense. "Because the truth matters, Ward."

Clint's shoulders twitched slightly at the shortened use of his name. Baumgartner had been using that tactic all day. He'd ignored it as best he could but like a boxer dealing with his opponent's flicking jab for ten rounds, he was losing his patience.

"Whose truth?" he demanded. "Yours? Salter's?"

"*The* truth," said Baumgartner.

"That's what I'm trying to find here."

Baumgartner reached up and scratched his cheek. "The truth is a slippery beast, Ward. Sometimes it takes a lie to find it."

"No," said Clint. "Truth is simple. It is an objective fact. People are the slippery ones."

"You think so, huh? With that mindset, you wouldn't have survived the politics of being chief for more than a week."

"If I had to be chief, I'd eat my gun the first day."

Baumgartner cracked a smile. "Damned if that isn't the truth."

"What did you mean about a lie to find the truth?"

"I thought you didn't believe that."

"I don't. I want to know what you meant."

"Try this, then," Baumgartner said. "Basil Pershing killed Isaac Hermitage. He killed Hudson Dorsey. Daniel Kerley, too, and others beyond that. He killed James Lockett. That's the truth I know."

"So?"

"The truth the rest of the world knows is very different. Hermitage's case was officially attributed to Etherton, with exceptional clearance, same as James Lockett's. Dorsey's status as a drowning victim was reclassified as homicide, assigned to Etherton by virtue of the missing ring finger. Kerley's death remained a suicide, if a suspicious one. Many consider him an unofficial victim of Karl Etherton."

"I'm waiting for a point," said Clint, impatiently.

"We couldn't undo those official truths," Baumgartner said. "They were like cement that had already set. Dusty and I weren't satisfied with that. We believed we could still tell the truth about Basil Pershing. Even if it took a lie to do it."

"What did you do?" Clint asked.

Part IV

2007

*"No man is justified in doing
evil on the ground of expediency."*

- Theodore Roosevelt,
New York City Police Commissioner, 1895-97

Chapter 43

Sergeant Robert Baumgartner walked through the Major Crimes bullpen on his way to lunch. As he strolled past desks, he made sure to greet those detectives who glanced up at him. The ones who were deep in concentration, he left alone. Breaking a homicide investigator's train of thought was a cardinal sin.

He stopped by the Property Crimes unit to see if Detective Tom Farrell wanted to join him. His friend had been promoted a few months prior, so he wasn't surprised to see the magnetic dot next to his name on the status board slid over to Out with a notation of interview. Farrell was obviously working diligently to make his bones.

Baumgartner decided to call Darla from the car. Her workday was as unpredictable as his could be, but she might be able to take a lunch break.

He walked down the hall and out the west doors. His city-issued Impala sat in one of the premiere parking spaces near the employee entrance. As a Major Crimes sergeant, he didn't merit one of those slots. However, his lieutenant was on a two-week vacation in Europe, so he took advantage of the man's absence to use his spot.

Baumgartner got into the car and pulled out, watching carefully for pedestrians. As he swung the wheel to straighten his course, his phone chimed, playing "The Old Gray Mare." It was the ringtone he'd set for his former partner, Dusty Maragas. He smiled at the sound. Every time she called, his joke never failed to amuse him.

He punched the answer button. "Dusty," he said, by way of greeting.

"You alone?" Maragas asked him.

Baumgartner's smile faded. "I'm in the car. Why?"

"No one else is there?" she asked.

"No. What's going on?"

"Find a place to pull over," Maragas said. "We need to talk."

Baumgartner frowned but did as directed. He slid the Impala into an empty metered space a block away from the Public Safety Building. "I'm parked," he said. "What the hell is going on?"

"I'm at the suspicious death on Elm," she said. "Patrol responded to make a notification to Jennifer Terreri. They found her on the living room floor inside, lying in the middle of a busted coffee table. They couldn't tell if she fell or was assaulted."

"Which was it?"

"She was struck. There's blunt force trauma. She was knocked down. This table was cheaply constructed, and it shattered. One of the wooden shards cut her head, which bled a lot. My guess is it was the first blow that killed her, though."

"The husband's a suspect?"

"That's the reason I'm calling. You know that motorcycle crash up on Alberta?"

"No," said Baumgartner. He didn't keep up on patrol calls.

"It's a fatal. Traffic collision investigators are out on it. The driver of the motorcycle was Christopher Terreri. That's why patrol was here. It was the notification they were making."

Baumgartner nodded slowly. It sounded like Maragas had caught a ground ball on this case. Husband assaults wife, flees on motorcycle, crashes and dies. Clean. All that was left was for Maragas to go through the motions and wrap it up.

"All right," he said. "Thanks for the update." He dropped the car into gear and looked over his shoulder for any traffic.

"I think you should come up here, Bob."

Baumgartner froze.

Maragas never called him by his first name anymore. Not since he made sergeant. Especially not when his first assignment was the Major Crimes unit. Commanding former co-workers was difficult enough. Maragas wanted him to be successful and calling him by his title reinforced his role with the other detectives.

If she was using his first name now…

"I think you should come up here," she repeated, "and stop by your house on the way."

***

Baumgartner entered his house and closed the door behind him. He paused in the entryway and listened. There wasn't anyone there, not even a dog. Baumgartner lived by himself.

However, he felt like a stranger at this moment, like he didn't belong in his own home. He'd never illegally broken into a house, but the sensation of being alone inside someone else's residence had to be like this. Baumgartner wasn't a thief. He wasn't about to burgle his abode, so he wasn't afraid to be caught by the police since he had every right to be there.

He was, however, about to blatantly commit a criminal act under the color of his badge. The severity of the first, when he stole the DNA filled tissues from Basil Pershing, could be rationalized by the heat of the moment.

He and Maragas had found a second serial killer lurking in the monied shadows of the South Hill. They wanted to put him away and were frustrated by their inability to do so. Grabbing the tissues, while still wrong, reflected that desperate state of mind.

That excuse couldn't be applied to what they were about to do.

Baumgartner steeled himself and headed toward the kitchen.

Two years had passed since that moment in Pershing's living room. Since Baumgartner took the tissues and placed them in a paper evidence bag, he'd stored them in the back of his freezer.

He thought about moving once or twice during the past couple of years, especially after the promotion to sergeant. The evidence hiding behind a stack of frozen pizza boxes kept him in the same house, however. Baumgartner didn't want to risk moving and either losing the evidence or letting others know about it.

Baumgartner placed his hand on the freezer door. He could back out now and avoid the slippery slope of noble cause corruption. He'd read about it in preparation for the oral board portion of his test. Throughout the nation, police departments battled moral turpitude in their ranks. It didn't always start as selfishness with eyes toward greed, power, or sex. Usually, corruption began because a cop thought he was doing the right thing.

Like today.

Baumgartner yanked open the freezer door and reached in.

Only three people knew Baumgartner took the tissues—Maragas, Lieutenant Salter, and Basil Pershing. Maragas was still in the Major Crimes unit, but Salter transferred a year ago to square away the Support Services section. The lieutenant didn't want to leave the unit, but the chief placed personnel where he wanted them.

Maragas and Salter knew Baumgartner kept the stolen evidence in his freezer.

Baumgartner wondered if Basil Pershing even remembered the tissues.

***

The small brown rancher sat further back from Elm Street than its neighbors. The lots were roughly the same size, so that meant more grass was in the front yard of Jennifer Terreri's home.

Baumgartner parked at the end of the block, not out of caution, but because of the lack of available space. Several patrol cars were interspersed with civilian cars, likely belonging to the locals.

Two lines of yellow caution tape were strung around the Terreri property to mark the inner and outer crime scene. An older officer with a clipboard stood on the sidewalk at the outer perimeter.

Baumgartner nodded as he approached. "Afternoon."

The officer dipped his chin in response, then jotted the sergeant's name into the crime scene log. Everyone who entered and exited the two perimeters was recorded.

"She's inside," the officer said.

Baumgartner briefly wondered if the officer meant Dusty Maragas or the dead woman before deciding it didn't matter. He ducked underneath the outer perimeter.

At the far edge of the property, a group of crime scene technicians huddled together. They chatted casually as if they had all the time in the world. The evidence van sat curbside behind them.

Baumgartner finished the walk up the pathway to the home, ducked under the second line of caution tape, and entered the house. His heart pounded as adrenaline spiked in his system. He'd been in plenty of homicide scenes before. This was the only one he was intimidated to enter.

"Dusty?" he called. He heard the stress in his voice.

"In here."

Baumgartner passed through the entryway, walked by the kitchen and bathroom, before finding Maragas standing in the living room. She wore a black pantsuit and red shirt. Latex gloves covered her hands.

He forced a smile to hide his nervousness. "Good to see you."

"What's wrong with you?" she asked. "Are you all right?"

Baumgartner waved away her questions as he turned to study the crime scene.

A woman lay on the floor in the middle of a broken, wooden coffee table. It had collapsed under her body which

Baumgartner found surprising because Jennifer Terreri was a thin woman. She was tall, though. He couldn't estimate Jennifer's size since he'd always felt it difficult to judge height while a victim was on the ground. She wore a Harley-Davidson T-shirt and blue cutoff shorts. Her feet were bare.

Outside, a small black dog stood at the sliding glass window. The puppy wagged its tail as it watched Baumgartner.

The rest of the house reminded Baumgartner of hundreds of homes he'd been in throughout the city—cheap furniture, a big-screen television, family photos on the wall. The only oddity was the Hummel figurines scattered about the room. They were on the end tables, the fireplace mantel, and three clustered together on the windowsill. Eleven ceramic statues lined the shelf in front of the TV.

Baumgartner leaned in to consider one of the statues in front of the television. He disliked the cherubic faces of the children who stood frozen in poses the designers likely considered nostalgic. At the end of the figurine line, a dust ring remained on the shelf. He pointed at it. "One of them is missing."

"You bring it?" Maragas whispered hoarsely from behind him. Her voice was ragged from the years of smoking.

Baumgartner stiffened, but his finger remained pointed at the dust ring. "Did you hear what I said?"

"Yeah, I heard." Her voice remained soft, but it gained a sense of urgency now. "We don't have much time. Did you bring it?"

He glanced around, checking for others in the house. "Anyone else in here?"

She smirked. "Jesus, Bob. Would I have asked otherwise? Now, give it to me." Maragas held out her hand.

Baumgartner stared at her short, manicured nails, her fingers adorned by a pair of simple silver rings. His eyes fixed on her empty ring finger. His stomach churned with a deep blackness that felt like it descended a mile into the ground.

"No." He spoke the word bluntly, surprised at how firm his voice sounded.

Maragas narrowed her eyes. She impatiently opened and closed her hand twice. "This is no time for argument."

"No," he repeated. "I can't."

"Then don't," Maragas snapped. "I will. Give me the goddamn tissues."

Baumgartner slowly shook his head. "Salter was right," he said. "This is wrong."

Maragas stepped closer to him, her scowl furious. "What's wrong is that son of a bitch living large in his big house up on the South Hill for the past two years. We should have done him back then when it was clean."

"But we didn't." Baumgartner's gaze lighted upon the dead woman amidst the shattered table. "And this isn't clean."

"It's as clean as it gets," said Maragas tersely.

Baumgartner waved a hand at the victim. "How's this work, huh? You plant the DNA and sell this as Pershing? There's no connection."

"The DNA is the connection."

"How do you get his DNA for comparison?" Baumgartner asked. Maybe if he kept her talking, she'd change her mind, he thought.

"I've got a CI whose always been good. She'll put him here."

Baumgartner rolled his eyes. "Your CI just *happens* to be here and *happens* to know him?"

Maragas glanced around, mirroring Baumgartner's earlier concern for eavesdroppers. She dropped her voice before replying, "Do you think I'm an idiot, Bob? The CI will say she was walking past. She'll see his car in the driveway and someone matching his general description exit the house."

"That's pretty convenient."

"Sometimes cases break that way," said Maragas, her tone still low and dangerous. "Now, give me the tissues and get out of here."

Baumgartner's gaze drifted back to the row of ceramic figurines. The missing one suddenly made sense to him. "You're going to plant one of these at his house, aren't you? To tie him to the scene with something physical."

Maragas didn't answer.

"What's the idea there, Dusty?" Baumgartner said. "Serial killers take trophies?"

Maragas took another half-step closer to Baumgartner, dropping her voice even lower. "What's your problem, Bob? Why are you suddenly being a dick? You knew this day was coming. You knew I was looking for a chance. It's what we both wanted."

"I don't want it."

"Then why'd you keep the tissues all this time?"

Baumgartner fell silent. The truth he told himself was that he kept them out of loyalty to her. At the same time, he had to wonder if he wanted to keep the possibility alive for his own sake. He wanted to see Pershing face justice. He just wasn't sure how far he was willing to go to make that happen.

Until today.

"I can't do it," he whispered. "*We* can't."

Maragas's hot glare burned into him. "You've forgotten what a piece of shit he is. How arrogant he is with his false front."

"I remember."

"I don't think so. If you did, I'd already have Forensics in here photographing the scene and collecting those tissues."

"Dusty…"

Maragas held up a finger to silence him. "Those stripes have dulled your memory. You need to see him again, to remember. So, that's what we'll do. Tomorrow, I'm taking you up to see that prick. Once you get it in your head again that *he's fucking evil*, Bob, you'll give me the tissues and we'll finally get this done."

"I'm not going to change my—"

"Get out of my scene, Sergeant," Maragas snapped. "One of us has a job to do."

Baumgartner watched her for a moment, but her expression was hard and unwavering. He lifted his hands in surrender. "Fine." He turned to go. When he neared the front door, Maragas called after him.

"Tomorrow!"

Chapter 44

Baumgartner sat on his back porch, sipping his third beer. The remainder of his work day had flitted past in a blur and he had virtually no memory of it. Darla had called him on his way home, suggesting they spend the night together, but he had begged off. He knew he'd be poor company. Besides, hiding in the arms of a woman tonight wasn't going to change his dilemma.

He had to face it.

This was a day he'd always known would come and yet had hoped it wouldn't. At least, that's what he told himself. Now, three beers in, he was more willing to admit there was more to it. A part of him still wondered if Maragas was right. The end has to justify the means, right?

Only Salter hadn't thought so. In the midst of orchestrating a lie he believed was justified by the outcome it created, the lieutenant had gone out of the way to admonish Baumgarter against it.

When it's your turn, you have to do better.

He respected Salter, but the hypocrisy was plain. The lieutenant was asking Baumgartner to do what he himself couldn't do.

Or chose not to.

Baumgartner understood the fury that drove Maragas. The idea of Pershing getting away with such evil ate at him, too. That the man hid behind status, wealth, and military service made it even worse. He did deserve to go to prison for whatever years he had left.

No matter the cost.

Those last four words resonated with him as he took a swig of his beer. He wondered if Maragas was right about tomorrow. Would seeing Pershing again bring his outrage roiling up again? Enough that he'd be willing to do what she wanted?

Or maybe it was what he wanted, too. Deep down.

Baumgartner tilted his bottle again, finishing off the beer. He stood, but instead of retrieving another, he took a few steps to the gas barbecue on the patio. Methodically, he turned the gauges to get the propane flowing. Then he hit the ignitor button. An electric crackle sizzled in the air, but nothing happened. He pressed the button again. This time, flames burst into existence and began to lick the underside of the grill.

Don't let this moment make you question who you are.

Salter's gravelly voice rang in his ears as he pulled the folded evidence bag from his jacket pocket. Underneath the lieutenant's pronouncement, he could hear all of Maragas's arguments, too. They'd been getting louder with each beer.

Baumgartner placed the bag on the center rack. The edges immediately began smoking. A moment later, flames leapt up the sides and raced toward the center, engulfing the paper in an orange ball. Within fifteen seconds, all that remained were large chunks of light, black ash. Pieces broke away and drifted upward, fluttering in the heat.

Another of Salter's warnings came to him then.

Once the lie is told, it can't stop.

Baumgartner closed the lid to the grill and let the paper sack burn.

* * *

Maragas was waiting at her desk for him when he arrived in the morning. Despite finishing the six pack the night before, he'd set his alarm so that he'd be in an hour early. He knew the conversation he had coming with Maragas would be easier if no one was around. His plan seemed to have paid off, as all the other desks in Major Crimes were dark except for hers.

"You look like shit," she said. "Rough night?"

Baumgartner nodded wordlessly.

"You have something for me?" Maragas asked.

"No," Baumgartner said, his voice scratchy and tired.

Maragas stood. "Then let's go."

"Dusty…"

Maragas lowered her voice. "You owe me this much, Bob."

Baumgartner sighed but it came out more as a groan.

"Come on," said Maragas, already walking. "We'll get coffee on the way."

***

When they pulled into the driveway, the house looked dark. A few exterior lights were on, but none shone behind any of the windows.

"It's too early," Baumgartner said. He clutched a McDonald's coffee between his hands, grateful for the caffeine.

"You really give a damn about waking him up?" scoffed Maragas.

"No," he admitted.

"Me, neither."

Maragas pulled the unmarked police vehicle all the way up to the garage. The two of them exited the car and went to the door. Maragas glanced at the large door knocker, shrugged, and pressed the doorbell.

They waited for thirty seconds with no response. Maragas rang the bell again, twice this time. A few seconds later, Baumgartner saw a light appear inside. Out of habit, the two of them shifted to the sides of the doorway, avoiding the fatal funnel.

Baumgartner heard the shuffle of feet, then the loud click of the lock disengaging. Without thinking about it, his hand drifted toward his gun. He looked over at Maragas to see her palm already resting on the butt of her weapon.

The door opened partway. A black man in his forties stared out at them, his eyes bleary with sleep. Baumgartner's eyes narrowed in confusion.

"Can I help you?" the homeowner demanded.

"Sorry for disturbing you, sir," Maragas said smoothly. "I'm Detective Maragas. This is Sergeant Baumgartner. We're here to speak with Basil Pershing."

The man rubbed his eyes, his demeanor softening. "Pershing? That's the doctor we bought the house from."

"He sold the house to you?" Maragas asked. "When was that?"

The man considered. "A little over a year ago." He eyed the two of them. "You people don't keep track of where people live?"

"I didn't check," Maragas said. "He lived here last time we spoke."

"What do you want with him, anyway?"

"Just to talk," Maragas told him. "He may have some information that can help us."

The man's eyebrows went up slightly. "Information, huh? Well, you best hurry where that's concerned."

"What's that mean?" Maragas asked. "You know where he is?"

"I do. When we bought the place, we dealt mostly with his lawyer. The doctor had health issues. He was already in a care facility."

"What kind of issues?"

"Dementia of some kind. He's out at Evergreen Gardens, if I remember correctly."

Baumgartner listened to Maragas thank the man, apologize again for disturbing him so early, then he walked woodenly back to the car.

***

"This feels like déjà vu," muttered Baumgartner, as he and Maragas trailed behind a nurse.

"It's not a hospice," Maragas said.

Baumgartner glanced around. Evergreen Gardens was a luxurious building that seemed more to Baumgartner like a high-end resort for seniors than a memory care facility. Expensive furnishings decorated the spacious common areas. The few rooms he glanced into looked like a suite at the Davenport Hotel. Even the staff seemed like they came from wealthy stock.

When they reached their destination, the nurse paused at the closed door. She gave the two of them an imploring look. "Dr. Pershing is a solitary patient who likes to be left alone, especially after he's eaten his breakfast. You're certain you need to disturb him?"

"Absolutely certain," said Maragas.

"What can we expect?" Baumgartner asked her. He dropped his eyes to the small silver nametag on her uniform. "Is he… still all there, Julie?"

Nurse Julie tilted her head and lifted one hand slightly. "Some days are better than others. Alzheimer's is a progressive disease, but it doesn't have the same steep decline as something like cancer. Instead, patients plateau for a while before dropping off, often because of a medical event of some kind. They will usually recover somewhat and plateau again, but the new normal will be lower than before. Think of it like a staircase rather than a straight downhill decline."

"A staircase to Hell," muttered Maragas.

Julie lifted her brow. "That's a bit grim for my taste."

"Does he know who he is?" Baumgartner asked her.

"Yes. I hope what you need from him isn't recent, though. If you ask him what he had for breakfast an hour ago or what movie he watched last week, you might get an answer, but it won't be the right one."

"He'll lie?"

"He'll cope," Julie said.

"What we want to know is from a long time ago," said Maragas quietly.

Julie glanced at her. The nurse's expression bore suspicion and she looked torn. They'd both shown her their badges upon arrival and explained their purpose as only needing to ask a few simple questions. Baumgartner got the distinct feeling that Julie sensed there was more to the situation, though.

The nurse stepped closer to the door, raising her hand to knock. "I'll come in with you," she said.

"I'd rather you not," said Maragas. "In our experience, witnesses are reluctant to be entirely forthcoming when someone else is present. Especially if what they need to share is… embarrassing."

Julie considered. "I'll wait outside then," she said.

Maragas nodded her agreement.

Julie knocked, waited two beats, then cracked open the door. "Mr. Pershing, it's Julie. You have some visitors."

She pushed open the door.

Maragas stepped through the opening. Baumgartner followed, making sure Julie pulled the door shut behind them. He'd been in a multitude of different rooms in his life, many of them populated by the dead or dying. His nose was attuned to the smell of death, even when it rode on the undercurrents. He smelt it here, too, despite the light, airy scent of lilac camouflaging it.

He spotted Basil Pershing, seated in a chair in front of a chessboard. The man appeared to be a withered version of his former self. His hair had gone nearly white. He'd lost weight, turning his already thin frame gaunt. His shoulders rounded, almost as if preparing to admit defeat.

It was his eyes Baumgartner focused on.

They were clouded with confusion at first. Pershing watched Maragas approach but skipped his gaze past her to land on Baumgartner. He followed the sergeant as he lumbered forward.

"You!" Pershing spat, his voice frail.

"You remember us?" Maragas asked.

Pershing swung his attention to her briefly, then back to Baumgartner. "I remember him. Amherst, right?"

Baumgartner shook his head. "Don't play games. I'm Sergeant Baumgartner."

"That's what I said."

Baumgartner stared at him inquisitively.

Pershing scowled. "What are you looking at, you fat bastard?"

"I'm not fat," Baumgartner said reflexively.

Pershing sniffed and turned his attention back to his chessboard.

Maragas snapped her fingers. "Over here," she said. "I have some questions for you."

Pershing eyed her with suspicion and rancor. "You can't speak to me like that, missy. I'm a doctor."

"You're a patient."

"I'm a veteran. A war hero."

Maragas leaned closer to him and lowered her voice. "You're a sadistic killer who has been piling up bodies since 1951. So you can fuck off with all that pretense. It's just us here now."

Pershing's face pinched with anger. "Don't make me call the nurse. They work for me. They'll make you leave."

"Mr. Pershing, who is the President right now?"

"Don't be stupid. It's Bush."

"Which Bush?"

Pershing blinked, confusion flashing across his face. Then his expression grew hard again. "President Bush. Why are you asking me this? Are you a census taker?"

"We're police detectives. You know us."

"I know that." Pershing glanced over at Baumgartner again. "Where's your partner? The thin one. Pierce?"

Baumgartner stared into Pershing's eyes, looking for deception. In one moment, he thought he saw some; in the next, it seemed like sincerity.

He's not acting. Who in the hell would fake their way into a memory care facility?

"You remember Josephine Banfield?" Maragas asked. "Shirley Jensen?"

Pershing scowled at her. "Of course, I do. They were my friends."

"And yet you tortured and killed them."

Pershing blinked. "No. That was Etherton."

"He told us everything before he died, Basil. About what you did."

"Don't address me by my first name. We're not friends."

"Etherton made peace with what he'd done," Maragas said. "He got a chance to tell the truth."

Pershing stared at her, not speaking.

"Hudson Dorsey," Maragas whispered. "Daniel Kerley. Isaac Hermitage. You remember them?"

"I don't remember their names," said Pershing. His eyes seemed to glaze momentarily as he spoke. "I never wanted to know their names. Their names didn't matter. Only their presence. Their purpose."

"James Lockett," Maragas continued. "Why'd you cut around his ring finger? Was it to make us think he was Etherton's, like the others? Were you just being cute? Or were you already slipping?"

Pershing's expression cleared. He gave his head a short shake. "You're trying to trick me."

"I'm trying to give you a chance to set the record straight," said Maragas. "Do you really want Karl Etherton getting credit for everything you did?"

"Who cares about credit?" Pershing muttered. "The act itself is all that matters. The glorious act."

"The act of killing?" Maragas pressed. "Is that what you mean?"

Pershing looked back to the chess board in front of him. He stared at the pieces for several moments. Then he reached out and shifted a pawn forward. When he looked up again, he seemed genuinely surprised to see them.

"I'd like my breakfast now," he said. "Will you tell the nurse?"

<h1 align="center">Chapter 45</h1>

In the car, Maragas slapped the steering wheel repeatedly with the palms of her hands, cursing. Baumgartner sat quietly, waiting for her to finish. She eventually stopped and stared out the windshield, breathing heavily.

"He shouldn't get to forget," Maragas said.

Baumgartner didn't know how to reply, so he maintained his silence. As far as he could see, this was the end of the line. Maragas would let this go now. She'd work the Jennifer Terreri case straight and—

"It can still work," she said. "With the DNA and what he said to us. It could still work."

Baumgartner shook his head. "No, Dusty, it won't."

"Don't wimp out on me now, Bob. You heard him. You saw him. I don't care what shape he's in, he needs to pay for what he did to those people."

"It's over," said Baumgartner. "I wish it wasn't, but it is." Baumgartner wondered if that were entirely true, but he knew he needed to say it. For her sake, if not his own.

"All I need to do is—"

"I burned the tissues," Baumgartner said.

Maragas snapped her gaze to him. "You *what*?"

Baumgartner stared at her evenly, waiting.

A bevy of emotions passed across his partner's face. Disbelief. Rage. Betrayal. She dropped her eyes and stared down into her lap. When she looked up again, her expression was desperate. "He *confessed*. We've got that."

Baumgartner lifted his hands and dropped them. "Diminished capacity. It'll never get past a judge."

"You can't be sure of that."

Baumgartner gave her a knowing look.

Maragas turned back to the steering wheel and struck it again. This time a short blast of the horn resulted from the blow.

"Fuck!" Maragas yelled.

***

Baumgartner sat in the booth across from Salter. The two men sipped beers at the Maxwell House Tavern, remaining mostly quiet while an eclectic mix of music ranging from the seventies to the nineties played from the jukebox. It took only a few words exchanged to bring Salter up to speed on the case. Baumgartner was grateful for that. He didn't want to talk about it any more than he had to.

The remainder of the day had been uneventful. Maragas returned to working on the Terreri homicide, going through the motions of what was a simple case. Husband murders wife, then flees on his motorcycle, only to splat himself on the roadway. Case solved.

He knew the deaths would impact the families left behind. He'd seen it all too often in his career. At least most of their questions would be answered, though. They would know and understand what occurred. He couldn't imagine Jennifer Terreri's parents puzzling why a seventy-year-old doctor murdered their daughter on the same day her husband died.

Baumgartner took a drink of beer.

"You did the right thing," Salter assured him. "A defense attorney would have torn that frame-up to shreds."

Baumgartner glanced up at the lieutenant. "So, it was right because otherwise we would have been caught?"

"Don't be salty, Bob." Salter lifted his mug and took a long drink, then wiped his lip. "It's two separate things. You did the right thing, full stop. And if you'd gone through with it, a defense attorney would have ripped through it like tissue paper."

Baumgartner winced at the lieutenant's word choice.

"There's another bullet you dodged," Salter told him. "The CODIS system has been utilizing low use periods to run all unmatched DNA against known DNA entries. It's automated now. They're chipping away at the backlog."

Baumgartner stared at him, realization setting in. "So, if we'd submitted the tissues or DNA from Pershing..."

"They'd both eventually ping against the unmatched DNA from previous cases we put on Etherton," Salter finished. "You'd undo everything we did in oh-five. High risk with minimal rewards. Besides, what did I tell you about that?"

Baumgartner didn't answer, but the words were as clear in his mind as the day he'd first heard them.

Once the lie is told, it can't stop.

The door to the tavern opened and Maragas walked in. The place was mostly empty, so she located them with ease. Baumgartner slid over to make room for her. As she sat, he could smell the cigarette smoke on her. The only bartender on duty, Roxy, drew Maragas a beer without being told.

"What's he doing here?" Maragas asked.

"He's as much a part of this as we are," Baumgartner said. "Don't be that way."

"Don't tell me how to be, Sergeant." Maragas smirked. "My freezer's full of unopened packs of Marlboro Reds I'm trying to keep from smoking, and nothing else."

Baumgartner smirked in return.

No one in the booth spoke as Roxy approached and plunked a beer onto the table in front of Maragas. The detective lifted it and took a long sip. Roxy returned to the bar.

"So, that's it?" Baumgartner asked, keeping his voice low. "It's done?"

"You were expecting a parade?" asked Maragas. "Making sergeant wasn't enough for you?"

Baumgartner glanced around but no one was within two tables of them. An Alan Jackson song started up on the juke, further camouflaging their conversation. "I just want to know this is over," he said. "That you're done."

"Oh, I'm fucking done," Maragas assured him. "Count on that."

"What's that mean?"

Maragas took another long pull on her beer. "Don't you worry. Hard part's already done, Bob."

"Not the hardest part," Salter said. His gaze drifted back and forth between the two of them. "That will come later, when you have to live with it all. Question if you did the right thing."

A coldness washed over Baumgartner. Why did doing the right thing—instead of framing and putting away a serial killer—feel so hollow? Pershing had taken… how many lives was it? Baumgartner was in no mood to count them or speculate on those killed they hadn't discovered, but he imagined the burden of those murders far outweighed the transgression they'd committed a couple of years ago and the one they'd considered today.

Didn't it?

"Once the lie starts, it can't stop," Maragas said. The sarcasm in her tone was unmistakable. "Right, Lieutenant? Even if it's a noble lie?"

"Better to preserve this noble lie than do what you almost did. Even if it worked, that would have haunted you, Dusty. All the way to your grave."

"You're wrong about that," Maragas said. "He was pure evil. I wouldn't have lost a moment of sleep over it."

"I'd envy you that peace," said Salter. "If I believed you."

Maragas didn't answer. She picked up her glass to take another drink. Before it reached her lips, Salter lifted his own glass.

"A toast," he said grimly.

She paused, waiting. Both of them looked at Baumgartner.

Reluctantly, he lifted his beer. He and Maragas waited while Salter thought for a moment. When the lieutenant spoke, his voice carried a weight laced with shame and satisfaction alike.

"I won't say their names," he said, "but this case has claimed many lives. Victims, for certain. Cops, too. Not just death, but hours and days of lives dedicated to its grimy details. So, here is to the dead and to the living. May we all rest in peace."

Salter lifted his glass an inch higher. Baumgartner thrust his forward as well. After a moment's reluctance, Maragas pushed hers in so all three glasses clinked together.

"Now, it's done," Salter whispered hoarsely, and they drank.

Epilogue

2023

And there is the silence of the dead.
If we who are in life cannot speak
Of profound experiences,
Why do you marvel that the dead
Do not tell you of death?
Their silence shall be interpreted
As we approach them.

Edgar Lee Masters, "Silence"
American Poet, 1868-1950

Chapter 46

Clint watched Baumgartner, waiting for him to finish. The former chief sat silently, staring out at the lake. Ribbons of amber and violet slashed across the water as the sun sank behind the low, distant hills. At the dock, Darla's boat banged into the rubber guard as she returned from fishing.

"Basil Pershing died nine weeks later," Baumgartner said quietly. "His obituary was a laundry list of positives. Doctor. Church leader. Purple Heart recipient."

Down at the dock, Darla hopped off the boat, holding a line of rope.

"Dusty rarely spoke to me after that case," Baumgartner continued, his tone one of dutiful resignation. "She retired right after. She got to enjoy retirement for all of four years before the emphysema got her." Baumgartner's voice thickened. "Salter didn't even make it that long. He died just two years later, still on the job."

Clint remembered. The funeral was heavily attended. He was relatively certain, if they could have, the brass would have declared the man's passing a line of duty death so all the stops could be pulled out for the service. That would have been difficult, however, since Salter passed away in his own bed.

"I made lieutenant off the position he vacated," Baumgartner said. "How ironic is that?"

Still riding the rocket ship, Clint thought, but held his tongue. Instead, he said, "You come off awfully heroic in this account. That's convenient."

"There's nothing convenient about you sitting here."

"I'll bet not." Clint eyed him carefully. "Was Salter right, do you think? About testifying? How hard it'd be?" He didn't mention the reason he asked—that he was starting to see such testimony in the former chief's future.

Baumgartner glanced his way, then went back to watching Darla tie off the boat. "You've never had to do it?"

Clint's lip curled. "*Had* to do it? I never *chose* to do it. It's corrupt."

"Corrupt? You mean, like conducting a two-year, off-book, secret investigation into another cop?" Baumgartner's words were flat, but Clint heard the accusation in them all the same.

"I took my hit. Same as everybody else."

"Days off," the former chief said. "Compared to what happened to everyone else, you might as well have gotten away scot-free."

"Don't make this about me."

"But it is," Baumgartner said. "Otherwise, you wouldn't be here. You'd be spending your time trying to find out who murdered Melanie Paz. Instead, you're weaving conspiracy theories, getting ready to tilt at windmills. All for revenge."

"Revenge? For what?"

"You tell me, Ward."

Clint's jaw tightened. "I am doing my job. I was assigned to review cold cases. Melanie Paz was one of those cases. There was some mutilation to her body, which led me to search the other unsolved files for the same. That's when I saw the similarities and broadened my search."

Baumgartner's eyes never left Darla as she finished securing the boat to the dock and headed their direction. "Similarities, huh? Well, I can see where you get that from fifty-one and seventy-four. Even from our case in oh-three, James Lockett. However, Pershing was already dead in 2016, when Paz was murdered. How the hell did you find any meaningful similarities there?"

"The mutilation was the only one," Clint admitted, "but once I knew about all the other cases, I started looking for connections and found plenty."

"I'm not surprised. You'd find connections between the Lincoln assassination and JFK's. Same number of letters in their names and all that."

Clint scowled. "Don't be ridiculous."

"Oh, those assassinations weren't a result of conspiracies?"

"Of course, they were, but don't think you'll distract me. We're talking about this conspiracy." He jabbed a finger downward into the arm of the wicker chair.

Darla approached on the pathway. Her eyes lighted on the two of them. "Still at it, huh?" she said. Clint heard some resentment hiding in her pleasant tone. "Should I set out an extra plate for dinner?"

"No," Baumgartner said. "We're almost done."

Darla nodded easily, not breaking stride. She slowed only long enough to drag her fingers along Baumgartner's forearm as she strolled past.

Baumgartner waited until the slider door behind them snapped shut. Then he asked, "I'm almost afraid to ask, but what connections do you think you found, Ward?"

"They're real," Clint insisted. The former chief's continued use of his shortened name still caused him to bristle, but he forced down any response. Instead, he listed his findings. "Elio Paz, her brother, tried and failed to become a police officer with this department. You know who the academy lieutenant was at the time? Tom Farrell, your right-hand man."

Baumgartner smirked. "That's weak, and it makes no sense."

"I didn't say it made sense. I said it was a connection. Here's something more concrete: Paz's boyfriend, Hector Martinez, worked as a caregiver at Evergreen Gardens from 2004 to 2008, which overlaps with when Pershing was there. Martinez delivered meals, took care of laundry, and helped the patients to and from the common areas and their rooms." Clint gave Baumgartner a hard, triumphant smile. "His duties gave him lots of time to interact with the patients. Some of it in private."

Baumgartner watched him, waiting.

"Go ahead," Clint challenged. "Call that coincidence."

"You're saying, what? Pershing mentored Martinez?"

Clint nodded. "Just like Etherton did for him."

"I don't think it works that way."

"No one knows for certain how it works," Clint said. "For all the public fascination and all the scholarship about serial killers, we still know very little about them. My theory is as good as any other out there. Trust me, I've read all of them."

"What's your theory, exactly?"

"Serial killers are like any other species. They need to reproduce. The only method available to them is asexual—they must train the next generation. That's what Etherton was doing, and that's what Pershing did with Martinez."

Baumgartner shook his head. "Now you're just making shit up to fit what you want the truth to be."

"I didn't make up where Martinez worked. Or that Pershing was a patient there."

"Coincidences don't equal truth."

"The truth is Hector Martinez murdered Melanie Paz."

"Do you have any more proof than what the original detective found?" Baumgartner asked.

Clint waved a hand tersely. "I'll find it. I'll dig deeper than Hollander did. Besides, after all this, I have the advantage." He tapped his temple. "I know he did it."

"You *believe* he did," Baumgartner corrected. "It isn't the same thing. Even if he did, who's to say he wouldn't have killed anyway, without your farfetched idea of mentorship?" Baumgartner scoffed. "How does that conversation even happen, Ward? Does Martinez just sidle up to him one day and say, 'Here's your applesauce, Mr. Pershing. By the way, do you happen to be a sexual sadist who murders people? Because I'd like to be your apprentice'. It's ridiculous."

"Like-minded people have a way of finding each other. Look at pedophiles."

Baumgartner ignored his comment. "Besides, if Martinez really was some kind of budding serial killer, wouldn't it be Etherton who'd interest him? All those murders, official and unofficial are publicly laid on *his* doorstep. Seems to me that'd be the kind of person an acolyte would want to study."

"I'm sure he did."

"Why don't you pull Martinez's library records, then? See if he checked out all the true crime books on Etherton?" Baumgartner dropped his chin and gave him a knowing look. "See, I can weave crazy connections, too, except about Etherton."

Clint refused to be cowed. "Only difference is, I'm right."

Baumgartner waved a hand. "Martinez is a coincidence."

"I hate coincidences."

"I hate Brussell sprouts," said Baumgartner. "but I've come to terms with the fact they exist."

"Martinez killed Melanie Paz. I'm sure of it."

"Then arrest him."

"I can't. He went to prison in 2019 for sexual assault. Six months later, someone stabbed him to death during a brawl in the yard."

Baumgartner lifted his hands. "So none of this was about solving a murder, was it, Ward? It was about you stitching together a grand conspiracy so you could get back at the department for perceived slights."

"Perceived?" Clint scoffed. "I'm stuck in the cold case squad for no good reason. Before that, I was punished for bringing down the most corrupt officer this department has ever known."

"Stop making yourself out to be the victim," Baumgartner snapped. "You're the only one on this department who came out of the Garrett situation virtually unscathed."

"Sure didn't feel *unscathed* when I served my suspension."

Baumgartner began counting on his fingers. "Gary Stone, dead. Ray Zielinski, prison. Tom Farrell, forced retirement. Jun Yang, off the job. Not to mention, the department was put under a consent decree." He shook his head. "You got off easy."

"Easy," Clint scoffed. "You don't know shit."

"I'll tell you what I do know," Baumgartner said. "You're often the smartest guy in the room, Ward. But not every room, and not every time. Your problem—and your greatest strength—is that you focus too much on the trees and never the forest. That's your talent and your curse. Most people are the opposite. They miss most of the trees and only vaguely see the forest. Sometimes the forest is what you *need* to see, but you just can't."

"I see the forest fine."

"No, you don't. What you see is a labyrinth of conspiracy trees, not the real forest."

Clint sniffed derisively. "You sound like someone trying to do an impression of their mentor and failing. I don't need your recycled advice. All I need from you I've already got—the facts."

"What are you going to do with these facts, Ward?"

"Oh, I'm going to blow the entire saga wide open. Expose the whole damn twisted circus."

Baumgartner didn't seem surprised or worried. He glanced back out at the lake again, thinking. Then he said, "You've said you don't believe in coincidence, right?"

"Not generally, no."

"Well, maybe it's a coincidence you were assigned to the cold case files, or that you came upon all these cases and made the connections you did. Do you think that might be true?"

"It's no coincidence," Clint said. "I did my job."

"Something you can always be counted on to do," Baumgartner agreed. "That's why I assigned you as shadow on the Garrett shooting, way back when. That was no coincidence."

"That was because I'm black and so is Garrett."

"Partially," Baumgartner admitted. "I needed the optics. Most of my reasoning was that you would do what you do best, Ward—work the case like a dog with a bone. That's what you did."

Clint shrugged. "No other way to work a case than to do it right, is there?"

"I suppose not." Baumgartner turned back to meet his gaze. "So, then maybe you stumbled on all this history. What if you were put in a position to find it? What if they created a situation where they knew you'd discover these cases?"

Clint squinted. "Now you sound like the one weaving conspiracies."

"I said dog and bone a few seconds ago, didn't I? Well, if you put a dog in a room and throw a bone in the corner, is there any surprise when he finds it?"

"What's your point?"

"Maybe this is all a coincidence. Or maybe they all but assigned these cases to you. If they did…" He trailed off, shaking his head sadly. "If they did, Ward, then it was for a reason."

"Yeah, so I could solve it."

"No, so you could impale yourself with it."

Clint stared at him, scowling. "That's ridiculous. There's no way anyone set this up for me to find. You're trying to work me."

"I'm trying to *help* you. You should let this sit. That's the smart move, but I know what you're going to do. You won't be able to let this go. You'll run it up the flagpole, just like you did when I was chief. It's your nature. Trust me, it isn't going *anywhere*. Hatcher is chief now. It's a whole new world. People might not be as patient with your idiosyncrasies and holy wars as I was. You will find yourself out of Major Crimes completely. Maybe even off the job."

"You're saying I should drop it?" Clint asked derisively.

"It's a choice."

"A bad choice."

A trace of a grin crossed Baumgartner's mouth. "There are bad choices," he said, "and then there are bad choices."

"Nice try," Clint scoffed. "I'm not letting this go. You're just worried about your own ass in a sling."

Baumgartner shrugged. "Go forward if you want. Bang your head against the wall. You won't accomplish what you think you will."

"I don't want to *accomplish* anything. This isn't a crusade. All I want is to solve these cases."

"They've all been solved. As far as anyone cares."

"I care. I want to solve them right."

"That's the problem."

"Since when is knocking down a case a problem?"

"You're not knocking down any cases," Baumgartner said. "Don't you see? Everything I gave you adds up to *nothing*. Just what Salter told me, much of which was told to him by Pierce, and some of that was about what Amherst did. It's all hearsay of the worst kind. Juries don't convict based on the telephone game."

"I've got you," Clint said.

"I won't testify."

"You will if you get subpoenaed."

"I'll show up, but I won't testify."

"You'd really do that?" Clint asked, accusingly. "Get up on the stand and plead the fifth?"

"I've done worse, and for better reasons."

Clint shook his head in disgust. "Maybe you really are corrupt."

"That's not a black and white word," Baumgartner said. "Just like it's not a black and white world."

"You know what that sounds like to me? Like something people tell themselves so their own dirt doesn't look so bad to them."

"I'm not surprised you'd see it that way." He turned slightly in his chair to face Clint. "Here's the deal—this is a no-win situation for you. You've got no evidence."

"I'll exhume Lockett and get DNA from the 2003 case. When I match it to Pershing, that'll be the first domino to fall. Then—"

"Pershing is dead," Baumgartner reminded him.

"I'll dig up that motherfucker, too," Clint snapped.

"He's been embalmed. All the DNA has been washed away."

"So, what? I'll get it from his bone marrow."

"Extracting DNA from bone marrow is no easy task. Our lab doesn't have the capability to do that analysis."

"Don't tell me my job," Clint said. "There are other labs in the country that have the equipment. The one in Texas is good."

"They're expensive. Over ten grand, and that was when I retired. Not to mention the cost of exhumation, which is already pricey."

"So, we're putting a price tag on truth now?"

"There's only so much money any chief is going to spend without proof, Ward. You have nothing." Baumgartner gave him a look Clint imagined was supposed to be fatherly. "Besides, if all of this were to come out, who would it benefit?"

"Certainly not you."

"This isn't about me," Baumgartner said, an edge creeping into his tone. "You'd impact all of the families of all those victims. Throw their lives into emotional upheaval, force them to relive what happened to their loved ones again. For what?"

"They'll know the truth."

"What truth? That another, different but still terrible man committed all these murders? The goddamn apprentice to the man they *thought* killed their family member did those same horrible things. What changes with that knowledge, except they get to live through all that grief all over again?" Baumgartner shook his head. "No, Ward, you're doing this for you. So you can point at the system you've been railing against your whole life and finally say, 'See, I was right. There is a conspiracy.'"

"There is!"

"It doesn't matter. The scandal you'll cause will hurt the department, yes. Probably not as badly as the Garrett situation did, but people haven't forgotten that one yet, so this new one will still be bad."

"I don't care about any of that."

"You should."

"It's above my pay grade and outside my circle of give-a-shit."

"Listen to me," Baumgartner said. "The department took its hits thanks to the Garrett disaster. Public opinion, the consent decree, all of that. We got through it because of my decisions and leadership."

"Don't break your arm patting yourself on the back," Clint said acidly. "Remember that list of people you threw in my face a few minutes ago?"

"I remember everything," Baumgartner said. "If you didn't already know that, then today should have proved it to you. Trust me, things could have gone much worse than they did. We got bloody but the decisions I made kept us from being mortally wounded. One of those decisions was putting you on the Garrett shooting to shadow the county investigation. I'm glad I made that choice. It was the right one. Like I said earlier, you have a special skill set."

Baumgartner leaned forward.

"But, Ward, if I were in charge today, this specific series of cold cases is something I would *never* assign to you."

"Why not?"

"Same reason I would assign you to just about any other case. Because you'll solve it. That is almost always a good thing. Here, it isn't. The public needs to have faith in its police department. They need to believe that, most of the time, we're going to catch the bad men who do bad things. All that will happen if this comes out is to undermine that belief."

"It's a lie."

"It's a lie that hurts no one and helps most. It's a lie based on a truth, too, Ward."

"Now you're talking in circles," Clint said.

"You think life is a straight line?" Baumgartner asked. "No. The truth is, Etherton was a killer. We caught him, in the end. The spirit of that truth exists within the version the public knows. It serves its purpose. It's a necessary fiction that rests on a deeper truth."

Clint scoffed. "Sounds like someone has thoroughly bought his own bullshit. Or is that Salter speaking?"

"Don't demean Gus. He challenged me to do better when it was my turn. That is why I tried to be a different sort of man as a lieutenant, a captain, and eventually chief. So no one would ever be entangled in something like this again."

"Yet here we are."

"I can't undo the past," Baumgartner said. "When the prospect of doing so only hurts everyone around, I'm prone to let it alone."

"Fortunate I'm not so inclined."

"All right," Baumgartner said. "Forget the public good for the moment. Look at it from a strictly mercenary standpoint— with the way you go about your work, this case might hurt the department, but it will destroy you."

"I've changed."

"Really? Is that why you're banished to cold cases instead of working the rotation?"

Clint scowled. "I can be smarter."

Baumgartner was quiet for a second. Then he said, "You ever hear the story about the frog and scorpion?"

"Everyone knows that fucking story," Clint snapped.

Baumgartner turned over his hands. "You are who you are, Ward. If you push forward with this, it will be the end of you."

"Maybe, but along the way, I'll expose the truth."

"If anyone believes you," said Baumgartner. "Your personnel jacket isn't exactly clean. When you go crying wolf, people are going to take a hard look at the messenger."

"These are the department's secrets. They need to be aired."

"No, they aren't. They are the secrets of our dead. Pierce. Amherst. Salter and Maragas. They, and everyone else touched by these events, are gone."

"That's exactly why," Clint said. "Someone has to speak for the dead. That's me."

Baumgartner looked at him sadly. "Sometimes, Wardell, the dead need to remain silent. And at peace."

Clint noted the sudden shift to the proper use of his full name. He narrowed his eyes suspiciously but didn't reply.

The former chief stared at him for a few moments, then rose from the wicker chair. He didn't extend his hand toward Clint.

"I'm finished talking about this," he said. "It's time for you to go."

Chapter 47

At home, Clint stayed up late into the night, furiously writing out notes from his interview with Baumgartner. He pushed aside any other thoughts than to document all he could remember. Out of habit, he wrote in the secret shorthand he'd developed years ago. NSA codebreakers might be able to decipher his notes but no one at the police department stood a chance.

Sometime after one in the morning, he finished. Carefully, he collected his notes and put them into his lock box. After securing the lock, he went through his routine to prepare for bed. By the time he slid between the cool sheets, he hoped sleep would be waiting for him.

As usual, his brain whirred.

Baumgartner's warnings rang off the walls of his mind palace. The assertion this case would go nowhere. That there was no profit in taking it forward. It would put families back through emotional turmoil. How doing so would destroy him.

All the doom saying bounced around in his head, unresolved. Examining it repeatedly kept him awake long into the night.

Eventually, he managed to drift off for a few hours of sleep.

His alarm woke him. Clint rose and went through his morning routine, meticulously preparing himself for the day. The sleep, as little as he got, refreshed him. While he brushed his teeth, he thought about Baumgartner's logic.

Was the former chief right?

Even if he was, would doing the right thing be worth the cost?

He considered that. Doing the right thing was an end unto itself, was it not? He'd always thought so. However, if Baumgartner was correct, nothing positive would result from the truth of these cases coming to light. Families would relive trauma. The agency would suffer, and so would Clint.

Who benefits? It was a question he often asked and one that frequently gave him a new line of investigation into a case. A worthwhile thread to follow. If Baumgartner's assessment was to be believed, the answer here was… no one.

Clint dressed, taking the time to knot his tie perfectly and ensure his shoelaces were of equal length. Then he headed for the door. As he reached for the knob, he paused. After a moment, he went and retrieved his notes from the lockbox.

Just in case.

When he arrived at the station, it was still early by detective standards. Only a few people were present. Just one other desk light was turned on in the Major Crimes bullpen, that belonging to Detective Marty Hill. Clint briefly considered asking his colleague for advice but rejected the idea. If even a quarter of what Baumgartner claimed was true, the fallout would be considerable. He didn't want to do that to one of the only detectives he considered a friend.

Clint dropped into his chair and set the notes on his desk. He stared down at them.

There are bad choices, he thought, and then there are bad choices.

He needed to make one of those bad choices now. Either shred his notes, close the Paz file, and move on. Or…

Baumgartner had suggested the world today was a different place than even a few years ago, Clint remembered. Maybe the man was onto something, albeit unintentionally. Maybe the world had changed enough that the former chief's predictions were skewed. People might actually believe Clint, see the points he was trying to make. Chief Hatcher was progressive. Hell, too much so for Clint's taste at times, but in this instance, such a tendency might work in his favor.

Maybe things will be different this time.

Clint's body tensed.

He hesitated, thinking it through one last time in a flash.

Then he grabbed his notes and headed down the hall toward the chief's office. The soles of his shoes thudded dully on the linoleum floor with every step. He didn't pass anyone along the way.

The desk where the chief's secretary usually sat was empty, though he immediately saw signs that Marilyn was already at work. Her computer was on, as was her desk lamp. Clint figured she must have gone for coffee, which was a stroke of luck. For three successive chiefs now, Marilyn had guarded the door to the leader's office as if it were the inner sanctum of the Vatican.

Clint walked past her desk and turned right in the short hallway beyond. He saw the chief's door was cracked open about four inches. Light came from within. He heard a female voice murmuring, "Yes, thank you." Clint strode purposefully toward the door and rapped sharply on it three times. Then he poked his head into the larger gap his knocking had created.

"Chief?" he asked.

Chief Dana Hatcher sat behind a mahogany desk. She lowered the phone receiver in her hand, replacing it on the cradle. Then she motioned for him to enter.

"Wardell," she said. "Come in. I've been expecting you."

Afterword and Acknowledgments

Some stories have the oddest of catalysts.

In 2014, Frank was living about forty-five minutes north of Spokane. While driving home from the city that summer, he saw a man hitchhiking along Highway 2. The man was dressed in ragged jeans, a dirty T-shirt, and dirty, scuffed boots. His flannel shirt was tied around his waist by the sleeves. On his back was a battered backpack.

What stuck out the most was the man's age. He was at least sixty-five and could have easily been a decade older.

Frank's first inclination was to pull to the side of the road and give the man a lift. He even let off the accelerator briefly to do so. Then twenty years of law enforcement experience came to bear.

"What are you thinking, picking up a hitchhiker? What would you tell your son or daughter to do in this situation?"

Frank kept driving. As he drove, he wondered why he'd even considered picking up that man. It wasn't something he did. The situation wasn't an emergency. No one was hurt or out in extreme weather. There was no exigency other than someone wanting to get further down the road. To his usual way of thinking, that need didn't outweigh the potential risk involved in picking up a stranger.

But the moment bothered him.

The trip home lasted another twenty minutes. In that time, Frank realized it had been the man's age that caused him to lower his usual defenses. This fact surprised him. The idea someone was less dangerous merely because they'd lived a certain number of years was illogical. Yet, this bias he'd almost succumbed to is one much of society holds. Dusty Maragas talks about this in the book. The train of thought she shares with Baumgartner—that a jerk at thirty is probably a jerk at seventy—is the same one that occurred to Frank on that drive home. Since his mind often resides in the realm of crime fiction, the next question came easily—what if a murderer continued to commit murders from youth to old age, becoming a generational serial killer? How invisible might he be to the police and victims, simply due to being elderly?

Those questions were the genesis of this story.

Some ideas die on the vine if they don't see the page by a certain point. This one, though, continued to grow in dribs and drabs. Slowly, piece by piece, and over about eight or so years, a general framework emerged—three separate time periods, three sets of detectives each linked by one partner, and the idea of the student killer posing as a victim and later framing his master.

Beyond that, the framework was quite bare when Frank brought the core idea to Colin with the intent that it live in the Charlie-316 universe. Once Colin agreed to the fit, our collaboration took what was the partial skeleton of a story, added the rest of the bones to complete it, and then all the muscles and organs and skin were hung on it, too. Our usual process kicked in and we took on this ambitious book.

For both of us, this was the first time writing anything of significant length in a time neither of us lived in (1951) or one we knew only as kids (1974). To meet that challenge, we did research and we relied on bits of advice we'd received from a fellow author, James Ziskin. To the discerning reader: we recognize there are some factual errors and anachronisms. These are intentional and used for dramatic purposes. Our authorial intent was to capture the feel of the time, even some details were slightly out of their real-history time frame, and we hope to have done exactly that.

The authors wish to thank:

The large number of subject matter experts who lent their knowledge and experience to this book. Contributions ranged from large to small, from academics to retired cops who lived in the eras we wrote about, and every one of them was crucial to making The Silence of the Dead as good as it could be. So, thank you to: Nick Stanley, Pam Stanley, Bill Scheres, John Grasso, Marty Hill, RJ Beam, Judi Carl, Ron Graves, Susan and Bob Walker, and Julie McFadden, RN.

Our combined crew of beta readers, who read this monster of a book and gave valuable feedback: Kristi Scalise, John Emery, Gary Felix, Brad Hallock, Suzanne Peckham, Ron Sarich, Anne Graham, Paula Dunn, Susan Bryson, and Jiver Freecloud.

Frank Zafiro
Colin Conway
July 2024

About the Authors

Frank Zafiro writes gritty crime fiction from both sides of the badge. He was a police officer in Spokane, Washington, from 1993 to 2013, retiring as a captain. Frank is the author of over fifty novels. These include the River City series, SpoCompton series, and Stefan Kopriva mysteries. He also co-authored the Charlie-316 series with Colin Conway and the Bricks & Cam Jobs with Eric Beetner. In addition to writing, Frank hosts the crime fiction podcast Wrong Place, Write Crime. He is an avid hockey fan and a tortured guitarist. He currently lives in Redmond, Oregon. You can keep up with him at frankzafiro.com.

Colin Conway is the creator of the 509 Crime Stories, the Cozy Up series, and the co-creator of the Charlie-316 series (written with Frank Zafiro). He served in the U.S. Army and later was an officer for the Spokane Police Department. He lives in Eastern Washington with his girlfriend and a codependent Vizsla that rules their world. Follow his journey at colinconway.com.